THE FIRST MEN I

◆

A MODERN UTOPIA

The First Men
in the Moon

◆

A Modern Utopia

——◆——

H. G. WELLS

with an Introduction by
DAVID STUART DAVIES

For my husband
ANTHONY JOHN RANSON
with love from your wife, the publisher.
Eternally grateful for your unconditional love.

Readers who are interested in other titles from
Wordsworth Editions are invited to visit our website at
www.wordsworth-editions.com

First published in 2017 by Wordsworth Editions Limited
8B East Street, Ware, Hertfordshire SG12 9HJ

ISBN 978 1 84022 744 4

Wordsworth Editions
is the company founded in 1987 by
MICHAEL TRAYLER

Typeset in Great Britain by Anthony Gray
Printed and bound by Clays Ltd, St Ives plc

Contents

GENERAL INTRODUCTION

Wordsworth Classics are inexpensive editions designed to appeal to the general reader and students. We commissioned teachers and specialists to write wide-ranging, jargon-free Introductions intended to assist the understanding of our readers rather than interpret the stories for them. In the same spirit, because the pleasures of reading are inseparable from the surprises, secrets and revelations that all narratives contain, we strongly advise you to enjoy these two novels before turning to the Introduction.

KEITH CARABINE
General Adviser
Rutherford College, University of Kent at Canterbury

BIOGRAPHY OF THE AUTHOR

Herbert George Wells, known as 'Bertie' or 'H. G.', was born on 21 September 1866 in Atlas House, on the High Street of what was then the Kentish market town of Bromley. His father Joseph, a former gardener, kept a shop and played professional cricket; after his father broke his leg when Wells was ten, Wells's mother Sarah returned to domestic service at the country house Uppark, near Midhurst, in Sussex.

Wells's elder brothers had both been apprenticed to drapers, a trade that Sarah Wells considered to be highly respectable. Wells was apprenticed to drapers in Windsor and Southsea but was much keener to continue to be educated, and he persuaded his mother to let him become a pupil-teacher at Midhurst Grammar School. Wells's exam results at Midhurst were so strong that he won a scholarship, aimed at increasing the number of science teachers in Britain, at the Normal School (now Imperial College London), under 'Darwin's bulldog', the biologist T. H. Huxley. Wells drew extensively on his experiences as a student for his 1900 novel *Love and Mr Lewisham*. Ill-fed, poor and increasingly discontented by both the quality of the teaching he received and the social organisation of the world, Wells became more and more interested in politics and in imaginative literature, especially Plato, Blake and Carlyle. He also began writing, providing articles and a time-travel story, 'The Chronic Argonauts', for the college magazine the *Science Schools Journal*.

Wells failed his final exams and found work as a teacher in Wales. After being fouled in a rugby game, he suffered severe kidney damage, and for much of the 1890s Wells feared he would die prematurely. Returning to London and completing his degree, he worked as a correspondence tutor and in 1893 wrote his first books *Honours Physiography* and *A Textbook of Biology*. His writing branched out into literary journalism and popular scientific writing, and in 1895 alone Wells published four further books: *Select Conversations with an Uncle*, *The Wonderful Visit*, *The Stolen Bacillus and Other Incidents* and his masterpiece, *The Time Machine*. This first 'scientific romance' was swiftly followed by *The Island of Doctor Moreau* (1896), *The Invisible Man* (1897) and *The War of the Worlds* (1898). None has ever been out of print since; Wells was swiftly hailed as a man of genius by his contemporaries. Both sociable and irascible, Wells became friends, and fell out with, other writers such as George Gissing, Joseph Conrad, Stephen Crane, George Bernard Shaw, Arnold Bennett, Ford Madox Ford and Henry James, whom Wells would later cruelly lampoon in his 1915 novel *Boon*, the climax of a long disagreement between the two writers about the purpose and nature of the novel.

Wells never wanted to be limited to writing scientific romances, and during this period he also wrote realistic prose fiction set in a recognisable real world, whose disorganisation and unfairness these novels sought to diagnose: *The Wheels of Chance* (1896), *Kipps* (1905), *Tono-Bungay*, *Ann Veronica* (both 1909) and *The History of Mr Polly* (1910). Wells's early-twentieth-century science fiction, such as *The Food of the Gods* (1905) and *In the Days of the Comet* (1906), increasingly showed a vision of the world as Wells would want to order it. His political and utopian writing from *Anticipations of the Reactions of Mechanical and Scientific Progress upon Human Life and Thought* (1901) and *A Modern Utopia* (1905) also demonstrated Wells's commitment to creating a utopian government, a World State that would ensure that mankind would never go to war.

Following the First World War, Wells's passion for this project intensified, and he embarked on an ambitious collaborative project to write the first history of the world, hoping that if future generations were better educated, then rivalries between nations would be unnecessary, and world government would follow. *The Outline of*

History (1919) was Wells's best-selling book in his own lifetime, selling millions of copies internationally, and was followed by the school version *A Short History of the World* (1922) and by equivalents for science, *The Science of Life* (1930), and social science, *The Work, Wealth and Happiness of Mankind* (1931). At its height, Wells's fame was as much as a thinker and public intellectual as a novelist. He met or corresponded with the greatest figures of the first half of the twentieth century, notably: Winston Churchill, Lenin and Stalin, Theodore and Franklin Roosevelt, Albert Einstein and Sigmund Freud. His later novels from *The New Machiavelli* (1911) onward tend to be more overtly engaged with Wells's 'Open Conspiracy' to convert his readership to his own political point of view, often at a cost to these books' literary merit and subsequent afterlife.

Wells had married his cousin Isabel in 1891, but the couple proved incompatible and he left her for his pupil Amy Catherine Robbins, whom he rechristened 'Jane'. In spite of Wells's many infidelities, which Jane seemed prepared to tolerate, the couple were happily married until Jane's death from cancer in 1928; and they had two sons, Gip and Frank. An affair with the writer Amber Reeves produced a daughter, Anna Jane, and Wells's long affair with novelist Rebecca West saw the birth of a further son, Anthony West. Wells also enjoyed liaisons with, amongst others, Dorothy Richardson, Elizabeth von Arnim, Margaret Sanger and, following Jane's death, Odette Keun and Moura Budberg.

Wells's writing was prophetic in both senses of the term: as exhorting humankind to mend its ways, and in foreseeing the future. His writing imagined before they existed the aeroplane, the tank, space travel, the atomic bomb and the internet. In later life, the emphasis of his political writing turned more towards the rights of the individual, and his 1940 book *The Rights of Man: Or, What Are We Fighting For?* is a key text in the history of human rights.

Wells often despaired of his warnings ever being sufficiently heeded, declaring that his epitaph should be: 'God *damn* you, you fools – I told you so.' None the less, the influence of his hundred and fifty books and pamphlets of science fiction, novels, politics, utopia, history, biography and autobiography has been enormous throughout the twentieth century and into the twenty-first.

Simon J. James

Professor of English Literature at Durham University
and author of *Maps of Utopia: H. G. Wells,
Modernity and the End of Culture*

INTRODUCTION

> 'Life!' And immediately it poured upon us that our vast
> journey had not been in vain, that we had come to no
> arid waste of minerals, but a world that lived and moved!
>
> *The First Men in the Moon*

It was in the nineteenth century that writers gradually began to create
what we would regard today as the science-fiction genre. This was
partly due, of course, to the great leaps that were being made at the
time in all fields of scientific endeavour from medicine to industry and
from transport to communication. Knowledge spread, taking on form
and substance, during this remarkably progressive century. It was as
though civilisation was shaking off its yoke of ignorance and beginning
to realise that it could reach for the stars. The growing curiosity with
our world prompted thoughts concerning other worlds also. The
nineteenth century began with horse-drawn carriages, gas lamps and
musical boxes and ended with motor cars, railway engines, electric
lighting, phonographs, the telephone and numerous other inventions
which enhanced the material state of mankind. Similarly there were
giant strides in medicine and our understanding of how the human
body functions. The further and faster science and technology advances,
the more it prompts authors to stretch their and our imaginations.
Writers are artistic dreamers and when a new door opens just a whisker
the creative scribbler will crowbar it wide.

Isaac Asimov, the great exponent of the science-fiction genre in the
twentieth century, stated that:

> True science fiction, by its modern definition (or at least by my
> modern definition), could not have been written prior to the nine-
> teenth century, because it was only with the coming of the Industrial
> Revolution in the last decades of the eighteenth century that the rate
> of technological change became great enough to notice in a single
> lifetime – in those areas of the globe affected by that revolution.'[1]

1 Isaac Asimov, 'The History of Science Fiction', an article in the volume
   Asimov on Science Fiction, Doubleday, 1981, p. 212

However, the development of science fiction was not due to technological advances alone; it was also due to man's increasing curiosity about his world, its limits and more importantly its possibilities. There was a fascination and an inquisitiveness about what constitutes life and death – and, indeed, what happens after death.

Symptomatic of these considerations was Charles Darwin's *On the Origin of Species*, published in 1859, which ruminated on the existence of God and his role in controlling the universe. Darwin introduced the theory that populations evolve over the course of generations through a process of natural selection. It presented a body of evidence that the diversity of life arose by common descent through a branching pattern of evolution.

It could be claimed that Mary Shelley's *Frankenstein* (1818), which encapsulates these concerns, was the first science-fiction novel. The increasing fascination with death, 'that undiscover'd country, from whose bourn no traveller returns', gave rise to the popularity of the ghost story.[2] But other writers looked not to the spirit world for their subject matter, but to other fantastic realms, either those in the future, or hidden from our view, beyond the confines of our known world.

Jules Verne (1828–1905) was the pioneer in this field of fiction. Indeed he is regarded as the 'Father of Science Fiction', a nomenclature coined in the early part of the twentieth century and one that has in recent years been attributed to H. G. Wells. Indeed the connection between the two men is strong. Verne referred to his works as 'scientific romances', as Wells did to his. Verne's stories took his characters on *A Journey to the Centre of the Earth* (1864), down to *Twenty Thousand Leagues Under the Sea* (1869–70), *Around the World in Eighty Days* (1873) and *From the Earth to the Moon* (1865).

Verne lit the pathway for other writers to follow, and follow they did. The greatest of these was Herbert George Wells (1866–1946). While it is true to state that Wells is now best remembered for his science-fiction novels, he was a prolific writer in many genres. The range of his writings is remarkable. For example his novels, *Kipps: The Story of a Simple Soul* (1905), a rags-to-riches study in class differences, and *The History of Mr Polly* (1910), inspired by Wells's early experiences in the drapery trade, have been compared favourably to the works of Charles Dickens; while his bestselling two-volume work, *The Outline of History* (1920), began a new vogue for popularising world history. In his fiction, even the 'scientific romances', he always exhibited a concern for the

2 William Shakespeare, *Hamlet*, 3, 1, 79–80

common man and how, in its various ways and manifestations, society treated, controlled and conditioned him. As a result, his fantasies were imbued with a perceptive realism which had resonances for the man in the street – the regular reader.

*   *   *

Herbert George Wells was born at Atlas House, 46 High Street, Bromley, in Kent, on 21 September 1866. Known as 'Bertie' in the family, he was the fourth and last child of Joseph Wells, who at the time of his son's birth was a shopkeeper and professional cricketer, and his wife Sarah Neal, a former domestic servant.

A defining incident in young Wells's life was an accident in 1874 that left him bedridden with a broken leg. To pass the time he started reading books from the local library, brought to him by his father. He soon became devoted to the fabulous and intriguing other worlds and lives to which these books gave him access: they fired his imagination and stimulated his desire to write. Later that year he entered Thomas Morley's Commercial Academy, a private school founded in 1849. The teaching was erratic. Wells later stated that the curriculum mostly focused on producing copperplate handwriting and doing the sort of sums useful to tradesmen. This ethos may well have been why, in his early teens, Wells went to work as a draper's assistant. He hated the job and eventually quit, much to his mother's dismay. In turning to teaching, Wells found a way to continue his own studies. He eventually won a scholarship to the Normal School of Science (later the Royal College of Science in South Kensington, now part of Imperial College London), where he learned about physics, chemistry, astronomy and biology, among other subjects. Wells also devoted a great deal of his time to becoming a writer. While at the college, he penned a short story about time travel called 'The Chronic Argonauts'. The tale was first published by the Royal College of Science in 1888 and combined Wells's new-found interest in science with his old love of literature and writing. This story foreshadowed his future literary success and was in many ways a dry run for his first full-length novel *The Time Machine* (1895).

Wells became an overnight literary sensation with the publication of this remarkable work. While providing an entertaining and exciting read, the novel also explored social and scientific topics ranging from class conflict to evolution. These themes were to recur in many of his other popular works. The success of this novel triggered an incredibly industrious and creative period of about six years when Wells wrote his most memorable and brilliantly conceived 'scientific romances'. In quick succession, he published *The Island of Doctor Moreau* (1896), *The Invisible Man* (1897), *The War of the Worlds* (1898) and *The First Men in the Moon* (1901).

Politically, Wells supported socialist ideals and his concerns and observations about the nature and stratification of society infiltrate all his novels, not least the two which are featured in this volume. At first glance, *The First Men in the Moon* appears to be a whimsical late-Victorian romp featuring two rather comical characters who take a trip to the moon, encounter strange creatures and experience exciting and fascinating adventures. That at least is the surface premise, but Wells gives the reader much more to chew on than this fairground thrill-imbued candy floss. In other words the novel has a literary duality which allows it to be enjoyed on more than one level by readers with differing demands and tastes in their fantasy fiction.

The frontispiece illustration for the first edition shows the two main characters floating out of control above the ground, coats flapping in the air, experiencing weightlessness for the first time in some rural location in Britain. The comical cartoon nature of this drawing strikes the note of whimsy which runs through the narrative, especially in the early stages. However, to some extent this is misleading, for the author also presents serious socio-political points along the way. The two protagonists, Bedford, a retired somewhat disreputable businessman, and Cavor, a would-be writer and reclusive physicist, take off for the moon thanks to Cavor's invention of a gravity-resisting material, which he has named Cavorite after himself. When these astronauts land on the moon, they encounter a breed of strange insect-like creatures who live beneath the lunar landscape. These are Selenites, natives of the moon. Cavor and Bedford are captured by them and imprisoned. Eventually one of the two men escapes and returns to earth while the other remains behind.

In many ways, the narrative has strong similarities to Georges Méliès's French silent fantasy film *A Trip to the Moon* (*Le Voyage dans la Lune*), which was made only a year after Wells's novel was published. Some critics have suggested that this movie was actually inspired by Jules Verne's novels *From the Earth to the Moon* and *Around the Moon*, but the fact that it was made so quickly on the heels of Wells's work and that the lunar creatures were named Selenites in Méliès's two-reeler, just as they are in *The First Men in the Moon*, suggests Wells's later work was the main influence on the film scenario.

There had been various novels describing trips to the moon in the

nineteenth century before Wells dipped his nib in ink and produced
this work. Along with the already mentioned two titles by Jules Verne,
in 1864 there appeared an intriguing book written by Chrysostom
Trueman, a pseudonym of the unidentified UK author who listed
himself as 'editor' of this story, which was entitled *The History of a
Voyage to the Moon*.[3] The tale is divided into two parts. In part one,
'The Voyage', the central characters learn how to create a new 'Power
Source' – an anti-gravity element capable of propelling the spaceship
they have had constructed by an eccentric inventor– and travel to the
moon. In part two, 'The Ideal Life', they discover a utopian society on
the moon inhabited by 'amnesiac reincarnations of select Earthmen',
who are gregarious, peace loving and a mere four feet tall. Trans-
portation on the planet is by means of giant roc-like birds. The space
travellers, in strong contrast to most visitors to other worlds in the
nineteenth century, neither leave nor destroy the world they have
discovered. One can see at first glance that there are certain similarities
between this vision and that of Wells, especially in the first part where
the anti-gravity element is very similar to the one Cavor invents.

Interestingly, soon after the publication of *The First Men in the Moon*,
Wells was accused by the Irish writer Robert Cromie of having stolen
ideas and details from his own novel *A Plunge into Space* (1890), which
also used an anti-gravity device similar to that in Chrysostom Trueman's book. Both of these works have certain elements in common with
Wells's novel, including the construction of a globular spaceship built in
secret after the discovery of a method to overcome earth's gravity. Wells
simply responded to this claim by stating: 'I have never heard of Mr
Cromie nor of the book he attempts to advertise by insinuations of
plagiarism on my part.'[4] And that appeared to be the end of the matter.

Indeed, the significance of the similarity of Trueman's and Cromie's
novels can easily be over emphasised. Their reiterations of the conventions of an interplanetary fantastic voyage are not remarkably
original, while their depictions of a new 'Power Source', and of the
spaceship that conveys their main characters to the moon, are not
markedly more innovative or detailed than those found, highly
condensed, in other early fictional works of space travel such as J. L.

3   'Chrystostom Trueman', pseud., ed., *The History of a Voyage to the Moon*,
    Lockwood, 1864; quoted in *The Encyclopedia of Science Fiction*, edited by Clute
    and Nicholls, p. 1242

4   Introduction to *The First Men in the Moon*, China Miéville and Patrick
    Parrinder (eds), Penguin Random House, 2005, p. xvii

Riddell's *Orrin Lindsay's Plan of Aerial Navigation, with a Narrative of his Explorations in the Higher Regions of the Atmosphere, and his Wonderful Voyage Round the Moon* (1847), or, much more expansively, in Elbert Perce's *Gulliver Joi: His Three Voyages; Being an Account of his Marvelous Adventures in Kailoo, Hydrogenia and Ejario* (1851). It is perhaps fair to say that these imaginative authors were all singing from the same hymn sheet, but it is how they interpreted the material that made the real difference.

If there was a kind of familiarity of plot in all these stories of men flying off into outer space, the question arises: what makes H. G. Wells's novel more interesting and why has it achieved the popularity and longevity denied the other books? The answer might well be summed up in the words of the Irish comedian Frank Carson, who, after reciting a series of tired jokes, would announce with pride, 'It's the way I tell 'em.' In Wells's case, with *The First Men in the Moon*, it was indeed the way that he told it. We might clarify the statement further by explaining that he made his narrative funnier and more thought-provoking than the rest.

This point was emphasised by one of Wells's biographers, the left-wing politician Michael Foot, in his book *The History of Mr Wells* (1995):

> Others had attempted the journey before HG, but he added an independence of his own which no one else could match. According to true Wellsian doctrine, the first man on the moon – or, rather, his bosom spheroid companion – was not some contrived superman but an authentic ne'er-do-well London East Ender who, despite all his natural fears and alarms, still knows what's what and can pluck up courage to stride across the universe.[5]

Daringly, Wells's other central character is the clichéd figure of the absent-minded professor, Dr Cavor, a standard incumbent in so many science-fiction sagas. It is Cavor who is the inventor of the propulsion system that will send his rocketless ship to the moon. He was of the same breed as the protagonists of *The Invisible Man* and *The Time Machine*: amateur boffins who ploughed their own inventive furrow. Wells's concept of scientific benefactors seems to revolve around workshop eccentrics of this sort. Jules Verne was more realistic in his comprehension that only a large-scale effort by a huge team, well financed and with a broad range of skills, could ever turn a lunar expedition into a reality.

5 Michael Foot, *The History of Mr Wells*, Black Swan, London, 1995, p. 39

Soon after its publication *The First Men in the Moon* was criticised for the implausibility of its scientific claims – by Jules Verne among others. Somewhat naïvely the Frenchman asked Wells to produce this mysterious flying metal that defied the law of gravity. If such demands were made on all the writers of science-fiction novels, there would be few left to delight and astound us. For novelists, there is a more important force than Newton's Law – the power of the imagination. On this scale, Wells stands out today, just as he did over a century ago. He gave us a story that, long after real men went to the real moon, still exerts a gravitational pull of its own on countless readers.

If Wells is vague on his applied science, he makes up for it in his storytelling skills. His narrator, the scheming Bedford, sets an amusing tone from the outset. He is evading creditors and trying to put together his life after a failed business venture. There is no sense of adventure in his motives. He is not particularly interested in reaching for the stars but rather reaching for profits. His interest in his neighbour's scientific theories is pecuniary, pure and simple. He is little better than a scoundrel, a belligerent man wanting to exploit technology for financial gain, but the author manages to make him a lovable one all the same, if only for his persistence in self-justification. Bedford is, at the time that the two men meet, attempting to write a play and this helps in making him a plausible narrator, one who uses a natural voice which engages and entertains the readers and draws them into this fantastical tale.

In many ways Bedford also represents the typical imperialist Victorian explorer adventurer who seeks new territory to conquer, to subjugate its natives and plunder its riches. It is his plan to revisit the moon for the sole purpose of retrieving more of the gold they have discovered below its surface. He intends to return 'in a bigger sphere with guns', which echoes the colonial policy at the time: confiscating riches by force. Bedford exhibits no curiosity concerning the Selenites and the structure of their society. He is merely an interplanetary conqueror on the grab.

By contrast his colleague Cavor is as idealistic as Bedford is mercenary; he is a pacifist inspired by the notion that science is for man's benefit and well-being. Wells makes use of this contrast in temperaments to impart some bite and irony into their dialogues. Cavor's humanitarian stance is expressed in his concerns about what will happen when the two men return to earth:

It was I who found the way here, but to find a way isn't always to be master of a way. If I take my secret back to earth, what will happen? I do not see how I can keep my secret for a year, for even part of a year.

Sooner or later it must come out, even if other men rediscover it. And then . . . Governments and powers will struggle to get hither, they will fight against one another and against these moon people; it will only spread warfare and multiply the occasions of war . . . No! Science has toiled too long forging weapons for fools to use. It is time she held her hand. Let him find it out for himself again – in a thousand years' time.

Wells's concept of the moon and its organisational structure has elements of his prognostications about the future organisation of society in *The Time Machine*. His explorers in *The First Men in the Moon* discover that lunar inhabitants living underground are strictly stratified and hierarchical, a situation that provides a fine basis for social commentary. These insectoid creatures, the Selenites (or 'Moonies', as Cavor whimsically dubs them), have a highly organised caste system much like terrestrial ants. It is only after Bedford has departed that Cavor learns more about the Selenite race, their history and their individual functions. He attempts to convey this information to earth in a series of radio transmissions. Cavor maintains that the Selenites have much greater 'intelligence, morality and social wisdom than men'. The academic Selenites are reminiscent of the creature described in one of Wells's early articles, 'The Man of the Year Million' (1893), in which the author thought that natural selection would eventually reshape the human.[6] He would become a creature with a huge head and eyes, delicate hands and a much reduced body, permanently immersed in nutrient fluids, having been forced to retreat beneath the earth's surface after the cooling of the sun.

In this work – as in so many of his best-known tales – Wells sets up a conflict between his protagonists and the amorphous surrounding social forces – the Selenites, in this instance. The creatures in these stories are rarely distinguished for their individuality and personal qualities. They are characterised forces, ideas and philosophies. In *The Time Machine*, we have the repressed but savage Morlocks, who are presented as the working class who have to toil underground so that the rich upper class can live in luxury; the mysterious aliens of *The War of the Worlds* are colourless aggressors, who wish to conquer by power and destroy all opposition; and the desperate packs of mutant creatures in *The Island of Dr Moreau* have been damaged and degraded by the dangerous march of science which cares little for the consequences of

6 This article was published in the periodical *Pall Mall Budget* on 18 November 1893.

experimentation on the individual. Usually these collectives betray some affinity with the less desirable traits of the Victorian society in which Wells came of age. Either they stand out for the oppressiveness of their class structures, or their imperialistic tendencies, or for some other aspect that would have been all too familiar to Wells's readers. It is to the author's credit that he could craft such well-paced adventures on the basis of so little individualised villainy.

The entire narrative of *The First Men in the Moon* is pretty much a warning against imperialism and how mindless society can become if people are restricted to one station in life. This is best seen in Cavor's recounting of a young Selenite being raised in a bottle in preparation for its lifetime of duty: 'That wretched-looking hand-tentacle sticking out of its jar seemed to have a sort of limp appeal for lost possibilities.' However, the true message of this book comes from its depiction of humanity's desire not to grow complacent, but rather continually to expand, explore and discover. At its heart, *The First Men in the Moon* is about the strength of the human spirit.

Perhaps we should not be surprised, then, that the inhabitants of the moon in this novel bear a strong resemblance to the insect colonies on earth. For this author, the most scary enemies are the depersonalised ones. The hordes, the unnamed masses, the mobs – these are what frightened H. G. Wells. Yet he portrays his lunar society with such a sensitivity to its inner logic, that one surmises that the novelist was both repelled and attracted by what he was describing.

This emotional conflict is played out in human terms in the final stages of Wells's plot. Our author's two protagonists take different paths, one returning to Earth and the other staying on the Moon. Normally this parting of the ways would indicate the conclusion of the story, but Wells added a section in which Bedford, now back on terra firma, receives, in a fragmented form, the radio messages from Cavor from across the void. While this coda adds nothing to the narrative track of the tale, it does throw light on the way an alternative form of society can function. Although this addition appears disconnected to the previous part of the book, it does give Wells more scope to mull over issues of social and political structure that he could hardly have developed in the earlier chapters, where the conflicts and rapid pacing of the story hardly allowed him time for such musings. It no doubt entertained Wells greatly to create this stratified society where a creature is aware of his limited function and seemingly accepts it without complaint. Whether he thought that human society was in danger of moving in this direction is open for debate. Under Cavor's tuition, some of the Selenites learn to speak English, and through their conversations the inventor learns of the strict order of the race:

'In the moon . . . every citizen knows his place. He is born to that place, and the elaborate discipline of training and education and surgery he undergoes fits him at last so completely to it that he has neither ideas nor organs for any purpose beyond it.'

The creatures are moulded to one specific role in life, a task in the great scheme of things, and there is no opportunity to change or progress. Not only does the mind resign itself to this fate, but the body morphs into the shape best suited to the role. When there are no tasks for the manual workers, they are drugged with opiate mushrooms until their services are required again. The intellectual Selenites, those 'beings with big heads on whom the intellectual labours fall, form a sort of aristocracy'. At their head is 'that marvellous ganglion the Grand Lunar', whose brain case measured 'many yards in diameter'. This supreme being is anxious to know the history and the ways of earthlings, and it is perhaps in Cavor's explanation and description of warfare as carried out on earth, and the Grand Lunar's incredulity at such senseless barbarity, that Wells makes his sharpest point:

'But what good is this war?' asked the Grand Lunar, sticking to his theme.
'Oh! as for *good*!' said I; 'It thins the population!'

*   *   *

Wells's fascination with the function and make-up of society as illustrated by his representation of the Selenite world in *The First Men in the Moon* continued to stay with him all his life. He returned to the subject of utopian/dystopian worlds in many of his other works. He expounded his views in great detail in *A Modern Utopia* (1904), which is not so much a novel as an intellectual treatise. In this work, contemplations concerning the nature of society and the ways in which a utopian way of life may be achieved take precedence over characterisation and plot. The premise of this novel is that there is a planet exactly like Earth, with the same geography and biology, where 'all the men and women that you know and I' exist 'in duplicate'. However, while these doppel-gangers have 'different habits, different traditions, different knowledge, different ideas, different clothing, and different appliances', they all speak the same language: 'Indeed, should we be in Utopia at all, if we could not talk to everyone?'

Wells's utopia is a world in which the problems of humanity have been solved. People live healthy, happy lives in cities where all human needs are met. Science and technology frees people from toil and enables them to enjoy security and innovation. However, this utopia is neither democratic nor equal. Wells advocates a scientific kind of socialism, rooted in the naïve notion that the world is orderly, knowable and controllable like a machine.

A Modern Utopia is presented as a tale told by a sketchily described character known only as 'the Owner of the Voice'. Wells warns his readers that this narrator 'is not to be taken as the Voice of the ostensible author who fathers these pages'. The storyteller is accompanied by another character known as 'the botanist'. Interspersed in the narrative are discursive passages on various aspects of the author's version of an ideal society, creating what Wells called in his preface 'a sort of shot-silk texture between philosophical discussion on the one hand and imaginative narrative on the other'. In addition, there are frequent comparisons to and discussions of previous literary visions of utopian societies, drawing on the works of Plato, More and Bacon.

The novel, if we must call it that, begins in an exciting traditional fashion – traditional for a 'scientific romance' at least. While walking in the Swiss Alps, two English travellers fall into a space-warp, and suddenly find themselves in another world. In many ways it is the same as our own – even down to the characters who inhabit it. However, the travellers discover that this new planet is nevertheless somehow radically different. They have landed on a utopian Earth controlled by a single World Government. Here, as they soon learn, not only do all the inhabitants share a common language, but there is sexual, economic and racial equality, and society is ruled by socialist ideals enforced by an austere, voluntary élite. Beginning as 'a tale', the narrative now moves into a discussion and analysis of this new world. As a result, the promise that this may provide the thrills and shocks characteristic of Wells's other scientific romances such as The War of the Worlds or The Time Machine fades.

Northrop Frye (1912–91), the Canadian critic who was regarded as one of the most influential literary theorists of the twentieth century, stated that A Modern Utopia, in terms of the classification of literary genres, is not a novel at all but 'an anatomy'.[7] By this phrase, one assumes he means that Wells dissects the nature of a utopian society

7 Quoted by Michael Sherborne in H. G. Wells: Another Kind of Life, Peter Owen, 2010, p. 165

and the human and civil mechanics which make it work and analyses
them in detail. In doing so, he presents an intriguing set of proposals
indicating how man could better himself, but in the process rather loses
the sense of what a novel should be. Imaginative it is, certainly, taking
us into the realm of fantasy, but there is no real drama, passion or
excitement. The reader does not become emotionally involved in the
lives and dilemmas of the major characters.

In many ways, *A Modern Utopia* is a dramatised treatment of an earlier
work by Wells, *Anticipations of the Reaction of Mechanical and Scientific
Progress upon Human Life and Thought*, generally known as *Anticipations*,
written in 1901. He referred to this book as, 'the keystone to the main
arch of my work'.[8] In *Anticipations* he took the revolution in transport
facilitated by the 'mechanical revolution' as his point of departure; Wells
told his readers that they were living through a reorganisation of human
society that would alter every dimension of life. It is true to say that at
the time of writing, in the early days of the new century – the twentieth
century – he was correct.

In *A Modern Utopia*, Wells identifies the key ways in which his utopia
is meant to be different from the many classical and contemporary
utopias to which he frequently refers. His ideal society is to be dynamic,
not static, and one that is not a perfect and unchanging ideal, but rather
an evolving social organism, adjusting its character to maintain its
purposes through changing times and circumstances. In one way or
another, Wells's utopia insists upon a socialist ethos in that it must
account for everyone, not just the able and admirable citizens found in
other utopias. It must offer everyone maximum freedom, not maximum
uniformity. Indeed some of the statements made in the book could
easily come from a left-wing political manifesto:

The modern Utopia will give a universal security indeed, and exercise
the minimum of compulsions to toil, but it will offer some acutely
desirable prizes. The aim of all these devices, the minimum wage, the
standard of life, provision for all the feeble and unemployed and so
forth, is not to rob life of incentives but to change their nature, to
make life not less energetic, but less panic-stricken and violent and
base, to shift the incidence of the struggle for existence from our
lower to our higher emotions, so to anticipate and neutralise the
motives of the cowardly and bestial, that the ambitious and energetic

8   H. G. Wells, *An Experiment in Autobiography*, Faber & Faber, London, 1988,
    p. 643

imagination which is man's finest quality may become the incentive and determining factor in survival.

This is certainly political science fiction, a blending together of two strands: the scientifc romance and an imaginative socialist ideology. It is a society without poverty, with free choice of occupation and interest, a meritocracy of 'voluntary noblemen', called samurai, who assume the key leadership and administrative positions. Strictly non-hereditary, this nobility operates rather like a combination of Plato's 'Guardians' and the imperial Chinese civil service. The samurai are 'noblemen', but unfortunately Wells does not explain how they achieve this status. However, with this nobility there is a system of differentiation. The narrator's double describes the ascetic Rule by which the samurai live; this includes a ban on alcohol and drugs and a mandatory annual one-week solitary ramble in the wilderness. He also explains the social theory of Utopia, which distinguished four 'main classes of mind': The Poetic, the Kinetic, the Dull and the Base. Poetic minds are creative or inventive; kinetic minds are able, but not particularly inventive; the Dull have 'inadequate imagination'; and the Base are mired in egotism and lack 'moral sense'.

While women in this utopia are free and officially equal, Wells cannot quite bring himself to discard the attitudes of his sex and his time. Though he argues that women are inferior to men only because they are kept economically inferior, which he proposes to remedy by making motherhood a paid occupation, his reasons for that economic inferiority must be regarded as Victorian sexism.

This new world is vegetarian also. The narrator is told:

'In all the round world of Utopia there is no meat. There used to be. But now we cannot stand the thought of slaughterhouses. And, in a population that is all educated, and at about the same level of physical refinement, it is practically impossible to find anyone who will hew a dead ox or pig. We never settled the hygienic question of meat-eating at all. This other aspect decided us. I can still remember, as a boy, the rejoicings over the closing of the last slaughterhouse.'

The novel champions negative eugenics by advocating the prevention of the procreation of certain 'types', namely congenital invalids and certain antisocial individuals such as violent criminals and drug (including alcohol) abusers. Wells insists on the celibacy or chastity of these groups and provides island prisons for those who break the prohibition. This is a Wellsian hobby horse that he has ridden before, notably in *The Time Machine*.

He sums up his reasoning in *A Modern Utopia*:

> . . . it is a conceivable and possible thing that this margin of futile struggling, pain and discomfort and death might be reduced to nearly nothing without checking physical and mental evolution, with indeed an acceleration of physical and mental evolution, by preventing the birth of those who would in the unrestricted interplay of natural forces be born to suffer and fail.

The book does not end in a totally negative fashion for our traveller/narrator returns to his own world, where he is overwhelmed by the imperfection of its dirt and noise and unequal suffering. Yet, even here, he sees a hope for the future:

> The face of a girl who is passing westward, a student girl, rather carelessly dressed, her books in a carrying-strap, comes across my field of vision. The westward sun of London glows upon her face. She has eyes that dream, surely no sensuous nor personal dream.
>
> After all, after all, dispersed, hidden, disorganised, undiscovered, unsuspected even by themselves, the samurai of Utopia are in this world, the motives that are developed and organised there stir dumbly here and stifle in ten thousand futile hearts . . .

The book was received with mixed responses by the intelligensia. Joseph Conrad complained to Wells that he did not 'take sufficient account of human imbecility which is cunning and perfidious'.[9] Marie-Louise Berneri, anarchist and author, was also critical, stating that 'Wells commits the faults of his forerunners by introducing a vast amount of legislation into his utopia', and observes that the author's concept of freedom turns out to be 'a very narrow one'.[10] However, at the memorial service held at the Royal Institution on 30 October 1946, shortly after Wells's death, William Beveridge, the noted progressive British economist and social reformer, architect of the post-war welfare state, read passages from *A Modern Utopia*, calling it the work that had influenced him the most. It is also interesting to note that following the book's publication several Samurai Societies were formed in response

9 Joseph Conrad, *The Collected Letters of Joseph Conrad*, Volume 3: 1903–7, edited by Frederick R. Karl and Laurence Davies, Cambridge University Press, Cambridge, p. 64
10 Marie-Louise Berneri, *Journey through Utopia*, Routledge & Kegan Paul, 1950, p. 295

to *A Modern Utopia*, and Wells met with one of them in April 1907 at
the New Reform Club.

A Modern Utopia remains a fascinating, if fanciful, read, although its
depiction of a world enlightened by science and led by an altruistic
intellectual and creative élite is a somewhat naïve concept rather than a
prescription for a real future.

*   *   *

Following the early years of the twentieth century, H. G. Wells
provided the occasional flashes of storytelling genius in some lively
novels, but a great deal of his writing was concerned with political,
utopian ideas. All too often the message rather than the story took the
upper hand. For example, in his last book, *Mind at the End of Its Tether*
(1945), he considered the idea that humanity being replaced by another
species might not be a bad idea. G. K. Chesterton quipped: 'Mr Wells
is a born storyteller who has sold his birthright for a pot of message.'[11]
Nevertheless, the astute reader cannot fail to be entranced, intrigued
and entertained by the two novels presented in this volume. They
certainly provide food for thought – a rarity in fiction these days.

FURTHER READING

Biographies

Batchelor, John, *H. G. Wells*, Cambridge, Cambridge University
    Press, 1985

Brome, Vincent, *H. G. Wells: A Biography*, Longmans, Green & Co.,
    London, New York and Toronto, 1951

Foot, Michael, *H. G.: History of Mr Wells*, Black Swan, London, 1996

Sherborne, Michael, *H. G. Wells: Another Kind of Life*, Peter Owen,
    London, 2010

Smith, David C., *H. G. Wells: Desperately Mortal: A Biography*, Yale
    University Press, New Haven and London, 1986

11 Chesterton's reference is to the biblical 'mess of pottage', implying that
    Wells had sold out his artistic birthright in mid-career. Quoted by
    Christopher Rolfe & Patrick Parrinder in *H. G. Wells under Revision*:
    Proceedings of the International H. G. Wells Symposium, London,
    July 1986, Susquehanna University Press, 1990, p. 9.

West, Anthony, *H. G. Wells: Aspects of a Life*, Hutchinson, London, 1984

H. G. Wells

Wells, H. G., *An Experiment in Autobiography: Discoveries and Conclusions of a Very Ordinary Brain (Since 1866)*, 2 volumes (1934), Faber & Faber, London, 2008

Wells, H. G., *H. G. Wells: Literary Criticism*, edited by Patrick Parrinder and Robert Philmus, Harvester, Sussex, 1980

Critical Works

Beaumont, Matthew, *The Spectre of Utopia: Utopian and Science Fiction at the Fin-de-Siècle*, Peter Lang, Bern, 2012

Bergonzi, Bernard, *The Early H. G. Wells: A Study of the Scientific Romances*, Manchester University Press, Manchester, 1961

Dryden, Linda, *The Modern Gothic and Literary Doubles: Stevenson, Wilde and Wells*, Palgrave, Basingstoke, 2003

Dryden, Linda, *Joseph Conrad and H. G. Wells: The Fin-de-Siècle Literary Scene*, Palgrave, Basingstoke, 2015

Haynes, Roslynn D., *H. G. Wells, Discoverer of the Future: The Influence of Science on His Thought*, New York University Press, New York, 1980

Huntington, John, *The Logic of Fantasy: H. G. Wells and Science Fiction*, Columbia University Press, New York, 1982

James, Simon J., *Maps of Utopia: H. G. Wells, Modernity and the End of Culture*, Oxford University Press, Oxford, 2012

McLean, Steven, *The Early Fiction of H. G. Wells: Fantasies of Science*, Palgrave, Basingstoke, 2009

Parrinder, Patrick, *H. G. Wells: The Critical Heritage*, Routledge & Kegan Paul, London, 1972

Parrinder, Patrick, *Shadows of the Future: H. G. Wells, Science Fiction, and Prophesy*, Syracuse University Press, Syracuse, 1995

Wagar, W. Warren, *H. G. Wells: Traversing Time*, Wesleyan University Press, Middletown, Conn., 2004

The First Men in the Moon

Three thousand stadia from the earth to the moon . . .
Marvel not, my comrade, if I appear to be talking to you
on super-terrestrial and aerial topics. The long and the
short of the matter is that I am running over the order of
a Journey I have lately made.

Lucian, Icaromenippus

The First Men
in the Moon

◆

H. G. WELLS

Contents

CHAPTER ONE

Mr Bedford Meets Mr Cavor at Lympne

A S I SIT DOWN TO WRITE here amidst the shadows of vine-leaves under the blue sky of southern Italy, it comes to me with a certain quality of astonishment that my participation in these amazing adventures of Mr Cavor was, after all, the outcome of the purest accident. It might have been anyone. I fell into these things at a time when I thought myself removed from the slightest possibility of disturbing experiences. I had gone to Lympne because I had imagined it the most uneventful place in the world. 'Here, at any rate,' said I, 'I shall find peace and a chance to work!'

And this book is the sequel. So utterly at variance is destiny with all the little plans of men.

I may perhaps mention here that very recently I had come an ugly cropper in certain business enterprises. Sitting now surrounded by all the circumstances of wealth, there is a luxury in admitting my extremity. I can admit, even, that to a certain extent my disasters were conceivably of my own making. It may be there are directions in which I have some capacity, but the conduct of business operations is not among these. But in those days I was young, and my youth among other objectionable forms took that of a pride in my capacity for affairs. I am young still in years, but the things that have happened to me have rubbed something of the youth from my mind. Whether they have brought any wisdom to light below it is a more doubtful matter.

It is scarcely necessary to go into the details of the speculations that landed me at Lympne, in Kent. Nowadays even about business transactions there is a strong spice of adventure. I took risks. In these things there is invariably a certain amount of give and take, and it fell to me finally to do the giving. Reluctantly enough. Even when I had got out of everything, one cantankerous creditor saw fit to be malignant. Perhaps you have met that flaming sense of outraged virtue, or perhaps you have only felt it. He ran me hard. It seemed to me, at last, that there was nothing for it but to write a play, unless I wanted to drudge for my living as a clerk. I have a certain imagination, and luxurious tastes, and I meant to make a vigorous fight for it before that fate overtook me. In addition to my belief in my powers as a businessman, I had always in those days had an idea that I was equal to writing a very good play. It is not, I believe, a very uncommon persuasion. I knew there is nothing a man can do outside legitimate business transactions that has such opulent possibilities, and very probably that biased my opinion. I had, indeed, got into the habit of regarding this unwritten drama as a convenient little reserve put by for a rainy day. That rainy day had come, and I set to work.

I soon discovered that writing a play was a longer business than I had supposed; at first I had reckoned ten days for it, and it was to have a *pied-à-terre* while it was in hand that I came to Lympne. I reckoned myself lucky in getting that little bungalow. I got it on a three years' agreement. I put in a few sticks of furniture, and while the play was in hand I did my own cooking. My cooking would have shocked Mrs Bond. And yet, you know, it had flavour. I had a coffeepot, a saucepan for eggs, and one for potatoes, and a frying-pan for sausages and bacon – such was the simple apparatus of my comfort. One cannot always be magnificent, but simplicity is always a possible alternative. For the rest I laid in an eighteen-gallon cask of beer on credit, and a trustful baker came each day. It was not, perhaps, in the style of Sybaris, but I have had worse times. I was a little sorry for the baker, who was a very decent man indeed, but even for him I hoped.

Certainly if anyone wants solitude, the place is Lympne. It is in the clay part of Kent, and my bungalow stood on the edge of an old sea cliff and stared across the flats of Romney Marsh at the sea. In very wet weather the place is almost inaccessible, and I have heard that at times the postman used to traverse the more succulent portions of his route with boards upon his feet. I never saw him doing so, but I can quite imagine it. Outside the doors of the few cottages and houses that make up the present village big birch besoms are stuck, to wipe off the worst of the clay, which will give some idea of the texture of the district. I doubt if the place would be there at all, if it were not a fading memory of things gone for ever. It was the big port of England in Roman times, Portus Lemanus, and now the sea is four miles away. All down the steep hill are boulders and masses of Roman brickwork, and from it old Watling Street, still paved in places, starts like an arrow to the north. I used to stand on the hill and think of it all, the galleys and legions, the captives and officials, the women and traders, the speculators like myself, all the swarm and tumult that came clanking in and out of the harbour. And now just a few lumps of rubble on a grassy slope, and a sheep or two – and me! And where the port had been were the levels of the marsh, sweeping round in a broad curve to distant Dungeness, and dotted here and there with tree clumps and the church towers of old mediaeval towns that are following Lemanus now towards extinction.

That outlook on the marsh was, indeed, one of the finest views I have ever seen. I suppose Dungeness was fifteen miles away; it lay like a raft on the sea, and farther westward were the hills by Hastings under the setting sun. Sometimes they hung close and clear, sometimes they were faded and low, and often the drift of the weather took them clean out of sight. And all the nearer parts of the marsh were laced and lit by ditches and canals.

The window at which I worked looked over the skyline of this crest, and it was from this window that I first set eyes on Cavor. It was just as I was struggling with my scenario, holding down my mind to the sheer hard work of it, and naturally enough he arrested my attention.

The sun had set, the sky was a vivid tranquillity of green and yellow, and against that he came out black – the oddest little figure.

He was a short, round-bodied, thin-legged little man, with a jerky quality in his motions; he had seen fit to clothe his extraordinary mind in a cricket cap, an overcoat, and cycling knickerbockers and stockings. Why he did so I do not know, for he never cycled and he never played cricket. It was a fortuitous concurrence of garments, arising I know not how. He gesticulated with his hands and arms, and jerked his head about and *buzzed*. He buzzed like something electric. You never heard such buzzing. And ever and again he cleared his throat with a most extraordinary noise.

There had been rain, and that spasmodic walk of his was enhanced by the extreme slipperiness of the footpath. Exactly as he came against the sun he stopped, pulled out a watch, hesitated. Then with a sort of convulsive gesture he turned and retreated with every manifestation of haste, no longer gesticulating, but going with ample strides that showed the relatively large size of his feet – they were, I remember, grotesquely exaggerated in size by adhesive clay – to the best possible advantage.

This occurred on the first day of my sojourn, when my play-writing energy was at its height and I regarded the incident simply as an annoying distraction – the waste of five minutes. I returned to my scenario. But when next evening the apparition was repeated with remarkable precision, and again the next evening, and indeed every evening when rain was not falling, concentration upon the scenario became a considerable effort. 'Confound the man,' I said, 'one would think he was learning to be a marionette!' and for several evenings I cursed him pretty heartily.

Then my annoyance gave way to amazement and curiosity. Why on earth should a man do this thing? On the fourteenth evening I could stand it no longer, and so soon as he appeared I opened the french window, crossed the verandah, and directed myself to the point where he invariably stopped.

He had his watch out as I came up to him. He had a chubby, rubicund face with reddish brown eyes – previously I had seen him only against the light. 'One moment, sir,' said I as he turned.

He stared. 'One moment,' he said, 'certainly. Or if you wish to speak to me for longer, and it is not asking too much – your moment is up – would it trouble you to accompany me?'

'Not in the least,' said I, placing myself beside him.

'My habits are regular. My time for intercourse – limited.'

'This, I presume, is your time for exercise?'

'It is. I come here to enjoy the sunset.'

'You don't.'

'Sir?'

'You never look at it.'

'Never look at it?'

'No. I've watched you thirteen nights, and not once have you looked at the sunset – not once.'

He knitted his brows like one who encounters a problem.

'Well, I enjoy the sunlight – the atmosphere – I go along this path, through that gate' – he jerked his head over his shoulder – 'and round – '

'You don't. You never have been. It's all nonsense. There isn't a way. Tonight for instance – '

'Oh! tonight! Let me see. Ah! I just glanced at my watch, saw that I had already been out just three minutes over the precise half-hour, decided there was not time to go round, turned – '

'You always do.'

He looked at me – reflected. 'Perhaps I do, now I come to think of it. But what was it you wanted to speak to me about?'

'Why, this!'

'This?'

'Yes. Why do you do it? Every night you come making a noise – '

'Making a noise?'

'Like this' – I imitated his buzzing noise.

He looked at me, and it was evident the buzzing awakened distaste. 'Do I do *that*?' he asked.

'Every blessed evening.'

'I had no idea.'

He stopped dead. He regarded me gravely. 'Can it be,' he said, 'that I have formed a Habit?'

'Well, it looks like it. Doesn't it?'

He pulled down his lower lip between finger and thumb. He regarded a puddle at his feet.

'My mind is much occupied,' he said. 'And you want to know *why*! Well, sir, I can assure you that not only do I not know why I do these things, but I did not even know I did them. Come to think, it is just as you say; I never *have* been beyond that field . . . And these things annoy you?'

For some reason I was beginning to relent towards him. 'Not *annoy*,' I said. 'But – imagine yourself writing a play!'

'I couldn't.'

'Well, anything that needs concentration.'

'Ah!' he said, 'of course,' and meditated. His expression became so eloquent of distress, that I relented still more. After all, there is a touch of aggression in demanding of a man you don't know why he hums on a public footpath.

'You see,' he said weakly, 'it's a habit.'

'Oh, I recognise that.'

'I must stop it.'

'But not if it puts you out. After all, I had no business – it's something of a liberty.'

'Not at all, sir,' he said, 'not at all. I am greatly indebted to you. I should guard myself against these things. In future I will. Could I trouble you – once again? That noise?'

'Something like this,' I said. 'Zuzzoo, zuzzoo. But really, you know – '

'I am greatly obliged to you. In fact, I know I am getting absurdly absent-minded. You are quite justified, sir – perfectly justified. Indeed, I am indebted to you. The thing shall end. And now, sir, I have already brought you farther than I should have done.'

'I do hope my impertinence – '

'Not at all, sir, not at all.'

We regarded each other for a moment. I raised my hat and wished him a good evening. He responded convulsively, and so we went our ways.

At the stile I looked back at his receding figure. His bearing had changed remarkably, he seemed limp, shrunken. The contrast with his former gesticulating, zuzzoing self took me in some absurd way as pathetic. I watched him out of sight. Then wishing very heartily I had kept to my own business, I returned to my bungalow and my play.

The next evening I saw nothing of him, nor the next. But he was very much in my mind, and it had occurred to me that as a sentimental comic character he might serve a useful purpose in the development of my plot.

The third day he called upon me.

For a time I was puzzled to think what had brought him. He made indifferent conversation in the most formal way, then abruptly he came to business. He wanted to buy me out of my bungalow.

'You see,' he said, 'I don't blame you in the least, but you've destroyed a habit, and it disorganises my day. I've walked past here for years – years. No doubt I've hummed . . . You've made all that impossible!'

I suggested he might try some other direction.

'No. There is no other direction. This is the only one. I've enquired. And now – every afternoon at four – I come to a dead wall.'

'But, my dear sir, if the thing is so important to you . . . '

'It's vital. You see, I'm – I'm an investigator – I am engaged in a scientific research. I live – ' he paused and seemed to think. 'Just over there,' he said, and pointed suddenly dangerously near my eye. 'The house with white chimneys you see just over the trees. And my circumstances are abnormal – abnormal. I am on the point of completing one of the most important – demonstrations – I can assure you one of *the most important* demonstrations that have ever been made. It requires constant thought, constant mental ease and activity. And the afternoon was my brightest time! – effervescing with new ideas – new points of view.'

'But why not come by still?'

'It would be all different. I should be self-conscious. I should think of you at your play – watching me irritated – instead of thinking of my work. No! I must have the bungalow.'

I meditated. Naturally, I wanted to think the matter over thoroughly before anything decisive was said. I was generally ready enough for business in those days, and selling always attracted me; but in the first place it was not my bungalow, and even if I sold it to him at a good price I might get inconvenienced in the delivery of goods if the current owner got wind of the transaction, and in the second I was, well – undischarged. It was clearly a business that required delicate handling. Moreover, the possibility of his being in pursuit of some valuable invention also interested me. It occurred to me that I would like to know more of this research, not with any dishonest intention, but simply with an idea that to know what it was would be a relief from play-writing. I threw out feelers.

He was quite willing to supply information. Indeed, once he was fairly under way the conversation became a monologue. He talked like a man long pent up, who has had it over with himself again and again. He talked for nearly an hour, and I must confess I found it a pretty stiff bit of listening. But through it all there was the undertone of satisfaction one feels when one is neglecting work one has set oneself. During that first interview I gathered very little of the drift of his work. Half his words were technicalities entirely strange to me, and he illustrated one or two points with what he was pleased to call elementary mathematics, computing on an envelope with a copying-ink pencil, in a manner that made it hard even to seem to understand. 'Yes,' I said, 'yes. Go on!' Nevertheless I made out enough to convince me that he was no mere crank playing at discoveries. In spite of his crank-like appearance there was a force about him that made that impossible. Whatever it was, it was a thing with mechanical possibilities. He told me of a work-shed he had, and of three assistants – originally jobbing carpenters – whom he had trained. Now, from the work-shed to the patent office is clearly only one step. He invited me to see those things. I accepted readily, and took care, by a remark or so, to underline that. The proposed transfer of the bungalow remained very conveniently in suspense.

At last he rose to depart, with an apology for the length of his call. Talking over his work was, he said, a pleasure enjoyed only too rarely. It was not often he found such an intelligent listener as myself, he mingled very little with professional scientific men.

'So much pettiness,' he explained; 'so much intrigue! And really, when one has an idea – a novel, fertilising idea – I don't want to be uncharitable, but – '

I am a man who believes in impulses. I made what was perhaps a rash proposition. But you must remember, that I had been alone, play-writing in Lympne, for fourteen days, and my compunction for his ruined walk still hung about me. 'Why not,' said I, 'make this your new habit? In the place of the one I spoilt? At least, until we can settle about the bungalow. What you want is to turn over your work in your mind. That you have always done during your afternoon walk. Unfortunately that's over – you can't get things back as they were. But why not come and talk about your work to me; use me as a sort of wall against which you may throw your thoughts and catch them again? It's certain I don't know enough to steal your ideas myself – and I know no scientific men – '

I stopped. He was considering. Evidently the thing attracted him. 'But I'm afraid I should bore you,' he said.

'You think I'm too dull?'

'Oh, no; but technicalities – '

'Anyhow, you've interested me immensely this afternoon.'

'Of course it *would* be a great help to me. Nothing clears up one's ideas so much as explaining them. Hitherto – '

'My dear sir, say no more.'

'But really can you spare the time?'

'There is no rest like change of occupation,' I said, with profound conviction.

The affair was over. On my verandah steps he turned. 'I am already greatly indebted to you,' he said.

I made an interrogative noise.

'You have completely cured me of that ridiculous habit of humming,' he explained.

I think I said I was glad to be of any service to him, and he turned away.

Immediately the train of thought that our conversation had suggested must have resumed its sway. His arms began to wave in their former fashion. The faint echo of 'zuzzoo' came back to me on the breeze . . .

Well, after all, that was not my affair . . .

He came the next day, and again the next day after that, and delivered two lectures on physics to our mutual satisfaction. He talked with an air of being extremely lucid about the 'ether' and 'tubes of force', and 'gravitational potential', and things like that, and I sat in my other folding-chair and said, 'Yes,' 'Go on,' 'I follow you,' to keep him going. It was tremendously difficult stuff, but I do not think he ever suspected how much I did not understand him. There were moments when I doubted whether I was well employed, but at any rate I was resting from that confounded play. Now and then things gleamed on me clearly for a space, only to vanish just when I thought I had hold of them. Sometimes my attention failed altogether, and I would give it up and sit and stare at him, wondering whether, after all, it would not be better to use him as a central figure in a good farce and let all this other stuff slide. And then, perhaps, I would catch on again for a bit.

At the earliest opportunity I went to see his house. It was large and carelessly furnished; there were no servants other than his three assistants, and his dietary and private life were characterised by a philosophical simplicity. He was a water-drinker, a vegetarian, and all those logical disciplinary things. But the sight of his equipment settled many doubts. It looked like business from cellar to attic – an amazing little place to find in an out-of-the-way village. The ground-floor rooms contained benches and apparatus, the bakehouse and scullery boiler had developed into respectable furnaces, dynamos occupied the cellar, and there was a gasometer in the garden. He showed it to me with all the confiding zest of a man who has been living too much alone. His seclusion was overflowing now in an excess of confidence, and I had the good luck to be the recipient.

The three assistants were creditable specimens of the class of 'handy-men' from which they came. Conscientious if unintelligent, strong, civil, and willing. One, Spargus, who did the cooking and all the metal work, had been a sailor; a second, Gibbs, was a joiner; and the third was an ex-jobbing gardener, and now general assistant. They were the merest labourers. All the intelligent work was done by Cavor. Theirs was the darkest ignorance compared even with my muddled impression.

And now, as to the nature of these enquiries. Here, unhappily, comes a grave difficulty. I am no scientific expert, and if I were to attempt to set forth in the highly scientific language of Mr Cavor the aim to which his experiments tended, I am afraid I should confuse not only the reader but myself, and almost certainly I should make some blunder that would bring upon me the mockery of every up-to-date student of mathematical physics in the country. The best thing I can do therefore is, I think, to give my impressions in my own inexact language, without any attempt to wear a garment of knowledge to which I have no claim.

The object of Mr Cavor's search was a substance that should be 'opaque' – he used some other word I have forgotten, but 'opaque' conveys the idea – to 'all forms of radiant energy'. 'Radiant energy', he made me understand, was anything like light or heat, or those Rontgen Rays there was so much talk about a year or so ago, or the electric waves of Marconi, or gravitation. All these things, he said, *radiate* out from centres, and act on bodies at a distance, whence comes the term 'radiant energy'. Now almost all substances are opaque to some form or other of radiant energy. Glass, for example, is transparent to light, but much less so to heat, so that it is useful as a fire-screen; and alum is transparent to light, but blocks heat completely. A solution of iodine in carbon bisulphide, on the other hand, completely blocks light, but is quite transparent to heat. It will hide a fire from you, but permit all its warmth to reach you. Metals are not only opaque to light and heat, but also to electrical energy, which passes through both iodine solution and glass almost as though they were not interposed. And so on.

Now all known substances are 'transparent' to gravitation. You can use screens of various sorts to cut off the light or heat, or electrical influence of the sun, or the warmth of the earth from anything; you can screen things by sheets of metal from Marconi's rays, but nothing will cut off the gravitational attraction of the sun or the gravitational attraction of the earth. Yet why there should be nothing is hard to say. Cavor did not see why such a substance should not exist, and certainly I could not tell him. I had never thought of such a possibility before. He showed me by calculations on paper, which Lord Kelvin, no doubt, or Professor Lodge, or Professor Karl Pearson, or any of those great scientific people might have understood, but which simply reduced me to a hopeless muddle, that not only was such a substance possible, but that it must satisfy certain conditions. It was an amazing piece of reasoning. Much as it amazed and exercised me at the time, it would be impossible to reproduce it here. 'Yes,' I said to it all, 'yes; go on!' Suffice it for this story that he believed he might be able to manufacture this possible substance opaque to gravitation out of a complicated alloy of metals and something new – a new element, I fancy – called, I believe, *helium*, which was sent to him from London in sealed stone jars. Doubt has been thrown upon this detail, but I am almost certain it was *helium* he had sent him in sealed stone jars. It was certainly something very gaseous and thin. If only I had taken notes . . .

But then, how was I to foresee the necessity of taking notes?

Anyone with the merest germ of an imagination will understand the extraordinary possibilities of such a substance, and will sympathise a little with the emotion I felt as this understanding emerged from the haze of abstruse phrases in which Cavor expressed himself. Comic relief in a play indeed! It was some time before I would believe that I had interpreted him aright, and I was very careful not to ask questions that would have enabled him to gauge the profundity of misunderstanding into which he dropped his daily exposition. But no one reading the story of it here will sympathise fully, because from my barren narrative it will be impossible to gather the strength of my conviction that this astonishing substance was positively going to be made.

I do not recall that I gave my play an hour's consecutive work at any time after my visit to his house. My imagination had other things to do. There seemed no limit to the possibilities of the stuff; whichever way I tried I came on miracles and revolutions. For example, if one wanted to lift a weight, however enormous, one had only to get a sheet of this substance beneath it, and one might lift it with a straw. My first natural impulse was to apply this principle to guns and ironclads, and all the material and methods of war, and from that to shipping, locomotion, building, every conceivable form of human industry. The chance that had brought me into the very birth-chamber of this new time – it was an epoch, no less – was one of those chances that come once in a thousand years. The thing unrolled, it expanded and expanded. Among other things I saw in it my redemption as a businessman. I saw a parent company, and daughter companies, applications to right of us, applications to left, rings and trusts, privileges, and concessions spreading and spreading, until one vast, stupendous Cavorite company ran and ruled the world.

And I was in it!

I took my line straight away. I knew I was staking everything, but I jumped there and then.

'We're on absolutely the biggest thing that has ever been invented,' I said, and put the accent on 'we'. 'If you want to keep me out of this, you'll have to do it with a gun. I'm coming down to be your fourth labourer tomorrow.'

He seemed surprised at my enthusiasm, but not a bit suspicious or hostile. Rather, he was self-depreciatory.

He looked at me doubtfully. 'But do you really think – ?' he said. 'And your play! How about that play?'

'It's vanished!' I cried. 'My dear sir, don't you see what you've got? Don't you see what you're going to do?'

That was merely a rhetorical turn, but positively, he didn't. At first I could not believe it. He had not had the beginning of the inkling of an idea. This astonishing little man had been working on purely theoretical grounds the whole time; when he said it was 'the most important' research the world had ever seen, he simply meant it squared up so many theories, settled so much that was in doubt; he had troubled no more about the application of the stuff he was going to turn out than if he had been a machine that makes guns. This was a possible substance, and he was going to make it! *V'la tout*, as the Frenchman says.

Beyond that, he was childish; if he made it, it would go down to posterity as Cavorite or Cavorine, and he would be made an FRS, and his portrait given away as a scientific worthy with *Nature*, and things like that. And that was all he saw! He would have dropped this bombshell into the world as though he had discovered a new species of gnat, if it had not happened that I had come along. And there it would have lain and fizzled, like one or two other little things these scientific people have lit and dropped about us.

When I realised this, it was I did the talking, and Cavor who said, 'Go on!' I jumped up. I paced the room, gesticulating like a boy of twenty. I tried to make him understand his duties and responsibilities in the matter – *our* duties and responsibilities in the matter. I assured him we might make wealth enough to work any sort of social revolution we fancied, we might own and order the whole world. I told him of companies and patents, and the case for secret processes. All these things seemed to take him much as his mathematics had taken me. A look of perplexity came into his ruddy little face. He stammered something about indifference to wealth, but I brushed all that aside. He had got to be rich, and it was no good his stammering. I gave him to understand the sort of man I was, and that I had had very considerable business experience. I did not tell him I was an undischarged bankrupt at the time, because that was temporary, but I think I reconciled my evident poverty with my financial claims. And quite insensibly, in the way such projects grow, the understanding of a Cavorite monopoly grew up between us. He was to make the stuff, and I was to make the boom.

I stuck like a leech to the 'we' – 'you' and 'I' didn't exist for me.

His idea was that the profits I spoke of might go to endow research, but that, of course, was a matter we had to settle later. 'That's all right,' I shouted, 'that's all right.' The great point, as I insisted, was to get the thing done.

'Here is a substance,' I cried, 'no home, no factory, no fortress, no ship can dare to be without – more universally applicable even than a patent medicine. There isn't a solitary aspect of it, not one of its ten thousand possible uses that will not make us rich, Cavor, beyond the dreams of avarice!'

'No!' he said. 'I begin to see. It's extraordinary how one gets new points of view by talking over things!'

'And as it happens you have just talked to the right man!'

'I suppose no one,' he said, 'is absolutely *averse* to enormous wealth. Of course there is one thing – '

He paused. I stood still.

'It is just possible, you know, that we may not be able to make it after all! It may be one of those things that are a theoretical possibility, but a practical absurdity. Or when we make it, there may be some little hitch – !'

'We'll tackle the hitch when it comes,' said I.

CHAPTER TWO

The First Making of Cavorite

But Cavor's fears were groundless, so far as the actual making was concerned. On the 14th of October, 1899, this incredible substance was made!

Oddly enough, it was made at last by accident, when Mr Cavor least expected it. He had fused together a number of metals and certain other things – I wish I knew the particulars now! – and he intended to leave the mixture a week and then allow it to cool slowly. Unless he had miscalculated, the last stage in the combination would occur when the stuff sank to a temperature of 60°F. But it chanced that, unknown to Cavor, dissension had arisen about the furnace tending. Gibbs, who had previously seen to this, had suddenly attempted to shift it to the man who had been a gardener, on the score that coal was soil, being dug, and therefore could not possibly fall within the province of a joiner; the man who had been a jobbing gardener alleged, however, that coal was a metallic or ore-like substance, let alone that he was cook. But Spargus insisted on Gibbs doing the coaling, seeing that he was a joiner and that coal is notoriously fossil wood. Consequently Gibbs ceased to replenish the furnace, and no one else did so, and Cavor was too much immersed in certain interesting problems concerning a Cavorite flying machine (neglecting the resistance of the air and one or two other points) to perceive that anything was wrong. And the premature birth of his invention took place just as he was coming across the field to my bungalow for our afternoon talk and tea.

I remember the occasion with extreme vividness. The water was boiling, and everything was prepared, and the sound of his 'zuzzoo' had brought me out upon the verandah. His active little figure was black against the autumnal sunset, and to the right the chimneys of his house just rose above a gloriously tinted group of trees. Remoter rose the Wealden Hills, faint and blue, while to the left the hazy marsh spread out spacious and serene. And then –

The chimneys jerked heavenward, smashing into a string of bricks as they rose, and the roof and a miscellany of furniture followed. Then overtaking them came a huge white flame. The trees about the building swayed and whirled and tore themselves to pieces, that sprang towards the flare. My ears were smitten with a clap of thunder that left me deaf on one side for life, and all about me windows smashed, unheeded.

I took three steps from the verandah towards Cavor's house, and even as I did so came the wind.

Instantly my coat tails were over my head, and I was progressing in great leaps and bounds, and quite against my will, towards him. In the same moment the discoverer was seized, whirled about, and flew through the screaming air. I saw one of my chimney pots hit the ground within six yards of me, leap a score of feet, and so hurry in great strides towards the focus of the disturbance. Cavor, kicking and flapping, came down again, rolled over and over on the ground for a space, struggled up and was lifted and borne forward at an enormous velocity, vanishing at last among the labouring, lashing trees that writhed about his house.

A mass of smoke and ashes, and a square of bluish shining substance rushed up towards the zenith. A large fragment of fencing came sailing past me, dropped edgeways, hit the ground and fell flat, and then the worst was over. The aerial commotion fell swiftly until it was a mere strong gale, and I became once more aware that I had breath and feet. By leaning back against the wind I managed to stop, and could collect such wits as still remained to me.

In that instant the whole face of the world had changed. The tranquil sunset had vanished, the sky was dark with scurrying clouds, everything was flattened and swaying with the gale. I glanced back to see if my bungalow was still in a general way standing, then staggered forwards towards the trees amongst which Cavor had vanished, and through whose tall and leaf-denuded branches shone the flames of his burning house.

I entered the copse, dashing from one tree to another and clinging to them, and for a space I sought him in vain. Then amidst a heap of smashed branches and fencing that had banked itself against a portion of his garden wall I perceived something stir. I made a run for this, but before I reached it a brown object separated itself, rose on two muddy legs, and protruded two drooping, bleeding hands. Some tattered ends of garment fluttered out from its middle portion and streamed before the wind.

For a moment I did not recognise this earthy lump, and then I saw that it was Cavor, caked in the mud in which he had rolled. He leant forward against the wind, rubbing the dirt from his eyes and mouth.

He extended a muddy lump of hand, and staggered a pace towards me. His face worked with emotion, little lumps of mud kept falling from it. He looked as damaged and pitiful as any living creature I have ever seen, and his remark therefore amazed me exceedingly. 'Gratulate me,' he gasped; 'gratulate me!'

'Congratulate you! said I. 'Good heavens! What for?'

'I've done it.'

'You *have*. What on earth caused that explosion?'

A gust of wind blew his words away. I understood him to say that it wasn't an explosion at all. The wind hurled me into collision with him, and we stood clinging to one another.

'Try and get back to my bungalow,' I bawled in his ear. He did not hear me, and shouted something about 'three martyrs – science', and also something about 'not much good'. At the time he laboured under the impression that his three attendants had perished in the whirlwind. Happily this was incorrect. Directly he had left for my bungalow they had gone. Off to the public-house in Lympne to discuss the question of the furnaces over some trivial refreshment.

I repeated my suggestion of getting back to my bungalow, and this time he understood. We clung arm-in-arm and started, and managed at last to reach the shelter of as much roof as was left to me. For a space we sat in armchairs and panted. All the windows were broken, and the lighter articles of furniture were in great disorder, but no irrevocable damage was done. Happily the kitchen door had stood the pressure upon it, so that all my crockery and cooking materials had survived. The oil stove was still burning, and I put on the water to boil again for tea. And that prepared, I could turn on Cavor for his explanation.

'Quite correct,' he insisted; 'quite correct. I've done it, and it's all right.'

'But', I protested. 'All right! Why, there can't be a rick standing, or a fence or a thatched roof undamaged for twenty miles round . . . '

'It's all right – *really*. I didn't, of course, foresee this little upset. My mind was preoccupied with another problem, and I'm apt to disregard these practical side issues. But it's all right – '

'My dear sir,' I cried, 'don't you see you've done thousands of pounds' worth of damage?'

'There, I throw myself on your discretion. I'm not a practical man, of course, but don't you think they will regard it as a cyclone?'

'But the explosion – '

'It was not an explosion. It's perfectly simple. Only, as I say, I'm apt to overlook these little things. Its that zuzzoo business on a larger scale. Inadvertently I made this substance of mine, this Cavorite, in a thin, wide sheet . . . '

He paused. 'You are quite clear that the stuff is opaque to gravitation, that it cuts off things from gravitating towards each other?'

'Yes,' said I. 'Yes.'

'Well, so soon as it reached a temperature of 60°F, and the process of its manufacture was complete, the air above it, the portions of roof and ceiling and floor above it ceased to have weight. I suppose you know – everybody knows nowadays – that, as a usual thing, the air has weight, that it presses on everything at the surface of the earth, presses in all directions, with a pressure of fourteen and a half pounds to the square inch?'

'I know that,' said I. 'Go on.'

'I know that too,' he remarked. 'Only this shows you how useless knowledge is unless you apply it. You see, over our Cavorite this ceased to be the case, the air there ceased to exert any pressure, and the air round it and not over the Cavorite was exerting a pressure of fourteen pounds and a half to the square in upon this suddenly weightless air. Ah! you begin to see! The air all about the Cavorite crushed in upon the air above it with irresistible force. The air above the Cavorite was forced upward violently, the air that rushed in to replace it immediately lost weight, ceased to exert any pressure, followed suit, blew the ceiling through and the roof off . . .

'You perceive,' he said, 'it formed a sort of atmospheric fountain, a kind of chimney in the atmosphere. And if the Cavorite itself hadn't been loose and so got sucked up the chimney, does it occur to you what would have happened?'

I thought. 'I suppose,' I said, 'the air would be rushing up and up over that infernal piece of stuff now.'

'Precisely,' he said. 'A huge fountain – '

'Spouting into space! Good heavens! Why, it would have squirted all the atmosphere of the earth away! It would have robbed the world of air! It would have been the death of all mankind! That little lump of stuff!'

'Not exactly into space,' said Cavor, 'but as bad – practically. It would have whipped the air off the world as one peels a banana, and flung it thousands of miles. It would have dropped back again, of course – but on an asphyxiated world! From our point of view very little better than if it never came back!'

I stared. As yet I was too amazed to realise how all my expectations had been upset. 'What do you mean to do now?' I asked.

'In the first place, if I may borrow a garden trowel I will remove some of this earth with which I am encased, and then if I may avail myself of your domestic conveniences I will have a bath. This done, we will converse more at leisure. It will be wise, I think' – he laid a muddy hand on my arm – 'if nothing were said of this affair beyond ourselves. I know I have caused great damage – probably even dwelling-houses may be ruined here and there upon the countryside. But on the other hand, I cannot possibly pay for the damage I have done, and if the real cause of this is published, it will lead only to heartburning and the obstruction of my work. One cannot foresee *everything*, you know, and I cannot consent for one moment to add the burthen of practical considerations to my theorising. Later on, when you have come in with your practical mind, and Cavorite is floated – floated is the word, isn't it? – and it has realised all you anticipate for it, we may set matters right with these persons. But not now – not now. If no other explanation is offered, people, in the present unsatisfactory state of meteorological science, will ascribe all this to a cyclone; there might be a public subscription, and as my house has collapsed and been burnt, I should in that case receive a considerable share in the compensation, which would be extremely helpful to the prosecution of our researches. But if it is known that *I* caused this, there will be no public subscription, and everybody will be put out. Practically I should never get a chance of working in peace again. My three assistants may or may not have perished. That is a detail. If they have, it is no great loss; they were more zealous than able, and this premature event must be largely due to their joint neglect of the furnace. If they have not perished, I doubt if they have the intelligence to explain the affair. They will accept the cyclone story. And if during the temporary unfitness of my house for occupation, I may lodge in one of the untenanted rooms of this bungalow of yours – '

He paused and regarded me.

A man of such possibilities, I reflected, is no ordinary guest to entertain.

'Perhaps,' said I, rising to my feet, 'we had better begin by looking for a trowel,' and I led the way to the scattered vestiges of the greenhouse.

And while he was having his bath I considered the entire question alone. It was clear there were drawbacks to Mr Cavor's society I had not foreseen. The absent-mindedness that had just escaped depopulating the terrestrial globe, might at any moment result in some other grave inconvenience. On the other hand I was young, my affairs were in a mess, and I was in just the mood for reckless adventure – with a chance of something good at the end of it. I had quite settled in my mind that I was to have half at least in that aspect of the affair. Fortunately I held my bungalow, as I have already explained, on a three-year agreement, without being responsible for repairs; and my furniture, such as there was of it, had been hastily purchased, was unpaid for, insured, and altogether devoid of associations. In the end I decided to keep on with him, and see the business through.

Certainly the aspect of things had changed very greatly. I no longer doubted at all the enormous possibilities of the substance, but I began to have doubts about the gun-carriage and the patent boots.

We set to work at once to reconstruct his laboratory and proceed with our experiments. Cavor talked more on my level than he had ever done before, when it came to the question of how we should make the stuff next.

'Of course we must make it again,' he said, with a sort of glee I had not expected in him, 'of course we must make it again. We have caught a Tartar, perhaps, but we have left the theoretical behind us for good and all. If we can possibly avoid wrecking this little planet of ours, we will. But – there *must* be risks! There must be. In experimental work there always are. And here, as a practical man, *you* must come in. For my own part it seems to me we might make it edgeways, perhaps, and very thin. Yet I don't know. I have a certain dim perception of another method. I can hardly explain it yet. But curiously enough it came into my mind, while I was rolling over and over in the mud before the wind, and very doubtful how the whole adventure was to end, as being absolutely the thing I ought to have done.'

Even with my aid we found some little difficulty, and meanwhile we kept at work restoring the laboratory. There was plenty to do before it became absolutely necessary to decide upon the precise form and method of our second attempt. Our only hitch was the strike of the three labourers, who objected to my activity as a foreman. But that matter we compromised after two days' delay.

CHAPTER THREE

The Building of the Sphere

I remember the occasion very distinctly when Cavor told me of his idea of the sphere. He had had intimations of it before, but at the time it seemed to come to him in a rush. We were returning to the bungalow for tea, and on the way he fell humming. Suddenly he shouted, 'That's it! That finishes it! A sort of roller blind!'

'Finishes what?' I asked.

'Space – anywhere! The moon.'

'What do you mean?'

'Mean? Why – it must be a sphere! That's what I mean!'

I saw I was out of it, and for a time I let him talk in his own fashion. I hadn't the ghost of an idea then of his drift. But after he had taken tea he made it clear to me.

'It's like this,' he said. 'Last time I ran this stuff that cuts things off from gravitation into a flat tank with an overlap that held it down. And directly it had cooled and the manufacture was completed all that uproar happened, nothing above it weighed anything, the air went squirting up, the house squirted up, and if the stuff itself hadn't squirted up too, I don't know what would have happened! But suppose the substance is loose, and quite free to go up?'

'It will go up at once!'

'Exactly. With no more disturbance than firing a big gun.'

'But what good will that do?'

'I'm going up with it!'

I put down my teacup and stared at him.

'Imagine a sphere,' he explained, 'large enough to hold two people and their luggage. It will be made of steel lined with thick glass; it will contain a proper store of solidified air, concentrated food, water distilling apparatus, and so forth. And enamelled, as it were, on the outer steel – '

'Cavorite?'

'Yes.'

'But how will you get inside?'

'There was a similar problem about a dumpling.'

'Yes, I know. But how?'

'That's perfectly easy. An air-tight manhole is all that is needed. That, of course, will have to be a little complicated; there will have to be a valve, so that things may be thrown out, if necessary, without much loss of air.'

'Like Jules Verne's thing in *A Trip to the Moon*.'

But Cavor was not a reader of fiction.

'I begin to see,' I said slowly. 'And you could get in and screw yourself up while the Cavorite was warm, and as soon as it cooled it would become impervious to gravitation, and off you would fly – '

'At a tangent.'

'You would go off in a straight line – ' I stopped abruptly. 'What is to prevent the thing travelling in a straight line into space for ever?' I asked. 'You're not safe to get anywhere, and if you do – how will you get back?'

'I've just thought of that,' said Cavor. 'That's what I meant when I said the thing is finished. The inner glass sphere can be air-tight, and, except for the manhole, continuous, and the steel sphere can be made in sections, each section capable of rolling up after the fashion of a roller blind. These can easily be worked by springs, and released and checked by electricity conveyed by platinum wires fused through the glass. All that is merely a question of detail. So you see, that except for the thickness of the blind rollers, the Cavorite exterior of the sphere will consist of windows or blinds, whichever you like to call them. Well, when all these windows or blinds are shut, no light, no heat, no gravitation, no radiant energy of any sort will get at the inside of the sphere, it will fly on through space in a straight line, as you say. But open a window, imagine one of the windows open. Then at once any heavy body that chances to be in that direction will attract us – '

I sat taking it in.

'You see?' he said.

'Oh, I *see*.'

'Practically we shall be able to tack about in space just as we wish. Get attracted by this and that.'

'Oh, yes. *That's* clear enough. Only – '

'Well?'

'I don't quite see what we shall do it for! It's really only jumping off the world and back again.'

'Surely! For example, one might go to the moon.'

'And when one got there? What would you find?'

'We should see – Oh! consider the new knowledge.'

'Is there air there?'

'There may be.'

'It's a fine idea,' I said, 'but it strikes me as a large order all the same. The moon! I'd much rather try some smaller things first.'

'They're out of the question, because of the air difficulty.'

'Why not apply that idea of spring blinds – Cavorite blinds in strong steel cases – to lifting weights?'

'It wouldn't work,' he insisted. 'After all, to go into outer space is not so much worse, if at all, than a polar expedition. Men go on polar expeditions.'

'Not businessmen. And besides, they get paid for polar expeditions. And if anything goes wrong there are relief parties. But this – it's just firing ourselves off the world for nothing.'

'Call it prospecting.'

'You'll have to call it that . . . One might make a book of it perhaps,' I said.

'I have no doubt there will be minerals,' said Cavor.

'For example?'

'Oh! sulphur, ores, gold perhaps, possibly new elements.'

'Cost of carriage,' I said. 'You know you're not a practical man. The moon's a quarter of a million miles away.'

'It seems to me it wouldn't cost much to cart any weight anywhere if you packed it in a Cavorite case.'

I had not thought of that. 'Delivered free on head of purchaser, eh?'

'It isn't as though we were confined to the moon.'

'You mean?'

'There's Mars – clear atmosphere, novel surroundings, exhilarating sense of lightness. It might be pleasant to go there.'

'Is there air on Mars?'

'Oh, yes!'

'Seems as though you might run it as a sanatorium. By the way, how far is Mars?'

'Two hundred million miles at present,' said Cavor airily; 'and you go close by the sun.'

My imagination was picking itself up again. 'After all,' I said, 'there's something in these things. There's travel – '

An extraordinary possibility came rushing into my mind. Suddenly I saw, as in a vision, the whole solar system threaded with Cavorite liners and spheres *de luxe*. 'Rights of pre-emption', came floating into my head – planetary rights of pre-emption. I recalled the old Spanish monopoly in American gold. It wasn't as though it was just this planet or that – it was all of them. I stared at Cavor's rubicund face, and suddenly my imagination was leaping and dancing. I stood up, I walked up and down; my tongue was unloosened.

'I'm beginning to take it in,' I said; 'I'm beginning to take it in.' The transition from doubt to enthusiasm seemed to take scarcely any time at all. 'But this is tremendous!' I cried. 'This is Imperial! I haven't been dreaming of this sort of thing.'

Once the chill of my opposition was removed, his own pent-up excitement had play. He too got up and paced. He too gesticulated and shouted. We behaved like men inspired. We *were* men inspired.

'We'll settle all that!' he said in answer to some incidental difficulty that had pulled me up. 'We'll soon settle that! We'll start the drawings for mouldings this very night.'

'We'll start them now,' I responded, and we hurried off to the laboratory to begin upon this work forthwith.

I was like a child in Wonderland all that night. The dawn found us both still at work – we kept our electric light going heedless of the day. I remember now exactly how these drawings looked. I shaded and tinted while Cavor drew – smudged and haste-marked they were in every line, but wonderfully correct. We got out the orders for the steel blinds and frames we needed from that night's work, and the glass sphere was designed within a week. We gave up our afternoon conversations and our old routine altogether. We worked, and we slept and ate when we could work no longer for hunger and fatigue. Our enthusiasm infected even our three men, though they had no idea what the sphere was for. Through those days the man Gibbs gave up walking, and went everywhere, even across the room, at a sort of fussy run.

And it grew – the sphere. December passed, January – I spent a day with a broom sweeping a path through the snow from bungalow to laboratory – February, March. By the end of March the completion was in sight. In January had come a team of horses, a huge packing-case; we had our thick glass sphere now ready, and in position under the crane we had rigged to sling it into the steel shell. All the bars and blinds of the steel shell – it was not really a spherical shell, but polyhedral, with a roller blind to each facet – had arrived by February, and the lower half was bolted together. The Cavorite was half made by March, the metallic paste had gone through two of the stages in its manufacture, and we had plastered quite half of it on to the steel bars and blinds. It was astonishing how closely we kept to the lines of Cavor's first inspiration in working out the scheme. When the bolting together of the sphere was finished, he proposed to remove the rough roof of the temporary laboratory in which the work was done, and build a furnace about it. So the last stage of Cavorite making, in which the paste is heated to a dull red glow in a stream of helium, would be accomplished when it was already on the sphere.

And then we had to discuss and decide what provisions we were to take – compressed foods, concentrated essences, steel cylinders containing reserve oxygen, an arrangement for removing carbonic acid and waste from the air and restoring oxygen by means of sodium peroxide, water condensers, and so forth. I remember the little heap they made in the corner – tins, and rolls, and boxes – convincingly matter-of-fact.

It was a strenuous time, with little chance of thinking. But one day, when we were drawing near the end, an odd mood came over me. I had been bricking up the furnace all the morning, and I sat down by these possessions dead beat. Everything seemed dull and incredible.

'But look here, Cavor,' I said. 'After all! What's it all for?'

He smiled. 'The thing now is to go.'

'The moon,' I reflected. 'But what do you expect? I thought the moon was a dead world.'

He shrugged his shoulders.

'We're going to see.'

'*Are* we?' I said, and stared before me.

'You are tired,' he remarked. 'You'd better take a walk this afternoon.'

'No,' I said obstinately; 'I'm going to finish this brickwork.'

And I did, and ensured myself a night of insomnia.

I don't think I have ever had such a night. I had some bad times before my business collapse, but the very worst of those was sweet slumber compared to this infinity of aching wakefulness. I was suddenly in the most enormous funk at the thing we were going to do.

I do not remember before that night thinking at all of the risks we were running. Now they came like that array of spectres that once beleaguered Prague, and camped around me. The strangeness of what we were about to do, the unearthliness of it, overwhelmed me. I was like a man awakened out of pleasant dreams to the most horrible surroundings. I lay, eyes wide open, and the sphere seemed to get more flimsy and feeble, and Cavor more unreal and fantastic, and the whole enterprise madder and madder every moment.

I got out of bed and wandered about. I sat at the window and stared at the immensity of space. Between the stars was the void, the unfathomable darkness! I tried to recall the fragmentary knowledge of astronomy I had gained in my irregular reading, but it was all too vague to furnish any idea of the things we might expect. At last I got back to bed and snatched some moments of sleep – moments of nightmare rather – in which I fell and fell and fell for evermore into the abyss of the sky.

I astonished Cavor at breakfast. I told him shortly, 'I'm not coming with you in the sphere.'

I met all his protests with a sullen persistence. 'The thing's too mad,' I said, 'and I won't come. The thing's too mad.'

I would not go with him to the laboratory. I fretted about my bungalow for a time, and then took hat and stick and set out alone, I knew not whither. It chanced to be a glorious morning: a warm wind and deep blue sky, the first green of spring abroad, and multitudes of birds singing. I lunched on beef and beer in a little public-house near Elham, and startled the landlord by remarking apropos of the weather, 'A man who leaves the world when days of this sort are about is a fool!'

'That's what I says when I heerd on it!' said the landlord, and I found that for one poor soul at least this world had proved excessive, and there had been a throat-cutting. I went on with a new twist to my thoughts.

In the afternoon I had a pleasant sleep in a sunny place, and went on my way refreshed. I came to a comfortable-looking inn near Canterbury. It was bright with creepers, and the landlady was a clean old woman and took my eye. I found I had just enough money to pay for my lodging with her. I decided to stop the night there. She was a talkative body, and among many other particulars learnt she had never been to London. 'Canterbury's as far as ever I been,' she said. 'I'm not one of your gad-about sort.'

'How would you like a trip to the moon?' I cried.

'I never did hold with them ballooneys,' she said, evidently under the impression that this was a common excursion enough. 'I wouldn't go up in one – not for ever so.'

This struck me as being funny. After I had supped I sat on a bench by the door of the inn and gossiped with two labourers about brick-making, and motor cars, and the cricket of last year. And in the sky a faint new crescent, blue and vague as a distant Alp, sank westward over the sun.

The next day I returned to Cavor. 'I am coming,' I said. 'I've been a little out of order, that's all.'

That was the only time I felt any serious doubt of our enterprise. Nerves purely! After that I worked a little more carefully, and took a trudge for an hour every day. And at last, save for the heating in the furnace, our labours were at an end.

CHAPTER FOUR

Inside the Sphere

'Go on,' said Cavor, as I sat across the edge of the manhole, and looked down into the black interior of the sphere. We two were alone. It was evening, the sun had set, and the stillness of the twilight was upon everything.

I drew my other leg inside and slid down the smooth glass to the bottom of the sphere, then turned to take the cans of food and other impedimenta from Cavor. The interior was warm, the thermometer stood at eighty, and as we should lose little or none of this by radiation, we were dressed in shoes and thin flannels. We had, however, a bundle of thick woollen clothing and several thick blankets to guard against mischance. By Cavor's direction I placed the packages, the cylinders of oxygen, and so forth, loosely about my feet, and soon we had everything in. He walked about the roofless shed for a time seeking anything we had overlooked, and then crawled in after me. I noted something in his hand.

'What have you got there?' I asked.

'Haven't you brought anything to read?'

'Good Lord! No.'

'I forgot to tell you. There are uncertainties – The voyage may last – We may be weeks!'

'But – '

'We shall be floating in this sphere with absolutely no occupation.'

'I wish I'd known – '

He peered out of the manhole. 'Look!' he said. 'There's something there!'

'Is there time?'

'We shall be an hour.'

I looked out. It was an old number of *Tit-Bits* that one of the men must have brought. Farther away in the corner I saw a torn *Lloyd's News*. I scrambled back into the sphere with these things. 'What have you got?' I said.

I took the book from his hand and read, *The Works of William Shake-speare*.

He coloured slightly. 'My education has been so purely scientific – ' he said apologetically.

'Never read him?'

'Never.'

'He knew a little, you know – in an irregular sort of way.'

'Precisely what I am told,' said Cavor.

I assisted him to screw in the glass cover of the manhole, and then he pressed a stud to close the corresponding blind in the outer case. The little oblong of twilight vanished. We were in darkness.

For a time neither of us spoke. Although our case would not be impervious to sound, everything was very still. I perceived there was nothing to grip when the shock of our start should come, and I realised that I should be uncomfortable for want of a chair.

'Why have we no chairs?' I asked.

'I've settled all that,' said Cavor. 'We won't need them.'

'Why not?'

'You will see,' he said, in the tone of a man who refuses to talk.

I became silent. Suddenly it had come to me clear and vivid that I was a fool to be inside that sphere. Even now, I asked myself, is it too late to withdraw? The world outside the sphere, I knew, would be cold and inhospitable enough for me – for weeks I had been living on subsidies from Cavor – but after all, would it be as cold as the infinite zero, as inhospitable as empty space? If it had not been for the appearance of cowardice, I believe that even then I should have made him let me out. But I hesitated on that score, and hesitated, and grew fretful and angry, and the time passed.

There came a little jerk, a noise like champagne being uncorked in another room, and a faint whistling sound. For just one instant I had a sense of enormous tension, a transient conviction that my feet were pressing downward with a force of countless tons. It lasted for an infinitesimal time.

But it stirred me to action. 'Cavor!' I said into the darkness, 'my nerve's in rags . . . I don't think – '

I stopped. He made no answer.

'Confound it!' I cried; 'I'm a fool! What business have I here? I'm not coming, Cavor. The thing's too risky. I'm getting out.'

'You can't,' he said.

'Can't! We'll soon see about that!'

He made no answer for ten seconds. 'It's too late for us to quarrel now, Bedford,' he said. 'That little jerk was the start. Already we are flying as swiftly as a bullet up into the gulf of space.'

'I – ' I said, and then it didn't seem to matter what happened. For a time I was, as it were, stunned; I had nothing to say. It was just as if I had never heard of this idea of leaving the world before. Then I perceived an unaccountable change in my bodily sensations. It was a feeling of lightness, of unreality. Coupled with that was a queer sensation in the head, an apoplectic effect almost, and a thumping of blood vessels at the ears. Neither of these feelings diminished as time went on, but at last I got so used to them that I experienced no inconvenience.

I heard a click, and a little glow lamp came into being.

I saw Cavor's face, as white as I felt my own to be. We regarded one another in silence. The transparent blackness of the glass behind him made him seem as though he floated in a void.

'Well, we're committed,' I said at last.

'Yes,' he said, 'we're committed.'

'Don't move,' he exclaimed, at some suggestion of a gesture. 'Let your muscles keep quite lax – as if you were in bed. We are in a little universe of our own. Look at those things!'

He pointed to the loose cases and bundles that had been lying on the blankets in the bottom of the sphere. I was astonished to see that they were floating now nearly a foot from the spherical wall. Then I saw from his shadow that Cavor was no longer leaning against the glass. I thrust out my hand behind me, and found that I too was suspended in space, clear of the glass.

I did not cry out nor gesticulate, but fear came upon me. It was like being held and lifted by something – you know not what. The mere touch of my hand against the glass moved me rapidly. I understood what had happened, but that did not prevent my being afraid. We were cut off from all exterior gravitation, only the attraction of objects within our sphere had effect. Consequently everything that was not fixed to the glass was falling – slowly because of the slightness of our masses – towards the centre of gravity of our little world, which seemed to be somewhere about the middle of the sphere, but rather nearer to myself than Cavor, on account of my greater weight.

'We must turn round,' said Cavor, 'and float back to back, with the things between us.'

It was the strangest sensation conceivable, floating thus loosely in space, at first indeed horribly strange, and when the horror passed, not disagreeable at all, exceeding restful; indeed, the nearest thing in earthly experience to it that I know is lying on a very thick, soft feather bed. But the quality of utter detachment and independence! I had not reckoned on things like this. I had expected a violent jerk at starting, a giddy sense of speed. Instead I felt – as if I were disembodied. It was not like the beginning of a journey; it was like the beginning of a dream.

CHAPTER FIVE

The Journey to the Moon

Presently Cavor extinguished the light. He said we had not overmuch energy stored, and that what we had we must economise for reading. For a time, whether it was long or short I do not know, there was nothing but blank darkness.

A question floated up out of the void. 'How are we pointing?' I said. 'What is our direction?'

'We are flying away from the earth at a tangent, and as the moon is near her third quarter we are going somewhere towards her. I will open a blind – '

Came a click, and then a window in the outer case yawned open. The sky outside was as black as the darkness within the sphere, but the shape of the open window was marked by an infinite number of stars.

Those who have only seen the starry sky from the earth cannot imagine its appearance when the vague, half-luminous veil of our air has been withdrawn. The stars we see on earth are the mere scattered survivors that penetrate our misty atmosphere. But now at last I could realise the meaning of the hosts of heaven!

Stranger things we were presently to see, but that airless, star-dusted sky! Of all things, I think that will be one of the last I shall forget.

The little window vanished with a click, another beside it snapped open and instantly closed, and then a third, and for a moment I had to close my eyes because of the blinding splendour of the waning moon.

For a space I had to stare at Cavor and the white-lit things about me to season my eyes to light again, before I could turn them towards that pallid glare.

Four windows were open in order that the gravitation of the moon might act upon all the substances in our sphere. I found I was no longer floating freely in space, but that my feet were resting on the glass in the direction of the moon. The blankets and cases of provisions were also creeping slowly down the glass, and presently came to rest so as to block out a portion of the view. It seemed to me, of course, that I looked 'down' when I looked at the moon. On earth 'down' means earthward, the way things fall, and 'up' the reverse direction. Now the pull of gravitation was towards the moon, and for all I knew to the contrary our earth was overhead. And, of course, when all the Cavorite blinds were closed, 'down' was towards the centre of our sphere, and 'up' towards its outer wall.

It was curiously unlike earthly experience, too, to have the light coming *up* to one. On earth light falls from above, or comes slanting down sideways, but here it came from beneath our feet, and to see our shadows we had to look up.

At first it gave me a sort of vertigo to stand only on thick glass and look down upon the moon through hundreds of thousands of miles of vacant space; but this sickness passed very speedily. And then – the splendour of the sight!

The reader may imagine it best if he will lie on the ground some warm summer's night and look between his up-raised feet at the moon, but for some reason, probably because the absence of air made it so much more luminous, the moon seemed already considerably larger than it does from earth. The minutest details of its surface were acutely clear. And since we did not see it through air, its outline was bright and sharp, there was no glow or halo about it, and the stardust that covered the sky came right to its very margin, and marked the outline of its unilluminated part. And as I stood and stared at the moon between my feet, that perception of the impossible that had been with me off and on ever since our start, returned again with tenfold conviction.

'Cavor,' I said, 'this takes me queerly. Those companies we were going to run, and all that about minerals?'

'Well?'

'I don't see 'em here.'

'No,' said Cavor; 'but you'll get over all that.'

'I suppose I'm made to turn right side up again. Still, *this* – For a moment I could half believe there never was a world.'

'That copy of *Lloyd's News* might help you.'

I stared at the paper for a moment, then held it above the level of my face, and found I could read it quite easily. I struck a column of mean little advertisements. 'A gentleman of private means is willing to lend money,' I read. I knew that gentleman. Then somebody eccentric wanted to sell a Cutaway bicycle, 'quite new and cost 15 pounds', for five pounds; and a lady in distress wished to dispose of some fish knives and forks, 'a wedding present', at a great sacrifice. No doubt some simple soul was sagely examining these knives and forks, and another triumphantly riding off on that bicycle, and a third trustfully consulting that benevolent gentleman of means even as I read. I laughed, and let the paper drift from my hand.

'Are we visible from the earth?' I asked.

'Why?'

'I knew someone who was rather interested in astronomy. It occurred to me that it would be rather odd if – my friend – chanced to be looking through some telescope.'

'It would need the most powerful telescope on earth even now to see us as the minutest speck.'

For a time I stared in silence at the moon.

'It's a world,' I said; 'one feels that infinitely more than one ever did on earth. People perhaps – '

'People!' he exclaimed. '*No!* Banish all that! Think yourself a sort of ultra-arctic voyager exploring the desolate places of space. Look at it!'

He waved his hand at the shining whiteness below. 'It's dead – dead! Vast extinct volcanoes, lava wildernesses, tumbled wastes of snow, or frozen carbonic acid, or frozen air, and everywhere landslip seams and cracks and gulfs. Nothing happens. Men have watched this planet systematically with telescopes for over two hundred years. How much change do you think they have seen?'

'None.'

'They have traced two indisputable landslips, a doubtful crack, and one slight periodic change of colour, and that's all.'

'I didn't know they'd traced even that.'

'Oh, yes. But as for people!'

'By the way,' I asked, 'how small a thing will the biggest telescopes show upon the moon?'

'One could see a fair-sized church. One could certainly see any towns or buildings, or anything like the handiwork of men. There might perhaps be insects, something in the way of ants, for example, so that they could hide in deep burrows from the lunar light, or some new sort of creatures having no earthly parallel. That is the most probable thing, if we are to find life there at all. Think of the difference in conditions! Life must fit itself to a day as long as fourteen earthly days, a cloudless sun-blaze of fourteen days, and then a night of equal length, growing ever colder and colder under these cold, sharp stars. In that night there must be cold, the ultimate cold, absolute zero, 273°C below the earthly freezing point. Whatever life there is must hibernate through *that*, and rise again each day.'

He mused. 'One can imagine something worm-like,' he said, 'taking its air solid as an earthworm swallows earth, or thick-skinned monsters – '

'By the by,' I said, 'why didn't we bring a gun?'

He did not answer that question. 'No,' he concluded, 'we just have to go. We shall see when we get there.'

I remembered something. 'Of course, there's my minerals, anyhow,' I said; 'whatever the conditions may be.'

Presently he told me he wished to alter our course a little by letting the earth tug at us for a moment. He was going to open one earthward blind for thirty seconds. He warned me that it would make my head swim, and advised me to extend my hands against the glass to break my fall. I did as he directed, and thrust my feet against the bales of food cases and air cylinders to prevent their falling upon me. Then with a click the window flew open. I fell clumsily upon hands and face, and saw for a moment between my black extended fingers our mother earth – a planet in a downward sky.

We were still very near – Cavor told me the distance was perhaps eight hundred miles – and the huge terrestrial disc filled all heaven. But already it was plain to see that the world was a globe. The land below us was in twilight and vague, but westward the vast grey stretches of the Atlantic shone like molten silver under the receding day. I think I recognised the cloud-dimmed coastlines of France and Spain and the south of England, and then, with a click, the shutter closed again, and I found myself in a state of extraordinary confusion sliding slowly over the smooth glass.

When at last things settled themselves in my mind again, it seemed quite beyond question that the moon was 'down' and under my feet, and that the earth was somewhere away on the level of the horizon – the earth that had been 'down' to me and my kindred since the beginning of things.

So slight were the exertions required of us, so easy did the practical annihilation of our weight make all we had to do, that the necessity for taking refreshment did not occur to us for nearly six hours (by Cavor's chronometer) after our start. I was amazed at that lapse of time. Even then I was satisfied with very little. Cavor examined the apparatus for absorbing carbonic acid and water, and pronounced it to be in satisfactory order, our consumption of oxygen having been extraordinarily slight. And our talk being exhausted for the time, and there being nothing further for us to do, we gave way to a curious drowsiness that had come upon us, and spreading our blankets on the bottom of the sphere in such a manner as to shut out most of the moonlight, wished each other good-night, and almost immediately fell asleep.

And so, sleeping, and sometimes talking and reading a little, and at times eating, although without any keenness of appetite,[*] but for the most part in a sort of quiescence that was neither waking nor slumber, we fell through a space of time that had neither night nor day in it, silently, softly, and swiftly down towards the moon.

[*]   It is a curious thing, that while we were in the sphere we felt not the slightest desire for food, nor did we feel the want of it when we abstained. At first we forced our appetites, but afterwards we fasted completely. Altogether we did not consume one-hundredth part of the compressed provisions we had brought with us. The amount of carbonic acid we breathed was also unnaturally low, but why this was, I am quite unable to explain.

CHAPTER SIX

The Landing on the Moon

I remember how one day Cavor suddenly opened six of our shutters and blinded me so that I cried aloud at him. The whole area was moon, a stupendous scimitar of white dawn with its edge hacked out by notches of darkness, the crescent shore of an ebbing tide of darkness, out of which peaks and pinnacles came glittering into the blaze of the sun. I take it the reader has seen pictures or photographs of the moon and that I need not describe the broader features of that landscape, those spacious ringlike ranges vaster than any terrestrial mountains, their summits shining in the day, their shadows harsh and deep, the grey disordered plains, the ridges, hills, and craterlets, all passing at last from a blazing illumination into a common mystery of black. Athwart this world we were flying scarcely a hundred miles above its crests and pinnacles. And now we could see, what no eye on earth will ever see, that under the blaze of the day the harsh outlines of the rocks and ravines of the plains and crater floor grew grey and indistinct under a thickening haze, that the white of their lit surfaces broke into lumps and patches, and broke again and shrank and vanished, and that here and there strange tints of brown and olive grew and spread.

But little time we had for watching then. For now we had come to the real danger of our journey. We had to drop ever closer to the moon as we spun about it, to slacken our pace and watch our chance, until at last we could dare to drop upon its surface.

For Cavor that was a time of intense exertion; for me it was an anxious inactivity. I seemed perpetually to be getting out of his way. He leapt about the sphere from point to point with an agility that would have been impossible on earth. He was perpetually opening and closing the Cavorite windows, making calculations, consulting his chronometer by means of the glow lamp during those last eventful hours. For a long time we had all our windows closed and hung silently in darkness hurtling through space.

Then he was feeling for the shutter studs, and suddenly four windows were open. I staggered and covered my eyes, drenched and scorched and blinded by the unaccustomed splendour of the sun beneath my feet. Then again the shutters snapped, leaving my brain spinning in a darkness that pressed against the eyes. And after that I floated in another vast, black silence.

Then Cavor switched on the electric light, and told me he proposed to bind all our luggage together with the blankets about it, against the concussion of our descent. We did this with our windows closed, because in that way our goods arranged themselves naturally at the centre of the sphere. That too was a strange business; we two men floating loose in that spherical space, and packing and pulling ropes. Imagine it if you can! No up nor down, and every effort resulting in unexpected movements. Now I would be pressed against the glass with the full force of Cavor's thrust, now I would be kicking helplessly in a void. Now the star of the electric light would be overhead, now under foot. Now Cavor's feet would float up before my eyes, and now we would be crossways to each other. But at last our goods were safely bound together in a big soft bale, all except two blankets with head holes that we were to wrap about ourselves.

Then for a flash Cavor opened a window moonwards, and we saw that we were dropping towards a huge central crater with a number of minor craters grouped in a sort of cross about it. And then again Cavor flung our little sphere open to the scorching, blinding sun. I think he was using the sun's attraction as a brake. 'Cover yourself with a blanket,' he cried, thrusting himself from me, and for a moment I did not understand.

Then I hauled the blanket from beneath my feet and got it about me and over my head and eyes. Abruptly he closed the shutters again, snapped one open again and closed it, then suddenly began snapping them all open, each safely into its steel roller. There came a jar, and then we were rolling over and over, bumping against the glass and against the big bale of our luggage, and clutching at each other, and outside some white substance splashed as if we were rolling down a slope of snow . . .

Over, clutch, bump, clutch, bump, over . . .

Came a thud, and I was half buried under the bale of our possessions, and for a space everything was still. Then I could hear Cavor puffing and grunting, and the snapping of a shutter in its sash. I made an effort, thrust back our blanket-wrapped luggage, and emerged from beneath it. Our open windows were just visible as a deeper black set with stars.

We were still alive, and we were lying in the darkness of the shadow of the wall of the great crater into which we had fallen.

We sat getting our breath again, and feeling the bruises on our limbs. I don't think either of us had had a very clear expectation of such rough handling as we had received. I struggled painfully to my feet. 'And now,' said I, 'to look at the landscape of the moon! But – ! It's tremendously dark, Cavor!'

The glass was dewy, and as I spoke I wiped at it with my blanket. 'We're half an hour or so beyond the day,' he said. 'We must wait.'

It was impossible to distinguish anything. We might have been in a sphere of steel for all that we could see. My rubbing with the blanket simply smeared the glass, and as fast as I wiped it, it became opaque again with freshly condensed moisture mixed with an increasing quantity of blanket hairs. Of course I ought not to have used the blanket. In my efforts to clear the glass I slipped upon the damp surface, and hurt my shin against one of the oxygen cylinders that protruded from our bale.

The thing was exasperating – it was absurd. Here we were just arrived upon the moon, amidst we knew not what wonders, and all we could see was the grey and streaming wall of the bubble in which we had come.

'Confound it!' I said, 'but at this rate we might have stopped at home;' and I squatted on the bale and shivered, and drew my blanket closer about me.

Abruptly the moisture turned to spangles and fronds of frost. 'Can you reach the electric heater,' said Cavor. 'Yes – that black knob. Or we shall freeze.'

I did not wait to be told twice. 'And now,' said I, what are we to do?'

'Wait,' he said.

'Wait?'

'Of course. We shall have to wait until our air gets warm again, and then this glass will clear. We can't do anything till then. It's night here yet; we must wait for the day to overtake us. Meanwhile, don't you feel hungry?'

For a space I did not answer him, but sat fretting. I turned reluctantly from the smeared puzzle of the glass and stared at his face. 'Yes,' I said, 'I am hungry. I feel somehow enormously disappointed. I had expected – I don't know what I had expected, but not this.'

I summoned my philosophy, and rearranging my blanket about me sat down on the bale again and began my first meal on the moon. I don't think I finished it – I forget. Presently, first in patches, then running rapidly together into wider spaces, came the clearing of the glass, came the drawing of the misty veil that hid the moon world from our eyes.

We peered out upon the landscape of the moon.

CHAPTER SEVEN

Sunrise on the Moon

As we saw it first it was the wildest and most desolate of scenes. We were in an enormous amphitheatre, a vast circular plain; the floor of the giant crater. Its cliff-like walls closed us in on every side. From the westward the light of the unseen sun fell upon them, reaching to the very foot of the cliff, and showed a disordered escarpment of drab and greyish rock, lined here and there with banks and crevices of snow. This was perhaps a dozen miles away, but at first no intervening atmosphere diminished in the slightest the minutely detailed brilliancy with which these things glared at us. They stood out clear and dazzling against a background of starry blackness that seemed to our earthly eyes rather a gloriously spangled velvet curtain than the spaciousness of the sky.

The eastward cliff was at first merely a starless selvedge to the starry dome. No rosy flush, no creeping pallor, announced the commencing day. Only the Corona, the Zodiacal light, a huge cone-shaped, luminous haze, pointing up towards the splendour of the morning star, warned us of the imminent nearness of the sun.

Whatever light was about us was reflected by the westward cliffs. It showed a huge undulating plain, cold and grey, a grey that deepened eastward into the absolute raven darkness of the cliff shadow. Innumerable rounded grey summits, ghostly hummocks, billows of snowy substance, stretching crest beyond crest into the remote obscurity, gave us our first inkling of the distance of the crater wall. These hummocks looked like snow. At the time I thought they were snow. But they were not – they were mounds and masses of frozen air.

So it was at first, and then, sudden, swift, and amazing, came the lunar day.

The sunlight had crept down the cliff, it touched the drifted masses at its base and incontinently came striding with seven-leagued boots towards us. The distant cliff seemed to shift and quiver, and at the touch of the dawn a reek of grey vapour poured upward from the crater floor, whirls and puffs and drifting wraiths of grey, thicker and broader and denser, until at last the whole westward plain was steaming like a wet handkerchief held before the fire, and the westward cliffs were no more than a refracted glare beyond.

'It is air,' said Cavor. 'It must be air – or it would not rise like this – at the mere touch of a sunbeam. And at this pace . . . '

He peered upwards. 'Look!' he said.

'What?' I asked.

'In the sky. Already. On the blackness – a little touch of blue. See! The stars seem larger. And the little ones and all those dim nebulosities we saw in empty space – they are hidden!'

Swiftly, steadily, the day approached us. Grey summit after grey summit was overtaken by the blaze, and turned to a smoking white intensity. At last there was nothing to the west of us but a bank of surging fog, the tumultuous advance and ascent of cloudy haze. The distant cliff had receded farther and farther, had loomed and changed through the whirl, and foundered and vanished at last in its confusion.

Nearer came that steaming advance, nearer and nearer, coming as fast as the shadow of a cloud before the south-west wind. About us rose a thin anticipatory haze.

Cavor gripped my arm.

'What?' I said.

'Look! The sunrise! The sun!'

He turned me about and pointed to the brow of the eastward cliff, looming above the haze about us, scarce lighter than the darkness of the sky. But now its line was marked by strange reddish shapes, tongues of vermilion flame that writhed and danced. I fancied it must be spirals of vapour that had caught the light and made this crest of fiery tongues against the sky, but indeed it was the solar prominences I saw, a crown of fire about the sun that is forever hidden from earthly eyes by our atmospheric veil.

And then – the sun!

Steadily, inevitably came a brilliant line, came a thin edge of intolerable effulgence that took a circular shape, became a bow, became a blazing sceptre, and hurled a shaft of heat at us as though it was a spear.

It seemed verily to stab my eyes! I cried aloud and turned about blinded, groping for my blanket beneath the bale.

And with that incandescence came a sound, the first sound that had reached us from without since we left the earth, a hissing and rustling, the stormy trailing of the aerial garment of the advancing day. And with the coming of the sound and the light the sphere lurched, and blinded and dazzled we staggered helplessly against each other. It lurched again, and the hissing grew louder. I had shut my eyes perforce, I was making clumsy efforts to cover my head with my blanket, and this second lurch sent me helplessly off my feet. I fell against the bale, and opening my eyes had a momentary glimpse of the air just outside our glass. It was running – it was boiling – like snow into which a white-hot rod is thrust. What had been solid air had suddenly at the touch of the sun become a paste, a mud, a slushy liquefaction, that hissed and bubbled into gas.

There came a still more violent whirl of the sphere and we had clutched one another. In another moment we were spun about again. Round we went and over, and then I was on all fours. The lunar dawn had hold of us. It meant to show us little men what the moon could do with us.

I caught a second glimpse of things without, puffs of vapour, half-liquid slush, excavated, sliding, falling, sliding. We dropped into dark-ness. I went down with Cavor's knees in my chest. Then he seemed to fly away from me, and for a moment I lay with all the breath out of my body staring upward. A toppling crag of the melting stuff had splashed over us, buried us, and now it thinned and boiled off us. I saw the bubbles dancing on the glass above. I heard Cavor exclaiming feebly.

Then some huge landslip in the thawing air had caught us, and spluttering expostulation, we began to roll down a slope, rolling faster and faster, leaping crevasses and rebounding from banks, faster and faster, westward into the white-hot boiling tumult of the lunar day.

Clutching at one another we spun about, pitched this way and that, our bale of packages leaping at us, pounding at us. We collided, we gripped, we were torn asunder – our heads met, and the whole universe burst into fiery darts and stars! On the earth we should have smashed one another a dozen times, but on the moon, luckily for us, our weight was only one-sixth of what it is terrestrially, and we fell very mercifully. I recall a sensation of utter sickness, a feeling as if my brain were upside down within my skull, and then –

*   *   *

Something was at work upon my face, some thin feelers worried my ears. Then I discovered the brilliance of the landscape around was mitigated by blue spectacles. Cavor bent over me, and I saw his face upside down, his eyes also protected by tinted goggles. His breath came irregularly, and his lip was bleeding from a bruise. 'Better?' he said, wiping the blood with the back of his hand.

Everything seemed swaying for a space, but that was simply my giddiness. I perceived that he had closed some of the shutters in the outer sphere to save me from the direct blaze of the sun. I was aware that everything about us was very brilliant.

'Lord! I gasped. 'But this – !'

I craned my neck to see. I perceived there was a blinding glare outside, an utter change from the gloomy darkness of our first impressions. 'Have I been insensible long?' I asked.

'I don't know – the chronometer is broken. Some little time . . . My dear chap! I have been afraid . . . '

I lay for a space taking this in. I saw his face still bore evidences of emotion. For a while I said nothing. I passed an inquisitive hand over my contusions, and surveyed his face for similar damages. The back of my right hand had suffered most, and was skinless and raw. My forehead was bruised and had bled. He handed me a little measure with some of the restorative – I forget the name of it – he had brought with us. After a time I felt a little better. I began to stretch my limbs carefully. Soon I could talk.

'It wouldn't have done,' I said, as though there had been no interval.

'No! it *wouldn't*.'

He thought, his hands hanging over his knees. He peered through the glass and then stared at me.

'Good Lord!' he said. '*No!*'

'What has happened?' I asked after a pause. 'Have we jumped to the tropics?'

'It was as I expected. This air has evaporated – if it is air. At any rate, it has evaporated, and the surface of the moon is showing. We are lying on a bank of earthy rock. Here and there bare soil is exposed. A queer sort of soil!'

It occurred to him that it was unnecessary to explain. He assisted me into a sitting position, and I could see with my own eyes.

CHAPTER EIGHT

A Lunar Morning

The harsh emphasis, the pitiless black and white of scenery had altogether disappeared. The glare of the sun had taken upon itself a faint tinge of amber; the shadows upon the cliff of the crater wall were deeply purple. To the eastward a dark bank of fog still crouched and sheltered from the sunrise, but to the westward the sky was blue and clear. I began to realise the length of my insensibility.

We were no longer in a void. An atmosphere had arisen about us. The outline of things had gained in character, had grown acute and varied; save for a shadowed space of white substance here and there, white substance that was no longer air but snow, the arctic appearance had gone altogether. Everywhere broad rusty brown spaces of bare and tumbled earth spread to the blaze of the sun. Here and there at the edge of the snowdrifts were transient little pools and eddies of water, the only things stirring in that expanse of barrenness. The sunlight inundated the upper two blinds of our sphere and turned our climate to high summer, but our feet were still in shadow, and the sphere was lying upon a drift of snow.

And scattered here and there upon the slope, and emphasised by little white threads of unthawed snow upon their shady sides, were shapes like sticks, dry twisted sticks of the same rusty hue as the rock upon which they lay. That caught one's thoughts sharply. Sticks! On a lifeless world? Then as my eye grew more accustomed to the texture of their substance, I perceived that almost all this surface had a fibrous texture, like the carpet of brown needles one finds beneath the shade of pine trees.

'Cavor!' I said.

'Yes.'

'It may be a dead world now – but once – '

Something arrested my attention. I had discovered among these needles a number of little round objects. And it seemed to me that one of these had moved.

'Cavor,' I whispered.

'What?'

But I did not answer at once. I stared incredulous. For an instant I could not believe my eyes. I gave an inarticulate cry. I gripped his arm. I pointed. 'Look!' I cried, finding my tongue. 'There! Yes! And there!'

His eyes followed my pointing finger. 'Eh?' he said.

How can I describe the thing I saw? It is so petty a thing to state, and yet it seemed so wonderful, so pregnant with emotion. I have said that amidst the stick-like litter were these rounded bodies, these little oval bodies that might have passed as very small pebbles. And now first one and then another had stirred, had rolled over and cracked, and down the crack of each of them showed a minute line of yellowish green, thrusting outward to meet the hot encouragement of the newly risen sun. For a moment that was all, and then there stirred, and burst a third!

'It is a seed,' said Cavor. And then I heard him whisper very softly, '*Life!*'

'Life!' And immediately it poured upon us that our vast journey had not been made in vain, that we had come to no arid waste of minerals, but to a world that lived and moved! We watched intensely. I remember I kept rubbing the glass before me with my sleeve, jealous of the faintest suspicion of mist.

The picture was clear and vivid only in the middle of the field. All about that centre the dead fibres and seeds were magnified and distorted by the curvature of the glass. But we could see enough! One after another all down the sunlit slope these miraculous little brown bodies burst and gaped apart, like seed-pods, like the husks of fruits; opened eager mouths that drank in the heat and light pouring in a cascade from the newly risen sun.

Every moment more of these seed coats ruptured, and even as they did so the swelling pioneers overflowed their rent-distended seed-cases, and passed into the second stage of growth. With a steady assurance, a swift deliberation, these amazing seeds thrust a rootlet downward to the earth and a queer little bundle-like bud into the air. In a little while the whole slope was dotted with minute plantlets standing at attention in the blaze of the sun.

They did not stand for long. The bundle-like buds swelled and strained and opened with a jerk, thrusting out a coronet of little sharp tips, spreading a whorl of tiny, spiky, brownish leaves, that lengthened rapidly, lengthened visibly even as we watched. The movement was slower than any animal's, swifter than any plant's I have ever seen before. How can I suggest it to you – the way that growth went on? The leaf tips grew so that they moved onward even while we looked at them. The brown seed-case shrivelled and was absorbed with an equal rapidity. Have you ever on a cold day taken a thermometer into your warm hand

and watched the little thread of mercury creep up the tube? These moon plants grew like that.

In a few minutes, as it seemed, the buds of the more forward of these plants had lengthened into a stem and were even putting forth a second whorl of leaves, and all the slope that had seemed so recently a lifeless stretch of litter was now dark with the stunted olive-green herbage of bristling spikes that swayed with the vigour of their growing.

I turned about, and behold! along the upper edge of a rock to the eastward a similar fringe in a scarcely less forward condition swayed and bent, dark against the blinding glare of the sun. And beyond this fringe was the silhouette of a plant mass, branching clumsily like a cactus, and swelling visibly, swelling like a bladder that fills with air.

Then to the westward also I discovered that another such distended form was rising over the scrub. But here the light fell upon its sleek sides, and I could see that its colour was a vivid orange hue. It rose as one watched it; if one looked away from it for a minute and then back, its outline had changed; it thrust out blunt congested branches until in a little time it rose a coralline shape of many feet in height. Compared with such a growth the terrestrial puff-ball, which will sometimes swell a foot in diameter in a single night, would be a hopeless laggard. But then the puff-ball grows against a gravitational pull six times that of the moon. Beyond, out of gullies and flats that had been hidden from us, but not from the quickening sun, over reefs and banks of shining rock, a bristling beard of spiky and fleshy vegetation was straining into view, hurrying tumultuously to take advantage of the brief day in which it must flower and fruit and seed again and die. It was like a miracle, that growth. So, one must imagine, the trees and plants arose at the Creation and covered the desolation of the new-made earth.

Imagine it; imagine that dawn! The resurrection of the frozen air, the stirring and quickening of the soil, and then this silent uprising of vegetation, this unearthly ascent of fleshiness and spikes. Conceive it all lit by a blaze that would make the intensest sunlight of earth seem watery and weak. And still around this stirring jungle, wherever there was shadow, lingered banks of bluish snow. And to have the picture of our impression complete, you must bear in mind that we saw it all through a thick bent glass, distorting it as things are distorted by a lens, acute only in the centre of the picture, and very bright there, and towards the edges magnified and unreal.

CHAPTER NINE

Prospecting Begins

We ceased to gaze. We turned to each other, the same thought, the same question in our eyes. For these plants to grow, there must be some air, however attenuated, air that we also should be able to breathe.

'The manhole?' I said.

'Yes!' said Cavor, 'if it is air we see!'

'In a little while,' I said, 'these plants will be as high as we are. Suppose – suppose after all – Is it certain? How do you know that stuff is air? It may be nitrogen – it may be carbonic acid even!'

'That's easy,' he said, and set about proving it. He produced a big piece of crumpled paper from the bale, lit it, and thrust it hastily through the manhole valve. I bent forward and peered down through the thick glass for its appearance outside, that little flame on whose evidence depended so much!

I saw the paper drop out and lie lightly upon the snow. The pink flame of its burning vanished. For an instant it seemed to be extinguished. And then I saw a little blue tongue upon the edge of it that trembled, and crept, and spread!

Quietly the whole sheet, save where it lay in immediate contact with the snow, charred and shrivelled and sent up a quivering thread of smoke. There was no doubt left to me; the atmosphere of the moon was either pure oxygen or air, and capable therefore – unless its tenuity was excessive – of supporting our alien life. We might emerge – and live!

I sat down with my legs on either side of the manhole and prepared to unscrew it, but Cavor stopped me. 'There is first a little precaution,' he said. He pointed out that although it was certainly an oxygenated atmosphere outside, it might still be so rarefied as to cause us grave injury. He reminded me of mountain sickness, and of the bleeding that often afflicts aeronauts who have ascended too swiftly, and he spent some time in the preparation of a sickly-tasting drink which he insisted on my sharing. It made me feel a little numb, but otherwise had no effect on me. Then he permitted me to begin unscrewing.

Presently the glass stopper of the manhole was so far undone that the denser air within our sphere began to escape along the thread of the screw, singing as a kettle sings before it boils. Thereupon he made me desist. It speedily became evident that the pressure outside was very much less than it was within. How much less it was we had no means of telling.

I sat grasping the stopper with both hands, ready to close it again if, in spite of our intense hope, the lunar atmosphere should after all prove too rarefied for us, and Cavor sat with a cylinder of compressed oxygen at hand to restore our pressure. We looked at one another in silence, and then at the fantastic vegetation that swayed and grew visibly and noiselessly without. And ever that shrill piping continued.

My blood-vessels began to throb in my ears, and the sound of Cavor's movements diminished. I noted how still everything had become, because of the thinning of the air.

As our air sizzled out from the screw the moisture of it condensed in little puffs.

Presently I experienced a peculiar shortness of breath that lasted indeed during the whole of the time of our exposure to the moon's exterior atmosphere, and a rather unpleasant sensation about the ears and fingernails and the back of the throat grew upon my attention, and presently passed off again.

But then came vertigo and nausea that abruptly changed the quality of my courage. I gave the lid of the manhole half a turn and made a hasty explanation to Cavor; but now he was the more sanguine. He answered me in a voice that seemed extraordinarily small and remote, because of the thinness of the air that carried the sound. He recommended a nip of brandy, and set me the example, and presently I felt better. I turned the manhole stopper back again. The throbbing in my ears grew louder, and then I remarked that the piping note of the outrush had ceased. For a time I could not be sure that it had ceased.

'Well?' said Cavor, in the ghost of a voice.

'Well?' said I.

'Shall we go on?'

I thought. 'Is this all?'

'If you can stand it.'

By way of answer I went on unscrewing. I lifted the circular operculum from its place and laid it carefully on the bale. A flake or so of snow whirled and vanished as that thin and unfamiliar air took possession of our sphere. I knelt, and then seated myself at the edge of the manhole, peering over it. Beneath, within a yard of my face, lay the untrodden snow of the moon.

There came a little pause. Our eyes met.

'It doesn't distress your lungs too much?' said Cavor.

'No,' I said. 'I can stand this.'

He stretched out his hand for his blanket, thrust his head through its central hole, and wrapped it about him. He sat down on the edge of the manhole, he let his feet drop until they were within six inches of the lunar ground. He hesitated for a moment, then thrust himself forward, dropped these intervening inches, and stood upon the untrodden soil of the moon.

As he stepped forward he was refracted grotesquely by the edge of the glass. He stood for a moment looking this way and that. Then he drew himself together and leapt.

The glass distorted everything, but it seemed to me even then to be an extremely big leap. He had at one bound become remote. He seemed twenty or thirty feet off. He was standing high upon a rocky mass and gesticulating back to me. Perhaps he was shouting – but the sound did not reach me. But how the deuce had he done this? I felt like a man who has just seen a new conjuring trick.

In a puzzled state of mind I too dropped through the manhole. I stood up. Just in front of me the snowdrift had fallen away and made a sort of ditch. I made a step and jumped.

I found myself flying through the air, saw the rock on which he stood coming to meet me, clutched it and clung in a state of infinite amazement.

I gasped a painful laugh. I was tremendously confused. Cavor bent down and shouted in piping tones for me to be careful.

I had forgotten that on the moon, with only an eighth part of the earth's mass and a quarter of its diameter, my weight was barely a sixth what it was on earth. But now that fact insisted on being remembered.

'We are out of Mother Earth's leading-strings now,' he said.

With a guarded effort I raised myself to the top, and moving as cautiously as a rheumatic patient, stood up beside him under the blaze of the sun. The sphere lay behind us on its dwindling snowdrift thirty feet away.

As far as the eye could see over the enormous disorder of rocks that formed the crater floor, the same bristling scrub that surrounded us was starting into life, diversified here and there by bulging masses of a cactus form, and scarlet and purple lichens that grew so fast they seemed to crawl over the rocks. The whole area of the crater seemed to me then to be one similar wilderness up to the very foot of the surrounding cliff.

This cliff was apparently bare of vegetation save at its base, and with buttresses and terraces and platforms that did not very greatly attract our attention at the time. It was many miles away from us in every direction, we seemed to be almost at the centre of the crater, and we saw it through a certain haziness that drove before the wind. For there was even a wind now in the thin air, a swift yet weak wind that chilled exceedingly but exerted little pressure. It was blowing round the crater, as it seemed, to the hot illuminated side from the foggy darkness under the sunward wall. It was difficult to look into this eastward fog; we had to peer with half-closed eyes beneath the shade of our hands, because of the fierce intensity of the motionless sun.

'It seems to be deserted,' said Cavor, 'absolutely desolate.'

I looked about me again. I retained even then a clinging hope of some quasi-human evidence, some pinnacle of building, some house or engine, but everywhere one looked spread the tumbled rocks in peaks and crests, and the darting scrub and those bulging cacti that swelled and swelled, a flat negation as it seemed of all such hope.

'It looks as though these plants had it to themselves,' I said. 'I see no trace of any other creature.'

'No insects – no birds, no! Not a trace, not a scrap nor particle of animal life. If there was – what would they do in the night? . . . No; there's just these plants alone.'

I shaded my eyes with my hand. 'It's like the landscape of a dream. These things are less like earthly land plants than the things one imagines among the rocks at the bottom of the sea. Look at that yonder! One might imagine it a lizard changed into a plant. And the glare!'

'This is only the fresh morning,' said Cavor.

He sighed and looked about him. 'This is no world for men,' he said. 'And yet in a way – it appeals.'

He became silent for a time, then commenced his meditative humming.

I started at a gentle touch, and found a thin sheet of livid lichen lapping over my shoe. I kicked at it and it fell to powder, and each speck began to grow.

I heard Cavor exclaim sharply, and perceived that one of the fixed bayonets of the scrub had pricked him.

He hesitated, his eyes sought among the rocks about us. A sudden blaze of pink had crept up a ragged pillar of crag. It was a most extraordinary pink, a livid magenta.

'Look!' said I, turning, and behold Cavor had vanished.

For an instant I stood transfixed. Then I made a hasty step to look over the verge of the rock. But in my surprise at his disappearance I forgot once more that we were on the moon. The thrust of my foot that I made in striding would have carried me a yard on earth; on the moon it carried me six – a good five yards over the edge. For the moment the thing had something of the effect of those nightmares when one falls and falls. For while one falls sixteen feet in the first second of a fall on earth, on the moon one falls two, and with only a sixth of one's weight. I fell, or rather I jumped down, about ten yards I suppose. It seemed to take quite a long time, five or six seconds, I should think. I floated through the air and fell like a feather, knee-deep in a snowdrift in the bottom of a gully of blue-grey, white-veined rock.

I looked about me. 'Cavor!' I cried; but no Cavor was visible.

'Cavor!' I cried louder, and the rocks echoed me.

I turned fiercely to the rocks and clambered to the summit of them. 'Cavor!' I cried. My voice sounded like the voice of a lost lamb.

The sphere, too, was not in sight, and for a moment a horrible feeling of desolation pinched my heart.

Then I saw him. He was laughing and gesticulating to attract my attention. He was on a bare patch of rock twenty or thirty yards away. I could not hear his voice, but 'jump' said his gestures. I hesitated, the distance seemed enormous. Yet I reflected that surely I must be able to clear a greater distance than Cavor.

I made a step back, gathered myself together, and leapt with all my might. I seemed to shoot right up in the air as though I should never come down.

It was horrible and delightful, and as wild as a nightmare, to go flying off in this fashion. I realised my leap had been altogether too violent. I flew clean over Cavor's head and beheld a spiky confusion in a gully spreading to meet my fall. I gave a yelp of alarm. I put out my hands and straightened my legs.

I hit a huge fungoid bulk that burst all about me, scattering a mass of orange spores in every direction, and covering me with orange powder. I rolled over spluttering, and came to rest convulsed with breathless laughter.

I became aware of Cavor's little round face peering over a bristling hedge. He shouted some faded enquiry. 'Eh?' I tried to shout, but could not do so for want of breath. He made his way towards me, coming gingerly among the bushes.

'We've got to be careful,' he said. 'This moon has no discipline. She'll let us smash ourselves.'

He helped me to my feet. 'You exerted yourself too much,' he said, dabbing at the yellow stuff with his hand to remove it from my garments.

I stood passive and panting, allowing him to beat off the jelly from my knees and elbows and lecture me upon my misfortunes. 'We don't quite allow for the gravitation. Our muscles are scarcely educated yet. We must practise a little, when you have got your breath.'

I pulled two or three little thorns out of my hand, and sat for a time on a boulder of rock. My muscles were quivering, and I had that feeling of personal disillusionment that comes at the first fall to the learner of cycling on earth.

It suddenly occurred to Cavor that the cold air in the gully, after the brightness of the sun, might give me a fever. So we clambered back into the sunlight. We found that beyond a few abrasions I had received no serious injuries from my tumble, and at Cavor's suggestion we were presently looking round for some safe and easy landing-place for my next leap. We chose a rocky slab some ten yards off, separated from us by a little thicket of olive-green spikes.

'Imagine it there!' said Cavor, who was assuming the airs of a trainer, and he pointed to a spot about four feet from my toes. This leap I managed without difficulty, and I must confess I found a certain satisfaction in Cavor's falling short by a foot or so and tasting the spikes of the scrub. 'One has to be careful you see,' he said, pulling out his thorns, and with that he ceased to be my Mentor and became my fellow-learner in the art of lunar locomotion.

We chose a still easier jump and did it without difficulty, and then leapt back again, and to and fro several times, accustoming our muscles to the new standard. I could never have believed had I not experienced it, how rapid that adaptation would be. In a very little time indeed, certainly after fewer than thirty leaps, we could judge the effort necessary for a distance with almost terrestrial assurance.

And all this time the lunar plants were growing around us, higher and denser and more entangled, every moment thicker and taller, spiked plants, green cactus masses, fungi, fleshy and lichenous things, strangest radiate and sinuous shapes. But we were so intent upon our leaping, that for a time we gave no heed to their unfaltering expansion.

An extraordinary elation had taken possession of us. Partly, I think, it was our sense of release from the confinement of the sphere. Mainly, however, the thin sweetness of the air, which I am certain contained a much larger proportion of oxygen than our terrestrial atmosphere. In spite of the strange quality of all about us, I felt as adventurous and experimental as a cockney would do placed for the first time among mountains and I do not think it occurred to either of us, face to face though we were with the unknown, to be very greatly afraid.

We were bitten by a spirit of enterprise. We selected a lichenous kopje perhaps fifteen yards away, and landed neatly on its summit one after the other. 'Good!' we cried to each other; 'good!' and Cavor made three steps and went off to a tempting slope of snow a good twenty yards and more beyond. I stood for a moment struck by the grotesque effect of his soaring figure – his dirty cricket cap, and spiky hair, his little round body, his arms and his knickerbockered legs tucked up tightly – against the weird spaciousness of the lunar scene. A gust of laughter seized me, and then I stepped off to follow. Plump! I dropped beside him.

We made a few gargantuan strides, leapt three or four times more, and sat down at last in a lichenous hollow. Our lungs were painful. We sat holding our sides and recovering our breath, looking appreciation to one another. Cavor panted something about 'amazing sensations'. And then came a thought into my head. For the moment it did not seem a particularly appalling thought, simply a natural question arising out of the situation.

'By the way,' I said, 'where exactly is the sphere?'

Cavor looked at me. 'Eh?'

The full meaning of what we were saying struck me sharply.

'Cavor!' I cried, laying a hand on his arm, 'where is the sphere?'

CHAPTER TEN

Lost Men in the Woods

His face caught something of my dismay. He stood up and stared about him at the scrub that fenced us in and rose about us, straining upward in a passion of growth. He put a dubious hand to his lips. He spoke with a sudden lack of assurance. 'I think,' he said slowly, 'we left it . . . somewhere . . . about *there*.'

He pointed a hesitating finger that wavered in an arc.

'I'm not sure.' His look of consternation deepened. 'Anyhow,' he said, with his eyes on me, 'it can't be far.'

We had both stood up. We made unmeaning ejaculations, our eyes sought in the twining, thickening jungle round about us.

All about us on the sunlit slopes frothed and swayed the darting shrubs, the swelling cactus, the creeping lichens, and wherever the shade remained the snowdrifts lingered. North, south, east, and west spread an identical monotony of unfamiliar forms. And somewhere, buried already among this tangled confusion, was our sphere, our home, our only provision, our only hope of escape from this fantastic wilderness of ephemeral growths into which we had come.

'I think after all,' he said, pointing suddenly, 'it might be over there.'

'No,' I said. 'We have turned in a curve. See! here is the mark of my heels. It's clear the thing must be more to the eastward, much more. No! – the sphere must be over there.'

'I *think*,' said Cavor, 'I kept the sun upon my right all the time.'

'Every leap, it seems to *me*,' I said, 'my shadow flew before me.'

We stared into one another's eyes. The area of the crater had become enormously vast to our imaginations, the growing thickets already impenetrably dense.

'Good heavens! What fools we have been!'

'It's evident that we must find it again,' said Cavor, 'and that soon. The sun grows stronger. We should be fainting with the heat already if it wasn't so dry. And . . . I'm hungry.'

I stared at him. I had not suspected this aspect of the matter before. But it came to me at once – a positive craving. 'Yes,' I said with emphasis. 'I am hungry too.'

He stood up with a look of active resolution. 'Certainly we must find the sphere.'

As calmly as possible we surveyed the interminable reefs and thickets that formed the floor of the crater, each of us weighing in silence the chances of our finding the sphere before we were overtaken by heat and hunger.

'It can't be fifty yards from here,' said Cavor, with indecisive gestures. 'The only thing is to beat round about until we come upon it.'

'That is all we can do,' I said, without any alacrity to begin our hunt. 'I wish this confounded spike bush did not grow so fast!'

'That's just it,' said Cavor. 'But it *was* lying on a bank of snow.'

I stared about me in the vain hope of recognising some knoll or shrub that had been near the sphere. But everywhere was a confusing sameness, everywhere the aspiring bushes, the distending fungi, the dwindling snow banks, steadily and inevitably changed. The sun scorched and stung, the faintness of an unaccountable hunger mingled with our infinite perplexity. And even as we stood there, confused and lost amidst unprecedented things, we became aware for the first time of a sound upon the moon other than the air of the growing plants, the faint sighing of the wind, or those that we ourselves had made.

Boom . . . Boom . . . Boom . . .

It came from beneath our feet, a sound in the earth. We seemed to hear it with our feet as much as with our ears. Its dull resonance was muffled by distance, thick with the quality of intervening substance. No sound that I can imagine could have astonished us more, or have changed more completely the quality of things about us. For this sound, rich, slow, and deliberate, seemed to us as though it could be nothing but the striking of some gigantic buried clock.

Boom . . . Boom . . . Boom . . .

Sound suggestive of still cloisters, of sleepless nights in crowded cities, of vigils and the awaited hour, of all that is orderly and methodical in life, booming out pregnant and mysterious in this fantastic desert! To the eye everything was unchanged: the desolation of bushes and cacti waving silently in the wind, stretched unbroken to the distant cliffs, the still dark sky was empty overhead, and the hot sun hung and burned. And through it all, a warning, a threat, throbbed this enigma of sound.

Boom . . . Boom . . . Boom . . .

We questioned one another in faint and faded voices.

'A clock?'

'Like a clock!'

'What is it?'

'What can it be?'

'Count,' was Cavor's belated suggestion, and at that word the striking ceased.

The silence, the rhythmic disappointment of the silence, came as a fresh shock. For a moment one could doubt whether one had ever heard a sound. Or whether it might not still be going on. Had I indeed heard a sound?

I felt the pressure of Cavor's hand upon my arm. He spoke in an undertone, as though he feared to wake some sleeping thing. 'Let us keep together,' he whispered, 'and look for the sphere. We must get back to the sphere. This is beyond our understanding.'

'Which way shall we go?'

He hesitated. An intense persuasion of presences, of unseen things about us and near us, dominated our minds. What could they be? Where could they be? Was this arid desolation, alternately frozen and scorched, only the outer rind and mask of some subterranean world? And if so, what sort of world? What sort of inhabitants might it not presently disgorge upon us?

And then, stabbing the aching stillness as vivid and sudden as an unexpected thunderclap, came a clang and rattle as though great gates of metal had suddenly been flung apart.

It arrested our steps. We stood gaping helplessly. Then Cavor stole towards me.

'I do not understand!' he whispered close to my face. He waved his hand vaguely skyward, the vague suggestion of still vaguer thoughts.

'A hiding-place! If anything came . . . '

I looked about us. I nodded my head in assent to him.

We started off, moving stealthily with the most exaggerated precautions against noise. We went towards a thicket of scrub. A clangour like hammers flung about a boiler hastened our steps. 'We must crawl,' whispered Cavor.

The lower leaves of the bayonet plants, already overshadowed by the newer ones above, were beginning to wilt and shrivel so that we could thrust our way in among the thickening stems without serious injury. A stab in the face or arm we did not heed. At the heart of the thicket I stopped, and stared panting into Cavor's face.

'Subterranean,' he whispered. 'Below.'

'They may come out.'

'We must find the sphere!'

'Yes,' I said; 'but how?'

'Crawl till we come to it.'

'But if we don't?'

'Keep hidden. See what they are like.'

'We will keep together,' said I.

He thought. 'Which way shall we go?'

'We must take our chance.'

We peered this way and that. Then very circumspectly, we began to crawl through the lower jungle, making, so far as we could judge, a circuit, halting now at every waving fungus, at every sound, intent only on the sphere from which we had so foolishly emerged. Ever and again from out of the earth beneath us came concussions, beatings, strange, inexplicable, mechanical sounds; and once, and then again, we thought we heard something, a faint rattle and tumult, borne to us through the air. But fearful as we were we dared essay no vantage-point to survey the crater. For long we saw nothing of the beings whose sounds were so abundant and insistent. But for the faintness of our hunger and the drying of our throats that crawling would have had the quality of a very vivid dream. It was so absolutely unreal. The only element with any touch of reality was these sounds.

Figure it to yourself! About us the dreamlike jungle, with the silent bayonet leaves darting overhead, and the silent, vivid, sun-splashed lichens under our hands and knees, waving with the vigour of their growth as a carpet waves when the wind gets beneath it. Ever and again one of the bladder fungi, bulging and distending under the sun, loomed upon us. Ever and again some novel shape in vivid colour obtruded. The very cells that built up these plants were as large as my thumb, like beads of coloured glass. And all these things were saturated in the unmitigated glare of the sun, were seen against a sky that was bluish black and spangled still, in spite of the sunlight, with a few surviving stars. Strange! the very forms and texture of the stones were strange. It was all strange, the feeling of one's body was unprecedented, every other movement ended in a surprise. The breath sucked thin in one's throat, the blood flowed through one's ears in a throbbing tide – thud, thud, thud, thud . . .

And ever and again came gusts of turmoil, hammering, the clanging and throb of machinery, and presently – the bellowing of great beasts!

CHAPTER ELEVEN

The Mooncalf Pastures

So we two poor terrestrial castaways, lost in that wild-growing moon jungle, crawled in terror before the sounds that had come upon us. We crawled, as it seemed, a long time before we saw either Selenite or mooncalf, though we heard the bellowing and gruntulous noises of these latter continually drawing nearer to us. We crawled through stony ravines, over snow slopes, amidst fungi that ripped like thin bladders at our thrust, emitting a watery humour, over a perfect pavement of things like puff-balls, and beneath interminable thickets of scrub. And ever more helplessly our eyes sought for our abandoned sphere. The noise of the mooncalves would at times be a vast flat calf-like sound, at times it rose to an amazed and wrathy bellowing, and again it would become a clogged bestial sound, as though these unseen creatures had sought to eat and bellow at the same time.

Our first view was but an inadequate transitory glimpse, yet none the less disturbing because it was incomplete. Cavor was crawling in front at the time, and he first was aware of their proximity. He stopped dead, arresting me with a single gesture.

A crackling and smashing of the scrub appeared to be advancing directly upon us, and then, as we squatted close and endeavoured to judge of the nearness and direction of this noise, there came a terrific bellow behind us, so close and vehement that the tops of the bayonet scrub bent before it, and one felt the breath of it hot and moist. And, turning about, we saw indistinctly through a crowd of swaying stems the mooncalf's shining sides, and the long line of its back loomed out against the sky.

Of course it is hard for me now to say how much I saw at that time, because my impressions were corrected by subsequent observation. First of all impressions was its enormous size; the girth of its body was some fourscore feet, its length perhaps two hundred. Its sides rose and fell with its laboured breathing. I perceived that its gigantic, flabby body lay along the ground, and that its skin was of a corrugated white, dappling into blackness along the backbone. But of its feet we saw nothing. I think also that we saw then the profile at least of the almost brainless head, with its fat-encumbered neck, its slobbering omnivorous mouth, its little nostrils, and tight shut eyes. (For the mooncalf invariably shuts its eyes in the presence of the sun.) We had a glimpse of a vast red pit as it opened its mouth to bleat and bellow again; we had a breath from the pit, and then the monster heeled over like a ship, dragged forward along the ground, creasing all its leathery skin, rolled again, and so wallowed past us, smashing a path amidst the scrub, and was speedily hidden from our eyes by the dense interlacings beyond. Another appeared more distantly, and then another, and then, as though he was guiding these animated lumps of provender to their pasture, a Selenite came momentarily into ken. My grip upon Cavor's foot became convulsive at the sight of him, and we remained motionless and peering long after he had passed out of our range.

By contrast with the mooncalves he seemed a trivial being, a mere ant, scarcely five feet high. He was wearing garments of some leathery substance, so that no portion of his actual body appeared, but of this, of course, we were entirely ignorant. He presented himself, therefore, as a compact, bristling creature, having much of the quality of a complicated insect, with whiplike tentacles and a clanging arm projecting from his shining cylindrical body case. The form of his head was hidden by his enormous many-spiked helmet – we discovered afterwards that he used the spikes for prodding refractory mooncalves – and a pair of goggles of darkened glass, set very much at the side, gave a birdlike quality to the metallic apparatus that covered his face. His arms did not project beyond his body case, and he carried himself upon short legs that, wrapped though they were in warm coverings, seemed to our terrestrial eyes inordinately flimsy. They had very short thighs, very long shanks, and little feet.

In spite of his heavy-looking clothing, he was progressing with what would be, from the terrestrial point of view, very considerable strides, and his clanging arm was busy. The quality of his motion during the instant of his passing suggested haste and a certain anger, and soon after we had lost sight of him we heard the bellow of a mooncalf change abruptly into a short, sharp squeal followed by the scuffle of its acceleration. And gradually that bellowing receded, and then came to an end, as if the pastures sought had been attained.

We listened. For a space the moon world was still. But it was some time before we resumed our crawling search for the vanished sphere.

When next we saw mooncalves they were some little distance away from us in a place of tumbled rocks. The less vertical surfaces of the rocks were thick with a speckled green plant growing in dense mossy clumps, upon which these creatures were browsing. We stopped at the edge of the reeds amidst which we were crawling at the sight of them, peering out at then and looking round for a second glimpse of a Selenite. They lay against their food like stupendous slugs, huge, greasy hulls, eating greedily and noisily, with a sort of sobbing avidity. They seemed monsters of mere fatness, clumsy and overwhelmed to a degree that would make a Smithfield ox seem a model of agility. Their busy, writhing, chewing mouths, and eyes closed, together with the appetising sound of their munching, made up an effect of animal enjoyment that was singularly stimulating to our empty frames.

'Hogs!' said Cavor, with unusual passion. 'Disgusting hogs!' and after one glare of angry envy crawled off through the bushes to our right. I stayed long enough to see that the speckled plant was quite hopeless for human nourishment, then crawled after him, nibbling a quill of it between my teeth.

Presently we were arrested again by the proximity of a Selenite, and this time we were able to observe him more exactly. Now we could see that the Selenite covering was indeed clothing, and not a sort of crustacean integument. He was quite similar in his costume to the former one we had glimpsed, except that ends of something like wadding were protruding from his neck, and he stood on a promontory of rock and moved his head this way and that, as though he was surveying the crater. We lay quite still, fearing to attract his attention if we moved, and after a time he turned about and disappeared.

We came upon another drove of mooncalves bellowing up a ravine, and then we passed over a place of sounds, sounds of beating machinery as if some huge hall of industry came near the surface there. And while these sounds were still about us we came to the edge of a great open space, perhaps two hundred yards in diameter, and perfectly level. Save for a few lichens that advanced from its margin this space was bare, and presented a powdery surface of a dusty yellow colour. We were afraid to strike out across this space, but as it presented less obstruction to our crawling than the scrub, we went down upon it and began very circumspectly to skirt its edge.

For a little while the noises from below ceased and everything, save for the faint stir of the growing vegetation, was very still. Then abruptly there began an uproar, louder, more vehement, and nearer than any we had so far heard. Of a certainty it came from below. Instinctively we crouched as flat as we could, ready for a prompt plunge into the thicket beside us. Each knock and throb seemed to vibrate through our bodies. Louder grew this throbbing and beating, and that irregular vibration increased until the whole moon world seemed to be jerking and pulsing.

'Cover,' whispered Cavor, and I turned towards the bushes.

At that instant came a thud like the thud of a gun, and then a thing happened – it still haunts me in my dreams. I had turned my head to look at Cavor's face, and thrust out my hand in front of me as I did so. And my hand met nothing! Plunged suddenly into a bottomless hole!

My chest hit something hard, and I found myself with my chin on the edge of an unfathomable abyss that had suddenly opened beneath me, my hand extended stiffly into the void. The whole of that flat circular area was no more than a gigantic lid, that was now sliding sideways from off the pit it had covered into a slot prepared for it.

Had it not been for Cavor I think I should have remained rigid, hanging over this margin and staring into the enormous gulf below, until at last the edges of the slot scraped me off and hurled me into its depths. But Cavor had not received the shock that had paralysed me. He had been a little distance from the edge when the lid had first opened, and perceiving the peril that held me helpless, gripped my legs and pulled me backward. I came into a sitting position, crawled away from the edge for a space on all fours, then staggered up and ran after him across the thundering, quivering sheet of metal. It seemed to be swinging open with a steadily accelerated velocity, and the bushes in front of me shifted sideways as I ran.

I was none too soon. Cavor's back vanished amidst the bristling thicket, and as I scrambled up after him, the monstrous valve came into its position with a clang. For a long time we lay panting, not daring to approach the pit.

But at last very cautiously and bit by bit we crept into a position from which we could peer down. The bushes about us creaked and waved with the force of a breeze that was blowing down the shaft. We could see nothing at first except smooth vertical walls descending at last into an impenetrable black. And then very gradually we became aware of a number of very faint and little lights going to and fro.

For a time that stupendous gulf of mystery held us so that we forgot even our sphere. In time, as we grew more accustomed to the darkness, we could make out very small, dim, elusive shapes moving about among those needle-point illuminations. We peered amazed and incredulous, understanding so little that we could find no words to say. We could distinguish nothing that would give us a clue to the meaning of the faint shapes we saw.

'What can it be?' I asked; 'what can it be?'

'The engineering! . . . They must live in these caverns during the night, and come out during the day.'

'Cavor!' I said. 'Can they be – *that* – it was something like – men?'

'*That* was not a man.'

'We dare risk nothing!'

'We dare do nothing until we find the sphere!'

'We can do nothing until we find the sphere.'

He assented with a groan and stirred himself to move. He stared about him for a space, sighed, and indicated a direction. We struck out through the jungle. For a time we crawled resolutely, then with diminishing vigour.

Presently among great shapes of flabby purple there came a noise of trampling and cries about us. We lay close, and for a long time the sounds went to and fro and very near. But this time we saw nothing. I tried to whisper to Cavor that I could hardly go without food much longer, but my mouth had become too dry for whispering.

'Cavor,' I said, 'I must have food.'

He turned a face full of dismay towards me. 'It's a case for holding out,' he said.

'But I *must*,' I said, 'and look at my lips!'

'I've been thirsty some time.'

'If only some of that snow had remained!'

'It's clean gone! We're driving from arctic to tropical at the rate of a degree a minute . . . '

I gnawed my hand.

'The sphere!' he said. 'There is nothing for it but the sphere.'

We roused ourselves to another spurt of crawling. My mind ran entirely on edible things, on the hissing profundity of summer drinks, more particularly I craved for beer. I was haunted by the memory of a sixteen-gallon cask that had swaggered in my Lympne cellar. I thought of the adjacent larder, and especially of steak and kidney pie – tender steak and plenty of kidney, and rich, thick gravy between. Ever and again I was seized with fits of hungry yawning. We came to flat places overgrown with fleshy red things, monstrous coralline growths; as we pushed against them they snapped and broke. I noted the quality of the broken surfaces. The confounded stuff certainly looked of a biteable texture. Then it seemed to me that it smelt rather well.

I picked up a fragment and sniffed at it.

'Cavor,' I said in a hoarse undertone.

He glanced at me with his face screwed up. 'Don't,' he said. I put down the fragment, and we crawled on through this tempting fleshiness for a space.

'Cavor,' I asked, 'why *not*?'

'Poison,' I heard him say, but he did not look round.

We crawled some way before I decided.

'I'll chance it,' said I.

He made a belated gesture to prevent me. I stuffed my mouth full. He crouched watching my face, his own twisted into the oddest expression.

'It's good,' I said.

'O Lord!' he cried.

He watched me munch, his face wrinkled between desire and disapproval, then suddenly succumbed to appetite and began to tear off huge mouthfuls. For a time we did nothing but eat.

The stuff was not unlike a terrestrial mushroom, only it was much laxer in texture, and, as one swallowed it, it warmed the throat. At first we experienced a mere mechanical satisfaction in eating; then our blood began to run warmer, and we tingled at the lips and fingers, and then new and slightly irrelevant ideas came bubbling up in our minds.

'It's good,' said I. 'Infernally good! What a home for our surplus population! Our poor surplus population,' and I broke off another large portion. It filled me with a curiously benevolent satisfaction that there was such good food in the moon. The depression of my hunger gave way to an irrational exhilaration. The dread and discomfort in which I had been living vanished entirely. I perceived the moon no longer as a planet from which I most earnestly desired the means of escape, but as a possible refuge from human destitution. I think I forgot the Selenites, the mooncalves, the lid, and the noises completely so soon as I had eaten that fungus.

Cavor replied to my third repetition of my 'surplus population' remark with similar words of approval. I felt that my head swam, but I put this down to the stimulating effect of food after a long fast. 'Ess'lent discov'ry yours, Cavor,' said I. 'Se'nd on'y to the 'tato.'

'Whajer mean?' asked Cavor. ' 'Scovery of the moon – se'nd on'y to the 'tato?'

I looked at him, shocked at his suddenly hoarse voice, and by the badness of his articulation. It occurred to me in a flash that he was intoxicated, possibly by the fungus. It also occurred to me that he erred in imagining that he had discovered the moon; he had not discovered it, he had only reached it. I tried to lay my hand on his arm and explain this to him, but the issue was too subtle for his brain. It was also unexpectedly difficult to express. After a momentary attempt to understand me – I remember wondering if the fungus had made my eyes as fishy as his – he set off upon some observations on his own account.

'We are,' he announced with a solemn hiccup, 'the creashurs o' what we eat and drink.'

He repeated this, and as I was now in one of my subtle moods, I determined to dispute it. Possibly I wandered a little from the point. But Cavor certainly did not attend at all properly. He stood up as well as he could, putting a hand on my head to steady himself, which was disrespectful, and stood staring about him, quite devoid now of any fear of the moon beings.

I tried to point out that this was dangerous for some reason that was not perfectly clear to me, but the word 'dangerous' had somehow got mixed with 'indiscreet', and came out rather more like 'injurious' than either; and after an attempt to disentangle them, I resumed my argument, addressing myself principally to the unfamiliar but attentive coralline growths on either side. I felt that it was necessary to clear up this confusion between the moon and a potato at once – I wandered into a long parenthesis on the importance of precision of definition in argument. I did my best to ignore the fact that my bodily sensations were no longer agreeable.

In some way that I have now forgotten, my mind was led back to projects of colonisation. 'We must annex this moon,' I said. 'There must be no shilly-shally. This is part of the White Man's Burthen. Cavor – we are – *hic* – Satap – mean Satraps! Nempire Caesar never dreamt. B'in all the newspapers. Cavorecia. Bedfordecia. Bedfordecia – hic – Limited. Mean – unlimited! Practically.'

Certainly I was intoxicated.

I embarked upon an argument to show the infinite benefits our arrival would confer on the moon. I involved myself in a rather difficult proof that the arrival of Columbus was, on the whole, beneficial to America. I found I had forgotten the line of argument I had intended to pursue, and continued to repeat 'Similar to C'lumbus', to fill up time.

From that point my memory of the action of that abominable fungus becomes confused. I remember vaguely that we declared our intention of standing no nonsense from any confounded insects, that we decided it ill became men to hide shamefully upon a mere satellite, that we equipped ourselves with huge armfuls of the fungus – whether for missile purposes or not I do not know – and, heedless of the stabs of the bayonet scrub, we started forth into the sunshine.

Almost immediately we must have come upon the Selenites. There were six of them, and they were marching in single file over a rocky place, making the most remarkable piping and whining sounds. They all seemed to become aware of us at once, all instantly became silent and motionless, like animals, with their faces turned towards us.

For a moment I was sobered.

'Insects,' murmured Cavor, 'insects! And they think I'm going to crawl about on my stomach – on my vertebrated stomach!'

'Stomach,' he repeated slowly, as though he chewed the indignity.

Then suddenly, with a shout of fury, he made three vast strides and leapt towards them. He leapt badly; he made a series of somersaults in the air, whirled right over them, and vanished with an enormous splash amidst the cactus bladders. What the Selenites made of this amazing, and to my mind undignified irruption from another planet, I have no means of guessing. I seem to remember the sight of their backs as they ran in all directions, but I am not sure. All these last incidents before oblivion came are vague and faint in my mind. I know I made a step to follow Cavor, and tripped and fell headlong among the rocks. I was, I am certain, suddenly and vehemently ill. I seem to remember, a violent struggle and being gripped by metallic clasps . . .

My next clear recollection is that we were prisoners at we knew not what depths beneath the moon's surface; we were in darkness amidst strange distracting noises; our bodies were covered with scratches and bruises, and our heads racked with pain.

CHAPTER TWELVE

The Selenite's Face

I found myself sitting crouched together in a tumultuous darkness. For a long time I could not understand where I was, nor how I had come to this perplexity. I thought of the cupboard into which I had been thrust at times when I was a child, and then of a very dark and noisy bedroom in which I had slept during an illness. But these sounds about me were not the noises I had known, and there was a thin flavour in the air like the wind of a stable. Then I supposed we must still be at work upon the sphere, and that somehow I had got into the cellar of Cavor's house. I remembered we had finished the sphere, and fancied I must still be in it and travelling through space.

'Cavor,' I said, 'cannot we have some light?'

There came no answer.

'Cavor!' I insisted.

I was answered by a groan. 'My head!' I heard him say; 'my head!'

I attempted to press my hands to my brow, which ached, and discovered they were tied together. This startled me very much. I brought them up to my mouth and felt the cold smoothness of metal. They were chained together. I tried to separate my legs and made out they were similarly fastened, and also that I was fastened to the ground by a much thicker chain about the middle of my body.

I was more frightened than I had yet been by anything in all our strange experiences. For a time I tugged silently at my bonds. 'Cavor!' I cried out sharply. 'Why am I tied? Why have you tied me hand and foot?'

'I haven't tied you,' he answered. 'It's the Selenites.'

The Selenites! My mind hung on that for a space. Then my memories came back to me: the snowy desolation, the thawing of the air, the growth of the plants, our strange hopping and crawling among the rocks and vegetation of the crater. All the distress of our frantic search for the sphere returned to me . . . Finally the opening of the great lid that covered the pit!

Then as I strained to trace our later movements down to our present plight, the pain in my head became intolerable. I came to an insurmountable barrier, an obstinate blank.

'Cavor!'

'Yes?'

'Where are we?'

'How should I know?'

'Are we dead?'

'What nonsense!'

'They've got us, then!'

He made no answer but a grunt. The lingering traces of the poison seemed to make him oddly irritable.

'What do you mean to do?'

'How should I know what to do?'

'Oh, very well!' said I, and became silent. Presently, I was roused from a stupor. 'O *Lord*!' I cried; 'I wish you'd stop that buzzing!'

We lapsed into silence again, listening to the dull confusion of noises like the muffled sounds of a street or factory that filled our ears. I could make nothing of it, my mind pursued first one rhythm and then another, and questioned it in vain. But after a long time I became aware of a new and sharper element, not mingling with the rest but standing out, as it were, against that cloudy background of sound. It was a series of relatively very little definite sounds, tappings and rubbings, like a loose spray of ivy against a window or a bird moving about upon a box. We listened and peered about us, but the darkness was a velvet pall. There followed a noise like the subtle movement of the wards of a well-oiled lock. And then there appeared before me, hanging as it seemed in an immensity of black, a thin bright line.

'Look!' whispered Cavor very softly.

'What is it?'

'I don't know.'

We stared.

The thin bright line became a band, and broader and paler. It took upon itself the quality of a bluish light falling upon a whitewashed wall. It ceased to be parallel-sided; it developed a deep indentation on one side. I turned to remark this to Cavor, and was amazed to see his ear in a brilliant illumination – all the rest of him in shadow. I twisted my head round as well as my bonds would permit. 'Cavor,' I said, 'it's behind!'

His ear vanished – gave place to an eye!

Suddenly the crack that had been admitting the light broadened out, and revealed itself as the space of an opening door. Beyond was a sapphire vista, and in the doorway stood a grotesque outline silhouetted against the glare.

We both made convulsive efforts to turn, and failing, sat staring over our shoulders at this. My first impression was of some clumsy quadruped with lowered head. Then I perceived it was the slender pinched body and short and extremely attenuated bandy legs of a Selenite, with his head depressed between his shoulders. He was without the helmet and body covering they wear upon the exterior.

He was a blank, black figure to us, but instinctively our imaginations supplied features to his very human outline. I, at least, took it instantly that he was somewhat hunchbacked, with a high forehead and long features.

He came forward three steps and paused for a time. His movements seemed absolutely noiseless. Then he came forward again. He walked like a bird, his feet fell one in front of the other. He stepped out of the ray of light that came through the doorway, and it seemed as though he vanished altogether in the shadow.

For a moment my eyes sought him in the wrong place, and then I perceived him standing facing us both in the full light. Only the human features I had attributed to him were not there at all!

Of course I ought to have expected that, only I didn't. It came to me as an absolute, for a moment an overwhelming shock. It seemed as though it wasn't a face, as though it must needs be a mask, a horror, a deformity, that would presently be disavowed or explained. There was no nose, and the thing had dull bulging eyes at the side – in the silhouette I had supposed they were ears. There were no ears . . . I have tried to draw one of these heads, but I cannot. There was a mouth, downwardly curved, like a human mouth in a face that stares ferociously . . .

The neck on which the head was poised was jointed in three places, almost like the short joints in the leg of a crab. The joints of the limbs I could not see, because of the puttee-like straps in which they were swathed, and which formed the only clothing the being wore.

There the thing was, looking at us!

At the time my mind was taken up by the mad impossibility of the creature. I suppose he also was amazed, and with more reason, perhaps, for amazement than we. Only, confound him! he did not show it. We did at least know what had brought about this meeting of incompatible creatures. But conceive how it would seem to decent Londoners, for example, to come upon a couple of living things, as big as men and absolutely unlike any other earthly animals, careering about among the sheep in Hyde Park! It must have taken him like that.

Figure us! We were bound hand and foot, fagged and filthy; our beards two inches long, our faces scratched and bloody. Cavor you must imagine in his knickerbockers (torn in several places by the bayonet scrub) his Jaegar shirt and old cricket cap, his wiry hair wildly disordered, a tail to every quarter of the heavens. In that blue light his face did not look red but very dark, his lips and the drying blood upon my hands seemed black. If possible I was in a worse plight than he, on account of the yellow fungus into which I had jumped. Our jackets were unbuttoned, and our shoes had been taken off and lay at our feet. And we were sitting with our backs to this queer bluish light, peering at such a monster as Dürer might have invented.

Cavor broke the silence; started to speak, went hoarse, and cleared his throat. Outside began a terrific bellowing, as if a mooncalf were in trouble. It ended in a shriek, and everything was still again.

Presently the Selenite turned about, flickered into the shadow, stood for a moment retrospective at the door, and then closed it on us; and once more we were in that murmurous mystery of darkness into which we had awakened.

CHAPTER THIRTEEN

Mr Cavor Makes Some Suggestions

For a time neither of us spoke. To focus together all the things we had brought upon ourselves, seemed beyond my mental powers.

'They've got us,' I said at last.

'It was that fungus.'

'Well – if I hadn't taken it we should have fainted and starved.'

'We might have found the sphere.'

I lost my temper at his persistence, and swore to myself. For a time we hated one another in silence. I drummed with my fingers on the floor between my knees, and gritted the links of my fetters together. Presently I was forced to talk again.

'What do you make of it, anyhow?' I asked humbly.

'They are reasonable creatures – they can make things and do things. Those lights we saw . . . '

He stopped. It was clear he could make nothing of it.

When he spoke again it was to confess, 'After all, they are more human than we had a right to expect. I suppose – '

He stopped irritatingly.

'Yes?'

'I suppose, anyhow – on any planet where there is an intelligent animal – it will carry its brain case upward, and have hands, and walk erect . . . '

Presently he broke away in another direction.

'We are some way in,' he said. 'I mean – perhaps a couple of thousand feet or more.'

'Why?'

'It's cooler. And our voices are so much louder. That faded quality – it has altogether gone. And the feeling in one's ears and throat.'

I had not noted that, but I did now.

'The air is denser. We must be some depths – a mile even, we may be – inside the moon.'

'We never thought of a world inside the moon.'

'No.'

'How could we?'

'We might have done. Only – one gets into habits of mind.'

He thought for a time.

'*Now*,' he said, 'it seems such an obvious thing.'

'Of course! The moon must be enormously cavernous, with an atmosphere within, and at the centre of its caverns a sea.

'One knew that the moon had a lower specific gravity than the earth, one knew that it had little air or water outside, one knew, too, that it was sister planet to the earth, and that it was unaccountable that it should be different in composition. The inference that it was hollowed out was as clear as day. And yet one never saw it as a fact. Kepler, of course – '

His voice had the interest now of a man who has discerned a pretty sequence of reasoning.

'Yes,' he said, 'Kepler with his *sub-volvani* was right after all.'

'I wish you had taken the trouble to find that out before we came,' I said.

He answered nothing, buzzing to himself softly, as he pursued his thoughts. My temper was going.

'What do you think has become of the sphere, anyhow?' I asked.

'Lost,' he said, like a man who answers an uninteresting question.

'Among those plants?'

'Unless they find it.'

'And then?'

'How can I tell?'

'Cavor,' I said, with a sort of hysterical bitterness, 'things look bright for my Company . . . '

He made no answer.

'Good Lord!' I exclaimed. 'Just think of all the trouble we took to get into this pickle! What did we come for? What are we after? What was the moon to us or we to the moon? We wanted too much, we tried too much. We ought to have started the little things first. It was you proposed the moon! Those Cavorite spring blinds! I am certain we could have worked them for terrestrial purposes. Certain! Did you really understand what I proposed? A steel cylinder – '

'Rubbish!' said Cavor.

We ceased to converse.

For a time Cavor kept up a broken monologue without much help from me.

'If they find it,' he began, 'if they find it . . . what will they do with it? Well, that's a question. It may be that's *the* question. They won't understand it, anyhow. If they understood that sort of thing they would have come long since to the earth. Would they? Why shouldn't they?

But they would have sent something – they couldn't keep their hands off such a possibility. No! But they will examine it. Clearly they are intelligent and inquisitive. They will examine it – get inside it – trifle with the studs. Off! . . . That would mean the moon for us for all the rest of our lives. Strange creatures, strange knowledge . . . '

'As for strange knowledge – ' said I, and language failed me.

'Look here, Bedford,' said Cavor, 'you came on this expedition of your own free will.'

'You said to me, "Call it prospecting".'

'There's always risks in prospecting.'

'Especially when you do it unarmed and without thinking out every possibility.'

'I was so taken up with the sphere. The thing rushed on us, and carried us away.'

'Rushed on *me*, you mean.'

'Rushed on me just as much. How was *I* to know when I set to work on molecular physics that the business would bring me here – of all places?'

'It's this accursed science,' I cried. 'It's the very Devil. The mediaeval priests and persecutors were right and the Moderns are all wrong. You tamper with it – and it offers you gifts. And directly you take them it knocks you to pieces in some unexpected way. Old passions and new weapons – now it upsets your religion, now it upsets your social ideas, now it whirls you off to desolation and misery!'

'Anyhow, it's no use your quarrelling with me *now*. These creatures – these Selenites, or whatever we choose to call them – have got us tied hand and foot. Whatever temper you choose to go through with it in, you will have to go through with it . . . We have experiences before us that will need all our coolness.'

He paused as if he required my assent. But I sat sulking. 'Confound your science!' I said.

'The problem is communication. Gestures, I fear, will be different. Pointing, for example. No creatures but men and monkeys point.'

That was too obviously wrong for me. 'Pretty nearly every animal,' I cried, 'points with its eyes or nose.'

Cavor meditated over that. 'Yes,' he said at last, 'and we don't. There's such differences – such differences!'

'One might . . . But how can I tell? There is speech. The sounds they make, a sort of fluting and piping. I don't see how we are to imitate that. Is it their speech, that sort of thing? They may have different senses, different means of communication. Of course they are minds and we are minds; there must be something in common. Who knows how far we may not get to an understanding?'

'The things are outside us,' I said. 'They're more different from us than the strangest animals on earth. They are a different clay. What is the good of talking like this?'

Cavor thought. 'I don't see that. Where there are minds they will have something *similar* – even though they have been evolved on different planets. Of course if it was a question of instincts, if we or they are no more than animals – '

'Well, *are* they? They're much more like ants on their hind legs than human beings, and who ever got to any sort of understanding with ants?'

'But these machines and clothing! No, I don't hold with you, Bedford. The difference is wide – '

'It's insurmountable.'

'The resemblance must bridge it. I remember reading once a paper by the late Professor Galton on the possibility of communication between the planets. Unhappily, at that time it did not seem probable that that would be of any material benefit to me, and I fear I did not give it the attention I should have done – in view of this state of affairs. Yet . . . Now, let me see!

'His idea was to begin with those broad truths that must underlie all conceivable mental existences and establish a basis on those. The great principles of geometry, to begin with. He proposed to take some leading proposition of Euclid's, and show by construction that its truth was known to us, to demonstrate, for example, that the angles at the base of an isosceles triangle are equal, and that if the equal sides be produced the angles on the other side of the base are equal also, or that the square on the hypotenuse of a right-angled triangle is equal to the sum of the squares on the two other sides. By demonstrating our knowledge of these things we should demonstrate our possession of a reasonable intelligence . . . Now, suppose I . . . I might draw the geometrical figure with a wet finger, or even trace it in the air . . . '

He fell silent. I sat meditating his words. For a time his wild hope of communication, of interpretation, with these weird beings held me. Then that angry despair that was a part of my exhaustion and physical misery resumed its sway. I perceived with a sudden novel vividness the extraordinary folly of everything I had ever done. 'Ass!' I said; 'oh, ass, unutterable ass . . . I seem to exist only to go about doing preposterous things. Why did we ever leave the thing? . . . Hopping about looking for patents and concessions in the craters of the moon! . . . If only we had had the sense to fasten a handkerchief to a stick to show where we had left the sphere!'

I subsided, fuming.

'It is clear,' meditated Cavor, 'they are intelligent. One can hypotheticate certain things. As they have not killed us at once, they must have ideas of mercy. Mercy! at any rate of restraint. Possibly of intercourse. They may meet us. And this apartment and the glimpses we had of its guardian. These fetters! A high degree of intelligence . . . '

'I wish to heaven,' cried I, 'I'd thought even twice! Plunge after plunge. First one fluky start and then another. It was my confidence in you! *Why* didn't I stick to my play? That was what I was equal to. That was my world and the life I was made for. I could have finished that play. I'm certain . . . it was a good play. I had the scenario as good as done. Then . . . Conceive it! leaping to the moon! Practically – I've thrown my life away! That old woman in the inn near Canterbury had better sense.'

I looked up, and stopped in mid-sentence. The darkness had given place to that bluish light again. The door was opening, and several noiseless Selenites were coming into the chamber. I became quite still, staring at their grotesque faces.

Then suddenly my sense of disagreeable strangeness changed to interest. I perceived that the foremost and second carried bowls. One elemental need at least our minds could understand in common. They were bowls of some metal that, like our fetters, looked dark in that bluish light; and each contained a number of whitish fragments. All the cloudy pain and misery that oppressed me rushed together and took the shape of hunger. I eyed these bowls wolfishly, and, though it returned to me in dreams, at that time it seemed a small matter that at the end of the arms that lowered one towards me were not hands, but a sort of flap and thumb, like the end of an elephant's trunk.

The stuff in the bowl was loose in texture, and whitish brown in colour – rather like lumps of some cold soufflé, and it smelt faintly like mushrooms. From a partially divided carcass of a mooncalf that we presently saw, I am inclined to believe it must have been mooncalf flesh.

My hands were so tightly chained that I could barely contrive to reach the bowl; but when they saw the effort I made, two of them dexterously released one of the turns about my wrist. Their tentacle hands were soft and cold to my skin. I immediately seized a mouthful of the food. It had the same laxness in texture that all organic structures seem to have upon the moon; it tasted rather like a *gauffre* or a damp meringue, but in no way was it disagreeable. I took two other mouthfuls. 'I *wanted* – foo'!' said I, tearing off a still larger piece . . .

For a time we ate with an utter absence of self-consciousness. We ate and presently drank like tramps in a soup kitchen. Never before nor since have I been hungry to the ravenous pitch, and save that I have had this very experience I could never have believed that, a quarter of a million of miles out of our proper world, in utter perplexity of soul, surrounded, watched, touched by beings more grotesque and inhuman than the worst creations of a nightmare, it would be possible for me to eat in utter forgetfulness of all these things. They stood about us watching us, and ever and again making a slight elusive twittering that stood them, I suppose, in the stead of speech. I did not even shiver at their touch. And when the first zeal of my feeding was over, I could note that Cavor, too, had been eating with the same shameless abandon.

CHAPTER FOURTEEN

Experiments in Intercourse

When at last we had made an end of eating, the Selenites linked our hands closely together again, and then untwisted the chains about our feet and rebound them, so as to give us a limited freedom of movement. Then they unfastened the chains about our waists. To do all this they had to handle us freely, and ever and again one of their queer heads came down close to my face, or a soft tentacle-hand touched my head or neck. I don't remember that I was afraid then or repelled by their proximity. I think that our incurable anthropomorphism made us imagine there were human heads inside their masks. The skin, like everything else, looked bluish, but that was on account of the light; and it was hard and shiny, quite in the beetle-wing fashion, not soft, or moist, or hairy, as a vertebrated animal's would be. Along the crest of the head was a low ridge of whitish spines running from back to front, and a much larger ridge curved on either side over the eyes. The Selenite who untied me used his mouth to help his hands.

'They seem to be releasing us,' said Cavor. 'Remember we are on the moon! Make no sudden movements!'

'Are you going to try that geometry?'

'If I get a chance. But, of course, they may make an advance first.'

We remained passive, and the Selenites, having finished their arrangements, stood back from us, and seemed to be looking at us. I say seemed to be, because as their eyes were at the side and not in front, one had the same difficulty in determining the direction in which they were looking as one has in the case of a hen or a fish. They conversed with one another in their reedy tones, that seemed to me impossible to imitate or define. The door behind us opened wider, and, glancing over my shoulder, I saw a vague large space beyond, in which quite a little crowd of Selenites were standing. They seemed a curiously miscellaneous rabble.

'Do they want us to imitate those sounds?' I asked Cavor.

'I don't think so,' he said.

'It seems to me that they are trying to make us understand something.'

'I can't make anything of their gestures. Do you notice this one, who is worrying with his head like a man with an uncomfortable collar?'

'Let us shake our heads at him.'

We did that, and finding it ineffectual, attempted an imitation of the Selenites' movements. That seemed to interest them. At any rate they all set up the same movement. But as that seemed to lead to nothing, we desisted at last and so did they, and fell into a piping argument among themselves. Then one of them, shorter and very much thicker than the others, and with a particularly wide mouth, squatted down suddenly beside Cavor, and put his hands and feet in the same posture as Cavor's were bound, and then by a dexterous movement stood up.

'Cavor,' I shouted, 'they want us to get up!'

He stared open-mouthed. 'That's it!' he said.

And with much heaving and grunting, because our hands were tied together, we contrived to struggle to our feet. The Selenites made way for our elephantine heavings, and seemed to twitter more volubly. As soon as we were on our feet the thick-set Selenite came and patted each of our faces with his tentacles, and walked towards the open doorway. That also was plain enough, and we followed him. We saw that four of the Selenites standing in the doorway were much taller than the others, and clothed in the same manner as those we had seen in the crater, namely, with spiked round helmets and cylindrical body-cases, and that each of the four carried a goad with spike and guard made of that same dull-looking metal as the bowls. These four closed about us, one on either side of each of us, as we emerged from our chamber into the cavern from which the light had come.

We did not get our impression of that cavern all at once. Our attention was taken up by the movements and attitudes of the Selenites immediately about us, and by the necessity of controlling our motion, lest we should startle and alarm them and ourselves by some excessive stride. In front of us was the short, thick-set being who had solved the problem of asking us to get up, moving with gestures that seemed, almost all of them, intelligible to us, inviting us to follow him. His spout-like face turned from one of us to the other with a quickness that was clearly interrogative. For a time, I say, we were taken up with these things.

But at last the great place that formed a background to our movements asserted itself. It became apparent that the source of much, at least, of the tumult of sounds which had filled our ears ever since we had recovered from the stupefaction of the fungus was a vast mass of machinery in active movement, whose flying and whirling parts were visible indistinctly over the heads and between the bodies of the Selenites who walked about us. And not only did the web of sounds that filled the air proceed from this mechanism, but also the peculiar blue light that irradiated the whole place. We had taken it as a natural thing that a subterranean cavern should be artificially lit, and even now, though the fact was patent to my eyes, I did not really grasp its import until presently the darkness came. The meaning and structure of this huge apparatus we saw I cannot explain, because we neither of us learnt what it was for or how it worked. One after another, big shafts of metal flung out and up from its centre, their heads travelling in what seemed to me to be a parabolic path; each dropped a sort of dangling arm as it rose towards the apex of its flight and plunged down into a vertical cylinder, forcing this down before it. About it moved the shapes of tenders, little figures that seemed vaguely different from the beings about us. As each of the three dangling arms of the machine plunged down, there was a clank and then a roaring, and out of the top of the vertical cylinder came pouring this incandescent substance that lit the place, and ran over as milk runs over a boiling pot, and dripped luminously into a tank of light below. It was a cold blue light, a sort of phosphorescent glow but infinitely brighter, and from the tanks into which it fell it ran in conduits athwart the cavern.

Thud, thud, thud, thud, came the sweeping arms of this unintelligible apparatus, and the light substance hissed and poured. At first the thing seemed only reasonably large and near to us, and then I saw how exceedingly little the Selenites upon it seemed, and I realised the full immensity of cavern and machine. I looked from this tremendous affair to the faces of the Selenites with a new respect. I stopped, and Cavor stopped, and stared at this thunderous engine.

'But this is stupendous!' I said. 'What can it be for?'

Cavor's blue-lit face was full of an intelligent respect. 'I can't dream! Surely these beings – Men could not make a thing like that! Look at those arms, are they on connecting rods?'

The thick-set Selenite had gone some paces unheeded. He came back and stood between us and the great machine. I avoided seeing him, because I guessed somehow that his idea was to beckon us onward. He walked away in the direction he wished us to go, and turned and came back, and flicked our faces to attract our attention.

Cavor and I looked at one another.

'Cannot we show him we are interested in the machine?' I said.

'Yes,' said Cavor. 'We'll try that.' He turned to our guide and smiled, and pointed to the machine, and pointed again, and then to his head, and then to the machine. By some defect of reasoning he seemed to imagine that broken English might help these gestures. 'Me look 'im,' he said, 'me think 'im very much. Yes.'

His behaviour seemed to check the Selenites in their desire for our progress for a moment. They faced one another, their queer heads moved, the twittering voices came quick and liquid. Then one of them, a lean, tall creature, with a sort of mantle added to the puttee in which the others were dressed, twisted his elephant trunk of a hand about Cavor's waist, and pulled him gently to follow our guide, who again went on ahead.

Cavor resisted. 'We may just as well begin explaining ourselves now. They may think we are new animals, a new sort of mooncalf perhaps! It is most important that we should show an intelligent interest from the outset.'

He began to shake his head violently. 'No, no,' he said, 'me not come on one minute. Me look at 'im.'

'Isn't there some geometrical point you might bring in apropos of that affair?' I suggested, as the Selenites conferred again.

'Possibly a parabolic – ' he began.

He yelled loudly, and leaped six feet or more!

One of the four armed moon-men had pricked him with a goad!

I turned on the goad-bearer behind me with a swift threatening gesture, and he started back. This and Cavor's sudden shout and leap clearly astonished all the Selenites. They receded hastily, facing us. For one of those moments that seem to last for ever, we stood in angry protest, with a scattered semicircle of these inhuman beings about us.

'He pricked me!' said Cavor, with a catching of the voice.

'I saw him,' I answered.

'Confound it!' I said to the Selenites; 'we're not going to stand that! What on earth do you take us for?'

I glanced quickly right and left. Far away across the blue wilderness of cavern I saw a number of other Selenites running towards us; broad and slender they were, and one with a larger head than the others. The cavern spread wide and low, and receded in every direction into darkness. Its roof, I remember, seemed to bulge down as if with the weight of the vast thickness of rocks that prisoned us. There was no way out of it – no way out of it. Above, below, in every direction, was the unknown, and these inhuman creatures, with goads and gestures, confronting us, and we two unsupported men!

CHAPTER FIFTEEN

The Giddy Bridge

Just for a moment that hostile pause endured. I suppose that both we and the Selenites did some very rapid thinking. My clearest impression was that there was nothing to put my back against, and that we were bound to be surrounded and killed. The overwhelming folly of our presence there loomed over me in black, enormous reproach. Why had I ever launched myself on this mad, inhuman expedition?

Cavor came to my side and laid his hand on my arm. His pale and terrified face was ghastly in the blue light.

'We can't do anything,' he said. 'It's a mistake. They don't under-stand. We must go. As they want us to go.'

I looked down at him, and then at the fresh Selenites who were coming to help their fellows. 'If I had my hands free – '

'It's no use,' he panted.

'No.'

'We'll go.'

And he turned about and led the way in the direction that had been indicated for us.

I followed, trying to look as subdued as possible, and feeling at the chains about my wrists. My blood was boiling. I noted nothing more of that cavern, though it seemed to take a long time before we had marched across it, or if I noted anything I forgot it as I saw it. My thoughts were concentrated, I think, upon my chains and the Selenites, and particularly upon the helmeted ones with the goads. At first they marched parallel with us, and at a respectful distance, but presently they were overtaken by three others, and then they drew nearer, until they were within arm's length again. I winced like a beaten horse as they came near to us. The shorter, thicker Selenite marched at first on our right flank, but presently came in front of us again.

How well the picture of that grouping has bitten into my brain; the back of Cavor's downcast head just in front of me, and the dejected droop of his shoulders, and our guide's gaping visage, perpetually jerking about him, and the goad-bearers on either side, watchful, yet open-mouthed – a blue monochrome. And after all, I *do* remember one other thing besides the purely personal affair, which is, that a sort of gutter came presently across the floor of the cavern, and then ran along by the side of the path of rock we followed. And it was full of that same bright blue luminous stuff that flowed out of the great machine. I walked close beside it, and I can testify it radiated not a particle of heat. It was brightly shining, and yet it was neither warmer nor colder than anything else in the cavern.

Clang, clang, clang, we passed right under the thumping levers of another vast machine, and so came at last to a wide tunnel, in which we could even hear the pad, pad, of our shoeless feet, and which, save for the trickling thread of blue to the right of us, was quite unlit. The shadows made gigantic travesties of our shapes and those of the Selenites on the irregular wall and roof of the tunnel. Ever and again crystals in the walls of the tunnel scintillated like gems, ever and again the tunnel expanded into a stalactitic cavern, or gave off branches that vanished into darkness.

We seemed to be marching down that tunnel for a long time. 'Trickle, trickle,' went the flowing light very softly, and our footfalls and their echoes made an irregular paddle, paddle. My mind settled down to the question of my chains. If I were to slip off one turn *so*, and then to twist it *so* . . .

If I tried to do it very gradually, would they see I was slipping my wrist out of the looser turn? If they did, what would they do?

'Bedford,' said Cavor, 'it goes down. It keeps on going down.'

His remark roused me from my sullen preoccupation.

'If they wanted to kill us,' he said, dropping back to come level with me, 'there is no reason why they should not have done it.'

'No,' I admitted, 'that's true.'

'They don't understand us,' he said, 'they think we are merely strange animals, some wild sort of mooncalf birth, perhaps. It will be only when they have observed us better that they will begin to think we have minds – '

'When you trace those geometrical problems,' said I.

'It may be that.'

We tramped on for a space.

'You see,' said Cavor, 'these may be Selenites of a lower class.'

'The infernal fools!' said I viciously, glancing at their exasperating faces.

'If we endure what they do to us – '

'We've got to endure it,' said I.

'There may be others less stupid. This is the mere outer fringe of their world. It must go down and down, cavern, passage, tunnel, down at last to the sea – hundreds of miles below.'

His words made me think of the mile or so of rock and tunnel that might be over our heads already. It was like a weight dropping on my shoulders. 'Away from the sun and air,' I said. 'Even a mine half a mile deep is stuffy.'

'This is not, anyhow. It's probable – Ventilation! The air would blow from the dark side of the moon to the sunlit, and all the carbonic acid would well out there and feed those plants. Up this tunnel, for example, there is quite a breeze. And what a world it must be. The earnest we have in that shaft, and those machines – '

'And the goad,' I said. 'Don't forget the goad!'

He walked a little in front of me for a time.

'Even that goad – ' he said.

'Well?'

'I was angry at the time. But – it was perhaps necessary we should get on. They have different skins, and probably different nerves. They may not understand our objection – Just as a being from Mars might not like our earthly habit of nudging – '

'They'd better be careful how they nudge *me*.'

'And about that geometry. After all, their way is a way of understanding, too. They begin with the elements of life and not of thought. Food. Compulsion. Pain. They strike at fundamentals.'

'There's no doubt about *that*,' I said.

He went on to talk of the enormous and wonderful world into which we were being taken. I realised slowly from his tone, that even now he was not absolutely in despair at the prospect of going ever deeper into this inhuman planet-burrow. His mind ran on machines and invention, to the exclusion of a thousand dark things that beset me. It wasn't that he intended to make any use of these things, he simply wanted to know them.

'After all,' he said, 'this is a tremendous occasion. It is the meeting of two worlds! What are we going to see? Think of what is below us here.'

'We shan't see much if the light isn't better,' I remarked.

'This is only the outer crust. Down below – On this scale – There will be everything. Do you notice how different they seem one from another? The story we shall take back!'

'Some rare sort of animal,' I said, 'might comfort himself in that way while they were bringing him to the Zoo . . . It doesn't follow that we are going to be shown all these things.'

'When they find we have reasonable minds,' said Cavor, 'they will want to learn about the earth. Even if they have no generous emotions, they will teach in order to learn . . . And the things they must know! The unanticipated things!'

He went on to speculate on the possibility of their knowing things he had never hoped to learn on earth, speculating in that way, with a raw wound from that goad already in his skin! Much that he said I forget, for my attention was drawn to the fact that the tunnel along which we had been marching was opening out wider and wider. We seemed, from the feeling of the air, to be going out into a huge space. But how big the space might really be we could not tell, because it was unlit. Our little stream of light ran in a dwindling thread and vanished far ahead. Presently the rocky walls had vanished altogether on either hand. There was nothing to be seen but the path in front of us and the trickling hurrying rivulet of blue phosphorescence. The figures of Cavor and the guiding Selenite marched before me, the sides of their legs and heads that were towards the rivulet were clear and bright blue, their darkened sides, now that the reflection of the tunnel wall no longer lit them, merged indistinguishably in the darkness beyond.

And soon I perceived that we were approaching a declivity of some sort, because the little blue stream dipped suddenly out of sight.

In another moment, as it seemed, we had reached the edge. The shining stream gave one meander of hesitation and then rushed over. It fell to a depth at which the sound of its descent was absolutely lost to us. Far below was a bluish glow, a sort of blue mist – at an infinite distance below. And the darkness the stream dropped out of became utterly void and black, save that a thing like a plank projected from the edge of the cliff and stretched out and faded and vanished altogether. There was a warm air blowing up out of the gulf.

For a moment I and Cavor stood as near the edge as we dared, peering into a blue-tinged profundity. And then our guide was pulling at my arm.

Then he left me, and walked to the end of that plank and stepped upon it, looking back. Then when he perceived we watched him, he turned about and went on along it, walking as surely as though he was on firm earth. For a moment his form was distinct, then he became a blue blur, and then vanished into the obscurity. I became aware of some vague shape looming darkly out of the black.

There was a pause. 'Surely – !' said Cavor.

One of the other Selenites walked a few paces out upon the plank, and turned and looked back at us unconcernedly. The others stood ready to follow after us. Our guide's expectant figure reappeared. He was returning to see why we had not advanced.

'What is that beyond there?' I asked.

'I can't see.'

'We can't cross this at any price,' said I.

'I could not go three steps on it,' said Cavor, 'even with my hands free.'

We looked at each other's drawn faces in blank consternation.

'They can't know what it is to be giddy!' said Cavor.

'It's quite impossible for us to walk that plank.'

'I don't believe they see as we do. I've been watching them. I wonder if they know this is simply blackness for us. How can we make them understand?'

'Anyhow, we must make them understand.'

I think we said these things with a vague half hope the Selenites might somehow understand. I knew quite clearly that all that was needed was an explanation. Then as I saw their faces, I realised that an explanation was impossible. Just here it was that our resemblances were not going to bridge our differences. Well, I wasn't going to walk the plank, anyhow. I slipped my wrist very quickly out of the coil of chain that was loose, and then began to twist my wrists in opposite directions. I was standing nearest to the bridge, and as I did this two of the Selenites laid hold of me, and pulled me gently towards it.

I shook my head violently. 'No go,' I said, 'no use. You don't understand.'

Another Selenite added his compulsion. I was forced to step forward.

'I've got an idea,' said Cavor; but I knew his ideas.

'Look here!' I exclaimed to the Selenites. 'Steady on! It's all very well for you – '

I sprang round upon my heel. I burst out into curses. For one of the armed Selenites had stabbed me behind with his goad.

I wrenched my wrists free from the little tentacles that held them. I turned on the goad-bearer. 'Confound you!' I cried. 'I've warned you of that. What on earth do you think I'm made of, to stick that into me? If you touch me again – '

By way of answer he pricked me forthwith.

I heard Cavor's voice in alarm and entreaty. Even then I think he wanted to compromise with these creatures. 'I say, Bedford,' he cried, 'I know a way!' But the sting of that second stab seemed to set free some pent-up reserve of energy in my being. Instantly the link of the wrist-chain snapped, and with it snapped all considerations that had held us unresisting in the hands of these moon creatures. For that second, at least, I was mad with fear and anger. I took no thought of consequences.

I hit straight out at the face of the thing with the goad. The chain was twisted round my fist . . .

There came another of these beastly surprises of which the moon world is full.

My mailed hand seemed to go clean through him. He smashed like – like some softish sort of sweet with liquid in it! He broke right in! He squelched and splashed. It was like hitting a damp toadstool. The flimsy body went spinning a dozen yards, and fell with a flabby impact. I was astonished. I was incredulous that any living thing could be so flimsy. For an instant I could have believed the whole thing a dream.

Then it had become real and imminent again. Neither Cavor nor the other Selenites seemed to have done anything from the time when I had turned about to the time when the dead Selenite hit the ground. Everyone stood back from us two, everyone alert. That arrest seemed to last at least a second after the Selenite was down. Everyone must have been taking the thing in. I seem to remember myself standing with my arm half retracted, trying also to take it in. 'What next?' clamoured my brain; 'what next?' Then in a moment everyone was moving!

I perceived we must get our chains loose, and that before we could do this these Selenites had to be beaten off. I faced towards the group of the three goad-bearers. Instantly one threw his goad at me. It swished over my head, and I suppose went flying into the abyss behind.

I leaped right at him with all my might as the goad flew over me. He turned to run as I jumped, and I bore him to the ground, came down right upon him, and slipped upon his smashed body and fell. He seemed to wriggle under my foot.

I came into a sitting position, and on every hand the blue backs of the Selenites were receding into the darkness. I bent a link by main force and untwisted the chain that had hampered me about the ankles, and sprang to my feet, with the chain in my hand. Another goad, flung javelin-wise, whistled by me, and I made a rush towards the darkness out of which it had come. Then I turned back towards Cavor, who was still standing in the light of the rivulet near the gulf convulsively busy with his wrists, and at the same time jabbering nonsense about his idea.

'Come on!' I cried.

'My hands!' he answered.

Then, realising that I dared not run back to him, because my ill-calculated steps might carry me over the edge, he came shuffling towards me, with his hands held out before him.

I gripped his chains at once to unfasten them.

'Where are they?' he panted.

'Run away. They'll come back. They're throwing things! Which way shall we go?'

'By the light. To that tunnel. Eh?'

'Yes,' said I, and his hands were free.

I dropped on my knees and fell to work on his ankle bonds. Whack came something – I know not what – and splashed the livid streamlet into drops about us. Far away on our right a piping and whistling began.

I whipped the chain off his feet, and put it in his hand. 'Hit with that!' I said, and without waiting for an answer, set off in big bounds along the path by which we had come. I had a nasty sort of feeling that these things could jump out of the darkness on to my back. I heard the impact of his leaps come following after me.

We ran in vast strides. But that running, you must understand, was an altogether different thing from any running on earth. On earth one leaps and almost instantly hits the ground again, but on the moon, because of its weaker pull, one shot through the air for several seconds before one came to earth. In spite of our violent hurry this gave an effect of long pauses, pauses in which one might have counted seven or eight. 'Step,' and one soared off! All sorts of questions ran through my mind: 'Where are the Selenites? What will they do? Shall we ever get to that tunnel? Is Cavor far behind? Are they likely to cut him off?' Then whack, stride, and off again for another step.

I saw a Selenite running in front of me, his legs going exactly as a man's would go on earth, saw him glance over his shoulder, and heard him shriek as he ran aside out of my way into the darkness. He was, I think, our guide, but I am not sure. Then in another vast stride the walls of rock had come into view on either hand, and in two more strides I was in the tunnel, and tempering my pace to its low roof. I went on to a bend, then stopped and turned back, and plug, plug, plug, Cavor came into view, splashing into the stream of blue light at every stride, and grew larger and blundered into me. We stood clutching each other. For a moment, at least, we had shaken off our captors and were alone.

We were both very much out of breath. We spoke in panting, broken sentences.

'You've spoilt it all!' panted Cavor.

'Nonsense,' I cried. 'It was that or death!'

'What are we to do?'

'Hide.'

'How can we?'

'It's dark enough.'

'But where?'

'Up one of these side caverns.'

'And then?'

'Think.'

'Right – come on.'

We strode on, and presently came to a radiating dark cavern. Cavor was in front. He hesitated, and chose a black mouth that seemed to promise good hiding. He went towards it and turned.

'Its dark,' he said.

'Your legs and feet will light us. You're wet with that luminous stuff.'

'But – '

A tumult of sounds, and in particular a sound like a clanging gong, advancing up the main tunnel, became audible. It was horribly suggestive of a tumultuous pursuit. We made a bolt for the unlit side cavern forthwith. As we ran along it our way was lit by the irradiation of Cavor's legs. 'It's lucky,' I panted, 'they took off our boots, or we should fill this place with clatter.' On we rushed, taking as small steps as we could to avoid striking the roof of the cavern. After a time we seemed to be gaining on the uproar. It became muffled, it dwindled, it died away.

I stopped and looked back, and I heard the pad, pad of Cavor's feet receding. Then he stopped also. 'Bedford,' he whispered, 'there's a sort of light in front of us.'

I looked, and at first could see nothing. Then I perceived his head and shoulders dimly outlined against a fainter darkness. I saw, also, that this mitigation of the darkness was not blue, as all the other light within the moon had been, but a pallid grey, a very vague, faint white, the daylight colour. Cavor noted this difference as soon, or sooner, than I did, and I think, too, that it filled him with much the same wild hope.

'Bedford,' he whispered, and his voice trembled. 'That light – it is possible – '

He did not dare to say the thing he hoped. Then came a pause. Suddenly I knew by the sound of his feet that he was striding towards that pallor. I followed him with a beating heart.

CHAPTER SIXTEEN

Points of View

The light grew stronger as we advanced. In a little time it was nearly as strong as the phosphorescence on Cavor's legs. Our tunnel was expanding into a cavern, and this new light was at the farther end of it. I perceived something that set my hopes leaping and bounding.

'Cavor,' I said, 'it comes from above! I am certain it comes from above!'

He made no answer, but hurried on.

Indisputably it was a grey light, a silvery light.

In another moment we were beneath it. It filtered down through a chink in the walls of the cavern, and as I stared up, drip, came a drop of water upon my face. I started and stood aside – drip, fell another drop quite audibly on the rocky floor.

'Cavor,' I said, 'if one of us lifts the other, he can reach that crack!'

'I'll lift you,' he said, and incontinently hoisted me as though I was a baby.

I thrust an arm into the crack, and just at my fingertips found a little ledge by which I could hold. I could see the white light was very much brighter now. I pulled myself up by two fingers with scarcely an effort, though on earth I weigh twelve stone, reached to a still higher corner of rock, and so got my feet on the narrow ledge. I stood up and searched up the rocks with my fingers; the cleft broadened out upwardly. 'It's climbable,' I said to Cavor. 'Can you jump up to my hand if I hold it down to you?'

I wedged myself between the sides of the cleft, rested knee and foot on the ledge, and extended a hand. I could not see Cavor, but I could hear the rustle of his movements as he crouched to spring. Then whack and he was hanging to my arm – and no heavier than a kitten! I lugged him up until he had a hand on my ledge, and could release me.

'Confound it!' I said, 'anyone could be a mountaineer on the moon;' and so set myself in earnest to the climbing. For a few minutes I clambered steadily, and then I looked up again. The cleft opened out steadily, and the light was brighter. Only –

It was not daylight after all.

In another moment I could see what it was, and at the sight I could have beaten my head against the rocks with disappointment. For I beheld simply an irregularly sloping open space, and all over its slanting floor stood a forest of little club-shaped fungi, each shining gloriously with that pinkish silvery light. For a moment I stared at their soft radiance, then sprang forward and upward among them. I plucked up half a dozen and flung them against the rocks, and then sat down, laughing bitterly, as Cavor's ruddy face came into view.

'It's phosphorescence again!' I said. 'No need to hurry. Sit down and make yourself at home.' And as he spluttered over our disappointment, I began to lob more of these growths into the cleft.

'I thought it was daylight,' he said.

'Daylight!' cried I. 'Daybreak, sunset, clouds, and windy skies! Shall we ever see such things again?'

As I spoke, a little picture of our world seemed to rise before me, bright and little and clear, like the background of some old Italian picture. 'The sky that changes, and the sea that changes, and the hills and the green trees and the towns and cities shining in the sun. Think of a wet roof at sunset, Cavor! Think of the windows of a westward house!' He made no answer.

'Here we are burrowing in this beastly world that isn't a world, with its inky ocean hidden in some abominable blackness below, and outside that torrid day and that death stillness of night. And all these things that are chasing us now, beastly men of leather – insect men, that come out of a nightmare! After all, they're right! What business have we here smashing them and disturbing their world! For all we know the whole planet is up and after us already. In a minute we may hear them whimpering, and their gongs going. What are we to do? Where are we to go? Here we are as comfortable as snakes from Jamrach's loose in a Surbiton villa!'

'It was your fault,' said Cavor.

'My fault!' I shouted. 'Good Lord!'

'I had an idea!'

'Curse your ideas!'

'If we had refused to budge – '

'Under those goads?'

'Yes. They would have carried us!'

'Over that bridge?'

'Yes. They must have carried us from outside.'

'I'd rather be carried by a fly across a ceiling.'

'Good Heavens!'

I resumed my destruction of the fungi. Then suddenly I saw something that struck me even then.

'Cavor,' I said, 'these chains are of gold!'

He was thinking intently, with his hands gripping his cheeks. He turned his head slowly and stared at me, and when I had repeated my words, at the twisted chain about his right hand. 'So they are,' he said, 'so they are.' His face lost its transitory interest even as he looked. He hesitated for a moment, then went on with his interrupted meditation. I sat for a space puzzling over the fact that I had only just observed this, until I considered the blue light in which we had been, and which had taken all the colour out of the metal. And from that discovery I also started upon a train of thought that carried me wide and far. I forgot that I had just been asking what business we had in the moon. Gold –

It was Cavor who spoke first. 'It seems to me that there are two courses open to us.'

'Well.'

'Either we can attempt to make our way – fight our way if necessary – out to the exterior again, and then hunt for our sphere until we find it, or the cold of the night comes to kill us, or else – '

He paused. 'Yes?' I said, though I knew what was coming.

'We might attempt once more to establish some sort of understanding with the minds of the people in the moon.'

'So far as I'm concerned – it's the first.'

'I doubt.'

'I don't.'

'You see,' said Cavor, 'I do not think we can judge the Selenites by what we have seen of them. Their central world, their civilised world will be far below in the profounder caverns about their sea. This region of the crust in which we are is an outlying district, a pastoral region. At any rate, that is my interpretation. These Selenites we have seen may be only the equivalent of cowboys and engine-tenders. Their use of goads – in all probability mooncalf goads – the lack of imagination they show in expecting us to be able to do just what they can do, their indisputable brutality, all seem to point to something of that sort. But if we endured – '

'Neither of us could endure a six-inch plank across the bottomless pit for very long.'

'No,' said Cavor; 'but then – '

'I *won't*,' I said.

He discovered a new line of possibilities. 'Well, suppose we got ourselves into some corner, where we could defend ourselves against these hinds and labourers. If, for example, we could hold out for a week or so, it is probable that the news of our appearance would filter down to the more intelligent and populous parts – '

'If they exist.'

'They must exist, or whence came those tremendous machines?'

'That's possible, but it's the worst of the two chances.'

'We might write up inscriptions on walls – '

'How do we know their eyes would see the sort of marks we made?'

'If we cut them – '

'That's possible, of course.'

I took up a new thread of thought. 'After all,' I said, 'I suppose you don't think these Selenites so infinitely wiser than men.'

'They must know a lot more – or at least a lot of different things.'

'Yes, but – ' I hesitated.

'I think you'll quite admit, Cavor, that you're rather an exceptional man.'

'How?'

'Well, you – you're a rather lonely man – have been, that is. You haven't married.'

'Never wanted to. But why – '

'And you never grew richer than you happened to be?'

'Never wanted that either.'

'You've just rooted after knowledge?'

'Well, a certain curiosity is natural – '

'You think so. That's just it. You think every other mind wants to *know*. I remember once, when I asked you why you conducted all these researches, you said you wanted your FRS, and to have the stuff called Cavorite, and things like that. You know perfectly well you didn't do it for that; but at the time my question took you by surprise, and you felt you ought to have something to look like a motive. Really you conducted researches because you *had* to. It's your twist.'

'Perhaps it is – '

'It isn't one man in a million has that twist. Most men want – well, various things, but very few want knowledge for its own sake. *I* don't, I know perfectly well. Now, these Selenites seem to be a driving, busy sort of being, but how do you know that even the most intelligent will take an interest in us or our world? I don't believe they'll even know we have a world. They never come out at night – they'd freeze if they did. They've probably never seen any heavenly body at all except the blazing sun. How are they to know there is another world? What does it matter to them if they do? Well, even if they *have* had a glimpse of a few stars, or even of the earth crescent, what of that? Why should people living *inside* a planet trouble to observe that sort of thing? Men wouldn't have done it except for the seasons and sailing; why should the moon people? . . .

'Well, suppose there are a few philosophers like yourself. They are just the very Selenites who'll never have heard of our existence. Suppose a Selenite had dropped on the earth when you were at Lympne, you'd have been the last man in the world to hear he had come. You never read a newspaper! You see the chances against you. Well, it's for these chances we're sitting here doing nothing while precious time is flying. I tell you we've got into a fix. We've come unarmed, we've lost our sphere, we've got no food, we've shown ourselves to the Selenites, and made them think we're strange, strong, dangerous animals; and unless these Selenites are perfect fools, they'll set about now and hunt us till they find us, and when they find us they'll try to take us if they can, and kill us if they can't, and that's the end of the matter. If they take us, they'll probably kill us, through some misunderstanding. After we're done for, they may discuss us perhaps, but we shan't get much fun out of that.'

'Go on.'

'On the other hand, here's gold knocking about like cast iron at home. If only we can get some of it back, if only we can find our sphere again before they do, and get back, then – '

'Yes?'

'We might put the thing on a sounder footing. Come back in a bigger sphere with guns.'

'Good Lord!' cried Cavor, as though that was horrible.

I shied another luminous fungus down the cleft.

'Look here, Cavor,' I said, 'I've half the voting power anyhow in this affair, and this is a case for a practical man. I'm a practical man, and you are not. I'm not going to trust to Selenites and geometrical diagrams if I can help it . . . That's all. Get back. Drop all this secrecy – or most of it. And come again.'

He reflected. 'When I came to the moon,' he said, 'I ought to have come alone.'

'The question before the meeting,' I said, 'is how to get back to the sphere.'

For a time we nursed our knees in silence. Then he seemed to decide for my reasons.

'I think,' he said, 'one can get data. It is clear that while the sun is on this side of the moon the air will be blowing through this planet sponge from the dark side hither. On this side, at any rate, the air will be expanding and flowing out of the moon caverns into the craters . . . Very well, there's a draught here.'

'So there is.'

'And that means that this is not a dead end; somewhere behind us this cleft goes on and up. The draught is blowing up, and that is the way we have to go. If we try to get up any sort of chimney or gully there is, we shall not only get out of these passages where they are hunting for us – '

'But suppose the gully is too narrow?'

'We'll come down again.'

'Ssh!' I said suddenly; 'what's that?'

We listened. At first it was an indistinct murmur, and then one picked out the clang of a gong. 'They must think we are mooncalves,' said I, 'to be frightened at that.'

'They're coming along that passage,' said Cavor.

'They must be.'

'They'll not think of the cleft. They'll go past.'

I listened again for a space. 'This time,' I whispered, 'they're likely to have some sort of weapon.'

Then suddenly I sprang to my feet. 'Good heavens, Cavor!' I cried. 'But they *will*! They'll see the fungi I have been pitching down. They'll – !'

I didn't finish my sentence. I turned about and made a leap over the fungus tops towards the upper end of the cavity. I saw that the space turned upward and became a draughty cleft again, ascending to impenetrable darkness. I was about to clamber up into this, and then with a happy inspiration turned back.

'What are you doing?' asked Cavor.

'Go on!' said I, and went back and got two of the shining fungi, and putting one into the breast pocket of my flannel jacket, so that it stuck out to light our climbing, went back with the other for Cavor. The noise of the Selenites was now so loud that it seemed they must be already beneath the cleft. But it might be they would have difficulty in clambering into it, or might hesitate to ascend it against our possible resistance. At any rate, we had now the comforting knowledge of the enormous muscular superiority our birth in another planet gave us. In other minute I was clambering with gigantic vigour after Cavor's blue-lit heels.

CHAPTER SEVENTEEN

The Fight in the Cave of the Moon Butchers

I do not know how far we clambered before we came to the grating. It may be we ascended only a few hundred feet, but at the time it seemed to me we might have hauled and jammed and hopped and wedged ourselves through a mile or more of vertical ascent. Whenever I recall that time there comes into my head the heavy clank of our golden chains that followed every movement. Very soon my knuckles and knees were raw, and I had a bruise on one cheek. After a time the first violence of our efforts diminished, and our movements became more deliberate and less painful. The noise of the pursuing Selenites had died away altogether. It seemed almost as though they had not traced us up the crack after all, in spite of the tell-tale heap of broken fungi that must have lain beneath it. At times the cleft narrowed so much that we could scarce squeeze up it; at others it expanded into great drusy cavities, studded with prickly crystals or thickly beset with dull, shining fungoid pimples. Sometimes it twisted spirally, and at other times slanted down nearly to the horizontal direction. Ever and again there was the intermittent drip and trickle of water by us. Once or twice it seemed to us that small living things had rustled out of our reach, but what they were we never saw. They may have been venomous beasts for all I know, but they did us no harm, and we were now tuned to a pitch when a weird creeping thing more or less mattered little. And at last, far above, came the familiar bluish light again, and then we saw that it filtered through a grating that barred our way.

We whispered as we pointed this out to one another, and became more and more cautious in our ascent. Presently we were close under the grating, and by pressing my face against its bars I could see a limited portion of the cavern beyond. It was clearly a large space, and lit no doubt by some rivulet of the same blue light that we had seen flow from the beating machinery. An intermittent trickle of water dropped ever and again between the bars near my face.

My first endeavour was naturally to see what might be upon the floor of the cavern, but our grating lay in a depression whose rim hid all this from our eyes. Our foiled attention then fell back upon the suggestion of the various sounds we heard, and presently my eye caught a number of faint shadows that played across the dim roof far overhead.

Indisputably there were several Selenites, perhaps a considerable number, in this space, for we could hear the noises of their intercourse, and faint sounds that I identified as their footfalls. There was also a succession of regularly repeated sounds – chid, chid, chid – which began and ceased, suggestive of a knife or spade hacking at some soft substance. Then came a clank as if of chains, a whistle and a rumble as of a truck running over a hollowed place, and then again that chid, chid, chid resumed. The shadows told of shapes that moved quickly and rhythmically, in agreement with that regular sound, and rested when it ceased.

We put our heads close together, and began to discuss these things in noiseless whispers.

'They are occupied,' I said, 'they are occupied in some way.'

'Yes.'

'They're not seeking us, or thinking of us.'

'Perhaps they have not heard of us.'

'Those others are hunting about below. If suddenly we appeared here – '

We looked at one another.

'There might be a chance to parley,' said Cavor.

'No,' I said. 'Not as we are.'

For a space we remained, each occupied by his own thoughts.

Chid, chid, chid went the chopping, and the shadows moved to and fro.

I looked at the grating. 'It's flimsy,' I said. 'We might bend two of the bars and crawl through.'

We wasted a little time in vague discussion. Then I took one of the bars in both hands, and got my feet up against the rock until they were almost on a level with my head, and so thrust against the bar. It bent so suddenly that I almost slipped. I clambered about and bent the adjacent bar in the opposite direction, and then took the luminous fungus from my pocket and dropped it down the fissure.

'Don't do anything hastily,' whispered Cavor, as I twisted myself up through the opening I had enlarged. I had a glimpse of busy figures as I came through the grating, and immediately bent down, so that the rim of the depression in which the grating lay hid me from their eyes, and so lay flat, signalling advice to Cavor as he also prepared to come through. Presently we were side by side in the depression, peering over the edge at the cavern and its occupants.

It was a much larger cavern than we had supposed from our first glimpse of it, and we looked up from the lowest portion of its sloping floor. It widened out as it receded from us, and its roof came down and hid the remoter portion altogether. And lying in a line along its length, vanishing at last far away in that tremendous perspective, were a number of huge shapes, huge pallid hulls, upon which the Selenites were busy. At first they seemed big white cylinders of vague import. Then I noted the heads upon them lying towards us, eyeless and skinless like the heads of sheep at a butcher's, and perceived they were the carcasses of mooncalves being cut up, much as the crew of a whaler might cut up a moored whale. They were cutting off the flesh in strips, and on some of the farther trunks the white ribs were showing. It was the sound of their hatchets that made that chid, chid. Some way away a thing like a trolley cable, drawn and loaded with chunks of lax meat, was running up the slope of the cavern floor. This enormous long avenue of hulls that were destined to be food, gave us a sense of the vast populousness of the moon world second only to the effect of our first glimpse down the shaft.

It seemed to me at first that the Selenites must be standing on trestle-supported planks, and then I saw that the planks* and supports and their hatchets were really of the same leaden hue as my fetters had seemed – before white light came to bear on them. A number of very thick-looking crowbars lay about the floor, and had apparently assisted to turn the dead mooncalf over on its side. They were perhaps six feet long, with shaped handles, very tempting-looking weapons. The whole place was lit by three transverse streams of the blue fluid.

We lay for a long time noting all these things in silence. 'Well?' said Cavor at last.

I crouched over and turned to him. I had come upon a brilliant idea. 'Unless they lowered those bodies by a crane,' I said, 'we must be nearer the surface than I thought.'

'Why?'

'The mooncalf doesn't hop, and it hasn't got wings.'

He peered over the edge of the hollow again. 'I wonder now . . . ' he began. 'After all, we have never gone far from the surface – '

I stopped him by a grip on his arm. I had heard a noise from the cleft below us!

* I do not remember seeing any wooden things on the moon; doors, tables, everything corresponding to our terrestrial joinery was made of metal, and I believe for the most part of gold, which as a metal would, of course, naturally recommend itself – other things being equal – on account of the ease in working it, and its toughness and durability.

We twisted ourselves about, and lay as still as death, with every sense alert. In a little while I did not doubt that something was quietly ascending the cleft. Very slowly and quite noiselessly I assured myself of a good grip on my chain, and waited for that something to appear.

'Just look at those chaps with the hatchets again,' I said.

'They're all right,' said Cavor.

I took a sort of provisional aim at the gap in the grating. I could hear now quite distinctly the soft twittering of the ascending Selenites, the dab of their hands against the rock, and the falling of dust from their grips as they clambered.

Then I could see that there was something moving dimly in the blackness below the grating, but what it might be I could not distinguish. The whole thing seemed to hang fire just for a moment – then smash! I had sprung to my feet, struck savagely at something that had flashed out at me. It was the keen point of a spear. I have thought since that its length in the narrowness of the cleft must have prevented its being sloped to reach me. Anyhow, it shot out from the grating like the tongue of a snake, and missed and flew back and flashed again. But the second time I snatched and caught it, and wrenched it away, but not before another had darted ineffectually at me.

I shouted with triumph as I felt the hold of the Selenite resist my pull for a moment and give, and then I was jabbing down through the bars, amidst squeals from the darkness, and Cavor had snapped off the other spear, and was leaping and flourishing it beside me, and making inefficient jabs. Clang, clang, came up through the grating, and then an axe hurtled through the air and whacked against the rocks beyond, to remind me of the fleshers at the carcasses up the cavern.

I turned, and they were all coming towards us in open order waving their axes. They were short, thick, little beggars, with long arms, strikingly different from the ones we had seen before. If they had not heard of us before, they must have realised the situation with incredible swiftness. I stared at them for a moment, spear in hand. 'Guard that grating, Cavor,' I cried, howled to intimidate them, and rushed to meet them. Two of them missed with their hatchets, and the rest fled incontinently. Then the two also were sprinting away up the cavern, with hands clenched and heads down. I never saw men run like them!

I knew the spear I had was no good for me. It was thin and flimsy, only effectual for a thrust, and too long for a quick recover. So I only chased the Selenites as far as the first carcass, and stopped there and picked up one of the crowbars that were lying about. It felt comfortingly heavy, and equal to smashing any number of Selenites. I threw away my spear, and picked up a second crowbar for the other hand. I felt five times better than I had with the spear. I shook the two threateningly at the Selenites, who had come to a halt in a little crowd far away up the cavern, and then turned about to look at Cavor.

He was leaping from side to side of the grating, making threatening jabs with his broken spear. That was all right. It would keep the Selenites down – for a time at any rate. I looked up the cavern again. What on earth were we going to do now?

We were cornered in a sort of way already. But these butchers up the cavern had been surprised, they were probably scared, and they had no special weapons, only those little hatchets of theirs. And that way lay escape. Their sturdy little forms – ever so much shorter and thicker than the mooncalf herds – were scattered up the slope in a way that was eloquent of indecision. I had the moral advantage of a mad bull in a street. But for all that, there seemed a tremendous crowd of them. Very probably there was. Those Selenites down the cleft had certainly some infernally long spears. It might be they had other surprises for us . . . But, confound it! if we charged up the cave we should let them up behind us, and if we didn't those little brutes up the cave would probably get reinforced. Heaven alone knew what tremendous engines of warfare – guns, bombs, terrestrial torpedoes – this unknown world below our feet, this vaster world of which we had only pricked the outer cuticle, might not presently send up to our destruction. It became clear the only thing to do was to charge! It became clearer as the legs of a number of fresh Selenites appeared running down the cavern towards us.

'Bedford!' cried Cavor, and behold! he was halfway between me and the grating.

'Go back!' I cried. 'What are you doing – '

'They've got – it's like a gun!'

And struggling in the grating between those defensive spears appeared the head and shoulders of a singularly lean and angular Selenite, bearing some complicated apparatus.

I realised Cavor's utter incapacity for the fight we had in hand. For a moment I hesitated. Then I rushed past him whirling my crowbars, and shouting to confound the aim of the Selenite. He was aiming in the queerest way with the thing against his stomach. '*Chuzz!*' The thing wasn't a gun; it went off like crossbow more, and dropped me in the middle of a leap.

I didn't fall down, I simply came down a little shorter than I should have done if I hadn't been hit, and from the feel of my shoulder the thing might have tapped me and glanced off. Then my left hand hit again the shaft, and I perceived there was a sort of spear sticking half through my shoulder. The moment after I got home with the crowbar in my right hand, and hit the Selenite fair and square. He collapsed – he crushed and crumpled – his head smashed like an egg.

I dropped a crowbar, pulled the spear out of my shoulder, and began to jab it down the grating into the darkness. At each jab came a shriek and twitter. Finally I hurled the spear down upon them with all my strength, leapt up, picked up the crowbar again, and started for the multitude up the cavern.

'Bedford!' cried Cavor. 'Bedford!' as I flew past him.

I seem to remember his footsteps coming on behind me.

Step, leap . . . whack, step, leap . . . Each leap seemed to last ages. With each, the cave opened out and the number of Selenites visible increased. At first they seemed all running about like ants in a disturbed ant-hill, one or two waving hatchets and coming to meet me, more running away, some bolting sideways into the avenue of carcasses, then presently others came in sight carrying spears, and then others. I saw a most extraordinary thing, all hands and feet, bolting for cover. The cavern grew darker farther up. Flick! something flew over my head. Flick! As I soared in mid-stride I saw a spear hit and quiver in one of the carcasses to my left. Then, as I came down, one hit the ground before me, and I heard the remote chuzz! with which their things were fired. Flick, flick! for a moment it was a shower. They were volleying!

I stopped dead.

I don't think I thought clearly then. I seem to remember a kind of stereotyped phrase running through my mind: 'Zone of fire, seek cover!' I know I made a dash for the space between two of the carcasses, and stood there panting and feeling very wicked.

I looked round for Cavor, and for a moment it seemed as if he had vanished from the world. Then he came out of the darkness between the row of the carcasses and the rocky wall of the cavern. I saw his little face, dark and blue, and shining with perspiration and emotion.

He was saying something, but what it was I did not heed. I had realised that we might work from mooncalf to mooncalf up the cave until we were near enough to charge home. It was charge or nothing. 'Come on!' I said, and led the way.

'Bedford!' he cried unavailingly.

My mind was busy as we went up that narrow alley between the dead bodies and the wall of the cavern. The rocks curved about – they could not enfilade us. Though in that narrow space we could not leap, yet with our earth-born strength we were still able to go very much faster than the Selenites. I reckoned we should presently come right among them. Once we were on them, they would be nearly as formidable as black beetles. Only! – there would first of all be a volley. I thought of a stratagem. I whipped off my flannel jacket as I ran.

'Bedford!' panted Cavor behind me.

I glanced back. 'What?' said I.

He was pointing upward over the carcasses. 'White light!' he said. 'White light again!'

I looked, and it was even so, a faint white ghost of light in the remoter cavern roof. That seemed to give me double strength.

'Keep close,' I said. A flat, long Selenite dashed out of the darkness, and squealed and fled. I halted, and stopped Cavor with my hand. I hung my jacket over my crowbar, ducked round the next carcass, dropped jacket and crowbar, showed myself, and darted back.

'Chuzz – flick,' just one arrow came. We were close on the Selenites, and they were standing in a crowd, broad, short, and tall together, with a little battery of their shooting implements pointing down the cave. Three or four other arrows followed the first, then their fire ceased.

I stuck out my head, and escaped by a hair's-breadth. This time I drew a dozen shots or more, and heard the Selenites shouting and twittering as if with excitement as they shot. I picked up jacket and crowbar again.

'*Now!*' said I, and thrust out the jacket.

'Chuzz-zz-zz-zz! Chuzz!' In an instant my jacket had grown a thick beard of arrows, and they were quivering all over the carcass behind us. Instantly I slipped the crowbar out of the jacket, dropped the jacket – for all I know to the contrary it is lying up there in the moon now – and rushed out upon them.

For a minute perhaps it was massacre. I was too fierce to discriminate, and the Selenites were probably too scared to fight. At any rate they made no sort of fight against me. I saw scarlet, as the saying is. I remember I seemed to be wading among those leathery, thin things as a man wades through tall grass, mowing and hitting, first right, then left; smash. Little drops of moisture flew about. I trod on things that crushed and piped and went slippery. The crowd seemed to open and close and flow like water. They seemed to have no combined plan whatever. There were spears flew about me, I was grazed over the ear by one. I was stabbed once in the arm and once in the cheek, but I only found that out afterwards, when the blood had had time to run and cool and feel wet.

What Cavor did I do not know. For a space it seemed that this fighting had lasted for an age, and must needs go on for ever. Then suddenly it was all over, and there was nothing to be seen but the backs of heads bobbing up and down as their owners ran in all directions . . . I seemed altogether unhurt. I ran forward some paces, shouting, then turned about. I was amazed.

I had come right through them in vast flying strides, they were all behind me, and running hither and thither to hide.

I felt an enormous astonishment at the evaporation of the great fight into which I had hurled myself, and not a little exultation. It did not seem to me that I had discovered the Selenites were unexpectedly flimsy, but that I was unexpectedly strong. I laughed stupidly. This fantastic moon!

I glanced for a moment at the smashed and writhing bodies that were scattered over the cavern floor, with a vague idea of further violence, then hurried on after Cavor.

CHAPTER EIGHTEEN

In the Sunlight

Presently we saw that the cavern before us opened upon a hazy void. In another moment we had emerged upon a sort of slanting gallery, that projected into a vast circular space, a huge cylindrical pit running vertically up and down. Round this pit the slanting gallery ran without any parapet or protection for a turn and a half, and then plunged high above into the rock again. Somehow it reminded me then of one of those spiral turns of the railway through the St Gothard. It was all tremendously huge. I can scarcely hope to convey to you the Titanic proportion of all that place, the Titanic effect of it. Our eyes followed up the vast declivity of the pit wall, and overhead and far above we beheld a round opening set with faint stars, and half of the lip about it well nigh blinding with the white light of the sun. At that we cried aloud simultaneously.

'Come on!' I said, leading the way.

'But there?' said Cavor, and very carefully stepped nearer the edge of the gallery. I followed his example, and craned forward and looked down, but I was dazzled by that gleam of light above, and I could see only a bottomless darkness with spectral patches of crimson and purple floating therein. Yet if I could not see, I could hear. Out of this darkness came a sound, a sound like the angry hum one can hear if one puts one's ear outside a hive of bees, a sound out of that enormous hollow, it may be, four miles beneath our feet . . .

For a moment I listened, then tightened my grip on my crowbar, and led the way up the gallery.

'This must be the shaft we looked down upon,' said Cavor. 'Under that lid.'

'And below there, is where we saw the lights.'

'The lights!' said he. 'Yes – the lights of the world that now we shall never see.'

'We'll come back,' I said, for now we had escaped so much I was rashly sanguine that we should recover the sphere.

His answer I did not catch.

'Eh?' I asked.

'It doesn't matter,' he answered, and we hurried on in silence.

I suppose that slanting lateral way was four or five miles long, allowing for its curvature, and it ascended at a slope that would have made it almost impossibly steep on earth, but which one strode up easily under lunar conditions. We saw only two Selenites during all that portion of our flight, and directly they became aware of us they ran headlong. It was clear that the knowledge of our strength and violence had reached them. Our way to the exterior was unexpectedly plain. The spiral gallery straightened into a steeply ascendent tunnel, its floor bearing abundant traces of the mooncalves, and so straight and short in proportion to its vast arch, that no part of it was absolutely dark. Almost immediately it began to lighten, and then far off and high up, and quite blindingly brilliant, appeared its opening on the exterior, a slope of Alpine steepness surmounted by a crest of bayonet shrub, tall and broken down now, and dry and dead, in spiky silhouette against the sun.

And it is strange that we men, to whom this very vegetation had seemed so weird and horrible a little time ago, should now behold it with the emotion a home-coming exile might feel at sight of his native land. We welcomed even the rareness of the air that made us pant as we ran, and which rendered speaking no longer the easy thing that it had been, but an effort to make oneself heard. Larger grew the sunlit circle above us, and larger, and all the nearer tunnel sank into a rim of indistinguishable black. We saw the dead bayonet shrub no longer with any touch of green in it, but brown and dry and thick, and the shadow of its upper branches high out of sight made a densely interlaced pattern upon the tumbled rocks. And at the immediate mouth of the tunnel was a wide trampled space where the mooncalves had come and gone.

We came out upon this space at last into a light and heat that hit and pressed upon us. We traversed the exposed area painfully, and clambered up a slope among the scrub stems, and sat down at last panting in a high place beneath the shadow of a mass of twisted lava. Even in the shade the rock felt hot.

The air was intensely hot, and we were in great physical discomfort, but for all that we were no longer in a nightmare. We seemed to have come to our own province again, beneath the stars. All the fear and stress of our flight through the dim passages and fissures below had fallen from us. That last fight had filled us with an enormous confidence in ourselves so far as the Selenites were concerned. We looked back almost incredulously at the black opening from which we had just emerged. Down there it was, in a blue glow that now in our memories seemed the next thing to absolute darkness, we had met with things like mad mockeries of men, helmet-headed creatures, and had walked in fear before them, and had submitted to them until we could submit no longer. And behold, they had smashed like wax and scattered like chaff, and fled and vanished like the creatures of a dream!

I rubbed my eyes, doubting whether we had not slept and dreamt these things by reason of the fungus we had eaten, and suddenly discovered the blood upon my face, and then that my shirt was sticking painfully to my shoulder and arm.

'Confound it!' I said, gauging my injuries with an investigatory hand, and suddenly that distant tunnel mouth became, as it were, a watching eye.

'Cavor!' I said; 'what are they going to do now? And what are we going to do?'

He shook his head, with his eyes fixed upon the tunnel. 'How can one tell what they will do?'

'It depends on what they think of us, and I don't see how we can begin to guess that. And it depends upon what they have in reserve. It's as you say, Cavor, we have touched the merest outside of this world. They may have all sorts of things inside here. Even with those shooting things they might make it bad for us . . .

'Yet after all,' I said, 'even if we *don't* find the sphere at once, there is a chance for us. We might hold out. Even through the night. We might go down there again and make a fight for it.'

I stared about me with speculative eyes. The character of the scenery had altered altogether by reason of the enormous growth and subsequent drying of the scrub. The crest on which we sat was high, and commanded a wide prospect of the crater landscape, and we saw it now all sere and dry in the late autumn of the lunar afternoon. Rising one behind the other were long slopes and fields of trampled brown where the mooncalves had pastured, and far away in the full blaze of the sun a drove of them basked slumberously, scattered shapes, each with a blot of shadow against it like sheep on the side of a down. But never a sign of a Selenite was to be seen. Whether they had fled on our emergence from the interior passages, or whether they were accustomed to retire after driving out the mooncalves, I cannot guess. At the time I believed the former was the case.

'If we were to set fire to all this stuff,' I said, 'we might find the sphere among the ashes.'

Cavor did not seem to hear me. He was peering under his hand at the stars, that still, in spite of the intense sunlight, were abundantly visible in the sky. 'How long do you think we've have been here?' he asked at last.

'Been where?'

'On the moon.'

'Two earthly days, perhaps.'

'More nearly ten. Do you know, the sun is past its zenith, and sinking in the west. In four days' time or less it will be night.'

'But – we've only eaten once!'

'I know that. And – But there are the stars!'

'But why should time seem different because we are on a smaller planet?'

'I don't know. There it is!'

'How does one tell time?'

'Hunger – fatigue – all those things are different. Everything is different – everything. To me it seems that since first we came out of the sphere has been only a question of hours – long hours – at most.'

'Ten days,' I said; 'that leaves – ' I looked up at the sun for a moment, and then saw that it was halfway from the zenith to the western edge of things. 'Four days! . . . Cavor, we musn't sit here and dream. How do you think we may begin?'

I stood up. 'We must get a fixed point we can recognise – we might hoist a flag, or a handkerchief, or something – and quarter the ground, and work round that.'

He stood up beside me.

'Yes,' he said, 'there is nothing for it but to hunt the sphere. Nothing. We may find it – certainly we may find it. And if not – '

'We must keep on looking.'

He looked this way and that, glanced up at the sky and down at the tunnel, and astonished me by a sudden gesture of impatience. 'Oh! but we have done foolishly! To have come to this pass! Think how it might have been, and the things we might have done!'

'We might do something yet.'

'Never the thing we might have done. Here below our feet is a world. Think of what that world must be! Think of that machine we saw, and the lid and the shaft! They were just remote outlying things, and those creatures we have seen and fought with no more than ignorant peasants, dwellers in the outskirts, yokels and labourers half akin to brutes. Down below! Caverns beneath caverns, tunnels, structures, ways . . . It must open out, and be greater and wider and more populous as one descends. Assuredly. Right down at the last the central sea that washes round the core of the moon. Think of its inky waters under the spare lights – if, indeed, their eyes need lights! Think of the cascading tributaries pouring down their channels to feed it! Think of the tides upon its surface, and the rush and swirl of its ebb and flow! perhaps they have ships that go upon it, perhaps down there are mighty cities and swarming ways, and wisdom and order passing the wit of man. And we may die here upon it, and never see the masters who *must* be – ruling over these things! We may freeze and die here, and the air will freeze and thaw upon us, and then – ! Then they will come upon us, come on our stiff and silent bodies, and find the sphere we cannot find, and they will understand at last too late all the thought and effort that ended here in vain!'

His voice for all that speech sounded like the voice of someone heard in a telephone, weak and far away.

'But the darkness,' I said.

'One might get over that.'

'How?'

'I don't know. How am I to know? One might carry a torch, one might have a lamp – The others – might understand.'

He stood for a moment with his hands held down and a rueful face, staring out over the waste that defied him. Then with a gesture of renunciation he turned towards me with proposals for the systematic hunting of the sphere.

'We can return,' I said.

He looked about him. 'First of all we shall have to get to earth.'

'We could bring back lamps to carry and climbing irons, and a hundred necessary things.'

'Yes,' he said.

'We can take back an earnest of success in this gold.'

He looked at my golden crowbars, and said nothing for a space. He stood with his hands clasped behind his back, staring across the crater. At last he sighed and spoke. 'It was I found the way here, but to find a way isn't always to be master of a way. If I take my secret back to earth, what will happen? I do not see how I can keep my secret for a year, for even a part of a year. Sooner or later it must come out, even if other men rediscover it. And then . . . Governments and powers will struggle to get hither, they will fight against one another, and against these moon people; it will only spread warfare and multiply the occasions of war. In a little while, in a very little while, if I tell my secret, this planet to its deepest galleries will be strewn with human dead. Other things are doubtful, but that is certain . . . It is not as though man had any use for the moon. What good would the moon be to men? Even of their own planet what have they made but a battleground and theatre of infinite folly? Small as his world is, and short as his time, he has still in his little life down there far more than he can do. No! Science has toiled too long forging weapons for fools to use. It is time she held her hand. Let him find it out for himself again – in a thousand years' time.'

'There are methods of secrecy,' I said.

He looked up at me and smiled. 'After all,' he said, 'why should one worry? There is little chance of our finding the sphere, and down below things are brewing. It's simply the human habit of hoping till we die that makes us think of return. Our troubles are only beginning. We have shown these moon folk violence, we have given them a taste of our quality, and our chances are about as good as a tiger's that has got loose and killed a man in Hyde Park. The news of us must be running down from gallery to gallery, down towards the central parts . . . No sane beings will ever let us take that sphere back to earth after so much as they have seen of us.'

'We aren't improving our chances,' said I, 'by sitting here.'

We stood up side by side.

'After all,' he said, 'we must separate. We must stick up a hand-kerchief on these tall spikes here and fasten it firmly, and from this as a centre we must work over the crater. You must go westward, moving out in semicircles to and fro towards the setting sun. You must move first with your shadow on your right until it is at right angles with the direction of your handkerchief, and then with your shadow on your left. And I will do the same to the east. We will look into every gully, examine every skerry of rocks; we will do all we can to find my sphere. If we see the Selenites we will hide from them as well as we can. For drink we must take snow, and if we feel the need of food, we must kill a mooncalf if we can, and eat such flesh as it has – raw – and so each will go his own way.'

'And if one of us comes upon the sphere?'

'He must come back to the white handkerchief, and stand by it and signal to the other.'

'And if neither – ?'

Cavor glanced up at the sun. 'We go on seeking until the night and cold overtake us.'

'Suppose the Selenites have found the sphere and hidden it?'

He shrugged his shoulders.

'Or if presently they come hunting us?'

He made no answer.

'You had better take a club,' I said.

He shook his head, and stared away from me across the waste.

But for a moment he did not start. He looked round at me shyly, hesitated. '*Au revoir*,' he said.

I felt an odd stab of emotion. A sense of how we had galled each other, and particularly how I must have galled him, came to me. 'Confound it,' thought I, 'we might have done better!' I was on the point of asking him to shake hands – for that, somehow, was how I felt just then – when he put his feet together and leapt away from me towards the north. He seemed to drift through the air as a dead leaf would do, fell lightly, and leapt again. I stood for a moment watching him, then faced westward reluctantly, pulled myself together, and with something of the feeling of a man who leaps into icy water, selected a leaping point, and plunged forward to explore my solitary half of the moon world. I dropped rather clumsily among rocks, stood up and looked about me, clambered on to a rocky slab, and leapt again . . .

When presently I looked for Cavor he was hidden from my eyes, but the handkerchief showed out bravely on its headland, white in the blaze of the sun.

I determined not to lose sight of that handkerchief whatever might betide.

CHAPTER NINETEEN

Mr Bedford Alone

In a little while it seemed to me as though I had always been alone on the moon. I hunted for a time with a certain intentness, but the heat was still very great, and the thinness of the air felt like a hoop about one's chest. I came presently into a hollow basin bristling with tall, brown, dry fronds about its edge, and I sat down under these to rest and cool. I intended to rest for only a little while. I put down my clubs beside me, and sat resting my chin on my hands. I saw with a sort of colourless interest that the rocks of the basin, where here and there the crackling dry lichens had shrunk away to show them, were all veined and splattered with gold, that here and there bosses of rounded and wrinkled gold projected from among the litter. What did that matter now? A sort of languor had possession of my limbs and mind, I did not believe for a moment that we should ever find the sphere in that vast desiccated wilderness. I seemed to lack a motive for effort until the Selenites should come. Then I supposed I should exert myself, obeying that unreasonable imperative that urges a man before all things to preserve and defend his life, albeit he may preserve it only to die more painfully in a little while.

Why had we come to the moon?

The thing presented itself to me as a perplexing problem. What is this spirit in man that urges him for ever to depart from happiness and security, to toil, to place himself in danger, to risk even a reasonable certainty of death? It dawned upon me up there in the moon as a thing I ought always to have known, that man is not made simply to go about being safe and comfortable and well fed and amused. Almost any man, if you put the thing to him, not in words, but in the shape of opportunities, will show that he knows as much. Against his interest, against his happiness, he is constantly being driven to do unreasonable things. Some force not himself impels him, and go he must. But why? Why? Sitting there in the midst of that useless moon gold, amidst the things of another world, I took count of all my life. Assuming I was to die a castaway upon the moon, I failed altogether to see what purpose I had served. I got no light on that point, but at any rate it was clearer to me than it had ever been in my life before that I was not serving my own purpose, that all my life I had in truth never served the purposes

of my private life. Whose purposes, what purposes, was I serving? . . .
I ceased to speculate on why we had come to the moon, and took a
wider sweep. Why had I come to the earth? Why had I a private life at
all? . . . I lost myself at last in bottomless speculations . . .

My thoughts became vague and cloudy, no longer leading in definite
directions. I had not felt heavy or weary – I cannot imagine one doing so
upon the moon – but I suppose I was greatly fatigued. At any rate I slept.

Slumbering there rested me greatly, I think, and the sun was setting
and the violence of the heat abating, through all the time I slumbered.
When at last I was roused from my slumbers by a remote clamour, I felt
active and capable again. I rubbed my eyes and stretched my arms. I
rose to my feet – I was a little stiff – and at once prepared to resume my
search. I shouldered my golden clubs, one on each shoulder, and went
on out of the ravine of the gold-veined rocks.

The sun was certainly lower, much lower than it had been; the air was
very much cooler. I perceived I must have slept some time. It seemed to
me that a faint touch of misty blueness hung about the western cliff. I
leapt to a little boss of rock and surveyed the crater. I could see no signs
of mooncalves or Selenites, nor could I see Cavor, but I could see my
handkerchief far off, spread out on its thicket of thorns. I looked about
me, and then leapt forward to the next convenient viewpoint.

I beat my round in a semicircle, and back again in a still remoter
crescent. It was very fatiguing and hopeless. The air was really very
much cooler, and it seemed to me that the shadow under the westward
cliff was growing broad. Ever and again I stopped and reconnoitred, but
there was no sign of Cavor, no sign of Selenites; and it seemed to me
the mooncalves must have been driven into the interior again – I could
see none of them. I became more and more desirous of seeing Cavor.
The winged outline of the sun had sunk now, until it was scarcely the
distance of its diameter from the rim of the sky. I was oppressed by the
idea that the Selenites would presently close their lids and valves, and
shut us out under the inexorable onrush of the lunar night. It seemed to
me high time that he abandoned his search, and that we took counsel
together. I felt how urgent it was that we should decide soon upon our
course. We had failed to find the sphere, we no longer had time to seek
it, and once these valves were closed with us outside, we were lost men.
The great night of space would descend upon us – that blackness of the
void which is the only absolute death. All my being shrank from that
approach. We must get into the moon again, though we were slain in
doing it. I was haunted by a vision of our freezing to death, of our
hammering with our last strength on the valve of the great pit.

I took no thought any more of the sphere. I thought only of finding Cavor again. I was half inclined to go back into the moon without him, rather than seek him until it was too late. I was already halfway back towards our handkerchief, when suddenly –

I saw the sphere!

I did not find it so much as it found me. It was lying much farther to the westward than I had gone, and the sloping rays of the sinking sun reflected from its glass had suddenly proclaimed its presence in a dazzling beam. For an instant I thought this was some new device of the Selenites against us, and then I understood.

I threw up my arms, shouted a ghostly shout, and set off in vast leaps towards it. I missed one of my leaps and dropped into a deep ravine and twisted my ankle, and after that I stumbled at almost every leap. I was in a state of hysterical agitation, trembling violently, and quite breathless long before I got to it. Three times at least I had to stop with my hands resting on my side and in spite of the thin dryness of the air, the perspiration was wet upon my face.

I thought of nothing but the sphere until I reached it, I forgot even my trouble of Cavor's whereabouts. My last leap flung me with my hands hard against its glass; then I lay against it panting, and trying vainly to shout, 'Cavor! here is the sphere!' When I had recovered a little I peered through the thick glass, and the things inside seemed tumbled. I stooped to peer closer. Then I attempted to get in. I had to hoist it over a little to get my head through the manhole. The screw stopper was inside, and I could see now that nothing had been touched, nothing had suffered. It lay there as we had left it when we had dropped out amidst the snow. For a time I was wholly occupied in making and remaking this inventory. I found I was trembling violently. It was good to see that familiar dark interior again! I cannot tell you how good. Presently I crept inside and sat down among the things. I looked through the glass at the moon world and shivered. I placed my gold clubs upon the table, and sought out and took a little food; not so much because I wanted it, but because it was there. Then it occurred to me that it was time to go out and signal for Cavor. But I did not go out and signal for Cavor forthwith. Something held me to the sphere.

After all, everything was coming right. There would be still time for us to get more of the magic stone that gives one mastery over men. Away there, close handy, was gold for the picking up; and the sphere would travel as well half full of gold as though it were empty. We could go back now, masters of ourselves and our world, and then –

I roused myself at last, and with an effort got myself out of the sphere.

I shivered as I emerged, for the evening air was growing very cold. I stood in the hollow staring about me. I scrutinised the bushes round me very carefully before I leapt to the rocky shelf hard by, and took once more what had been my first leap in the moon. But now I made it with no effort whatever.

The growth and decay of the vegetation had gone on apace, and the whole aspect of the rocks had changed, but still it was possible to make out the slope on which the seeds had germinated, and the rocky mass from which we had taken our first view of the crater. But the spiky shrub on the slope stood brown and sere now, and thirty feet high, and cast long shadows that stretched out of sight, and the little seeds that clustered in its upper branches were brown and ripe. Its work was done, and it was brittle and ready to fall and crumple under the freezing air, so soon as the nightfall came. And the huge cacti, that had swollen as we watched them, had long since burst and scattered their spores to the four quarters of the moon. Amazing little corner in the universe – the landing place of men!

Some day, thought I, I will have an inscription standing there right in the midst of the hollow. It came to me, if only this teeming world within knew of the full import of the moment, how furious its tumult would become!

But as yet it could scarcely be dreaming of the significance of our coming. For if it did, the crater would surely be an uproar of pursuit, instead of as still as death! I looked about for some place from which I might signal Cavor, and saw that same patch of rock to which he had leapt from my present standpoint, still bare and barren in the sun. For a moment I hesitated at going so far from the sphere. Then with a pang of shame at that hesitation, I leapt . . .

From this vantage point I surveyed the crater again. Far away at the top of the enormous shadow I cast was the little white handkerchief fluttering on the bushes. It was very little and very far, and Cavor was not in sight. It seemed to me that by this time he ought to be looking for me. That was the agreement. But he was nowhere to be seen.

I stood waiting and watching, hands shading my eyes, expecting every moment to distinguish him. Very probably I stood there for quite a long time. I tried to shout, and was reminded of the thinness of the air. I made an undecided step back towards the sphere. But a lurking dread of the Selenites made me hesitate to signal my whereabouts by hoisting one of our sleeping-blankets on to the adjacent scrub. I searched the crater again.

It had an effect of emptiness that chilled me. And it was still; any sound from the Selenites in the world beneath, even had died away. It was as still as death. Save for the faint stir of the shrub about me in the little breeze that was rising, there was no sound nor shadow of a sound. And the breeze blew chill.

Confound Cavor!

I took a deep breath. I put my hands to the sides of my mouth. 'Cavor!' I bawled, and the sound was like some manikin shouting far away.

I looked at the handkerchief, I looked behind me at the broadening shadow of the westward cliff, I looked under my hand at the sun. It seemed to me that almost visibly it was creeping down the sky.

I felt I must act instantly if I was to save Cavor. I whipped off my vest and flung it as a mark on the sere bayonets of the shrubs behind me, and then set off in a straight line towards the handkerchief. Perhaps it was a couple of miles away – a matter of a few hundred leaps and strides. I have already told how one seemed to hang through those lunar leaps. In each suspense I sought Cavor, and marvelled why he should be hidden. In each leap I could feel the sun setting behind me. Each time I touched the ground I was tempted to go back.

A last leap and I was in the depression below our handkerchief, a stride, and I stood on our former vantage point within arms' reach of it. I stood up straight and scanned the world about me, between its lengthening bars of shadow. Far away, down a long declivity, was the opening of the tunnel up which we had fled, and my shadow reached towards it, stretched towards it, and touched it, like a finger of the night.

Not a sign of Cavor, not a sound in all the stillness, only the stir and waving of the scrub and of the shadows increased. And suddenly and violently I shivered. 'Cav –' I began, and realised once more the uselessness of the human voice in that thin air.

Silence. The silence of death.

Then it was my eye caught something – a little thing lying, perhaps fifty yards away down the slope, amidst a litter of bent and broken branches. What was it? I knew, and yet for some reason I would not know. I went nearer to it. It was the little cricket-cap Cavor had worn. I did not touch it, I stood looking at it.

I saw then that the scattered branches about it had been forcibly smashed and trampled. I hesitated, stepped forward, and picked it up.

I stood with Cavor's cap in my hand, staring at the trampled reeds and thorns about me. On some of them were little smears of something dark, something that I dared not touch. A dozen yards away, perhaps, the rising breeze dragged something into view, something small and vividly white.

It was a little piece of paper crumpled tightly, as though it had been clutched tightly. I picked it up, and on it were smears of red. My eye caught faint pencil marks. I smoothed it out, and saw uneven and broken writing ending at last in a crooked streak upon the paper.

I set myself to decipher this.

'I have been injured about the knee, I think my kneecap is hurt, and I cannot run or crawl,' it began – pretty distinctly written.

Then less legibly: 'They have been chasing me for some time, and it is only a question of' – the word 'time' seemed to have been written here and erased in favour of something illegible – 'before they get me. They are beating all about me.'

Then the writing became convulsive. 'I can hear them,' I guessed the tracing meant, and then it was quite unreadable for a space. Then came a little string of words that were quite distinct: 'a different sort of Selenite altogether, who appears to be directing the – The writing became a mere hasty confusion again.

'They have larger brain cases – much larger, and slenderer bodies, and very short legs. They make gentle noises, and move with organised deliberation . . .

'And though I am wounded and helpless here, their appearance still gives me hope – ' That was like Cavor. 'They have not shot at me or attempted . . . injury. I intend – '

Then came the sudden streak of the pencil across the paper, and on the back and edges – blood!

And as I stood there stupid, and perplexed, with this dumbfounding relic in my hand, something very soft and light and chill touched my hand for a moment and ceased to be, and then a thing, a little white speck, drifted athwart a shadow. It was a tiny snowflake, the first snowflake, the herald of the night.

I looked up with a start, and the sky had darkened almost to blackness, and was thick with a gathering multitude of coldly watchful stars. I looked eastward, and the light of that shrivelled world was touched with sombre bronze; westward, and the sun robbed now by a thickening white mist of half its heat and splendour, was touching the crater rim, was sinking out of sight, and all the shrubs and jagged and tumbled rocks stood out against it in a bristling disorder of black shapes. Into the great lake of darkness westward, a vast wreath of mist was sinking. A cold wind set all the crater shivering. Suddenly, for a moment, I was in a puff of falling snow, and all the world about me grey and dim.

And then it was I heard, not loud and penetrating as at first, but faint and dim like a dying voice, that tolling, that same tolling that had welcomed the coming of the day: Boom! . . . Boom! . . . Boom! . . .

It echoed about the crater, it seemed to throb with the throbbing of the greater stars, the blood-red crescent of the sun's disc sank as it tolled out: Boom! . . . Boom! . . . Boom! . . .

What had happened to Cavor? All through that tolling I stood there stupidly, and at last the tolling ceased.

And suddenly the open mouth of the tunnel down below there, shut like an eye and vanished out of sight.

Then indeed was I alone.

Over me, around me, closing in on me, embracing me ever nearer, was the Eternal; that which was before the beginning, and that which triumphs over the end; that enormous void in which all light and life and being is but the thin and vanishing splendour of a falling star, the cold, the stillness, the silence – the infinite and final Night of space.

The sense of solitude and desolation became the sense of an overwhelming presence that stooped towards me, that almost touched me.

'No,' I cried. '*No!* Not yet! not yet! Wait! Wait! Oh, wait!' My voice went up to a shriek. I flung the crumpled paper from me, scrambled back to the crest to take my bearings, and then, with all the will that was in me, leapt out towards the mark I had left, dim and distant now in the very margin of the shadow.

Leap, leap, leap, and each leap was seven ages.

Before me the pale serpent-girdled section of the sun sank and sank, and the advancing shadow swept to seize the sphere before I could reach it. I was two miles away, a hundred leaps or more, and the air about me was thinning out as it thins under an air-pump, and the cold was gripping at my joints. But had I died, I should have died leaping. Once, and then again my foot slipped on the gathering snow as I leapt and shortened my leap; once I fell short into bushes that crashed and smashed into dusty chips and nothingness, and once I stumbled as I dropped and rolled head over heels into a gully, and rose bruised and bleeding and confused as to my direction.

But such incidents were as nothing to the intervals, those awful pauses when one drifted through the air towards that pouring tide of night. My breathing made a piping noise, and it was as though knives were whirling in my lungs. My heart seemed to beat against the top of my brain. 'Shall I reach it? O Heaven! Shall I reach it?'

My whole being became anguish.

'Lie down!' screamed my pain and despair; 'lie down!'

The nearer I struggled, the more awfully remote it seemed. I was numb, I stumbled, I bruised and cut myself and did not bleed.

It was in sight.

I fell on all fours, and my lungs whooped.

I crawled. The frost gathered on my lips, icicles hung from my moustache, I was white with the freezing atmosphere.

I was a dozen yards from it. My eyes had become dim. 'Lie down!' screamed despair; 'lie down!'

I touched it, and halted. 'Too late!' screamed despair; 'lie down!'

I fought stiffly with it. I was on the manhole lip, a stupefied, half-dead being. The snow was all about me. I pulled myself in. There lurked within a little warmer air.

The snowflakes – the air flakes – danced in about me, as I tried with chilling hands to thrust the valve in and spun it tight and hard. I sobbed. 'I will,' I chattered in my teeth. And then, with fingers that quivered and felt brittle, I turned to the shutter studs.

As I fumbled with the switches – for I had never controlled them before – I could see dimly through the steaming glass the blazing red streamers of the sinking sun, dancing and flickering through the snowstorm, and the black forms of the scrub thickening and bending and breaking beneath the accumulating snow. Thicker whirled the snow and thicker, black against the light. What if even now the switches overcame me?

Then something clicked under my hands, and in an instant that last vision of the moon world was hidden from my eyes. I was in the silence and darkness of the interplanetary sphere.

CHAPTER TWENTY

Mr Bedford in Infinite Space

It was almost as though I had been killed. Indeed, I could imagine a man suddenly and violently killed would feel very much as I did. One moment, a passion of agonising existence and fear; the next darkness and stillness, neither light nor life nor sun, moon nor stars, the blank infinite. Although the thing was done by my own act, although I had already tasted this very effect in Cavor's company, I felt astonished, dumbfounded, and overwhelmed. I seemed to be borne upward into an enormous darkness. My fingers floated off the studs, I hung as if I were annihilated, and at last very softly and gently I came against the bale and the golden chain, and the crowbars that had drifted to the middle of the sphere.

I do not know how long that drifting took. In the sphere of course, even more than on the moon, one's earthly time sense was ineffectual. At the touch of the bale it was as if I had awakened from a dreamless sleep. I immediately perceived that if I wanted to keep awake and alive I must get a light or open a window, so as to get a grip of something with my eyes. And besides, I was cold. I kicked off from the bale, therefore, clawed on to the thin cords within the glass, crawled along until I got to the manhole rim, and so got my bearings for the light and blind studs, took a shove off, and flying once round the bale, and getting a scare from something big and flimsy that was drifting loose, I got my hand on the cord quite close to the studs, and reached them. I lit the little lamp first of all to see what it was I had collided with, and discovered that old copy of *Lloyd's News* had slipped its moorings, and was adrift in the void. That brought me out of the infinite to my own proper dimensions again. It made me laugh and pant for a time, and suggested the idea of a little oxygen from one of the cylinders. After that I lit the heater until I felt warm, and then I took food. Then I set to work in a very gingerly fashion on the Cavorite blinds, to see if I could guess by any means how the sphere was travelling.

The first blind I opened I shut at once, and hung for a time flattened and blinded by the sunlight that had hit me. After thinking a little I started upon the windows at right angles to this one, and got the huge crescent moon and the little crescent earth behind it, the second time. I was amazed to find how far I was from the moon. I had reckoned that not only should I have little or none of the 'kick-off' that the earth's atmosphere had given us at our start, but that the tangential 'fly off' of the moon's spin would be at least twenty-eight times less than the earth's. I had expected to discover myself hanging over our crater, and on the edge of the night, but all that was now only a part of the outline of the white crescent that filled the sky. And Cavor – ?

He was already infinite.

I tried to imagine what could have happened to him. But at that time I could think of nothing but death. I seemed to see him, bent and smashed at the foot of some interminably high cascade of blue. And all about him the stupid insects stared . . .

Under the inspiring touch of the drifting newspaper I became practical again for a while. It was quite clear to me that what I had to do was to get back to earth, but as far as I could see I was drifting away from it. Whatever had happened to Cavor, even if he was still alive, which seemed to me incredible after that bloodstained scrap, I was powerless to help him. There he was, living or dead behind the mantle of that rayless night, and there he must remain at least until I could summon our fellow men to his assistance. Should I do that? Something of the sort I had in my mind; to come back to earth if it were possible, and then as maturer consideration might determine, either to show and explain the sphere to a few discreet persons, and act with them, or else to keep my secret, sell my gold, obtain weapons, provisions, and an assistant, and return with these advantages to deal on equal terms with the flimsy people of the moon, to rescue Cavor, if that were still possible, and at any rate to procure a sufficient supply of gold to place my subsequent proceedings on a firmer basis. But that was hoping far; I had first to get back.

I set myself to decide just exactly how the return to earth could be contrived. As I struggled with that problem I ceased to worry about what I should do when I got there. At last my only care was to get back.

I puzzled out at last that my best chance would be to drop back towards the moon as near as I dared in order to gather velocity, then to shut my windows, and fly behind it, and when I was past to open my earthward windows, and so get off at a good pace homeward. But whether I should ever reach the earth by that device, or whether I might not simply find myself spinning about it in some hyperbolic or parabolic curve or other, I could not tell. Later I had a happy inspiration, and by opening certain windows to the moon, which had appeared in the sky in front of the earth, I turned my course aside so as to head off the earth, which it had become evident to me I must pass behind without some such expedient. I did a very great deal of complicated thinking over these problems – for I am no mathematician – and in the end I am certain it was much more my good luck than my reasoning that enabled me to hit the earth. Had I known then, as I know now, the mathematical chances there were against me, I doubt if I should have troubled even to touch the studs to make any attempt. And having puzzled out what I considered to be the thing to do, I opened all my moonward windows, and squatted down – the effort lifted me for a time some feet or so into the air, and I hung there in the oddest way – and waited for the crescent to get bigger and bigger until I felt I was near enough for safety. Then I would shut the windows, fly past the moon with the velocity I had got from it – if I did not smash upon it – and so go on towards the earth.

And that is what I did.

At last I felt my moonward start was sufficient. I shut out the sight of the moon from my eyes, and in a state of mind that was, I now recall, incredibly free from anxiety or any distressful quality, I sat down to begin a vigil in that little speck of matter in infinite space that would last until I should strike the earth. The heater had made the sphere tolerably warm, the air had been refreshed by the oxygen, and except for that faint congestion of the head that was always with me while I was away from earth, I felt entire physical comfort. I had extinguished the light again, lest it should fail me in the end; I was in darkness, save for the earth-shine and the glitter of the stars below me. Everything was so absolutely silent and still that I might indeed have been the only being in the universe, and yet, strangely enough, I had no more feeling of loneliness or fear than if I had been lying in bed on earth. Now, this seems all the stranger to me, since during my last hours in that crater of the moon, the sense of my utter loneliness had been an agony . . .

Incredible as it will seem, this interval of time that I spent in space has no sort of proportion to any other interval of time in my life. Sometimes it seemed as though I sat through immeasurable eternities like some god upon a lotus leaf, and again as though there was a momentary pause as I leapt from moon to earth. In truth, it was altogether some weeks of earthly time. But I had done with care and anxiety, hunger or fear, for that space. I floated, thinking with a strange breadth and freedom of all that we had undergone, and of all my life and motives, and the secret issues of my being. I seemed to myself to have grown greater and greater, to have lost all sense of movement; to be floating amidst the stars, and always the sense of earth's littleness and the infinite littleness of my life upon it, was implicit in my thoughts.

I can't profess to explain the things that happened in my mind. No doubt they could all be traced directly or indirectly to the curious physical conditions under which I was living. I set them down here just for what they are worth, and without any comment. The most prominent quality of it was a pervading doubt of my own identity. I became, if I may so express it, dissociate from Bedford; I looked down on Bedford as a trivial, incidental thing with which I chanced to be connected. I saw Bedford in many relations – as an ass or as a poor beast, where I had hitherto been inclined to regard him with a quiet pride as a very spirited or rather forcible person. I saw him not only as an ass, but as the son of many generations of asses. I reviewed his school-days and his early manhood, and his first encounter with love, very much as one might review the proceedings of an ant in the sand. Something of that period of lucidity I regret still hangs about me, and I doubt if I shall ever recover the full-bodied self-satisfaction of my early days. But at the time the thing was not in the least painful, because I had that extraordinary persuasion that, as a matter of fact, I was no more Bedford than I was anyone else, but only a mind floating in the still serenity of space. Why should I be disturbed about this Bedford's shortcomings? I was not responsible for him or them.

For a time I struggled against this really very grotesque delusion. I tried to summon the memory of vivid moments, of tender or intense emotions to my assistance; I felt that if I could recall one genuine twinge of feeling the growing severance would be stopped. But I could not do it. I saw Bedford rushing down Chancery Lane, hat on the back of his head, coat tails flying out, *en route* for his public examination. I saw him dodging and bumping against, and even saluting, other similar little creatures in that swarming gutter of people. Me? I saw Bedford that same evening in the sitting-room of a certain lady, and his hat was on the table beside him, and it wanted brushing badly, and he was in tears. Me? I saw him with that lady in various attitudes and emotions – I never felt so detached before . . . I saw him hurrying off to Lympne to write a play, and accosting Cavor, and in his shirt sleeves working at the sphere, and walking out to Canterbury because he was afraid to come! Me? I did not believe it.

I still reasoned that all this was hallucination due to my solitude, and the fact that I had lost all weight and sense of resistance. I endeavoured to recover that sense by banging myself about the sphere, by pinching my hands and clasping them together. Among other things, I lit the light, captured that torn copy of *Lloyd's*, and read those convincingly realistic advertisements about the Cutaway bicycle, and the gentleman of private means, and the lady in distress who was selling those 'forks and spoons'. There was no doubt they existed surely enough, and, said I, 'This is your world, and you are Bedford, and you are going back to live among things like that for all the rest of your life.' But the doubts within me could still argue: 'It is not you that is reading, it is Bedford, but you are not Bedford, you know. That's just where the mistake comes in.'

'Confound it!' I cried; 'and if I am not Bedford, what am I?'

But in that direction no light was forthcoming, though the strangest fancies came drifting into my brain, queer remote suspicions, like shadows seen from faraway. Do you know, I had a sort of idea that really I was something quite outside not only the world, but all worlds, and out of space and time, and that this poor Bedford was just a peephole through which I looked at life? . . .

Bedford! However I disavowed him, there I was most certainly bound up with him, and I knew that wherever or whatever I might be, I must needs feel the stress of his desires, and sympathise with all his joys and sorrows until his life should end. And with the dying of Bedford – what then? . . .

Enough of this remarkable phase of my experiences! I tell it here simply to show how one's isolation and departure from this planet touched not only the functions and feeling of every organ of the body, but indeed also the very fabric of the mind, with strange and un-anticipated disturbances. All through the major portion of that vast space journey I hung thinking of such immaterial things as these, hung dissociated and apathetic, a cloudy megalomaniac, as it were, amidst the stars and planets in the void of space; and not only the world to which I was returning, but the blue-lit caverns of the Selenites, their helmet faces, their gigantic and wonderful machines, and the fate of Cavor, dragged helpless into that world, seemed infinitely minute and altogether trivial things to me.

Until at last I began to feel the pull of the earth upon my being, drawing me back again to the life that is real for men. And then, indeed, it grew clearer and clearer to me that I was quite certainly Bedford after all, and returning after amazing adventures to this world of ours, and with a life that I was very likely to lose in this return. I set myself to puzzle out the conditions under which I must fall to earth.

CHAPTER TWENTY-ONE

Mr Bedford at Littlestone

My line of flight was about parallel with the surface as I came into the upper air. The temperature of the sphere began to rise forthwith. I knew it behoved me to drop at once. Far below me, in a darkling twilight, stretched a great expanse of sea. I opened every window I could, and fell – out of sunshine into evening, and out of evening into night. Vaster grew the earth and vaster, swallowing up the stars, and the silvery translucent starlit veil of cloud it wore spread out to catch me. At last the world seemed no longer a sphere but flat, and then concave. It was no longer a planet in the sky, but the world of Man. I shut all but an inch or so of earthward window, and dropped with a slackening velocity. The broadening water, now so near that I could see the dark glitter of the waves, rushed up to meet me. The sphere became very hot. I snapped the last strip of window, and sat scowling and biting my knuckles, waiting for the impact . . .

The sphere hit the water with a huge splash: it must have sent it fathoms high. At the splash I flung the Cavorite shutters open. Down I went, but slower and slower, and then I felt the sphere pressing against my feet, and so drove up again as a bubble drives. And at the last I was floating and rocking upon the surface of the sea, and my journey in space was at an end.

The night was dark and overcast. Two yellow pinpoints far away showed the passing of a ship, and nearer was a red glare that came and went. Had not the electricity of my glow-lamp exhausted itself, I could have got picked up that night. In spite of the inordinate fatigue I was beginning to feel, I was excited now, and for a time hopeful, in a feverish, impatient way, that so my travelling might end.

But at last I ceased to move about, and sat, wrists on knees, staring at a distant red light. It swayed up and down, rocking, rocking. My excitement passed. I realised I had yet to spend another night at least in the sphere. I perceived myself infinitely heavy and fatigued. And so I fell asleep.

A change in my rhythmic motion awakened me. I peered through the refracting glass, and saw that I had come aground upon a huge shallow of sand. Far away I seemed to see houses and trees, and seaward a curve, vague distortion of a ship hung between sea and sky.

I stood up and staggered. My one desire was to emerge. The manhole was upward, and I wrestled with the screw. Slowly I opened the manhole. At last the air was singing in again as once it had sung out. But this time I did not wait until the pressure was adjusted. In another moment I had the weight of the window on my hands, and I was open, wide open, to the old familiar sky of earth.

The air hit me on the chest so that I gasped. I dropped the glass screw. I cried out, put my hands to my chest, and sat down. For a time I was in pain. Then I took deep breaths. At last I could rise and move about again.

I tried to thrust my head through the manhole, and the sphere rolled over. It was as though something had lugged my head down directly it emerged. I ducked back sharply, or I should have been pinned face under water. After some wriggling and shoving I managed to crawl out upon sand, over which the retreating waves still came and went.

I did not attempt to stand up. It seemed to me that my body must be suddenly changed to lead. Mother Earth had her grip on me now – no Cavorite intervening. I sat down heedless of the water that came over my feet.

It was dawn, a grey dawn, rather overcast but showing here and there a long patch of greenish grey. Some way out a ship was lying at anchor, a pale silhouette of a ship with one yellow light. The water came rippling in in long shallow waves. Away to the right curved the land, a shingle bank with little hovels, and at last a lighthouse, a sailing mark and a point. Inland stretched a space of level sand, broken here and there by pools of water, and ending a mile away perhaps in a low shore of scrub. To the north-east some isolated watering-place was visible, a row of gaunt lodging-houses, the tallest things that I could see on earth, dull dabs against the brightening sky. What strange men can have reared these vertical piles in such an amplitude of space I do not know. There they are, like pieces of Brighton lost in the waste.

For a long time I sat there, yawning and rubbing my face. At last I struggled to rise. It made me feel that I was lifting a weight. I stood up.

I stared at the distant houses. For the first time since our starvation in the crater I thought of earthly food. 'Bacon,' I whispered, 'eggs. Good toast and good coffee . . . And how the devil am I going to get all this stuff to Lympne?' I wondered where I was. It was an east shore anyhow, and I had seen Europe before I dropped.

I heard footsteps scrunching in the sand, and a little round-faced, friendly-looking man in flannels, with a bathing towel wrapped about his shoulders, and his bathing dress over his arm, appeared up the beach. I knew instantly that I must be in England. He was staring most intently at the sphere and me. He advanced staring. I dare say I looked a ferocious savage enough – dirty, unkempt, to an indescribable degree; but it did not occur to me at the time. He stopped at a distance of twenty yards. 'Hel-lo, my man!' he said doubtfully.

'Hello yourself!' said I.

He advanced, reassured by that. 'What on earth is that thing?' he asked.

'Can you tell me where I am?' I asked.

'That's Littlestone,' he said, pointing to the houses; 'and that's Dungeness! Have you just landed? What's that thing you've got? Some sort of machine?'

'Yes.'

'Have you floated ashore? Have you been wrecked or something? What is it?'

I meditated swiftly. I made an estimate of the little man's appearance as he drew nearer. 'By Jove!' he said, 'you've had a time of it! I thought you – Well – Where were you cast away? Is that thing a sort of floating thing for saving life?'

I decided to take that line for the present. I made a few vague affirmatives. 'I want help,' I said hoarsely. 'I want to get some stuff up the beach – stuff I can't very well leave about.' I became aware of three other pleasant-looking young men with towels, blazers, and straw hats, coming down the sands towards me. Evidently the early bathing section of this Littlestone.

'Help!' said the young man: 'rather!' He became vaguely active. 'What particularly do you want done?' He turned round and gesticulated. The three young men accelerated their pace. In a minute they were about me, plying me with questions I was indisposed to answer. 'I'll tell all that later,' I said. 'I'm dead beat. I'm a rag.'

'Come up to the hotel,' said the foremost little man. 'We'll look after that thing there.'

I hesitated. 'I can't,' I said. 'In that sphere there's two big bars of gold.'

They looked incredulously at one another, then at me with a new enquiry. I went to the sphere, stooped, crept in, and presently they had the Selenites' crowbars and the broken chain before them. If I had not been so horribly fagged I could have laughed at them. It was like kittens round a beetle. They didn't know what to do with the stuff. The fat little man stooped and lifted the end of one of the bars, and then dropped it with a grunt. Then they all did.

'It's lead, or gold!' said one.

'Oh, it's *gold*!' said another.

'Gold, right enough,' said the third.

Then they all stared at me, and then they all stared at the ship lying at anchor.

'I say!' cried the little man. 'But where did you get that?'

I was too tired to keep up a lie. 'I got it in the moon.'

I saw them stare at one another.

'Look here!' said I, 'I'm not going to argue now. Help me carry these lumps of gold up to the hotel – I guess, with rests, two of you can manage one, and I'll trail this chain thing – and I'll tell you more when I've had some food.'

'And how about that thing?'

'It won't hurt there,' I said. 'Anyhow – confound it! – it must stop there now. If the tide comes up, it will float all right.'

And in a state of enormous wonderment, these young men most obediently hoisted my treasures on their shoulders, and with limbs that felt like lead I headed a sort of procession towards that distant fragment of 'seafront'. Halfway there we were reinforced by two awestricken little girls with spades, and later a lean little boy, with a penetrating sniff, appeared. He was, I remember, wheeling a bicycle, and he accompanied us at a distance of about a hundred yards on our right flank, and then I suppose, gave us up as uninteresting, mounted his bicycle and rode off over the level sands in the direction of the sphere.

I glanced back after him.

'*He* won't touch it,' said the stout young man reassuringly, and I was only too willing to be reassured.

At first something of the grey of the morning was in my mind, but presently the sun disengaged itself from the level clouds of the horizon and lit the world, and turned the leaden sea to glittering waters. My spirits rose. A sense of the vast importance of the things I had done and had yet to do came with the sunlight into my mind. I laughed aloud as the foremost man staggered under my gold. When indeed I took my place in the world, how amazed the world would be!

If it had not been for my inordinate fatigue, the landlord of the Littlestone hotel would have been amusing, as he hesitated between my gold and my respectable company on the one hand and my filthy appearance on the other. But at last I found myself in a terrestrial bathroom once more with warm water to wash myself with, and a change of raiment, preposterously small indeed, but anyhow clean, that the genial little man had lent me. He lent me a razor too, but I could not screw up my resolution to attack even the outposts of the bristling beard that covered my face.

I sat down to an English breakfast and ate with a sort of languid appetite – an appetite many weeks old and very decrepit – and stirred myself to answer the questions of the four young men. And I told them the truth.

'Well,' said I, 'as you press me – I got it in the moon.'

'The moon?'

'Yes, the moon in the sky.'

'But how do you mean?'

'What I say, confound it!'

'Then you have just come from the moon?'

'Exactly! through space – in that ball.' And I took a delicious mouthful of egg. I made a private note that when I went back to the moon I would take a box of eggs.

I could see clearly that they did not believe one word of what I told them, but evidently they considered me the most respectable liar they had ever met. They glanced at one another, and then concentrated the fire of their eyes on me. I fancy they expected a clue to me in the way I helped myself to salt. They seemed to find something significant in my peppering my egg. These strangely shaped masses of gold they had staggered under held their minds. There the lumps lay in front of me, each worth thousands of pounds, and as impossible for anyone to steal as a house or a piece of land. As I looked at their curious faces over my coffee-cup, I realised something of the enormous wilderness of explanations into which I should have to wander to render myself comprehensible again.

'You don't *really* mean – ' began the youngest young man, in the tone of one who speaks to an obstinate child.

'Just pass me that toast-rack,' I said, and shut him up completely.

'But look here, I say,' began one of the others. 'We're not going to believe that, you know.'

'Ah, well,' said I, and shrugged my shoulders.

'He doesn't want to tell us,' said the youngest young man in a stage aside; and then, with an appearance of great sang-froid, 'You don't mind if I take a cigarette?'

I waved him a cordial assent, and proceeded with my breakfast. Two of the others went and looked out of the farther window and talked inaudibly. I was struck by a thought. 'The tide,' I said, 'is running out?'

There was a pause, a doubt who should answer me.

'It's near the ebb,' said the fat little man.

'Well, anyhow,' I said, 'it won't float far.'

I decapitated my third egg, and began a little speech. 'Look here,' I said. 'Please don't imagine I'm surly or telling you uncivil lies, or anything of that sort. I'm forced, almost, to be a little short and mysterious. I can quite understand this is as queer as it can be, and that your imaginations must be going it. I can assure you, you're in at a memorable time. But I can't make it clear to you now – it's impossible. I give you my word of honour I've come from the moon, and that's all I can tell you . . . All the same, I'm tremendously obliged to you, you know, tremendously. I hope that my manner hasn't in any way given you offence.'

'Oh, not in the least!' said the youngest young man affably. 'We can quite understand,' and staring hard at me all the time, he heeled his chair back until it very nearly upset, and recovered with some exertion. 'Not a bit of it,' said the fat young man.

'Don't you imagine *that*!' and they all got up and dispersed, and walked about and lit cigarettes, and generally tried to show they were perfectly amiable and disengaged, and entirely free from the slightest curiosity about me and the sphere. 'I'm going to keep an eye on that ship out there all the same,' I heard one of them remarking in an undertone. If only they could have forced themselves to it, they would, I believe, even have gone out and left me. I went on with my third egg.

'The weather,' the fat little man remarked presently, 'has been immense, has it not? I don't know *when* we have had such a summer . . . '

Phoo – whizz! Like a tremendous rocket!

And somewhere a window was broken . . .

'What's that?' said I.

'It isn't – ?' cried the little man, and rushed to the corner window.

All the others rushed to the window likewise. I sat staring at them.

Suddenly I leapt up, knocked over my third egg, rushed for the window also. I had just thought of something. 'Nothing to be seen there,' cried the little man, rushing for the door.

'It's that boy!' I cried, bawling in hoarse fury; 'it's that accursed boy!' and turning about I pushed the waiter aside – he was just bringing me some more toast – and rushed violently out of the room and down and out upon the queer little esplanade in front of the hotel.

The sea, which had been smooth, was rough now with hurrying cat's-paws, and all about where the sphere had been was tumbled water like the wake of a ship. Above, a little puff of cloud whirled like dispersing smoke, and the three or four people on the beach were staring up with interrogative faces towards the point of that unexpected report. And that was all! Boots and waiter and the four young men in blazers came rushing out behind me. Shouts came from windows and doors, and all sorts of worrying people came into sight – agape.

For a time I stood there, too overwhelmed by this new development to think of the people.

At first I was too stunned to see the thing as any definite disaster – I was just stunned, as a man is by some accidental violent blow. It is only afterwards he begins to appreciate his specific injury.

'Good Lord!'

I felt as though somebody was pouring funk out of a can down the back of my neck. My legs became feeble. I had got the first intimation of what the disaster meant for me. There was that confounded boy – sky high! I was utterly 'left'. There was the gold in the coffee-room – my only possession on earth. How would it all work out? The general effect was of a gigantic unmanageable confusion.

'I say,' said the voice of the little man behind. 'I *say*, you know.'

I wheeled about, and there were twenty or thirty people, a sort of irregular investment of people, all bombarding me with dumb inter-rogation, with infinite doubt and suspicion. I felt the compulsion of their eyes intolerably. I groaned aloud.

'I *can't*!' I shouted. 'I tell you I can't! I'm not equal to it! You must puzzle and – and be damned to you!'

I gesticulated convulsively. He receded a step as though I had threatened him. I made a bolt through them into the hotel. I charged back into the coffee-room, rang the bell furiously. I gripped the waiter as he entered. 'D'ye hear?' I shouted. 'Get help and carry these bars up to my room right away.'

He failed to understand me, and I shouted and raved at him. A scared-looking little old man in a green apron appeared, and further two of the young men in flannels. I made a dash at them and commandeered their services. As soon as the gold was in my room I felt free to quarrel. 'Now get out,' I shouted; 'all of you get out if you don't want to see a man go mad before your eyes!' And I helped the waiter by the shoulder as he hesitated in the doorway. And then, as soon as I had the door locked on them all, I tore off the little man's clothes again, shied them right and left, and got into bed forthwith. And there I lay swearing and panting and cooling for a very long time.

At last I was calm enough to get out of bed and ring up the round-eyed waiter for a flannel nightshirt, a soda and whisky, and some good cigars. And these things being procured me, after an exasperating delay that drove me several times to the bell, I locked the door again and proceeded very deliberately to look the entire situation in the face.

The net result of the great experiment presented itself as an absolute failure. It was a rout, and I was the sole survivor. It was an absolute collapse, and this was the final disaster. There was nothing for it but to save myself, and as much as I could in the way of prospects from our *débâcle*. At one fatal crowning blow all my vague resolutions of return and recovery had vanished. My intention of going back to the moon, of getting a sphereful of gold, and afterwards of having a fragment of Cavorite analysed and so recovering the great secret – perhaps, finally, even of recovering Cavor's body – all these ideas vanished altogether.

I was the sole survivor, and that was all.

I think that going to bed was one of the luckiest ideas I have ever had in an emergency. I really believe I should either have got loose-headed or done some fatal indiscreet thing. But there, locked in and secure from all interruptions, I could think out the position in all its bearings and make my arrangements at leisure.

Of course, it was quite clear to me what had happened to the boy. He had crawled into the sphere, meddled with the studs, shut the Cavorite windows, and gone up. It was highly improbable he had screwed the manhole stopper, and, even if he had, the chances were a thousand to one against his getting back. It was fairly evident that he would gravitate with my bales to somewhere near the middle of the sphere and remain there, and so cease to be a legitimate terrestrial interest, however remarkable he might seem to the inhabitants of some remote quarter of space. I very speedily convinced myself on that point. And as for any responsibility I might have in the matter, the more I reflected upon that, the clearer it became that if only I kept quiet about things, I need not trouble myself about that. If I was faced by sorrowing parents demanding their lost boy, I had merely to demand my lost sphere – or ask them what they meant. At first I had had a vision of weeping parents and guardians, and all sorts of complications; but now I saw that I simply had to keep my mouth shut, and nothing in that way could arise. And, indeed, the more I lay and smoked and thought, the more evident became the wisdom of impenetrability.

It is within the right of every British citizen, provided he does not commit damage nor indecorum, to appear suddenly wherever he pleases, and as ragged and filthy as he pleases, and with whatever amount of virgin gold he sees fit to encumber himself, and no one has any right at all to hinder and detain him in this procedure. I formulated that at last to myself, and repeated it over as a sort of private Magna Carta of my liberty.

Once I had put that issue on one side, I could take up and consider in an equable manner certain considerations I had scarcely dared to think of before, namely, those arising out of the circumstances of my bankruptcy. But now, looking at this matter calmly and at leisure, I could see that if only I suppressed my identity by a temporary assumption of some less well-known name, and if I retained the two months' beard that had grown upon me, the risks of any annoyance from the spiteful creditor to whom I have already alluded became very small indeed. From that to a definite course of rational worldly action was plain sailing. It was all amazingly petty, no doubt, but what was there remaining for me to do?

Whatever I did I was resolved that I would keep myself level and right side up.

I ordered up writing materials, and addressed a letter to the New Romney Bank – the nearest, the waiter informed me – telling the manager I wished to open an account with him, and requesting him to send two trustworthy persons properly authenticated in a cab with a good horse to fetch some hundredweight of gold with which I happened to be encumbered. I signed the letter 'Blake', which seemed to me to be a thoroughly respectable sort of name. This done, I got a Folkestone Blue Book, picked out an outfitter, and asked him to send a cutter to measure me for a dark tweed suit, ordering at the same time a valise, dressing bag, brown boots, shirts, hat (to fit), and so forth; and from a watchmaker I also ordered a watch. And these letters being despatched, I had up as good a lunch as the hotel could give, and then lay smoking a cigar, as calm and ordinary as possible, until in accordance with my instructions two duly authenticated clerks came from the bank and weighed and took away my gold. After which I pulled the clothes over my ears in order to drown any knocking, and went very comfortably to sleep.

I went to sleep. No doubt it was a prosaic thing for the first man back from the moon to do, and I can imagine that the young and imaginative reader will find my behaviour disappointing. But I was horribly fatigued and bothered, and, confound it! what else was there to do? There certainly was not the remotest chance of my being believed, if I had told my story then, and it would certainly have subjected me to intolerable annoyances. I went to sleep. When at last I woke up again I was ready to face the world as I have always been accustomed to face it since I came to years of discretion. And so I got away to Italy, and there it is I am writing this story. If the world will not have it as fact, then the world may take it as fiction. It is no concern of mine.

And now that the account is finished, I am amazed to think how completely this adventure is gone and done with. Everybody believes that Cavor was a not very brilliant scientific experimenter who blew up his house and himself at Lympne, and they explain the bang that followed my arrival at Littlestone by a reference to the experiments with explosives that are going on continually at the government establishment of Lydd, two miles away. I must confess that hitherto I have not acknowledged my share in the disappearance of Master Tommy Simmons, which was that little boy's name. That, perhaps, may prove a difficult item of corroboration to explain away. They account for my appearance in rags with two bars of indisputable gold upon the Littlestone beach in various ingenious ways – it doesn't worry me what they think of me. They say I have strung all these things together to avoid being questioned too closely as to the source of my wealth. I would like to see the man who could invent a story that would hold together like this one. Well, they must take it as fiction – there it is.

I have told my story – and now, I suppose, I have to take up the worries of this terrestrial life again. Even if one has been to the moon, one has still to earn a living. So I am working here at Amalfi, on the scenario of that play I sketched before Cavor came walking into my world, and I am trying to piece my life together as it was before ever I saw him. I must confess that I find it hard to keep my mind on the play when the moonshine comes into my room. It is full moon here, and last night I was out on the pergola for hours, staring away at the shining blankness that hides so much. Imagine it! tables and chairs, and trestles and bars of gold! Confound it! – if only one could hit on that Cavorite again! But a thing like that doesn't come twice in a life. Here I am, a little better off than I was at Lympne, and that is all. And Cavor has committed suicide in a more elaborate way than any human being ever did before. So the story closes as finally and completely as a dream. It fits in so little with all the other things of life, so much of it is so utterly remote from all human experience, the leaping, the eating, the breathing, and these weightless times, that indeed there are moments when, in spite of my moon gold, I do more than half believe myself that the whole thing was a dream . . .

CHAPTER TWENTY-TWO

The Astonishing Communication of Mr Julius Wendigee

When I had finished my account of my return to the earth at Littlestone, I wrote, 'The End', made a flourish, and threw my pen aside,
fully believing that the whole story of the First Men in the Moon was
done. Not only had I done this, but I had placed my manuscript in the
hands of a literary agent, had permitted it to be sold, had seen the
greater portion of it appear in the *Strand Magazine*, and was setting to
work again upon the scenario of the play I had commenced at Lympne
before I realised that the end was not yet. And then, following me
from Amalfi to Algiers, there reached me (it is now about six months
ago) one of the most astounding communications I have ever been
fated to receive. Briefly, it informed me that Mr Julius Wendigee, a
Dutch electrician, who has been experimenting with certain apparatus
akin to the apparatus used by Mr Tesla in America, in the hope of
discovering some method of communication with Mars, was receiving
day by day a curiously fragmentary message in English, which was
indisputably emanating from Mr Cavor in the moon.

At first I thought the thing was an elaborate practical joke by someone
who had seen the manuscript of my narrative. I answered Mr Wendigee
jestingly, but he replied in a manner that put such suspicion altogether
aside, and in a state of inconceivable excitement I hurried from Algiers
to the little observatory upon the St Gothard in which he was working.
In the presence of his record and his appliances – and above all of the
messages from Cavor that were coming to hand – my lingering doubts
vanished. I decided at once to accept a proposal he made to me to
remain with him, assisting him to take down the record from day to
day, and endeavouring with him to send a message back to the moon.
Cavor, we learnt, was not only alive, but free, in the midst of an almost
inconceivable community of these ant-like beings, these ant-men, in
the blue darkness of the lunar caves. He was lamed, it seemed, but
otherwise in quite good health – in better health, he distinctly said, than
he usually enjoyed on earth. He had had a fever, but it had left no bad
effects. But curiously enough he seemed to be labouring under a conviction that I was either dead in the moon crater or lost in the deep
of space.

His message began to be received by Mr Wendigee when that gentle-man was engaged in quite a different investigation. The reader will no doubt recall the little excitement that began the century, arising out an announcement by Mr Nikola Tesla, the American electrical celebrity, that he had received a message from Mars. His announcement renewed attention to a fact that had long been familiar to scientific people, namely: that from some unknown source in space, waves of electro-magnetic disturbance, entirely similar to those used by Signor Marconi for his wireless telegraphy, are constantly reaching the earth. Besides Tesla quite a number of other observers have been engaged in perfecting apparatus for receiving and recording these vibrations, though few would go so far as to consider them actual messages from some extraterrestrial sender. Among that few, however, we must certainly count Mr Wendi-gee. Ever since 1898 he had devoted himself almost entirely to this subject, and being a man of ample means he had erected an observatory on the flanks of Monte Rosa, in a position singularly adapted in every way for such observations.

My scientific attainments, I must admit, are not great, but so far as they enable me to judge, Mr Wendigee's contrivances for detecting and recording any disturbances in the electromagnetic conditions of space are singularly original and ingenious. And by a happy combination of circumstances they were set up and in operation about two months before Cavor made his first attempt to call up the earth. Consequently we have fragments of his communication even from the beginning. Unhappily, they are only fragments, and the most momentous of all the things that he had to tell humanity – the instructions, that is, for the making of Cavorite, if, indeed, he ever transmitted them – have throbbed themselves away unrecorded into space. We never succeeded in getting a response back to Cavor. He was unable to tell, therefore, what we had received or what we had missed; nor, indeed, did he certainly know that anyone on earth was really aware of his efforts to reach us. And the persistence he displayed in sending eighteen long descriptions of lunar affairs – as they would be if we had them complete – shows how much his mind must have turned back towards his native planet since he left it two years ago.

You can imagine how amazed Mr Wendigee must have been when he discovered his record of electromagnetic disturbances interlaced by Cavor's straightforward English. Mr Wendigee knew nothing of our wild journey moonward, and suddenly – this English out of the void!

It is well the reader should understand the conditions under which it would seem these messages were sent. Somewhere within the moon

Cavor certainly had access for a time to a considerable amount of electrical apparatus, and it would seem he rigged up – perhaps furtively – a transmitting arrangement of the Marconi type. This he was able to operate at irregular intervals: sometimes for only half an hour or so, sometimes for three or four hours at a stretch. At these times he transmitted his earthward message, regardless of the fact that the relative position of the moon and points upon the earth's surface is constantly altering. As a consequence of this and of the necessary imperfections of our recording instruments his communication comes and goes in our records in an extremely fitful manner; it becomes blurred; it 'fades out' in a mysterious and altogether exasperating way. And added to this is the fact that he was not an expert operator; he had partly forgotten, or never completely mastered, the code in general use, and as he became fatigued he dropped words and misspelt in a curious manner.

Altogether we have probably lost quite half of the communications he made, and much we have is damaged, broken, and partly effaced. In the abstract that follows the reader must be prepared therefore for a considerable amount of break, hiatus, and change of topic. Mr Wendigee and I are collaborating in a complete and annotated edition of the Cavor record, which we hope to publish, together with a detailed account of the instruments employed, beginning with the first volume in January next. That will be the full and scientific report, of which this is only the popular transcript. But here we give at least sufficient to complete the story I have told, and to give the broad outlines of the state of that other world so near, so akin, and yet so dissimilar to our own.

CHAPTER TWENTY-THREE

An Abstract of the Six Messages
First Received from Mr Cavor

The two earlier messages of Mr Cavor may very well be reserved for that larger volume. They simply tell, with greater brevity and with a difference in several details that is interesting, but not of any vital importance, the bare facts of the making of the sphere and our departure from the world. Throughout, Cavor speaks of me as a man who is dead, but with a curious change of temper as he approaches our landing on the moon. 'Poor Bedford', he says of me, and 'this poor young man'; and he blames himself for inducing a young man, 'by no means well equipped for such adventures', to leave a planet 'on which he was indisputably fitted to succeed' on so precarious a mission. I think he underrates the part my energy and practical capacity played in bringing about the realisation of his theoretical sphere. 'We arrived,' he says, with no more account of our passage through space than if we had made a journey of common occurrence in a railway train.

And then he becomes increasingly unfair to me. Unfair, indeed, to an extent I should not have expected in a man trained in the search for truth. Looking back over my previously written account of these things, I must insist that I have been altogether juster to Cavor than he has been to me. I have extenuated little and suppressed nothing. But his account is:

It speedily became apparent that the entire strangeness of our circumstances and surroundings – great loss of weight, attenuated but highly oxygenated air, consequent exaggeration of the results of muscular effort, rapid development of weird plants from obscure spores, lurid sky – was exciting my companion unduly. On the moon his character seemed to deteriorate. He became impulsive, rash, and quarrelsome. In a little while his folly in devouring some gigantic vesicles and his consequent intoxication led to our capture by the Selenites – before we had had the slightest opportunity of properly observing their ways . . .

(He says, you observe, nothing of his own concession to these same 'vesicles'.)

And he goes on from that point to say that 'We came to a difficult passage with them, and Bedford mistaking certain gestures of theirs' – pretty gestures they were! – 'gave way to a panic violence. He ran amuck, killed three, and perforce I had to flee with him after the outrage. Subsequently we fought with a number who endeavoured to bar our way, and slew seven or eight more. It says much for the tolerance of these beings that on my recapture I was not instantly slain. We made our way to the exterior and separated in the crater of our arrival, to increase our chances of recovering our sphere. But presently I came upon a body of Selenites, led by two who were curiously different, even in form, from any of these we had seen hitherto, with larger heads and smaller bodies, and much more elaborately wrapped about. And after evading them for some time I fell into a crevasse, cut my head rather badly, and displaced my patella, and, finding crawling very painful, decided to surrender – if they would still permit me to do so. This they did, and, perceiving my helpless condition, carried me with them again into the moon. And of Bedford I have heard or seen nothing more, nor, so far as I can gather, any Selenite. Either the night overtook him in the crater, or else, which is more probable, he found the sphere, and, desiring to steal a march upon me, made off with it – only, I fear, to find it uncontrollable, and to meet a more lingering fate in outer space.'

And with that Cavor dismisses me and goes on to more interesting topics. I dislike the idea of seeming to use my position as his editor to deflect his story in my own interest, but I am obliged to protest here against the turn he gives these occurrences. He said nothing about that gasping message on the bloodstained paper in which he told, or attempted to tell, a very different story. The dignified self-surrender is an altogether new view of the affair that has come to him, I must insist, since he began to feel secure among the lunar people; and as for the 'stealing a march' conception, I am quite willing to let the reader decide between us on what he has before him. I know I am not a model man – I have made no pretence to be. But am I *that*?

However, that is the sum of my wrongs. From this point I can edit Cavor with an untroubled mind, for he mentions me no more.

It would seem the Selenites who had come upon him carried him to some point in the interior down 'a great shaft' by means of what he describes as 'a sort of balloon'. We gather from the rather confused passage in which he describes this, and from a number of chance allusions and hints in other and subsequent messages, that this 'great shaft' is one of an enormous system of artificial shafts that run, each from what is called a lunar 'crater', downwards for very nearly a hundred miles towards the central portion of our satellite. These shafts communicate by transverse tunnels, they throw out abysmal caverns and expand into great globular places; the whole of the moon's substance for a hundred miles inward, indeed, is a mere sponge of rock. 'Partly,' says Cavor, 'this sponginess is natural, but very largely it is due to the enormous industry of the Selenites in the past. The enormous circular mounds of the excavated rock and earth it is that form these great circles about the tunnels known to earthly astronomers (misled by a false analogy) as volcanoes.'

It was down this shaft they took him, in this 'sort of balloon' he speaks of, at first into an inky blackness and then into a region of continually increasing phosphorescence. Cavor's despatches show him to be curiously regardless of detail for a scientific man, but we gather that this light was due to the streams and cascades of water – 'no doubt containing some phosphorescent organism' – that flowed ever more abundantly downward towards the Central Sea. And as he descended, he says, 'The Selenites also became luminous.' And at last far below him he saw, as it were, a lake of heatless fire, the waters of the Central Sea, glowing and eddying in strange perturbation, 'like luminous blue milk that is just on the boil'.

'This Lunar Sea,' says Cavor, in a later passage 'is not a stagnant ocean; a solar tide sends it in a perpetual flow around the lunar axis, and strange storms and boilings and rushings of its waters occur, and at times cold winds and thunderings that ascend out of it into the busy ways of the great ant-hill above. It is only when the water is in motion that it gives out light; in its rare seasons of calm it is black. Commonly, when one sees it, its waters rise and fall in an oily swell, and flakes and big rafts of shining, bubbly foam drift with the sluggish, faintly glowing current. The Selenites navigate its cavernous straits and lagoons in little shallow boats of a canoe-like shape; and even before my journey to the galleries about the Grand Lunar, who is Master of the Moon, I was permitted to make a brief excursion on its waters.

'The caverns and passages are naturally very tortuous. A large proportion of these ways are known only to expert pilots among the fishermen, and not infrequently Selenites are lost for ever in their labyrinths. In their remoter recesses, I am told, strange creatures lurk, some of them terrible and dangerous creatures that all the science of the moon has been unable to exterminate. There is particularly the Rapha, an inextricable mass of clutching tentacles that one hacks to pieces only to multiply; and the Tzee, a darting creature that is never seen, so subtly and suddenly does it slay . . . '

He gives us a gleam of description.

'I was reminded on this excursion of what I have read of the Mammoth Caves; if only I had had a yellow flambeau instead of the pervading blue light, and a solid-looking boatman with an oar instead of a scuttle-faced Selenite working an engine at the back of the canoe, I could have imagined I had suddenly got back to earth. The rocks about us were very various, sometimes black, sometimes pale blue and veined, and once they flashed and glittered as though we had come into a mine of sapphires. And below one saw the ghostly phosphorescent fishes flash and vanish in the hardly less phosphorescent deep. Then, presently, a long ultramarine vista down the turgid stream of one of the channels of traffic, and a landing stage, and then, perhaps, a glimpse up the enormous crowded shaft of one of the vertical ways.

'In one great place heavy with glistening stalactites a number of boats were fishing. We went alongside one of these and watched the long-armed Selenites winding in a net. They were little, hunchbacked insects, with very strong arms, short, bandy legs, and crinkled face-masks. As they pulled at it that net seemed the heaviest thing I had come upon in the moon; it was loaded with weights – no doubt of gold – and it took a long time to draw, for in those waters the larger and more edible fish lurk deep. The fish in the net came up like a blue moonrise – a blaze of darting, tossing blue.

'Among their catch was a many-tentaculate, evil-eyed black thing, ferociously active, whose appearance they greeted with shrieks and twitters, and which with quick, nervous movements they hacked to pieces by means of little hatchets. All its dissevered limbs continued to lash and writhe in a vicious manner. Afterwards, when fever had hold of me, I dreamt again and again of that bitter, furious creature rising so vigorous and active out of the unknown sea. It was the most active and malignant thing of all the living creatures I have yet seen in this world inside the moon . . .

*   *   *

'The surface of this sea must be very nearly two hundred miles (if not more) below the level of the moon's exterior; all the cities of the moon lie, I learnt, immediately above this Central Sea, in such cavernous spaces and artificial galleries as I have described, and they communicate with the exterior by enormous vertical shafts which open invariably in what are called by earthly astronomers the "craters" of the moon. The lid covering one such aperture I had already seen during the wanderings that had preceded my capture.

'Upon the condition of the less central portion of the moon I have not yet arrived at very precise knowledge. There is an enormous system of caverns in which the mooncalves shelter during the night; and there are abattoirs and the like – in one of these it was that I and Bedford fought with the Selenite butchers – and I have since seen balloons laden with meat descending out of the upper dark. I have as yet scarcely learnt as much of these things as a Zulu in London would learn about the British corn supplies in the same time. It is clear, however, that these vertical shafts and the vegetation of the surface must play an essential role in ventilating and keeping fresh the atmosphere of the moon. At one time, and particularly on my first emergence from my prison, there was certainly a cold wind blowing *down* the shaft, and later there was a kind of sirocco upward that corresponded with my fever. For at the end of about three weeks I fell ill of an indefinable sort of fever, and in spite of sleep and the quinine tabloids that very fortunately I had brought in my pocket, I remained ill and fretting miserably, almost to the time when I was taken into the presence of the Grand Lunar, who is Master of the Moon.

'I will not dilate on the wretchedness of my condition,' he remarks, 'during those days of ill-health.' And he goes on with great amplitude with details I omit here. 'My temperature,' he concludes, 'kept abnormally high for a long time, and I lost all desire for food. I had stagnant waking intervals, and sleep tormented by dreams, and at one phase I was, I remember, so weak as to be earth-sick and almost hysterical. I longed almost intolerably for colour to break the everlasting blue . . .'

He reverts again presently to the topic of this sponge-caught lunar atmosphere. I am told by astronomers and physicists that all he tells is in absolute accordance with what was already known of the moon's condition. Had earthly astronomers had the courage and imagination to push home a bold induction, says Mr Wendigee, they might have foretold almost everything that Cavor has to say of the general structure of the moon. They know now pretty certainly that moon and earth are not so much satellite and primary as smaller and greater sisters, made out of one mass, and consequently made of the same material. And since the density of the moon is only three-fifths that of the earth, there can be nothing for it but that she is hollowed out by a great system of caverns. There was no necessity, said Sir Jabez Flap, FRS, that most entertaining exponent of the facetious side of the stars, that we should ever have gone to the moon to find out such easy inferences, and points the pun with an allusion to Gruyère, but he certainly might have announced his knowledge of the hollowness of the moon before. And if the moon is hollow, then the apparent absence of air and water is, of course, quite easily explained. The sea lies within at the bottom of the caverns, and the air travels through the great sponge of galleries, in accordance with simple physical laws. The caverns of the moon, on the whole, are very windy places. As the sunlight comes round the moon the air in the outer galleries on that side is heated, its pressure increases, some flows out on the exterior and mingles with the evaporating air of the craters (where the plants remove its carbonic acid), while the greater portion flows round through the galleries to replace the shrinking air of the cooling side that the sunlight has left. There is, therefore, a constant eastward breeze in the air of the outer galleries, and an up-flow during the lunar day up the shafts, complicated, of course, very greatly by the varying shape of the galleries, and the ingenious contrivances of the Selenite mind . . .

CHAPTER TWENTY-FOUR

The Natural History of the Selenites

The messages of Cavor from the sixth up to the sixteenth are for the most part so much broken, and they abound so in repetitions, that they scarcely form a consecutive narrative. They will be given in full, of course, in the scientific report, but here it will be far more convenient to continue simply to abstract and quote as in the former chapter. We have subjected every word to a keen critical scrutiny, and my own brief memories and impressions of lunar things have been of inestimable help in interpreting what would otherwise have been impenetrably dark. And, naturally, as living beings, our interest centres far more upon the strange community of lunar insects in which he was living, it would seem, as an honoured guest than upon the mere physical condition of their world.

I have already made it clear, I think, that the Selenites I saw resembled man in maintaining the erect attitude, and in having four limbs, and I have compared the general appearance of their heads and the jointing of their limbs to that of insects. I have mentioned, too, the peculiar consequence of the smaller gravitation of the moon on their fragile slightness. Cavor confirms me upon all these points. He calls them 'animals', though of course they fall under no division of the classification of earthly creatures, and he points out 'the insect type of anatomy had, fortunately for men, never exceeded a relatively very small size on earth'. The largest terrestrial insects, living or extinct, do not, as a matter of fact, measure six inches in length; 'but here, against the lesser gravitation of the moon, a creature certainly as much an insect as vertebrate seems to have been able to attain to human and ultra-human dimensions'.

He does not mention the ant, but throughout his allusions the ant is continually being brought before my mind, in its sleepless activity, in its intelligence and social organisation, in its structure, and more particularly in the fact that it displays, in addition to the two forms, the male and the female form, that almost all other animals possess, a number of other sexless creatures, workers, soldiers, and the like, differing from one another in structure, character, power, and use, and yet all members of the same species. For these Selenites, also, have a great variety of forms. Of course, they are not only colossally greater in size than ants, but also, in Cavor's opinion at least, in intelligence, morality, and social wisdom are they colossally greater than men. And instead of the four or five different forms of ant that are found, there are almost innumerably different forms of Selenite. I had endeavoured to indicate the very considerable difference observable in such Selenites of the outer crust as I happened to encounter; the differences in size and proportions were certainly as wide as the differences between the most widely separated races of men. But such differences as I saw fade absolutely to nothing in comparison with the huge distinctions of which Cavor tells. It would seem the exterior Selenites I saw were, indeed, mostly engaged in kindred occupations – mooncalf herds, butchers, fleshers, and the like. But within the moon, practically unsuspected by me, there are, it seems, a number of other sorts of Selenite, differing in size, differing in the relative size of part to part, differing in power and appearance, and yet not different species of creatures, but only different forms of one species, and retaining through all their variations a certain common likeness that marks their specific unity. The moon is, indeed, a sort of vast ant-hill, only, instead of there being only four or five sorts of ant, there are many hundred different sorts of Selenite, and almost every gradation between one sort and another.

It would seem the discovery came upon Cavor very speedily. I infer rather than learn from his narrative that he was captured by the mooncalf herds under the direction of these other Selenites who 'have larger brain cases (heads?) and very much shorter legs'. Finding he would not walk even under the goad, they carried him into darkness, crossed a narrow, plank-like bridge that may have been the identical bridge I had refused, and put him down in something that must have seemed at first to be some sort of lift. This was the balloon – it had certainly been absolutely invisible to us in the darkness – and what had seemed to me a mere plank-walking into the void was really, no doubt, the passage of the gangway. In this he descended towards constantly more luminous caverns of the moon. At first they descended in silence – save for the twitterings of the Selenites – and then into a stir of windy movement. In a little while the profound blackness had made his eyes so sensitive that he began to see more and more of the things about him, and at last the vague took shape.

'Conceive an enormous cylindrical space,' says Cavor, in his seventh message, 'a quarter of a mile across, perhaps; very dimly lit at first and then brighter, with big platforms twisting down its sides in a spiral that vanishes at last below in a blue profundity; and lit even more brightly – one could not tell how or why. Think of the well of the very largest spiral staircase or lift-shaft that you have ever looked down, and magnify that by a hundred. Imagine it at twilight seen through blue glass. Imagine yourself looking down that; only imagine also that you feel extraordinarily light, and have got rid of any giddy feeling you might have on earth, and you will have the first conditions of my impression. Round this enormous shaft imagine a broad gallery running in a much steeper spiral than would be credible on earth, and forming a steep road protected from the gulf only by a little parapet that vanishes at last in perspective a couple of miles below.

'Looking up, I saw the very fellow of the downward vision; it had, of course, the effect of looking into a very steep cone. A wind was blowing down the shaft, and far above I fancy I heard, growing fainter and fainter, the bellowing of the mooncalves that were being driven down again from their evening pasturage on the exterior. And up and down the spiral galleries were scattered numerous moon people, pallid, faintly luminous beings, regarding our appearance or busied on unknown errands.

'Either I fancied it or a flake of snow came drifting down on the icy breeze. And then, falling like a snowflake, a little figure, a little man-insect, clinging to a parachute, drove down very swiftly towards the central places of the moon.

'The big-headed Selenite sitting beside me, seeing me move my head with the gesture of one who saw, pointed with his trunk-like "hand" and indicated a sort of jetty coming into sight very far below: a little landing-stage, as it were, hanging into the void. As it swept up towards us our pace diminished very rapidly, and in a few moments, as it seemed, we were abreast of it, and at rest. A mooring-rope was flung and grasped, and I found myself pulled down to a level with a great crowd of Selenites, who jostled to see me.

'It was an incredible crowd. Suddenly and violently there was forced upon my attention the vast amount of difference there is amongst these beings of the moon.

'Indeed, there seemed not two alike in all that jostling multitude. They differed in shape, they differed in size, they rang all the horrible changes on the theme of Selenite form! Some bulged and overhung, some ran about among the feet of their fellows. All of them had a grotesque and disquieting suggestion of an insect that has somehow contrived to mock humanity; but all seemed to present an incredible exaggeration of some particular feature: one had a vast right forelimb, an enormous antennal arm, as it were; one seemed all leg, poised, as it were, on stilts; another protruded the edge of his face mask into a nose-like organ that made him startlingly human until one saw his expressionless gaping mouth. The strange and (except for the want of mandibles and palps) most insect-like head of the mooncalf-minders underwent, indeed, the most incredible transformations: here it was broad and low, here high and narrow; here its leathery brow was drawn out into horns and strange features; here it was whiskered and divided, and there with a grotesquely human profile. One distortion was particularly conspicuous. There were several brain cases distended like bladders to a huge size, with the face mask reduced to quite small proportions. There were several amazing forms, with heads reduced to microscopic proportions and blobby bodies; and fantastic, flimsy things that existed, it would seem, only as a basis for vast, trumpet-like protrusions of the lower part of the mask. And oddest of all, as it seemed to me for the moment, two or three of these weird inhabitants of a subterranean world, a world sheltered by innumerable miles of rock from sun or rain, *carried umbrellas* in their tentaculate hands – real terrestrial-looking umbrellas! And then I thought of the parachutist I had watched descend.

'These moon people behaved exactly as a human crowd might have done in similar circumstances: they jostled and thrust one another, they shoved one another aside, they even clambered upon one another to get a glimpse of me. Every moment they increased in numbers, and pressed more urgently upon the discs of my ushers' – Cavor does not explain what he means by this – 'every moment fresh shapes emerged from the shadows and forced themselves upon my astounded attention. And presently I was signed and helped into a sort of litter, and lifted up on the shoulders of strong-armed bearers, and so borne through the twilight over this seething multitude towards the apartments that were provided for me in the moon. All about me were eyes, faces, masks, a leathery noise like the rustling of beetle wings, and a great bleating and cricket-like twittering of Selenite voices . . . '

*   *   *

We gather he was taken to a 'hexagonal apartment', and there for a space he was confined. Afterwards he was given a much more considerable liberty; indeed, almost as much freedom as one has in a civilised town on earth. And it would appear that the mysterious being who is the ruler and master of the moon appointed two Selenites 'with large heads' to guard and study him, and to establish whatever mental communications were possible with him. And, amazing and incredible as it may seem, these two creatures, these fantastic men insects, these beings of other world, were presently communicating with Cavor by means of terrestrial speech.

Cavor speaks of them as Phi-oo and Tsi-puff. Phi-oo, he says, was about five feet high; he had small slender legs about eighteen inches long, and slight feet of the common lunar pattern. On these balanced a little body, throbbing with the pulsations of his heart. He had long, soft, many-jointed arms ending in a tentacled grip, and his neck was many-jointed in the usual way, but exceptionally short and thick. His head, says Cavor – apparently alluding to some previous description that has gone astray in space – 'is of the common lunar type, but strangely modified. The mouth has the usual expressionless gape, but it is unusually small and pointing downward, and the mask is reduced to the size of a large flat nose-flap. On either side are the little eyes.

'The rest of the head is distended into a huge globe and the chitinous leathery cuticle of the mooncalf herds thins out to a mere membrane, through which the pulsating brain movements are distinctly visible. He is a creature, indeed, with a tremendously hypertrophied brain, and with the rest of his organism both relatively and absolutely dwarfed.'

In another passage Cavor compares the back view of him to Atlas supporting the world. Tsi-puff it seems was a very similar insect, but his 'face' was drawn out to a considerable length, and the brain hypertrophy being in different regions, his head was not round but pear-shaped, with the stalk downward. There were also litter-carriers, lopsided beings, with enormous shoulders, very spidery ushers, and a squat foot attendant in Cavor's retinue.

The manner in which Phi-oo and Tsi-puff attacked the problem of speech was fairly obvious. They came into this 'hexagonal cell' in which Cavor was confined, and began imitating every sound he made, beginning with a cough. He seems to have grasped their intention with great quickness, and to have begun repeating words to them and pointing to indicate the application. The procedure was probably always the same. Phi-oo would attend to Cavor for a space, then point also and say the word he had heard.

The first word he mastered was 'man', and the second 'Mooney' – which Cavor on the spur of the moment seems to have used instead of 'Selenite' for the moon race. As soon as Phi-oo was assured of the meaning of a word he repeated it to Tsi-puff, who remembered it infallibly. They mastered over one hundred English nouns at their first session.

Subsequently it seems they brought an artist with them to assist the work of explanation with sketches and diagrams – Cavor's drawings being rather crude. He was, says Cavor, 'a being with an active arm and an arresting eye', and he seemed to draw with incredible swiftness.

The eleventh message is undoubtedly only a fragment of a longer communication. After some broken sentences, the record of which is unintelligible, it goes on:

'But it will interest only linguists, and delay me too long, to give the details of the series of intent parleys of which these were the beginning, and, indeed, I very much doubt if I could give in anything like the proper order all the twistings and turnings that we made in our pursuit of mutual comprehension. Verbs were soon plain sailing – at least, such active verbs as I could express by drawings; some adjectives were easy, but when it came to abstract nouns, to prepositions, and the sort of hackneyed figures of speech, by means of which so much is expressed on earth, it was like diving in cork-jackets. Indeed, these difficulties were insurmountable until to the sixth lesson came a fourth assistant, a being with a huge football-shaped head, whose forte was clearly the pursuit of intricate analogy. He entered in a preoccupied manner, stumbling against a stool, and the difficulties that arose had to be presented to him with a certain amount of clamour and hitting and pricking before they reached his apprehension. But once he was involved his penetration was amazing. Whenever there came a need of thinking beyond Phi-oo's by no means limited scope, this prolate-headed person was in request, but he invariably told the conclusion to Tsi-puff, in order that it might be remembered; Tsi-puff was ever the arsenal for facts. And so we advanced again.

'It seemed long and yet brief – a matter of days – before I was positively talking with these insects of the moon. Of course, at first it was an intercourse infinitely tedious and exasperating, but imperceptibly it has grown to comprehension. And my patience has grown to meet its limitations, Phi-oo it is who does all the talking. He does it with a vast amount of meditative provisional "M'm-M'm" and has caught up one or two phrases, "If I may say", "If you understand", and beads all his speech with them.

'Thus he would discourse. Imagine him explaining his artist.

' "M'm-M'm – he – if I may say – draw. Eat little – drink little – draw. Love draw. No other thing. Hate all who not draw like him. Angry. Hate all who draw like him better. Hate most people. Hate all who not think all world for to draw. Angry. M'm. All things mean nothing to him – only draw. He like you . . . if you understand . . . New thing to draw. Ugly – striking. Eh?

' "He," – turning to Tsi-puff – "love remember words. Remember wonderful more than any. Think no, draw no – remember. Say" – here he referred to his gifted assistant for a word – "histories – all things. He hear once – say ever."

THE NATURAL HISTORY OF THE SELENITES 175

'It is more wonderful to me than I dreamt that anything ever could be again, to hear, in this perpetual obscurity, these extraordinary creatures – for even familiarity fails to weaken the inhuman effect of their appearance – continually piping a nearer approach to coherent earthly speech – asking questions, giving answers. I feel that I am casting back to the fable-hearing period of childhood again, when the ant and the grasshopper talked together and the bee judged between them . . . '

*   *   *

And while these linguistic exercises were going on Cavor seems to have experienced a considerable relaxation of his confinement. 'The first dread and distrust our unfortunate conflict aroused is being,' he said, 'continually effaced by the deliberate rationality of all I do.' . . . 'I am now able to come and go as I please, or I am restricted only for my own good. So it is I have been able to get at this apparatus, and, assisted by a happy find among the material that is littered in this enormous store-cave, I have contrived to despatch these messages. So far not the slightest attempt has been made to interfere with me in this, though I have made it quite clear to Phi-oo that I am signalling to the earth.

' "You talk to other?" he asked, watching me.

' "Others," said I.

' "Others," he said. "Oh yes, Men?"

'And I went on transmitting.'

*   *   *

Cavor was continually making corrections in his previous accounts of the Selenites as fresh facts flowed upon him to modify his conclusions, and accordingly one gives the quotations that follow with a certain amount of reservation. They are quoted from the ninth, thirteenth, and sixteenth messages, and, altogether vague and fragmentary as they are, they probably give as complete a picture of the social life of this strange community as mankind can now hope to have for many generations.

'In the moon,' says Cavor, 'every citizen knows his place. He is born to that place, and the elaborate discipline of training and education and surgery he undergoes fits him at last so completely to it that he has neither ideas nor organs for any purpose beyond it. "Why should he?" Phi-oo would ask. If, for example, a Selenite is destined to be a mathematician, his teachers and trainers set out at once to that end. They check any incipient disposition to other pursuits, they encourage his mathematical bias with a perfect psychological skill. His brain grows, or at least the mathematical faculties of his brain grow, and the rest of him only so much as is necessary to sustain this essential part of him. At last, save for rest and food, his one delight lies in the exercise and display of his facility, his one interest in its application, his sole society with other specialists in his own line. His brain grows continually larger, at least so far as the portions engaging in mathematics are concerned; they bulge ever larger and seem to suck all life and vigour from the rest of his frame. His limbs shrivel, his heart and digestive organs diminish, his insect face is hidden under its bulging contours. His voice becomes a mere stridulation for the stating of formula; he seems deaf to all but properly enunciated problems. The faculty of laughter, save for the sudden discovery of some paradox, is lost to him; his deepest emotion is the evolution of a novel computation. And so he attains his end.

'Or, again, a Selenite appointed to be a minder of mooncalves is from his earliest years induced to think and live mooncalf, to find his pleasure in mooncalf lore, his exercise in their tending and pursuit. He is trained to become wiry and active, his eye is indurated to the tight wrappings, the angular contours that constitute a "smart mooncalfishness". He takes at last no interest in the deeper part of the moon; he regards all Selenites not equally versed in mooncalves with indifference, derision, or hostility. His thoughts are of mooncalf pastures, and his dialect an accomplished mooncalf technique. So also he loves his work, and discharges in perfect happiness the duty that justifies his being. And so it is with all sorts and conditions of Selenites – each is a perfect unit in a world machine . . .

'These beings with big heads, on whom the intellectual labours fall, form a sort of aristocracy in this strange society, and at the head of them, quintessential of the moon, is that marvellous gigantic ganglion the Grand Lunar, into whose presence I am finally to come. The unlimited development of the minds of the intellectual class is rendered possible by the absence of any body skull in the lunar anatomy, that strange box of bone that clamps about the developing brain of man, imperiously insisting "thus far and no farther" to all his possibilities. They fall into three main classes differing greatly in influence and respect. There are administrators, of whom Phi-oo is one, Selenites of considerable initiative and versatility, responsible each for a certain cubic content of the moon's bulk; the experts like the football-headed thinker, who are trained to perform certain special operations; and the erudite, who are the repositories of all knowledge. To the latter class belongs Tsi-puff, the first lunar professor of terrestrial languages. With regard to these latter, it is a curious little thing to note that the unlimited growth of the lunar brain has rendered unnecessary the invention of all those mechanical aids to brain work which have distinguished the career of man. There are no books, no records of any sort, no libraries or inscriptions. All knowledge is stored in distended brains much as the honey-ants of Texas store honey in their distended abdomens. The lunar Somerset House and the lunar British Museum Library are collections of living brains . . .

'The less specialised administrators, I note, do for the most part take a very lively interest in me whenever they encounter me. They will come out of the way and stare at me and ask questions to which Phi-oo will reply. I see them going hither and thither with a retinue of bearers, attendants, shouters, parachute-carriers, and so forth – queer groups to see. The experts for the most part ignore me completely, even as they ignore each other, or notice me only to begin a clamorous exhibition of their distinctive skill. The erudite for the most part are rapt in an impervious and apoplectic complacency, from which only a denial of their erudition can rouse them. Usually they are led about by little watchers and attendants, and often there are small and active-looking creatures, small females usually, that I am inclined to think are a sort of wife to them; but some of the profounder scholars are altogether too great for locomotion, and are carried from place to place in a sort of sedan tub, wabbling jellies of knowledge that enlist my respectful astonishment. I have just passed one in coming to this place where I am permitted to amuse myself with these electrical toys, a vast, shaven, shaky head, bald and thin-skinned, carried on his grotesque stretcher. In front and behind came his bearers, and curious, almost trumpet-faced, news disseminators shrieked his fame.

'I have already mentioned the retinues that accompany most of the intellectuals: ushers, bearers, valets, extraneous tentacles and muscles, as it were, to replace the abortive physical powers of these hyper-trophied minds. Porters almost invariably accompany them. There are also extremely swift messengers with spider-like legs and "hands" for grasping parachutes, and attendants with vocal organs that could well nigh wake the dead. Apart from their controlling intelligence these subordinates are as inert and helpless as umbrellas in a stand. They exist only in relation to the orders they have to obey, the duties they have to perform.

'The bulk of these insects, however, who go to and fro upon the spiral ways, who fill the ascending balloons and drop past me clinging to flimsy parachutes are, I gather, of the operative class. "Machine hands", indeed, some of these are in actual nature – it is not a figure of speech, the single tentacle of the mooncalf herd is profoundly modified for clawing, lifting, guiding, the rest of them no more than necessary subordinate appendages to these important mechanisms, have enormously developed auditory organs; some whose work lies in delicate chemical operations project a vast olfactory organ; others again have flat feet for treadles with anchylosed joints; and others – who I have been told are glass-blowers – seem mere lung-bellows. But every one of these common Selenites I have seen at work is exquisitely adapted to the social need it meets. Fine work is done by fined-down workers, amazingly dwarfed and neat. Some I could hold on the palm of my hand. There is even a sort of turn-spit Selenite, very common, whose duty and only delight it is to apply the motive power for various small appliances. And to rule over these things and order any erring tendency there might be in some aberrant natures are the most muscular beings I have seen in the moon, a sort of lunar police, who must have been trained from their earliest years to give a perfect respect and obedience to the swollen heads.

'The making of these various sorts of operative must be a very curious and interesting process. I am very much in the dark about it, but quite recently I came upon a number of young Selenites confined in jars from which only the forelimbs protruded, who were being compressed to become machine-minders of a special sort. The extended "hand" in this highly developed system of technical education is stimulated by irritants and nourished by injection, while the rest of the body is starved. Phi-oo, unless I misunderstood him, explained that in the earlier stages these queer little creatures are apt to display signs of suffering in their various cramped situations, but they easily become indurated to their lot; and he took me on to where a number of flexible-minded messengers were being drawn out and broken in. It is quite unreasonable, I know, but such glimpses of the educational methods of these beings affect me disagreeably. I hope, however, that may pass off, and I may be able to see more of this aspect of their wonderful social order. That wretched-looking hand-tentacle sticking out of its jar seemed to have a sort of limp appeal for lost possibilities; it haunts me still, although, of course it is really in the end a far more humane proceeding than our earthly method of leaving children to grow into human beings, and then making machines of them.

'Quite recently, too – I think it was on the eleventh or twelfth visit I made to this apparatus – I had a curious light upon the lives of these operatives. I was being guided through a short cut hither, instead of going down the spiral, and by the quays to the Central Sea. From the devious windings of a long, dark gallery, we emerged into a vast, low cavern, pervaded by an earthy smell, and as things go in this darkness, rather brightly lit. The light came from a tumultuous growth of livid fungoid shapes – some indeed singularly like our terrestrial mushrooms, but standing as high or higher than a man.

' "Mooneys eat these?" said I to Phi-oo.

' "Yes, food."

' "Goodness me!" I cried; "what's that?"

'My eye had just caught the figure of an exceptionally big and ungainly Selenite lying motionless among the stems, face downward. We stopped.

' "Dead?" I asked. (For as yet I have seen no dead on the moon, and I have grown curious.)

' "*No!*" exclaimed Phi-oo. "Him – worker – no work to do. Get little drink then – make sleep – till we him want. What good him wake, eh? No want him walking about."

' "There's another!" cried I.

'And indeed all that huge extent of mushroom ground was, I found, peppered with these prostrate figures sleeping under an opiate until the moon had need of them. There were scores of them of all sorts, and we were able to turn over some of them, and examine them more precisely than I had been able to previously. They breathed noisily at my doing so, but did not wake. One, I remember very distinctly: he left a strong impression, I think, because some trick of the light and of his attitude was strongly suggestive of a drawn-up human figure. His forelimbs were long, delicate tentacles – he was some kind of refined manipulator – and the pose of his slumber suggested a submissive suffering. No doubt it was a mistake for me to interpret his expression in that way, but I did. And as Phi-oo rolled him over into the darkness among the livid fleshiness again I felt a distinctly unpleasant sensation, although as he rolled the insect in him was confessed.

'It simply illustrates the unthinking way in which one acquires habits of feeling. To drug the worker one does not want and toss him aside is surely far better than to expel him from his factory to wander starving in the streets. In every complicated social community there is necessarily a certain intermittency of employment for all specialised labour, and in this way the trouble of an "unemployed" problem is altogether anticipated. And yet, so unreasonable are even scientifically trained minds, I still do not like the memory of those prostrate forms amidst those quiet, luminous arcades of fleshy growth, and I avoid that short cut in spite of the inconveniences of the longer, more noisy, and more crowded alternative.

*   *   *

'My alternative route takes me round by a huge, shadowy cavern, very crowded and clamorous, and here it is I see peering out of the hexagonal openings of a sort of honeycomb wall, or parading a large open space behind, or selecting the toys and amulets made to please them by the dainty-tentacled jewellers who work in kennels below, the mothers of the moon world – the queen bees, as it were, of the hive. They are noble-looking beings, fantastically and sometimes quite beautifully adorned, with a proud carriage, and, save for their mouths, almost microscopic heads.

'Of the condition of the moon sexes, marrying and giving in marriage, and of birth and so forth among the Selenites, I have as yet been able to learn very little. With the steady progress of Phi-oo in English, however, my ignorance will no doubt as steadily disappear. I am of opinion that, as with the ants and bees, there is a large majority of the members in this community of the neuter sex. Of course on earth in our cities there are now many who never live that life of parentage which is the natural life of man. Here, as with the ants, this thing has become a normal condition of the race, and the whole of such replacement as is necessary falls upon this special and by no means numerous class of matrons, the mothers of the moon-world, large and stately beings beautifully fitted to bear the larval Selenite. Unless I misunderstand an explanation of Phi-oo's, they are absolutely incapable of cherishing the young they bring into the moon; periods of foolish indulgence alternate with moods of aggressive violence, and as soon as possible the little creatures, who are quite soft and flabby and pale coloured, are transferred to the charge of celibate females, women "workers" as it were, who in some cases possess brains of almost masculine dimensions.'

*   *   *

Just at this point, unhappily, this message broke off. Fragmentary and tantalising as the matter constituting this chapter is, it does nevertheless give a vague, broad impression of an altogether strange and wonderful world – a world with which our own may have to reckon we know not how speedily. This intermittent trickle of messages, this whispering of a record needle in the stillness of the mountain slopes, is the first warning of such a change in human conditions as mankind has scarcely imagined heretofore. In that satellite of ours there are new elements, new appliances, traditions, an overwhelming avalanche of new ideas, a strange race with whom we must inevitably struggle for mastery – gold as common as iron or wood . . .

CHAPTER TWENTY-FIVE

The Grand Lunar

The penultimate message describes, with occasionally elaborate detail, the encounter between Cavor and the Grand Lunar, who is the ruler or master of the moon. Cavor seems to have sent most of it without interference, but to have been interrupted in the concluding portion. The second came after an interval of a week.

The first message begins: 'At last I am able to resume this – it then becomes illegible for a space, and after a time resumes in mid-sentence.

The missing words of the following sentence are probably 'the crowd'. There follows quite clearly: 'grew ever denser as we drew near the palace of the Grand Lunar – if I may call a series of excavations a palace. Everywhere faces stared at me – blank, chitinous gapes and masks, eyes peering over tremendous olfactory developments, eyes beneath monstrous forehead plates; an undergrowth of smaller creatures dodged and yelped, and helmet faces poised on sinuous, long-jointed necks appeared craning over shoulders and beneath armpits. Keeping a welcome space about me marched a cordon of stolid, scuttle-headed guards, who had joined us on our leaving the boat in which we had come along the channels of the Central Sea. The quick-eyed artist with the little brain joined us also, and a thick bunch of lean porter-insects swayed and struggled under the multitude of conveniences that were considered essential to my state. I was carried in a litter during the final stage of our journey. This litter was made of some very ductile metal that looked dark to me, meshed and woven, and with bars of paler metal, and about me as I advanced there grouped itself a long and complicated procession.

'In front, after the manner of heralds, marched four trumpet-faced creatures making a devastating bray; and then came squat, resolute-moving ushers before and behind, and on either hand a galaxy of learned heads, a sort of animated encyclopaedia, who were, Phi-oo explained, to stand about the Grand Lunar for purposes of reference. (Not a thing in lunar science, not a point of view or method of thinking, that these wonderful beings did not carry in their heads!) Followed guards and porters, and then Phi-oo's shivering brain borne also on a litter. Then came Tsi-puff in a slightly less important litter; then myself on a litter of greater elegance than any other, and surrounded by my food and drink attendants. More trumpeters came next, splitting the ear with vehement outcries, and then several big brains, special correspondents one might well call them, or historiographers, charged with the task of observing and remembering every detail of this epoch-making inter- view. A company of attendants, bearing and dragging banners and masses of scented fungus and curious symbols, vanished in the darkness behind. The way was lined by ushers and officers in caparisons that gleamed like steel, and beyond their line, so far as my eyes could pierce the gloom, the heads of that enormous crowd extended.

'I will own that I am still by no means indurated to the peculiar effect of the Selenite appearance, and to find myself, as it were, adrift on this broad sea of excited entomology was by no means agreeable. Just for a space I had something very like what I should imagine people mean when they speak of the "horrors". It had come to me before in these lunar caverns, when on occasion I have found myself weaponless and with an undefended back, amidst a crowd of these Selenites, but never quite so vividly. It is, of course, as absolutely irrational a feeling as one could well have, and I hope gradually to subdue it. But just for a moment, as I swept forward into the welter of the vast crowd, it was only by gripping my litter tightly and summoning all my will-power that I succeeded in avoiding an outcry or some such manifestation. It lasted perhaps three I minutes; then I had myself in hand again.

'We ascended the spiral of a vertical way for some time, and then passed through a series of huge halls, dome-roofed and elaborately decorated. The approach to the Grand Lunar was certainly contrived to give one a vivid impression of his greatness. Each cavern one entered seemed greater and more boldly arched than its predecessor. This effect of progressive size was enhanced by a thin haze of faintly phosphorescent blue incense that thickened as one advanced, and robbed even the nearer figures of clearness. I seemed to advance continually to something larger, dimmer, and less material.

'I must confess that all this multitude made me feel extremely shabby and unworthy. I was unshaven and unkempt; I had brought no razor; I had a coarse beard over my mouth. On earth I have always been inclined to despise any attention to my person beyond a proper care for cleanliness; but under the exceptional circumstances in which I found myself, representing, as I did, my planet and my kind, and depending very largely upon the attractiveness of my appearance for a proper reception, I could have given much for something a little more artistic and dignified than the husks I wore. I had been so serene in the belief that the moon was uninhabited as to overlook such precautions altogether. As it was I was dressed in a flannel jacket, knickerbockers, and golfing stockings, stained with every sort of dirt the moon offered, slippers (of which the left heel was wanting), and a blanket, through a hole in which I thrust my head. (These clothes, indeed, I still wear.) Sharp bristles are anything but an improvement to my cast of features, and there was an unmended tear at the knee of my knickerbockers that showed conspicuously as I squatted in my litter; my right stocking, too, persisted in getting about my ankle. I am fully alive to the injustice my appearance did humanity, and if by any expedient I could have improvised something a little out of the way and imposing I would have done so. But I could hit upon nothing. I did what I could with my blanket – folding it somewhat after the fashion of a toga, and for the rest I sat as upright as the swaying of my litter permitted.

'Imagine the largest hall you have ever been in, imperfectly lit with blue light and obscured by a grey-blue fog, surging with metallic or livid-grey creatures of such a mad diversity as I have hinted. Imagine this hall to end in an open archway beyond which is a still larger hall, and beyond this yet another and still larger one, and so on. At the end of the vista, dimly seen, a flight of steps, like the steps of Ara Coeli at Rome, ascend out of sight. Higher and higher these steps appear to go as one draws nearer their base. But at last I came under a huge archway and beheld the summit of these steps, and upon it the Grand Lunar exalted on his throne.

'He was seated in what was relatively a blaze of incandescent blue. This, and the darkness about him, gave him an effect of floating in a blue-black void. He seemed a small, self-luminous cloud at first, brooding on his sombre throne; his brain case must have measured many yards in diameter. For some reason that I cannot fathom a number of blue searchlights radiated from behind the throne on which he sat, and immediately encircling him was a halo. About him, and little and indistinct in this glow, a number of body-servants sustained and supported him, and overshadowed and standing in a huge semicircle beneath him were his intellectual subordinates, his remembrancers and computators and searchers and servants, and all the distinguished insects of the court of the moon. Still lower stood ushers and messengers, and then all down the countless steps of the throne were guards, and at the base, enormous, various, indistinct, vanishing at last into an absolute black, a vast swaying multitude of the minor dignitaries of the moon. Their feet made a perpetual scraping whisper on the rocky floor, as their limbs moved with a rustling murmur.

'As I entered the penultimate hall the music rose and expanded into an imperial magnificence of sound, and the shrieks of the news-bearers died away . . .

'I entered the last and greatest hall . . .

'My procession opened out like a fan. My ushers and guards went right and left, and the three litters bearing myself and Phi-oo and Tsi-puff marched across a shiny darkness of floor to the foot of the giant stairs. Then began a vast throbbing hum, that mingled with the music. The two Selenites dismounted, but I was bidden remain seated – I imagine as a special honour. The music ceased, but not that humming, and by a simultaneous movement of ten thousand respectful heads my attention was directed to the enhaloed supreme intelligence that hovered above me.

'At first as I peered into the radiating glow this quintessential brain looked very much like an opaque, featureless bladder with dim, un-dulating ghosts of convolutions writhing visibly within. Then beneath its enormity and just above the edge of the throne one saw with a start minute elfin eyes peering out of the glow. No face, but eyes, as if they peered through holes. At first I could see no more than these two staring little eyes, and then below I distinguished the little dwarfed body and its insect-jointed limbs shrivelled and white. The eyes stared down at me with a strange intensity, and the lower part of the swollen globe was wrinkled. Ineffectual-looking little hand-tentacles steadied this shape on the throne . . .

'It was great. It was pitiful. One forgot the hall and the crowd.

'I ascended the staircase by jerks. It seemed to me that this darkly glowing brain case above us spread over me, and took more and more of the whole effect into itself as I drew nearer. The tiers of attendants and helpers grouped about their master seemed to dwindle and fade into the night. I saw that shadowy attendants were busy spraying that great brain with a cooling spray, and patting and sustaining it. For my own part, I sat gripping my swaying litter and staring at the Grand Lunar, unable to turn my gaze aside. And at last, as I reached a little landing that was separated only by ten steps or so from the supreme seat, the woven splendour of the music reached a climax and ceased, and I was left naked, as it were, in that vastness, beneath the still scrutiny of the Grand Lunar's eyes.

'He was scrutinising the first man he had ever seen . . .

'My eyes dropped at last from his greatness to the ant figures in the blue mist about him, and then down the steps to the massed Selenites, still and expectant in their thousands, packed on the floor below. Once again an unreasonable horror reached out towards me . . . And passed.

'After the pause came the salutation. I was assisted from my litter, and stood awkwardly while a number of curious and no doubt deeply symbolical gestures were vicariously performed for me by two slender officials. The encyclopaedic galaxy of the learned that had accompanied me to the entrance of the last hall appeared two steps above me and left and right of me, in readiness for the Grand Lunar's need, and Phi-oo's pale brain placed itself about halfway up to the throne in such a position as to communicate easily between us without turning his back on either the Grand Lunar or myself. Tsi-puff took up position behind him. Dexterous ushers sidled sideways towards me, keeping a full face to the Presence. I seated myself Turkish fashion, and Phi-oo and Tsi-puff also knelt down above me. There came a pause. The eyes of the nearer court went from me to the Grand Lunar and came back to me, and a hissing and piping of expectation passed across the hidden multitudes below and ceased.

'That humming ceased.

'For the first and last time in my experience the moon was silent.

'I became aware of a faint wheezy noise. The Grand Lunar was addressing me. It was like the rubbing of a finger upon a pane of glass.

'I watched him attentively for a time, and then glanced at the alert Phi-oo. I felt amidst these slender beings ridiculously thick and fleshy and solid; my head all jaw and black hair. My eyes went back to the Grand Lunar. He had ceased; his attendants were busy, and his shining superfices was glistening and running with cooling spray.

'Phi-oo meditated through an interval. He consulted Tsi-puff. Then he began piping his recognisable English – at first a little nervously, so that he was not very clear.

' "M'm – the Grand Lunar – wishes to say – wishes to say – he gathers you are – m'm – men – that you are a man from the planet earth. He wishes to say that he welcomes you – welcomes you – and wishes to learn – learn, if I may use the word – the state of your world, and the reason why you came to this."

'He paused. I was about to reply when he resumed. He proceeded to remarks of which the drift was not very clear, though I am inclined to think they were intended to be complimentary. He told me that the earth was to the moon what the sun is to the earth, and that the Selenites desired very greatly to learn about the earth and men. He then told me, no doubt in compliment also, the relative magnitude and diameter of earth and moon, and the perpetual wonder and speculation with which the Selenites had regarded our planet. I meditated with downcast eyes, and decided to reply that men too had wondered what might lie in the moon, and had judged it dead, little recking of such magnificence as I had seen that day. The Grand Lunar, in token of recognition, caused his long blue rays to rotate in a very confusing manner, and all about the great hall ran the pipings and whisperings and rustlings of the report of what I had said. He then proceeded to put to Phi-oo a number of enquiries which were easier to answer.

'He understood, he explained, that we lived on the surface of the earth, that our air and sea were outside the globe; the latter part, indeed, he already knew from his astronomical specialists. He was very anxious to have more detailed information of what he called this extraordinary state of affairs, for from the solidity of the earth there had always been a disposition to regard it as uninhabitable. He endeavoured first to ascertain the extremes of temperature to which we earth beings were exposed, and he was deeply interested by my descriptive treatment of clouds and rain. His imagination was assisted by the fact that the lunar atmosphere in the outer galleries of the night side is not infrequently very foggy. He seemed inclined to marvel that we did not find the sunlight too intense for our eyes, and was interested in my attempt to explain that the sky was tempered to a bluish colour through the refraction of the air, though I doubt if he clearly understood that. I explained how the iris of the human eyes can contract the pupil and save the delicate internal structure from the excess of sunlight, and was allowed to approach within a few feet of the Presence in order that this structure might be seen. This led to a comparison of the lunar and terrestrial eyes. The former is not only excessively sensitive to such light as men can see, but it can also *see* heat, and every difference in temperature within the moon renders objects visible to it.

'The iris was quite a new organ to the Grand Lunar. For a time he amused himself by flashing his rays into my face and watching my pupils contract. As a consequence, I was dazzled and blinded for some little time . . .

'But in spite of that discomfort I found something reassuring by insensible degrees in the rationality of this business of question and answer. I could shut my eyes, think of my answer, and almost forget that the Grand Lunar has no face . . .

'When I had descended again to my proper place the Grand Lunar asked how we sheltered ourselves from heat and storms, and I expounded to him the arts of building and furnishing. Here we wandered into misunderstandings and cross-purposes, due largely, I must admit, to the looseness of my expressions. For a long time I had great difficulty in making him understand the nature of a house. To him and his attendant

Selenites it seemed, no doubt, the most whimsical thing in the world that men should build houses when they might descend into excavations, and an additional complication was introduced by the attempt I made to explain that men had originally begun their homes in caves, and that they were now taking their railways and many establishments beneath the surface. Here I think a desire for intellectual completeness betrayed me. There was also a considerable tangle due to an equally unwise attempt on my part to explain about mines. Dismissing this topic at last in an incomplete state, the Grand Lunar enquired what we did with the interior of our globe.

'A tide of twittering and piping swept into the remotest corners of that great assembly when it was at last made clear that we men know absolutely nothing of the contents of the world upon which the immemorial generations of our ancestors had been evolved. Three times had I to repeat that of all the 4,000 miles of distance between the earth and its centre men knew only to the depth of a mile, and that very vaguely. I understood the Grand Lunar to ask why had I come to the moon seeing we had scarcely touched our own planet yet, but he did not trouble me at that time to proceed to an explanation, being too anxious to pursue the details of this mad inversion of all his ideas.

'He reverted to the question of weather, and I tried to describe the perpetually changing sky, and snow, and frost and hurricanes. "But when the night comes," he asked, "is it not cold?"

'I told him it was colder than by day.

' "And does not your atmosphere freeze?"

'I told him not; that it was never cold enough for that, because our nights were so short.

' "Not even liquefy?"

'I was about to say "No", but then it occurred to me that one part at least of our atmosphere, the water vapour of it, does sometimes liquefy and form dew, and sometimes freeze and form frost – a process perfectly analogous to the freezing of all the external atmosphere of the moon during its longer night. I made myself clear on this point, and from that the Grand Lunar went on to speak with me of sleep. For the need of sleep that comes so regularly every twenty-four hours to all things is part also of our earthly inheritance. On the moon they rest only at rare intervals, and after exceptional exertions. Then I tried to describe to him the soft splendours of a summer night, and from that I passed to a description of those animals that prowl by night and sleep by day. I told him of lions and tigers, and here it seemed as though we had come to a deadlock. For, save in their waters, there are no creatures in the moon not absolutely domestic and subject to his will, and so it has been for immemorial years. They have monstrous water creatures, but no evil beasts, and the idea of anything strong and large existing "outside" in the night is very difficult for them . . . '

The record is here too broken to transcribe for the space of perhaps twenty words or more.

'He talked with his attendants, as I suppose, upon the strange superficiality and unreasonableness of (man) who lives on the mere surface of a world, a creature of waves and winds, and all the chances of space, who cannot even unite to overcome the beasts that prey upon his kind, and yet who dares to invade another planet. During this aside I sat thinking, and then at his desire I told him of the different sorts of men. He searched me with questions. 'And for all sorts of work you have the same sort of men. But who thinks? Who governs?'

'I gave him an outline of the democratic method.

'When I had done he ordered cooling sprays upon his brow, and then requested me to repeat my explanation conceiving something had miscarried.

' "Do they not do different things, then?" said Phi-oo.

'Some, I admitted, were thinkers and some officials; some hunted, some were mechanics, some artists, some toilers. "But *all* rule," I said.

' "And have they not different shapes to fit them to their different duties?"

' "None that you can see," I said, "except, perhaps, for clothes. Their minds perhaps differ a little," I reflected.

' "Their minds must differ a great deal," said the Grand Lunar, "or they would all want to do the same things."

'In order to bring myself into a closer harmony with his preconceptions, I said that his surmise was right. "It was all hidden in the brain," I said; "but the difference was there. Perhaps if one could see the minds and souls of men they would be as varied and unequal as the Selenites." There were great men and small men, men who could reach out far and wide, men who could go swiftly; noisy, trumpet-minded men, and men who could remember without thinking . . . ' The record is indistinct for three words.

'He interrupted me to recall me to my previous statements. "But you said all men rule?" he pressed.

' "To a certain extent," I said, and made, I fear, a denser fog with my explanation.

'He reached out to a salient fact. "Do you mean," he asked, "that there is no Grand Earthly?"

'I thought of several people, but assured him finally there was none. I explained that such autocrats and emperors as we had tried upon earth had usually ended in drink, or vice, or violence, and that the large and influential section of the people of the earth to which I belonged, the Anglo-Saxons, did not mean to try that sort of thing again. At which the Grand Lunar was even more amazed.

' "But how do you keep even such wisdom as you have?" he asked; and I explained to him the way we helped our limited [a word omitted here, probably 'brains'] with libraries of books. I explained to him how our science was growing by the united labours of innumerable little men, and on that he made no comment save that it was evident we had mastered much in spite of our social savagery, or we could not have come to the moon. Yet the contrast was very marked. With knowledge the Selenites grew and changed; mankind stored their knowledge about them and remained brutes – equipped. He said this . . . [Here there is a short piece of the record indistinct.]

'He then caused me to describe how we went about this earth of ours, and I described to him our railways and ships. For a time he could not understand that we had had the use of steam only one hundred years, but when he did he was clearly amazed. (I may mention as a singular thing, that the Selenites use years to count by, just as we do on earth, though I can make nothing of their numeral system. That, however, does not matter, because Phi-oo understands ours.) From that I went on to tell him that mankind had dwelt in cities only for nine or ten thousand years, and that we were still not united in one brotherhood, but under many different forms of government. This astonished the Grand Lunar very much, when it was made clear to him. At first he thought we referred merely to administrative areas.

' "Our States and Empires are still the rawest sketches of what order will some day be," I said, and so I came to tell him . . . [At this point a length of record that probably represents thirty or forty words is totally illegible.]

'The Grand Lunar was greatly impressed by the folly of men in clinging to the inconvenience of diverse tongues. "They want to communicate, and yet not to communicate," he said, and then for a long time he questioned me closely concerning war.

'He was at first perplexed and incredulous. "You mean to say," he asked, seeking confirmation, "that you run about over the surface of your world – this world, whose riches you have scarcely begun to scrape – killing one another for beasts to eat?"

'I told him that was perfectly correct.

'He asked for particulars to assist his imagination.

' "But do not ships and your poor little cities get injured?" he asked, and I found the waste of property and conveniences seemed to impress him almost as much as the killing. "Tell me more," said the Grand Lunar; "make me see pictures. I cannot conceive these things."

'And so, for a space, though something loath, I told him the story of earthly War.

'I told him of the first orders and ceremonies of war, of warnings and ultimatums, and the marshalling and marching of troops. I gave him an idea of manoeuvres and positions and battle joined. I told him of sieges and assaults, of starvation and hardship in trenches, and of sentinels freezing in the snow. I told him of routs and surprises, and desperate last stands and faint hopes, and the pitiless pursuit of fugitives and the dead upon the field. I told, too, of the past, of invasions and massacres, of the Huns and Tartars, and the wars of Mahomet and the Caliphs, and of the Crusades. And as I went on, and Phi-oo translated, the Selenites cooed and murmured in a steadily intensified emotion.

'I told them an ironclad could fire a shot of a ton twelve miles, and go through 20 ft of iron – and how we could steer torpedoes under water. I went on to describe a Maxim gun in action, and what I could imagine of the Battle of Colenso. The Grand Lunar was so incredulous that he interrupted the translation of what I had said in order to have my verification of my account. They particularly doubted my description of the men cheering and rejoicing as they went into (? battle).

' "But surely they do not like it!" translated Phi-oo.

'I assured them men of my race considered battle the most glorious experience of life, at which the whole assembly was stricken with amazement.

' "But what good is this war?" asked the Grand Lunar, sticking to his theme.

' "Oh! as for *good*!" said I; "it thins the population!"

' "But why should there be a need – ?"

'There came a pause, the cooling sprays impinged upon his brow, and then he spoke again.'

*   *   *

[At this point a series of undulations that have been apparent as a perplexing complication as far back as Cavor's description of the silence that fell before the first speaking of the Grand Lunar become confusingly predominant in the record. These undulations are evidently the result of radiations proceeding from a lunar source, and their persistent approximation to the alternating signals of Cavor is curiously suggestive of some operator deliberately seeking to mix them in with his message and render it illegible. At first they are small and regular, so that with a little care and the loss of very few words we have been able to disentangle Cavor's message; then they become broad and larger, then suddenly they are irregular, with an irregularity that gives the effect at last of someone scribbling through a line of writing. For a long time nothing can be made of this madly zigzagging trace; then quite abruptly the interruption ceases, leaves a few words clear, and then resumes and continues for the rest of the message, completely obliterating whatever Cavor was attempting to transmit. Why, if this is indeed a deliberate intervention, the Selenites should have preferred to let Cavor go on transmitting his message in happy ignorance of their obliteration of its record, when it was clearly quite in their power and much more easy and convenient for them to stop his proceedings at any time, is a problem to which I can contribute nothing. The thing seems to have happened so, and that is all I can say. This last rag of his description of the Grand Lunar begins in mid-sentence.]

*   *   *

' . . . interrogated me very closely upon my secret. I was able in a little while to get to an understanding with them, and at last to elucidate what has been a puzzle to me ever since I realised the vastness of their science, namely, how it is they themselves have never discovered "Cavorite". I find they know of it as a theoretical substance, but they have always regarded it as a practical impossibility, because for some reason there is no helium in the moon, and helium – '

*   *   *

[Across the last letters of helium slashes the resumption of that obliterating trace. Note that word 'secret', for that, and that alone, I base my interpretation of the message that follows, the last message, as both Mr Wendigee and myself now believe it to be, that he is ever likely to send us.]

CHAPTER TWENTY-SIX

The Last Message Cavor Sent to the Earth

In this unsatisfactory manner the penultimate message of Cavor dies out. One seems to see him away there in the blue obscurity amidst his apparatus intently signalling us to the last, all unaware of the curtain of confusion that drops between us; all unaware, too, of the final dangers that even then must have been creeping upon him. His disastrous want of vulgar common sense had utterly betrayed him. He had talked of war, he had talked of all the strength and irrational violence of men, of their insatiable aggressions, their tireless futility of conflict. He had filled the whole moon world with this impression of our race, and then I think it is plain that he made the most fatal admission that upon himself alone hung the possibility – at least for a long time – of any further men reaching the moon. The line the cold, inhuman reason of the moon would take seems plain enough to me, and a suspicion of it, and then perhaps some sudden sharp realisation of it, must have come to him. One imagines him about the moon with the remorse of this fatal indiscretion growing in his mind. During a certain time I am inclined to guess the Grand Lunar was deliberating the new situation, and for all that time Cavor may have gone as free as ever he had gone. But obstacles of some sort prevented his getting to his electromagnetic apparatus again after that message I have just given. For some days we received nothing. Perhaps he was having fresh audiences, and trying to evade his previous admissions. Who can hope to guess?

And then suddenly, like a cry in the night, like a cry that is followed by a stillness, came the last message. It is the briefest fragment, the broken beginnings of two sentences.

The first was: 'I was mad to let the Grand Lunar know – '

There was an interval of perhaps a minute. One imagines some interruption from without. A departure from the instrument – a dreadful hesitation among the looming masses of apparatus in that dim, blue-lit cavern – a sudden rush back to it, full of a resolve that came too late. Then, as if it were hastily transmitted came: 'Cavorite made as follows: take – '

There followed one word, a quite unmeaning word as it stands: 'uless'. And that is all.

It may be he made a hasty attempt to spell 'useless' when his fate was close upon him. Whatever it was that was happening about that apparatus we cannot tell. Whatever it was we shall never, I know, receive another message from the moon. For my own part a vivid dream has come to my help, and I see, almost as plainly as though I had seen it in actual fact, a blue-lit shadowy dishevelled Cavor struggling in the grip of these insect Selenites, struggling ever more desperately and hopelessly as they press upon him, shouting, expostulating, perhaps even at last fighting, and being forced backwards step by step out of all speech or sign of his fellows, for evermore into the Unknown – into the dark, into that silence that has no end . . .

A Modern Utopia

A Modern Utopia

---◆---

H. G. WELLS

Contents

A Note to the Reader

This book is in all probability the last of a series of writings, of which –
disregarding certain earlier disconnected essays – my *Anticipations*
was the beginning. Originally I intended *Anticipations* to be my sole
digression from my art or trade (or what you will) of an imaginative
writer. I wrote that book in order to clear up the muddle in my own
mind about innumerable social and political questions, questions I
could not keep out of my work, which it distressed me to touch upon
in a stupid haphazard way, and which no one, so far as I knew, had
handled in a manner to satisfy my needs. But *Anticipations* did not
achieve its end. I have a slow constructive hesitating sort of mind, and
when I emerged from that undertaking I found I had still most of my
questions to state and solve. In *Mankind in the Making*, therefore, I
tried to review the social organisation in a different way, to consider it
as an educational process instead of dealing with it as a thing with a
future history, and if I made this second book even less satisfactory
from a literary standpoint than the former (and this is my opinion), I
blundered, I think, more edifyingly – at least from the point of view of
my own instruction. I ventured upon several themes with a greater
frankness than I had used in *Anticipations*, and came out of that second
effort guilty of much rash writing, but with a considerable development of formed opinion. In many matters I had shaped out at last a
certain personal certitude, upon which I feel I shall go for the rest of
my days. In this present book I have tried to settle accounts with a
number of issues left over or opened up by its two predecessors, to
correct them in some particulars, and to give the general picture of a
Utopia that has grown up in my mind during the course of these
speculations as a state of affairs at once possible and more desirable
than the world in which I live. But this book has brought me back to
imaginative writing again. In its two predecessors the treatment of
social organisation had been purely objective; here my intention has
been a little wider and deeper, in that I have tried to present not
simply an ideal, but an ideal in reaction with two personalities. Moreover, since this may be the last book of the kind I shall ever publish,
I have written into it as well as I can the heretical metaphysical
scepticism upon which all my thinking rests, and I have inserted certain

sections reflecting upon the established methods of sociological and economic science . . .

The last four words will not attract the butterfly reader, I know. I have done my best to make the whole of this book as lucid and entertaining as its matter permits, because I want it read by as many people as possible, but I do not promise anything but rage and confusion to him who proposes to glance through my pages just to see if I agree with him, or to begin in the middle, or to read without a constantly alert attention. If you are not already a little interested and open-minded with regard to social and political questions, and a little exercised in self-examination, you will find neither interest nor pleasure here. If your mind is 'made up' upon such issues your time will be wasted on these pages. And even if you are a willing reader you may require a little patience for the peculiar method I have this time adopted.

That method assumes an air of haphazard, but it is not so careless as it seems. I believe it to be – even now that I am through with the book – the best way to a sort of lucid vagueness which has always been my intention in this matter. I tried over several beginnings of a Utopian book before I adopted this. I rejected from the outset the form of the argumentative essay, the form which appeals most readily to what is called the 'serious' reader, the reader who is often no more than the solemnly impatient parasite of great questions. He likes everything in hard, heavy lines, black and white, yes and no, because he does not understand how much there is that cannot be presented at all in that way; wherever there is any effect of obliquity, of incommensurables, wherever there is any levity or humour or difficulty of multiplex present-ation, he refuses attention. Mentally he seems to be built up upon an invincible assumption that the Spirit of Creation cannot count beyond two, he deals only in alternatives. Such readers I have resolved not to attempt to please here. Even if I presented all my tri-clinic crystals as systems of cubes! Indeed I felt it would not be worth doing. But having rejected the 'serious' essay as a form, I was still greatly exercised, I spent some vacillating months, over the scheme of this book. I tried first a recognised method of viewing questions from divergent points that has always attracted me and which I have never succeeded in using, the discussion novel, after the fashion of Peacock's (and Mr Mallock's) development of the ancient dialogue; but this encumbered me with unnecessary characters and the inevitable complication of intrigue among them, and I abandoned it. After that I tried to cast the thing into a shape resembling a little the double personality of Boswell's Johnson, a sort of interplay between monologue and commentator; but that too, although it got nearer to the quality I sought, finally failed. Then I hesitated over what one might call 'hard narrative'. It will be evident to the experienced reader that by omitting certain speculative and metaphysical elements and by elaborating incident, this book might have been reduced to a straightforward story. But I did not want to omit as much on this occasion. I do not see why I should always pander to the vulgar appetite for stark stories. And in short, I made it this. I explain all this in order to make it clear to the reader that, however queer this book appears at the first examination, it is the outcome of trial and deliberation, it is intended to be as it is. I am aiming throughout at a sort of shot-silk texture between philosophical discussion on the one hand and imaginative narrative on the other.

H. G. WELLS

The Owner of the Voice

There are works, and this is one of them, that are best begun with a portrait of the author. And here, indeed, because of a very natural misunderstanding, this is the only course to take. Throughout these papers sounds a note, a distinctive and personal note, a note that tends at times towards stridency; and all that is not, as these words are, in Italics, is in one Voice. Now this Voice, and this is the peculiarity of the matter, is not to be taken as the Voice of the ostensible author who fathers these pages. You have to clear your mind of any preconceptions in that respect. The Owner of the Voice you must figure to yourself as a whitish plump man, a little under the middle size and age, with such blue eyes as many Irishmen have, and agile in his movements and with a slight tonsorial baldness – a penny might cover it – of the crown. His front is convex. He droops at times like most of us, but for the greater part he bears himself as valiantly as a sparrow. Occasionally his hand flies out with a fluttering gesture of illustration. And his Voice (which is our medium henceforth) is an unattractive tenor that becomes at times aggressive. Him you must imagine as sitting at a table reading a manuscript about Utopias, a manuscript he holds in two hands that are just a little fat at the wrist. The curtain rises upon him so. But afterwards, if the devices of this declining art of literature prevail, you will go with him through curious and interesting experiences. Yet, ever and again, you will find him back at that little table, the manuscript in his hand, and the expansion of his ratiocinations about Utopia conscientiously resumed. The entertainment before you is neither the set drama of the work of fiction you are accustomed to read, nor the set lecturing of the essay you are accustomed to evade, but a hybrid of these two. If you figure this owner of the Voice as sitting, a little nervously, a little modestly, on a stage, with table, glass of water and all complete, and myself as the intrusive chairman insisting with a bland ruthlessness upon his 'few words' of introduction before he recedes into the wings, and if furthermore you figure a sheet behind our friend on which moving pictures intermittently appear, and if finally you suppose his subject to be the story of the adventure of his soul among Utopian enquiries, you will be prepared for some at least of the difficulties of this unworthy but unusual work.

But over against this writer here presented, there is also another earthly person in the book, who gathers himself together into a distinct personality only after a preliminary complication with the reader. This person is spoken of as the botanist, and he is a leaner, rather taller, graver and much less garrulous man. His face is weakly handsome and done in tones of grey, he is fairish and grey-eyed, and you would suspect him of dyspepsia. It is a justifiable suspicion. Men of this type, the chairman remarks with a sudden intrusion of exposition, are romantic with a shadow of meanness, they seek at once to conceal and shape their sensuous cravings beneath egregious sentimentalities, they get into mighty tangles and troubles with women, and he has had his troubles. You will hear of them, for that is the quality of his type. He gets no personal expression in this book, the Voice is always that other's, but you gather much of the matter and something of the manner of his interpolations from the asides and the tenor of the Voice.

So much by way of portraiture is necessary to present the explorers of the Modern Utopia, which will unfold itself as a background to these two enquiring figures. The image of a cinematograph entertainment is the one to grasp. There will be an effect of these two people going to and fro in front of the circle of a rather defective lantern, which sometimes jams and sometimes gets out of focus, but which does occasionally succeed in displaying on a screen a momentary moving picture of Utopian conditions. Occasionally the picture goes out altogether, the Voice argues and argues, and the footlights return, and then you find yourself listening again to the rather too plump little man at his table laboriously enunciating propositions, upon whom the curtain rises now.

CHAPTER ONE

Topographical

The Utopia of a modern dreamer must needs differ in one fundamental aspect from the Nowheres and Utopias men planned before Darwin quickened the thought of the world. Those were all perfect and static States, a balance of happiness won for ever against the forces of unrest and disorder that inhere in things. One beheld a healthy and simple generation enjoying the fruits of the earth in an atmosphere of virtue and happiness, to be followed by other virtuous, happy, and entirely similar generations until the Gods grew weary. Change and development were dammed back by invincible dams for ever. But the Modern Utopia must be not static but kinetic, must shape not as a permanent state but as a hopeful stage, leading to a long ascent of stages. Nowadays we do not resist and overcome the great stream of things, but rather float upon it. We build now not citadels, but ships of state. For one ordered arrangement of citizens rejoicing in an equality of happiness safe and assured to them and their children for ever, we have to plan 'a flexible common compromise, in which a perpetually novel succession of individualities may converge most effectually upon a comprehensive onward development'. That is the first, most generalised difference between a Utopia based upon modern conceptions and all the Utopias that were written in the former time.

Our business here is to be Utopian, to make vivid and credible, if we can, first this facet and then that, of an imaginary whole and happy world. Our deliberate intention is to be not, indeed, impossible, but most distinctly impracticable, by every scale that reaches only between today and tomorrow. We are to turn our backs for a space upon the insistent examination of the thing that is, and face towards the freer air, the ampler spaces of the thing that perhaps might be, to the projection of a State or city 'worthwhile', to designing upon the sheet of our imaginations the picture of a life conceivably possible, and yet better worth living than our own. That is our present enterprise. We are going to lay down certain necessary starting propositions, and then we shall proceed to explore the sort of world these propositions give us . . .

It is no doubt an optimistic enterprise. But it is good for a while to be free from the carping note that must needs be audible when we discuss our present imperfections, to release ourselves from practical difficulties and the tangle of ways and means. It is good to stop by the track for a space, put aside the knapsack, wipe the brows, and talk a little of the upper slopes of the mountain we think we are climbing, would but the trees let us see it.

There is to be no enquiry here of policy and method. This is to be a holiday from politics and movements and methods. But for all that, we must needs define certain limitations. Were we free to have our untrammelled desire, I suppose we should follow Morris to his Nowhere, we should change the nature of man and the nature of things together; we should make the whole race wise, tolerant, noble, perfect – wave our hands to a splendid anarchy, every man doing as it pleases him, and none pleased to do evil, in a world as good in its essential nature, as ripe and sunny, as the world before the Fall. But that golden age, that perfect world, comes out into the possibilities of space and time. In space and time the pervading Will to Live sustains for evermore a perpetuity of aggressions. Our proposal here is upon a more practical plane at least than that. We are to restrict ourselves first to the limitations of human possibility as we know them in the men and women of this world today, and then to all the inhumanity, all the insubordination of nature. We are to shape our state in a world of uncertain seasons, sudden catastrophes, antagonistic diseases, and inimical beasts and vermin, out of men and women with like passions, like uncertainties of mood and desire to our own. And, moreover, we are going to accept this world of conflict, to adopt no attitude of renunciation towards it, to face it in no ascetic spirit, but in the mood of the Western peoples, whose purpose is to survive and overcome. So much we adopt in common with those who deal not in Utopias, but in the world of Here and Now.

Certain liberties, however, following the best Utopian precedents, we may take with existing fact. We assume that the tone of public thought may be entirely different from what it is in the present world. We permit ourselves a free hand with the mental conflict of life, within the possibilities of the human mind as we know it. We permit ourselves also a free hand with all the apparatus of existence that man has, so to speak, made for himself, with houses, roads, clothing, canals, machinery, with laws, boundaries, conventions, and traditions, with schools, with liter-ature and religious organisation, with creeds and customs, with every-thing, in fact, that it lies within man's power to alter. That, indeed, is the cardinal assumption of all Utopian speculations old and new; the *Republic* and *Laws* of Plato, and More's *Utopia*, Howells' implicit *Altruria*, and

Bellamy's future *Boston*, Comte's great *Western Republic*, Hertzka's *Freeland*, Cabet's *Icaria*, and Campanella's *City of the Sun*, are built, just as we shall build, upon that, upon the hypothesis of the complete emancipation of a community of men from tradition, from habits, from legal bonds, and that subtler servitude possessions entail. And much of the essential value of all such speculations lies in this assumption of emancipation, lies in that regard towards human freedom, in the undying interest of the human power of self-escape, the power to resist the causation of the past, and to evade, initiate, endeavour, and overcome.

2

There are very definite artistic limitations also. There must always be a certain effect of hardness and thinness about Utopian speculations. Their common fault is to be comprehensively jejune. That which is the blood and warmth and reality of life is largely absent; there are no individualities, but only generalised people. In almost every Utopia – except, perhaps, Morris's *News from Nowhere* – one sees handsome but characterless buildings, symmetrical and perfect cultivations, and a multitude of people, healthy, happy, beautifully dressed, but without any personal distinction whatever. Too often the prospect resembles the key to one of those large pictures of coronations, royal weddings, parliaments, conferences, and gatherings so popular in Victorian times, in which, instead of a face, each figure bears a neat oval with its index number legibly inscribed. This burthens us with an incurable effect of unreality, and I do not see how it is altogether to be escaped. It is a disadvantage that has to be accepted. Whatever institution has existed or exists, however irrational, however preposterous, has, by virtue of its contact with individualities, an effect of realness and rightness no untried thing may share. It has ripened, it has been christened with blood, it has been stained and mellowed by handling, it has been rounded and dented to the softened contours that we associate with life; it has been salted, maybe, in a brine of tears. But the thing that is merely proposed, the thing that is merely suggested, however rational, however necessary, seems strange and inhuman in its clear, hard, uncompromising lines, its unqualified angles and surfaces.

There is no help for it, there it is! The Master suffers with the last and least of his successors. For all the humanity he wins to, through his dramatic device of dialogue, I doubt if anyone has ever been warmed to desire himself a citizen in the Republic of Plato; I doubt if anyone could

stand a month of the relentless publicity of virtue planned by More . . .
No one wants to live in any community of intercourse really, save for
the sake of the individualities he would meet there. The fertilising
conflict of individualities is the ultimate meaning of the personal life,
and all our Utopias no more than schemes for bettering that interplay.
At least, that is how life shapes itself more and more to modern per-
ceptions. Until you bring in individualities, nothing comes into being,
and a Universe ceases when you shiver the mirror of the least of
individual minds.

3

No less than a planet will serve the purpose of a modern Utopia. Time
was when a mountain valley or an island seemed to promise sufficient
isolation for a polity to maintain itself intact from outward force; the
Republic of Plato stood armed ready for defensive war, and the New
Atlantis and the Utopia of More in theory, like China and Japan
through many centuries of effectual practice, held themselves isolated
from intruders. Such late instances as Butler's satirical *Erewhon*, and
Mr Stead's queendom of inverted sexual conditions in Central Africa,
found the Tibetan method of slaughtering the enquiring visitor a
simple, sufficient rule. But the whole trend of modern thought is
against the permanence of any such enclosures. We are acutely aware
nowadays that, however subtly contrived a State may be, outside your
boundary lines the epidemic, the breeding barbarian or the economic
power will gather its strength to overcome you. The swift march of
invention is all for the invader. Now perhaps you might still guard a
rocky coast or a narrow pass; but what of that near tomorrow when the
flying machine soars overhead, free to descend at this point or that? A
state powerful enough to keep isolated under modern conditions would
be powerful enough to rule the world, would be, indeed, if not actively
ruling, yet passively acquiescent in all other human organisations, and
so responsible for them altogether. World State, therefore, it must be.

That leaves no room for a modern Utopia in Central Africa, or in
South America, or round about the pole, those last refuges of ideality.
The floating isle of *La Cité Morellyste* no longer avails. We need a planet.
Lord Erskine, the author of a Utopia ('Armata') that might have been
inspired by Mr Hewins, was the first of all Utopists to perceive this – he
joined his twin planets pole to pole by a sort of umbilical cord. But the
modern imagination, obsessed by physics, must travel further than that.

Out beyond Sirius, far in the deeps of space, beyond the flight of a cannonball flying for a billion years, beyond the range of unaided vision, blazes the star that is *our* Utopia's sun. To those who know where to look, with a good opera-glass aiding good eyes, it and three fellows that seem in a cluster with it – though they are incredible billions of miles nearer – make just the faintest speck of light. About it go planets, even as our planets, but weaving a different fate, and in its place among them is Utopia, with its sister mate, the Moon. It is a planet like our planet, the same continents, the same islands, the same oceans and seas, another Fujiyama is beautiful there dominating another Yokohama – and another Matterhorn overlooks the icy disorder of another Theodule. It is so like our planet that a terrestrial botanist might find his every species there, even to the meanest pond weed or the remotest Alpine blossom . . .

Only when he had gathered that last and turned about to find his inn again, perhaps he would not find his inn!

Suppose now that two of us were actually to turn about in just that fashion. Two, I think, for to face a strange planet, even though it be a wholly civilised one, without some other familiar backing, dashes the courage overmuch. Suppose that we were indeed so translated even as we stood. You figure us upon some high pass in the Alps, and though I – being one easily made giddy by stooping – am no botanist myself, if my companion were to have a specimen tin under his arm – so long as it is not painted that abominable popular Swiss apple green – I would make it no occasion for quarrel! We have tramped and botanised and come to a rest, and, sitting among rocks, we have eaten our lunch and finished our bottle of Yvorne, and fallen into a talk of Utopias, and said such things as I have been saying. I could figure it myself upon that little neck of the Lucendro Pass, upon the shoulder of the Piz Lucendro, for there once I lunched and talked very pleasantly, and we are looking down upon the Val Bedretto, and Villa and Fontana and Airolo try to hide from us under the mountain side – three-quarters of a mile they are vertically below. (*Lantern.*) With that absurd nearness of effect one gets in the Alps, we see the little train a dozen miles away, running down the Biaschina to Italy, and the Lukmanier Pass beyond Piora left of us, and the San Giacomo right, mere footpaths under our feet . . .

And behold! in the twinkling of an eye we are in that other world!

We should scarcely note the change. Not a cloud would have gone from the sky. It might be the remote town below would take a different air, and my companion the botanist, with his educated observation, might almost see as much, and the train, perhaps, would be gone out of the picture, and the embanked straightness of the Ticino in the Ambri-Piotta meadows – that might be altered, but that would be all the visible change. Yet I have an idea that in some obscure manner we should come to feel at once a difference in things.

The botanist's glance would, under a subtle attraction, float back to Airolo. 'It's queer,' he would say quite idly, 'but I never noticed that building there to the right before.'

'Which building?'

'That to the right – with a queer sort of thing – '

'I see now. Yes. Yes, it's certainly an odd-looking affair . . . And big, you know! Handsome! I wonder – '

That would interrupt our Utopian speculations. We should both discover that the little towns below had changed – but how, we should not have marked them well enough to know. It would be indefinable, a change in the quality of their grouping, a change in the quality of their remote, small shapes.

I should flick a few crumbs from my knee, perhaps. 'It's odd,' I should say, for the tenth or eleventh time, with a motion to rise, and we should get up and stretch ourselves, and, still a little puzzled, turn our faces towards the path that clambers down over the tumbled rocks and runs round by the still clear lake and down towards the Hospice of St Gotthard – if perchance we could still find that path.

Long before we got to that, before even we got to the great high road, we should have hints from the stone cabin in the nape of the pass – it would be gone or wonderfully changed – from the very goats upon the rocks, from the little hut by the rough bridge of stone, that a mighty difference had come to the world of men.

And presently, amazed and amazing, we should happen on a man – no Swiss – dressed in unfamiliar clothing and speaking an unfamiliar speech . . .

4

Before nightfall we should be drenched in wonders, but still we should have wonder left for the thing my companion, with his scientific training, would no doubt be the first to see. He would glance up, with that proprietary eye of the man who knows his constellations down to the little Greek letters. I imagine his exclamation. He would at first doubt his eyes. I should enquire the cause of his consternation, and it would be hard to explain. He would ask me with a certain singularity of manner for Orion, and I should not find him; for the Great Bear, and it would have vanished. 'Where?' I should ask, and 'where?' seeking among that scattered starriness, and slowly I should acquire the wonder that possessed him.

Then, for the first time, perhaps, we should realise from this unfamiliar heaven that not the world had changed, but ourselves – that we had come into the uttermost deeps of space.

5

We need suppose no linguistic impediments to intercourse. The whole world will surely have a common language, that is quite elementarily Utopian; and since we are free of the trammels of convincing storytelling, we may suppose that language to be sufficiently our own to understand. Indeed, should we be in Utopia at all, if we could not talk to everyone? That accursed bar of language, that hostile inscription in the foreigner's eyes, 'deaf and dumb to you, sir, and so – your enemy', is the very first of the defects and complications one has fled the earth to escape.

But what sort of language would we have the world speak, if we were told the miracle of Babel was presently to be reversed?

If I may take a daring image, a mediaeval liberty, I would suppose that in this lonely place the Spirit of Creation spoke to us on this matter. 'You are wise men,' that Spirit might say – and I, being a suspicious, touchy, over-earnest man for all my predisposition to plumpness, would instantly scent the irony (while my companion, I fancy, might even plume himself), 'and to beget your wisdom is chiefly why the world was made. You are so good as to propose an acceleration of that tedious multitudinous evolution upon which I am engaged. I gather, a universal tongue would serve you there. While I sit here among these mountains – I have been filing away at them for this last aeon or so, just to attract your hotels, you know – will you be so kind – ? A few hints – ?'

Then the Spirit of Creation might transiently smile, a smile that would be like the passing of a cloud. All the mountain wilderness about us would be radiantly lit. (You know those swift moments, when warmth and brightness drift by, in lonely and desolate places.)

Yet, after all, why should two men be smiled into apathy by the Infinite? Here we are, with our knobby little heads, our eyes and hands and feet and stout hearts, and if not us or ours, still the endless multitudes about us and in our loins are to come at last to the World State and a greater fellowship and the universal tongue. Let us to the extent of our ability, if not answer that question, at any rate try to think ourselves within sight of the best thing possible. That, after all, is our purpose, to imagine our best and strive for it, and it is a worse folly and a worse sin than presumption, to abandon striving because the best of all our bests looks mean amidst the suns.

Now you as a botanist would, I suppose, incline to something as they say, '*scientific*'. You wince under that most offensive epithet – and I am able to give you my intelligent sympathy – though 'pseudo-scientific' and 'quasi-scientific' are worse by far for the skin. You would begin to talk of scientific languages, of Esperanto, La Langue Bleue, New Latin, Volapuk, and Lord Lytton, of the philosophical language of Archbishop Whateley, Lady Welby's work upon Significs and the like. You would tell me of the remarkable precisions, the encyclopaedic quality of chemical terminology, and at the word terminology I should insinuate a comment on that eminent American biologist, Professor Mark Baldwin, who has carried the language biological to such heights of expressive clearness as to be triumphantly and invincibly unreadable. (Which foreshadows the line of my defence.)

You make your ideal clear, a scientific language you demand, without ambiguity, as precise as mathematical formulae, and with every term in relations of exact logical consistency with every other. It will be a language with all the inflexions of verbs and nouns regular and all its constructions inevitable, each word clearly distinguishable from every other word in sound as well as spelling.

That, at any rate, is the sort of thing one hears demanded, and if only because the demand rests upon implications that reach far beyond the region of language, it is worth considering here. It implies, indeed, almost everything that we are endeavouring to repudiate in this particular work. It implies that the whole intellectual basis of mankind is established, that the rules of logic, the systems of counting and measurement, the general categories and schemes of resemblance and difference, are established for the human mind for ever – blank Comte-ism, in fact, of the blankest description. But, indeed, the science of logic and the whole framework of philosophical thought men have kept since the days of Plato and Aristotle, has no more essential permanence as a final expression of the human mind, than the Scottish Longer Catechism. Amidst the welter of modern thought, a philosophy long lost to men rises again into being, like some blind and almost formless embryo, that must presently develop sight, and form, and power, a philosophy in which this assumption is denied.*

All through this Utopian excursion, I must warn you, you shall feel the thrust and disturbance of that insurgent movement. In the reiterated use of 'Unique', you will, as it were, get the gleam of its integument; in the insistence upon individuality, and the individual difference as the significance of life, you will feel the texture of its shaping body. Nothing endures, nothing is precise and certain (except the mind of a pedant), perfection is the mere repudiation of that ineluctable marginal in-exactitude which is the mysterious inmost quality of Being. Being, indeed! – there is no being, but a universal becoming of individualities, and Plato turned his back on truth when he turned towards his museum of specific ideals. Heraclitus, that lost and misinterpreted giant, may perhaps be coming to his own . . .

There is no abiding thing in what we know. We change from weaker to stronger lights, and each more powerful light pierces our hitherto opaque foundations and reveals fresh and different opacities below. We can never foretell which of our seemingly assured fundamentals the next change will not affect. What folly, then, to dream of mapping out our minds in however general terms, of providing for the endless mysteries of the future a terminology and an idiom! We follow the vein, we mine and accumulate our treasure, but who can tell which way the vein may trend? Language is the nourishment of the thought of man, that serves only as it undergoes metabolism, and becomes thought and lives, and in its very living passes away. You scientific people, with your fancy of a terrible exactitude in language, of indestructible foundations built, as that Wordsworthian doggerel on the title-page of Nature says, 'for aye', are marvellously without imagination!

The language of Utopia will no doubt be one and indivisible; all mankind will, in the measure of their individual differences in quality, be brought into the same phase, into a common resonance of thought, but the language they will speak will still be a living tongue, an animated system of imperfections, which every individual man will infinitesimally modify. Through the universal freedom of exchange and movement, the

---

*   The serious reader may refer at leisure to Sidgwick's *Use of Words in Reasoning* (particularly), and to Bosanquet's *Essentials of Logic*, Bradley's *Principles of Logic*, and Sigwart's *Logik*; the lighter-minded may read and mark the temper of Professor Case in the British Encyclopaedia, article 'Logic' (Vol. XXX). I have appended to this book a rude sketch of a philosophy upon new lines, originally read by me to the Oxford Philosophical Society in 1903.

developing change in its general spirit will be a worldwide change; that is the quality of its universality. I fancy it will be a coalesced language, a synthesis of many. Such a language as English is a coalesced language; it is a coalescence of Anglo-Saxon and Norman French and Scholar's Latin, welded into one speech more ample and more powerful and beautiful than either. The Utopian tongue might well present a more spacious coalescence, and hold in the frame of such an uninflected or slightly inflected idiom as English already presents, a profuse vocabulary into which have been cast a dozen once separate tongues, superposed and then welded together through bilingual and trilingual compromises.* In the past ingenious men have speculated on the enquiry, 'Which language will survive?' The question was badly put. I think now that this wedding and survival of several in a common offspring is a far more probable thing.

6

This talk of languages, however, is a digression. We were on our way along the faint path that runs round the rim of the Lake of Lucendro, and we were just upon the point of coming upon our first Utopian man. He was, I said, no Swiss. Yet he would have been a Swiss on mother Earth, and here he would have the same face, with some difference, maybe, in the expression; the same physique, though a little better developed, perhaps – the same complexion. He would have different habits, different traditions, different knowledge, different ideas, different clothing, and different appliances, but, except for all that, he would be the same man. We very distinctly provided at the outset that the modern Utopia must have people inherently the same as those in the world.

There is more, perhaps, in that than appears at the first suggestion.

That proposition gives one characteristic difference between a modern Utopia and almost all its predecessors. It is to be a world Utopia, we have agreed, no less; and so we must needs face the fact that we are to have differences of race. Even the lower class of Plato's Republic was not specifically of different race. But this is a Utopia as wide as Christian charity, and white and black, brown, red and yellow, all tints of skin, all types of body and character, will be there. How we

* *Vide* an excellent article, *La Langue Française en l'an 2003*, par Léon Bollack, in *La Revue*, 15 juillet, 1903.

are to adjust their differences is a master question, and the matter is not even to be opened in this chapter. It will need a whole chapter even to glance at its issues. But here we underline that stipulation; every race of this planet earth is to be found in the strictest parallelism there, in numbers the same – only, as I say, with an entirely different set of traditions, ideals, ideas, and purposes, and so moving under those different skies to an altogether different destiny.

There follows a curious development of this to anyone clearly impressed by the uniqueness and the unique significance of individualities. Races are no hard and fast things, no crowd of identically similar persons, but massed sub-races, and tribes and families, each after its kind unique, and these again are clusterings of still smaller uniques and so down to each several person. So that our first convention works out to this, that not only is every earthly mountain, river, plant, and beast in that parallel planet beyond Sirius also, but every man, woman, and child alive has a Utopian parallel. From now onward, of course, the fates of these two planets will diverge, men will die here whom wisdom will save there, and perhaps conversely here we shall save men; children will be born to them and not to us, to us and not to them, but this, this moment of reading, is the starting moment, and for the first and last occasion the populations of our planets are abreast.

We must in these days make some such supposition. The alternative is a Utopia of dolls in the likeness of angels – imaginary laws to fit incredible people, an unattractive undertaking.

For example, we must assume there is a man such as I might have been, better informed, better disciplined, better employed, thinner and more active – and I wonder what he is doing! – and you, Sir or Madam, are in duplicate also, and all the men and women that you know and I. I doubt if we shall meet our doubles, or if it would be pleasant for us to do so; but as we come down from these lonely mountains to the roads and houses and living places of the Utopian World State, we shall certainly find, here and there, faces that will remind us singularly of those who have lived under our eyes.

There are some you never wish to meet again, you say, and some, I gather, you do. 'And One – !'

It is strange, but this figure of the botanist will not keep in place. It sprang up between us, dear reader, as a passing illustrative invention. I do not know what put him into my head, and for the moment, it fell in with my humour for a space to foist the man's personality upon you as yours and call you scientific – that most abusive word. But here he is, indisputably, with me in Utopia, and lapsing from our high speculative theme into halting but intimate confidences. He declares he has not come to Utopia to meet again with his sorrows.

What sorrows?

I protest, even warmly, that neither he nor his sorrows were in my intention.

He is a man, I should think, of thirty-nine, a man whose life has been neither tragedy nor a joyous adventure, a man with one of those faces that have gained interest rather than force or nobility from their commerce with life. He is something refined, with some knowledge, perhaps, of the minor pains and all the civil self-controls; he has read more than he has suffered, and suffered rather than done. He regards me with his blue-grey eye, from which all interest in this Utopia has faded.

'It is a trouble,' he says, 'that has come into my life only for a month or so – at least acutely again. I thought it was all over. There was someone – '

It is an amazing story to hear upon a mountain crest in Utopia, this Hampstead affair, this story of a Frognal heart. 'Frognal', he says, is the place where they met, and it summons to my memory the word on a board at the corner of a flint-dressed new road, an estate development road, with a vista of villas up a hill. He had known her before he got his professorship, and neither her 'people' nor his – he speaks that detestable middle-class dialect in which aunts and things with money and the right of intervention are called 'people'! – approved of the affair. 'She was, I think, rather easily swayed,' he says. 'But that's not fair to her, perhaps. She thought too much of others. If they seemed distressed, or if they seemed to think a course right – ' . . .

Have I come to Utopia to hear this sort of thing?

7

It is necessary to turn the botanist's thoughts into a worthier channel. It is necessary to override these modest regrets, this intrusive, petty love story. Does he realise this is indeed Utopia? Turn your mind, I insist, to this Utopia of mine, and leave these earthly troubles to their proper planet. Do you realise just where the propositions necessary to a modern Utopia are taking us? Everyone on earth will have to be here; – themselves, but with a difference. Somewhere here in this world is, for example, Mr Chamberlain, and the King is here (no doubt incognito), and all the Royal Academy, and Sandow, and Mr Arnold White.

But these famous names do not appeal to him.

My mind goes from this prominent and typical personage to that, and for a time I forget my companion. I am distracted by the curious side issues this general proposition trails after it. There will be so-and-so, and so-and-so. The name and figure of Mr Roosevelt jerks into focus, and obliterates an attempt to acclimatise the Emperor of the Germans. What, for instance, will Utopia do with Mr Roosevelt? There drifts across my inner vision the image of a strenuous struggle with Utopian constables, the voice that has thrilled terrestrial millions in eloquent protest. The writ of arrest, drifting loose in the conflict, comes to my feet; I impale the scrap of paper, and read – but can it be? – 'attempted disorganisation . . . incitements to disarrange . . . the balance of population.'

The trend of my logic for once has led us into a facetious alley. One might indeed keep in this key, and write an agreeable little Utopia, that like the holy families of the mediaeval artists (or Michelangelo's *Last Judgement*) should compliment one's friends in various degrees. Or one might embark upon a speculative treatment of the entire *Almanach de Gotha*, something on the lines of Epistemon's vision of the damned great, when

> Xerxes was a crier of mustard.
> Romulus was a salter and a patcher of patterns . . .

That incomparable catalogue! That incomparable catalogue! Inspired by the Muse of Parody, we might go on to the pages of *Who's Who*, and even, with an eye to the obdurate republic, to *Who's Who in America*, and make the most delightful and extensive arrangements. Now where shall we put this most excellent man? And this? . . .

But, indeed, it is doubtful if we shall meet any of these doubles during our Utopian journey, or know them when we meet them. I doubt if anyone will be making the best of both these worlds. The great men in this still unexplored Utopia may be but village Hampdens in our own, and earthly goatherds and obscure illiterates sit here in the seats of the mighty.

That again opens agreeable vistas left of us and right.

But my botanist obtrudes his personality again. His thoughts have travelled by a different route.

'I know,' he says, 'that she will be happier here, and that they will value her better than she has been valued upon earth.'

His interruption serves to turn me back from my momentary contemplation of those popular effigies inflated by old newspapers and windy report, the earthly great. He sets me thinking of more personal and intimate applications, of the human beings one knows with a certain approximation to real knowledge, of the actual common substance of life. He turns me to the thought of rivalries and tendernesses, of differences and disappointments. I am suddenly brought painfully against the things that might have been. What if instead of that Utopia of vacant ovals we meet relinquished loves here, and opportunities lost and faces as they might have looked to us?

I turn to my botanist almost reprovingly. 'You know, she won't be quite the same lady here that you knew in Frognal,' I say, and wrest myself from a subject that is no longer agreeable by rising to my feet.

'And besides,' I say, standing above him, 'the chances against our meeting her are a million to one . . . And we loiter! This is not the business we have come upon, but a mere incidental kink in our larger plan. The fact remains, these people we have come to see are people with like infirmities to our own – and only the conditions are changed. Let us pursue the tenor of our enquiry.'

With that I lead the way round the edge of the Lake of Lucendro towards our Utopian world. (*You figure him doing it.*) Down the mountain we shall go and down the passes, and as the valleys open the world will open – Utopia, where men and women are happy and laws are wise, and where all that is tangled and confused in human affairs has been unravelled and made right.

CHAPTER TWO

Concerning Freedoms

1

Now what sort of question would first occur to two men descending upon the planet of a Modern Utopia? Probably grave solicitude about their personal freedom. Towards the Stranger, as I have already remarked, the Utopias of the past displayed their least amiable aspect. Would this new sort of Utopian State, spread to the dimensions of a world, be any less forbidding?

We should take comfort in the thought that universal Toleration is certainly a modern idea, and it is upon modern ideas that this World State rests. But even suppose we are tolerated and admitted to this unavoidable citizenship, there will still remain a wide range of possibility ... I think we should try to work the problem out from an enquiry into first principles, and that we should follow the trend of our time and kind by taking up the question as one of 'Man *v.* the State', and discussing the compromise of Liberty.

The idea of individual liberty is one that has grown in importance and grows with every development of modern thought. To the classical Utopists freedom was relatively trivial. Clearly they considered virtue and happiness as entirely separable from liberty, and as being altogether more important things. But the modern view, with its deepening insistence upon individuality and upon the significance of its uniqueness, steadily intensifies the value of freedom, until at last we begin to see liberty as the very substance of life, that indeed it is life, and that only the dead things, the choiceless things, live in absolute obedience to law. To have free play for one's individuality is, in the modern view, the subjective triumph of existence, as survival in creative work and offspring is its objective triumph. But for all men, since man is a social creature, the play of will must fall short of absolute freedom. Perfect human liberty is possible only to a despot who is absolutely and universally obeyed. Then to will would be to command and achieve, and within the limits of natural law we could at any moment do exactly as it pleased us to do. All other liberty is a compromise between our own freedom of will and the wills of those with whom we come in contact. In an organised state each one of us has a more or less elaborate code of what he may do to others and to himself, and what others may do to him. He limits others by his rights, and is limited by the rights of others, and by considerations affecting the welfare of the community as a whole.

Individual liberty in a community is not, as mathematicians would say, always of the same sign. To ignore this is the essential fallacy of the cult called Individualism. But in truth, a general prohibition in a state may increase the sum of liberty, and a general permission may diminish it. It does not follow, as these people would have us believe, that a man is more free where there is least law and more restricted where there is most law. A socialism or a communism is not necessarily a slavery, and there is no freedom under Anarchy. Consider how much liberty we gain by the loss of the common liberty to kill. Thereby one may go to and fro in all the ordered parts of the earth, unencumbered by arms or armour, free of the fear of playful poison, whimsical barbers, or hotel trap-doors. Indeed, it means freedom from a thousand fears and precautions. Suppose there existed even the limited freedom to kill in vendetta, and think what would happen in our suburbs. Consider the inconvenience of two households in a modern suburb estranged and provided with modern weapons of precision, the inconvenience not only to each other, but to the neutral pedestrian, the practical loss of freedoms all about them. The butcher, if he came at all, would have to come round in an armoured cart . . .

It follows, therefore, in a modern Utopia, which finds the final hope of the world in the evolving interplay of unique individualities, that the State will have effectually chipped away just all those spendthrift liberties that waste liberty, and not one liberty more, and so have attained the maximum general freedom.

There are two distinct and contrasting methods of limiting liberty; the first is Prohibition, 'thou shalt not', and the second Command, 'thou shalt'. There is, however, a sort of prohibition that takes the form of a conditional command, and this one needs to bear in mind. It says if you do so-and-so, you must also do so-and-so; if, for example, you go to sea with men you employ, you must go in a seaworthy vessel. But the pure command is unconditional; it says, whatever you have done or are doing or want to do, you are to do this, as when the social system, working through the base necessities of base parents and bad laws, sends a child of thirteen into a factory. Prohibition takes one definite thing from the indefinite liberty of a man, but it still leaves him an unbounded choice of actions. He remains free, and you have merely taken a bucketful from the sea of his freedom. But compulsion destroys freedom altogether. In this Utopia of ours there may be many prohibitions, but no indirect compulsions – if one may so contrive it – and few or no commands. As far as I see it now, in this present discussion, I think, indeed, there should be no positive compulsions at all in Utopia, at any rate for the adult Utopian – unless they fall upon him as penalties incurred.

2

What prohibitions should we be under, we two Uitlanders in this Utopian world? We should certainly not be free to kill, assault, or threaten anyone we met, and in that we earth-trained men would not be likely to offend. And until we knew more exactly the Utopian idea of property we should be very chary of touching anything that might conceivably be appropriated. If it was not the property of individuals it might be the property of the State. But beyond that we might have our doubts. Are we right in wearing the strange costumes we do, in choosing the path that pleases us athwart this rock and turf, in coming striding with unfumigated rucksacks and snow-wet hobnails into what is conceivably an extremely neat and orderly world? We have passed our first Utopian now, with an answered vague gesture, and have noted, with secret satisfaction, there is no access of dismay; we have rounded a bend, and down the valley in the distance we get a glimpse of what appears to be a singularly well-kept road . . .

I submit that to the modern-minded man it can be no sort of Utopia worth desiring that does not give the utmost freedom of going to and fro. Free movement is to many people one of the greatest of life's privileges – to go wherever the spirit moves them, to wander and see – and though they have every comfort, every security, every virtuous discipline, they will still be unhappy if that is denied them. Short of damage to things cherished and made, the Utopians will surely have this right, so we may expect no unclimbable walls and fences, nor the discovery of any laws we may transgress in coming down these mountain places.

And yet, just as civil liberty itself is a compromise defended by prohibitions, so this particular sort of liberty must also have its qualifications. Carried to the absolute pitch the right of free movement ceases to be distinguishable from the right of free intrusion. We have already, in a comment on More's Utopia, hinted at an agreement with Aristotle's argument against communism, that it flings people into an intolerable continuity of contact. Schopenhauer carried out Aristotle in the vein of his own bitterness and with the truest of images when he likened human society to hedgehogs clustering for warmth, and unhappy when either too closely packed or too widely separated. Empedocles found no significance in life whatever except as an unsteady play of love and hate, of attraction and repulsion, of assimilation and the assertion of difference. So long as we ignore difference, so long as we ignore individuality and that I hold has been the common sin of all Utopias hitherto we can make absolute statements, prescribe communisms or individualisms, and all sorts of hard theoretic arrangements. But in the world of reality, which – to modernise Heraclitus and Empedocles – is nothing more nor less than the world of individuality, there are no absolute rights and wrongs, there are no qualitative questions at all, but only quantitative adjustments. Equally strong in the normal civilised man is the desire for freedom of movement and the desire for a certain privacy, for a corner definitely his, and we have to consider where the line of reconciliation comes.

The desire for absolute personal privacy is perhaps never a very strong or persistent craving. In the great majority of human beings, the gregarious instinct is sufficiently powerful to render any but the most temporary isolations not simply disagreeable, but painful. The savage has all the privacy he needs within the compass of his skull; like dogs and timid women, he prefers ill-treatment to desertion, and it is only a scarce and complex modern type that finds comfort and refreshment in lonely places and solitary occupations. Yet such there are, men who can neither sleep well nor think well, nor attain to a full perception of beautiful objects, who do not savour the best of existence until they are securely alone, and for the sake of these even it would be reasonable to draw some limits to the general right of free movement. But their particular need is only a special and exceptional aspect of an almost universal claim to privacy among modern people, not so much for the sake of isolation as for congenial companionship. We want to go apart from the great crowd, not so much to be alone as to be with those who appeal to us particularly and to whom we particularly appeal; we want to form households and societies with them, to give our individualities play in intercourse with them, and in the appointments and furnishings of that intercourse. We want gardens and enclosures and exclusive freedoms for our like and our choice, just as spacious as we can get them – and it is only the multitudinous uncongenial, anxious also for similar developments in some opposite direction, that checks this expansive movement of personal selection and necessitates a compromise on privacy.

Glancing back from our Utopian mountainside down which this discourse marches, to the confusions of old earth, we may remark that the need and desire for privacies there is exceptionally great at the present time, that it was less in the past, that in the future it may be less again, and that under the Utopian conditions to which we shall come when presently we strike yonder road, it may be reduced to quite manageable dimensions. But this is to be effected not by the suppression of individualities to some common pattern,* but by the broadening of public charity and the general amelioration of mind and manners. It is not by assimilation, that is to say, but by understanding that the modern Utopia achieves itself. The ideal community of man's past was one with a common belief, with common customs and common ceremonies, common manners and common formulae; men of the same society dressed in the same fashion, each according to his defined and understood grade, behaved in the same fashion, loved, worshipped, and died in the same fashion. They did or felt little that did not find a sympathetic publicity. The natural disposition of all peoples, white, black, or brown, a natural disposition that education seeks to destroy, is to insist upon uniformity, to make publicity extremely unsympathetic to even the most harmless departures from the code. To be dressed 'oddly', to behave 'oddly', to eat in a different manner or of different food, to commit, indeed, any breach of the established convention is to give offence and to incur hostility among unsophisticated men. But the disposition of the more original and enterprising minds at all times has been to make such innovations.

This is particularly in evidence in this present age. The almost cataclysmal development of new machinery, the discovery of new materials, and the appearance of new social possibilities through the organised pursuit of material science, has given enormous and unprecedented facilities to the spirit of innovation. The old local order has been broken up or is now being broken up all over the earth, and everywhere societies deliquesce, everywhere men are afloat amidst the wreckage of their flooded conventions, and still tremendously unaware of the thing that has happened. The old local orthodoxies of behaviour, of precedence, the old accepted amusements and employments, the old ritual of conduct in the important small things of the daily life and the old ritual of thought in the things that make discussion, are smashed up and scattered and mixed discordantly together, one use

* More's *Utopia*. 'Whoso will may go in, for there is nothing within the houses that is private or anie man's owne.'

with another, and no worldwide culture of toleration, no courteous admission of differences, no wider understanding has yet replaced them. And so publicity in the modern earth has become confusedly unsympathetic for everyone. Classes are intolerable to classes and sets to sets, contact provokes aggressions, comparisons, persecutions and discomforts, and the subtler people are excessively tormented by a sense of observation, unsympathetic always and often hostile. To live without some sort of segregation from the general mass is impossible in exact proportion to one's individual distinction.

Of course things will be very different in Utopia. Utopia will be saturated with consideration. To us, clad as we are in mountain-soiled tweeds and with no money but British bank-notes negotiable only at a practically infinite distance, this must needs be a reassuring induction. And Utopian manners will not only be tolerant, but almost universally tolerable. Endless things will be understood perfectly and universally that on earth are understood only by a scattered few; baseness of bearing, grossness of manner, will be the distinctive mark of no section of the community whatever. The coarser reasons for privacy, therefore, will not exist here. And that savage sort of shyness, too, that makes so many half-educated people on earth recluse and defensive, that too the Utopians will have escaped by their more liberal breeding. In the cultivated State we are assuming it will be ever so much easier for people to eat in public, rest and amuse themselves in public, and even work in public. Our present need for privacy in many things marks, indeed, a phase of transition from an ease in public in the past due to homogeneity, to an ease in public in the future due to intelligence and good breeding, and in Utopia that transition will be complete. We must bear that in mind throughout the consideration of this question.

Yet, after this allowance has been made, there still remains a considerable claim for privacy in Utopia. The room, or apartments, or home, or mansion, whatever it may be a man or woman maintains, must be private, and under his or her complete dominion; it seems harsh and intrusive to forbid a central garden plot or peristyle, such as one sees in Pompeii, within the house walls, and it is almost as difficult to deny a little private territory beyond the house. Yet if we concede that, it is clear that without some further provision we concede the possibility that the poorer townsman (if there are to be rich and poor in the world) will be forced to walk through endless miles of high fenced villa gardens before he may expand in his little scrap of reserved open country. Such is already the poor Londoner's miserable fate . . . Our Utopia will have, of course, faultless roads and beautifully arranged inter-urban communications, swift trains or motor services or what not, to diffuse its population, and without some anticipatory provisions, the prospect of the residential areas becoming a vast area of defensively walled villa Edens is all too possible.

This is a quantitative question, be it remembered, and not to be dismissed by any statement of principle. Our Utopians will meet it, I presume, by detailed regulations, very probably varying locally with local conditions. Privacy beyond the house might be made a privilege to be paid for in proportion to the area occupied, and the tax on these licences of privacy might increase as the square of the area affected. A maximum fraction of private enclosure for each urban and suburban square mile could be fixed. A distinction could be drawn between an absolutely private garden and a garden private and closed only for a day or a couple of days a week, and at other times open to the well-behaved public. Who, in a really civilised community, would grudge that measure of invasion? Walls could be taxed by height and length, and the enclosure of really natural beauties, of rapids, cascades, gorges, viewpoints, and so forth made impossible. So a reasonable compromise between the vital and conflicting claims of the freedom of movement and the freedom of seclusion might be attained . . .

And as we argue thus we draw nearer and nearer to the road that goes up and over the Gotthard crest and down the Val Tremola towards Italy.

What sort of road would that be?

3

Freedom of movement in a Utopia planned under modern conditions must involve something more than unrestricted pedestrian wanderings, and the very proposition of a World State speaking one common tongue carries with it the idea of a world population travelled and travelling to an extent quite beyond anything our native earth has seen. It is now our terrestrial experience that whenever economic and political developments set a class free to travel, that class at once begins to travel; in England, for example, above the five or six hundred pounds a year level, it is hard to find anyone who is not habitually migratory, who has not been frequently, as people say, 'abroad'. In the modern Utopia travel must be in the common texture of life. To go into fresh climates and fresh scenery, to meet a different complexion of humanity and a different type of home and food and apparatus, to mark unfamiliar trees and plants and flowers and beasts, to climb mountains, to see the snowy night of the North and the blaze of the tropical midday, to follow great rivers, to taste loneliness in desert places, to traverse the gloom of tropical forests and to cross the high seas, will be an essential part of the reward and adventure of life, even for the commonest people . . . This is a bright and pleasant particular in which a modern Utopia must differ again, and differ diametrically, from its predecessors.

We may conclude from what has been done in places upon our earth that the whole Utopian world will be open and accessible and as safe for the wayfarer as France or England is today. The peace of the world will be established for ever, and everywhere, except in remote and desolate places, there will be convenient inns, at least as convenient and trust-worthy as those of Switzerland today; the touring clubs and hotel associations that have tariffed that country and France so effectually will have had their fine Utopian equivalents, and the whole world will be habituated to the coming and going of strangers. The greater part of the world will be as secure and cheaply and easily accessible to everyone as is Zermatt or Lucerne to a Western European of the middle-class at the present time.

On this account alone no places will be so congested as these two are now on earth. With freedom to go everywhere, with easy access every-where, with no dread of difficulties about language, coinage, custom, or law, why should everyone continue to go to just a few special places? Such congestions are merely the measure of the general inaccessibility and insecurity and costliness of contemporary life, an awkward trans-itory phase in the first beginnings of the travel age of mankind.

No doubt the Utopian will travel in many ways. It is unlikely there will be any smoke-disgorging steam railway trains in Utopia, they are already doomed on earth, already threatened with that obsolescence that will endear them to the Ruskins of tomorrow, but a thin spider's web of inconspicuous special routes will cover the land of the world, pierce the mountain masses and tunnel under the seas. These may be double railways or monorails or what not – we are no engineers to judge between such devices – but by means of them the Utopian will travel about the earth from one chief point to another at a speed of two or three hundred miles or more an hour. That will abolish the greater distances . . . One figures these main communications as something after the manner of corridor trains, smooth-running and roomy, open from end to end, with cars in which one may sit and read, cars in which one may take refreshment, cars into which the news of the day comes printing itself from the wires beside the track; cars in which one may have privacy and sleep if one is so disposed, bathroom cars, library cars; a train as comfortable as a good club. There will be no distinctions of class in such a train, because in a civilised world there would be no offence between one kind of man and another, and for the good of the whole world such travelling will be as cheap as it can be, and well within the reach of any but the almost criminally poor.

Such great tramways as this will be used when the Utopians wish to travel fast and far; thereby you will glide all over the land surface of the planet; and feeding them and distributing from them, innumerable minor systems, clean little electric tramways I picture them, will spread out over the land in finer reticulations, growing close and dense in the urban regions and thinning as the population thins. And running beside these lighter railways, and spreading beyond their range, will be the smooth minor high roads such as this one we now approach, upon which independent vehicles, motor cars, cycles, and what not, will go. I doubt if we shall see any horses upon this fine, smooth, clean road; I doubt if there will be many horses on the high roads of Utopia, and, indeed, if they will use draught horses at all upon that planet. Why should they? Where the world gives turf or sand, or along special tracts, the horse will perhaps be ridden for exercise and pleasure, but that will be all the use for him; and as for the other beasts of burden, on the remoter mountain tracks the mule will no doubt still be a picturesque survival, in the desert men will still find a use for the camel, and the elephant may linger to play a part in the pageant of the East. But the burden of the minor traffic, if not the whole of it, will certainly be mechanical. This is what we shall see even while the road is still remote, swift and shapely motor cars going past, cyclists, and in these agreeable mountain regions there will also be pedestrians upon their way. Cycle tracks will abound in Utopia, sometimes following beside the great high roads, but oftener taking their own more agreeable line amidst woods and crops and pastures; and there will be a rich variety of footpaths and minor ways. There will be many footpaths in Utopia. There will be pleasant ways over the scented needles of the mountain pine woods, primrose-strewn tracks amidst the budding thickets of the lower country, paths running beside rushing streams, paths across the wide spaces of the corn land, and, above all, paths through the flowery garden spaces amidst which the houses in the towns will stand. And everywhere about the world, on road and path, by sea and land, the happy holiday Utopians will go.

The population of Utopia will be a migratory population beyond any earthly precedent, not simply a travelling population, but migratory.

The old Utopias were all localised, as localised as a parish councillor; but it is manifest that nowadays even quite ordinary people live over areas that would have made a kingdom in those former days, would have filled the Athenian of the 'Laws' with incredulous astonishment. Except for the habits of the very rich during the Roman Empire, there was never the slightest precedent for this modern detachment from place. It is nothing to us that we go eighty or ninety miles from home to place of business, or take an hour's spin of fifty miles to our weekend golf; every summer it has become a fixed custom to travel wide and far. Only the clumsiness of communications limit us now, and every facilitation of locomotion widens not only our potential, but our habitual range. Not only this, but we change our habitations with a growing frequency and facility; to Sir Thomas More we should seem a breed of nomads. That old fixity was of necessity and not of choice, it was a mere phase in the development of civilisation, a trick of rooting man learnt for a time from his new-found friends, the corn and the vine and the hearth; the untamed spirit of the young has turned for ever to wandering and the sea. The soul of man has never yet in any land been willingly adscript to the glebe. Even Mr Belloc, who preaches the happiness of a peasant proprietor, is so much wiser than his thoughts that he sails about the seas in a little yacht or goes afoot from Belgium to Rome. We are winning our freedom again once more, a freedom renewed and enlarged, and there is now neither necessity nor advantage in a permanent life servitude to this place or that. Men may settle down in our modern Utopia for love and the family at last, but first and most abundantly they will see the world.

And with this loosening of the fetters of locality from the feet of men, necessarily there will be all sorts of fresh distributions of the factors of life. On our own poor haphazard earth, wherever men work, wherever there are things to be grown, minerals to be won, power to be used, there, regardless of all the joys and decencies of life, the households needs must cluster. But in Utopia there will be wide stretches of cheerless or unhealthy or toilsome or dangerous land with never a household; there will be regions of mining and smelting, black with the smoke of furnaces and gashed and desolated by mines, with a sort of weird inhospitable grandeur of industrial desolation, and the men will come thither and work for a spell and return to civilisation again, washing and changing their attire in the swift gliding train. And by way of compensation there will be beautiful regions of the earth specially set apart and favoured for children; in them the presence of children will remit taxation, while in other less wholesome places the presence of children will be taxed; the lower passes and fore hills of these very Alps, for example, will be populous with homes, serving the vast arable levels of Upper Italy.

So we shall see, as we come down by our little lake in the lap of Lucendro, and even before we reach the road, the first scattered chalets and households in which these migrant people live, the upper summer homes. With the coming of summer, as the snows on the high Alps recede, a tide of households and schools, teachers and doctors, and all such attendant services will flow up the mountain masses, and ebb again when the September snows return. It is essential to the modern ideal of life that the period of education and growth should be prolonged to as late a period as possible and puberty correspondingly retarded, and by wise regulation the statesmen of Utopia will constantly adjust and readjust regulations and taxation to diminish the proportion of children reared in hot and stimulating conditions. These high mountains will, in the bright sweet summer, be populous with youth. Even up towards this high place where the snow is scarce gone until July, these households will extend, and below, the whole long valley of Urseren will be a scattered summer town.

One figures one of the more urban highways, one of those along which the light railways of the second order run, such as that in the valley of Urseren, into which we should presently come. I figure it as one would see it at night, a band a hundred yards perhaps in width, the footpath on either side shaded with high trees and lit softly with orange glowlights; while down the centre the tramway of the road will go, with sometimes a nocturnal tramcar gliding, lit and gay but almost noiselessly, past. Lantern-lit cyclists will flit along the track like fireflies, and ever and again some humming motor car will hurry by, to or from the Rhoneland or the Rhineland or Switzerland or Italy. Away on either side the lights of the little country homes up the mountain slopes will glow.

I figure it at night, because so it is we should see it first.

We should come out from our mountain valley into the minor road that runs down the lonely rock wilderness of the St Gotthard Pass, we should descend that nine miles of winding route, and so arrive towards twilight among the clustering homes and upland unenclosed gardens of Realp and Hospenthal and Andermatt. Between Realp and Andermatt, and down the Schoellenen gorge, the greater road would run. By the time we reached it, we should be in the way of understanding our adventure a little better. We should know already, when we saw those two familiar clusters of chalets and hotels replaced by a great dispersed multitude of houses – we should see their window lights, but little else – that we were the victims of some strange transition in space or time, and we should come down by dimly seen buildings into the part that would answer to Hospenthal, wondering and perhaps a little afraid. We should come out into this great main roadway – this roadway like an urban avenue – and look up it and down, hesitating whether to go along the valley Furka-ward, or down by Andermatt through the gorge that leads to Göschenen . . .

People would pass us in the twilight, and then more people; we should see they walked well and wore a graceful, unfamiliar dress, but more we should not distinguish.

'Good-night!' they would say to us in clear, fine voices. Their dim faces would turn with a passing scrutiny towards us.

We should answer out of our perplexity: 'Good-night!' – for by the conventions established in the beginning of this book, we are given the freedom of their tongue.

4

Were this a story, I should tell at length how much we were helped by the good fortune of picking up a Utopian coin of gold, how at last we adventured into the Utopian inn and found it all marvellously easy. You see us the shyest and most watchful of guests; but of the food they put before us and the furnishings of the house, and all our entertainment, it will be better to speak later. We are in a migratory world, we know, one greatly accustomed to foreigners; our mountain clothes are not strange enough to attract acute attention, though ill-made and shabby, no doubt, by Utopian standards; we are dealt with as we might best wish to be dealt with, that is to say as rather untidy, inconspicuous men. We look about us and watch for hints and examples, and, indeed, get through with the thing. And after our queer, yet not unpleasant, dinner, in which we remark no meat figures, we go out of the house for a breath of air and for quiet counsel one with another, and there it is we discover those strange constellations overhead. It comes to us then, clear and full, that our imagination has realised itself; we dismiss quite finally a Rip-Van-Winkle fancy we have entertained, all the unfamiliarities of our descent from the mountain pass gather together into one fullness of conviction, and we know, we know, we are in Utopia.

We wander under the trees by the main road, watching the dim passers-by as though they were the phantoms of a dream. We say little

to one another. We turn aside into a little pathway and come to a
bridge over the turbulent Reuss, hurrying down towards the Devil's
Bridge in the gorge below. Far away over the Furka ridge a pallid glow
preludes the rising of the moon.

Two lovers pass us whispering, and we follow them with our eyes.
This Utopia has certainly preserved the fundamental freedom, to love.
And then a sweet-voiced bell from somewhere high up towards Oberalp
chimes two-and-twenty times.

I break the silence. 'That might mean ten o'clock,' I say.

My companion leans upon the bridge and looks down into the dim
river below. I become aware of the keen edge of the moon like a needle
of incandescent silver creeping over the crest, and suddenly the river is
alive with flashes.

He speaks, and astonishes me with the hidden course his thoughts
have taken.

'We two were boy and girl lovers like that,' he says, and jerks a head
at the receding Utopians. 'I loved her first, and I do not think I have
ever thought of loving anyone but her.'

It is a curiously human thing, and, upon my honour, not one I had
designed, that when at last I stand in the twilight in the midst of a
Utopian township, when my whole being should be taken up with
speculative wonder, this man should be standing by my side, and lugging
my attention persistently towards himself, towards his limited futile
self. This thing perpetually happens to me, this intrusion of something
small and irrelevant and alive, upon my great impressions. The time I
first saw the Matterhorn, that Queen among the Alpine summits, I was
distracted beyond appreciation by the tale of a man who could not eat
sardines – always sardines did this with him and that; and my first
wanderings along the brown streets of Pompeii, an experience I had
anticipated with a strange intensity, was shot with the most stupidly
intelligent discourse on vehicular tariffs in the chief capitals of Europe
that it is possible to imagine. And now this man, on my first night in
Utopia, talks and talks and talks of his poor little love affair.

It shapes itself as the most trite and feeble of tragedies, one of those
stories of effortless submission to chance and custom in which Mr
Hardy or George Gissing might have found a theme. I do but half listen
at first – watching the black figures in the moonlit roadway pacing to
and fro. Yet – I cannot trace how he conveys the subtle conviction to
my mind – the woman he loves is beautiful.

They were boy and girl together, and afterwards they met again as
fellow students in a world of comfortable discretions. He seems to have

taken the decorums of life with a confiding good faith, to have been shy and innocent in a suppressed sort of way, and of a mental type not made for worldly successes; but he must have dreamt about her and loved her well enough. How she felt for him I could never gather; it seemed to be all of that fleshless friendliness into which we train our girls. Then abruptly happened stresses. The man who became her husband appeared, with a very evident passion. He was a year or so older than either of them, and he had the habit and quality of achieving his ends; he was already successful, and with the promise of wealth, and I, at least, perceived, from my botanist's phrasing, that his desire was for her beauty.

As my botanist talked I seemed to see the whole little drama, rather clearer than his words gave it me, the actors all absurdly in Hampstead middle-class raiment, meetings of a Sunday after church (the men in silk hats, frock coats, and tightly-rolled umbrellas), rare excursions into evening dress, the decorously vulgar fiction read in their homes, its ambling sentimentalities of thought, the amiably worldly mothers, the respectable fathers, the aunts, the 'people' – his 'people' and her 'people' – the piano music and the song, and in this setting our friend, 'quite clever' at botany and 'going in' for it 'as a profession', and the girl, gratuitously beautiful; so I figured the arranged and orderly environment into which this claw of an elemental force had thrust itself to grip.

The stranger who had come in got what he wanted; the girl considered that she thought she had never loved the botanist, had had only friendship for him – though little she knew of the meaning of those fine words – they parted a little incoherently and in tears, and it had not occurred to the young man to imagine she was not going off to conventional life in some other of the endless Frognals he imagined as the cellular tissue of the world.

But she wasn't.

He had kept her photograph and her memory sweet, and if ever he had strayed from the severest constancy, it seemed only in the end to strengthen with the stuff of experience, to enhance by comparative disappointment his imagination of what she might have meant to him . . . Then eight years afterwards they met again.

By the time he gets to this part of his story we have, at my initiative, left the bridge and are walking towards the Utopian guest house. The Utopian guest house! His voice rises and falls, and sometimes he holds my arm. My attention comes and goes. 'Good-night,' two sweet-voiced Utopians cry to us in their universal tongue, and I answer them 'Good-night.'

'You see,' he persists, 'I saw her only a week ago. It was in Lucerne, while I was waiting for you to come on from England. I talked to her three or four times altogether. And her face – the change in her! I can't get it out of my head – night or day. The miserable waste of her . . . '

Before us, through the tall pine stems, shine the lights of our Utopian inn.

He talks vaguely of ill-usage. 'The husband is vain, boastful, dishonest to the very confines of the law, and a drunkard. There are scenes and insults – '

'She told you?'

'Not much, but someone else did. He brings other women almost into her presence to spite her.'

'And it's going on?' I interrupt.

'Yes. *Now*.'

'Need it go on?'

'What do you mean?'

'Lady in trouble,' I say. 'Knight at hand. Why not stop this dismal grizzling and carry her off?' (*You figure the heroic sweep of the arm that belongs to the Voice.*) I positively forget for the moment that we are in Utopia at all.

'You mean?'

'Take her away from him! What's all this emotion of yours worth if it isn't equal to that!'

Positively he seems aghast at me.

'Do you mean elope with her?'

'It seems a most suitable case.'

For a space he is silent, and we go on through the trees. A Utopian tramcar passes and I see his face, poor bitted wretch! looking pinched and scared in its trailing glow of light.

'That's all very well in a novel,' he says. 'But how could I go back to my laboratory, mixed classes with young ladies, you know, after a thing like that? How could we live and where could we live? We might have a house in London, but who would call upon us? . . . Besides, you don't know her. She is not the sort of woman . . . Don't think I'm timid or conventional. Don't think I don't feel . . . Feel! *You* don't know what it is to feel in a case of this sort . . . '

He halts and then flies out viciously: 'Ugh! There are times when I could strangle him with my hands.'

Which is nonsense.

He flings out his lean botanising hands in an impotent gesture.

'My dear man!' I say, and say no more.

For a moment I forget we are in Utopia altogether.

Let us come back to Utopia. We were speaking of travel.

Besides roadways and railways and tramways, for those who go to and fro in the earth the Modern Utopians will have very many other ways of travelling. There will be rivers, for example, with a vast variety of boats; canals with diverse sorts of haulage; there will be lakes and lagoons; and when one comes at last to the borders of the land, the pleasure craft will be there, coming and going, and the swift great passenger vessels, very big and steady, doing thirty knots an hour or more, will trace long wakes as they go dwindling out athwart the restless vastness of the sea.

They will be just beginning to fly in Utopia. We owe much to M. Santos Dumont; the world is immeasurably more disposed to believe this wonder is coming, and coming nearly, than it was five years ago. But unless we are to suppose Utopian scientific knowledge far in advance of ours – and though that supposition was not proscribed in our initial undertaking, it would be inconvenient for us and not quite in the vein of the rest of our premises – they, too, will only be in the same experimental stage as ourselves. In Utopia, however, they will conduct research by the army corps while we conduct it – we don't conduct it! We let it happen. Fools make researches and wise men exploit them – that is our earthly way of dealing with the question, and we thank Heaven for an assumed abundance of financially impotent and sufficiently ingenious fools.

In Utopia, a great multitude of selected men, chosen volunteers, will be collaborating upon this new step in man's struggle with the elements. Bacon's visionary House of Saloman* will be a thing realised, and it will be humming with this business. Every university in the world will be urgently working for priority in this aspect of the problem or that. Reports of experiments, as full and as prompt as the telegraphic reports of cricket in our more sportive atmosphere, will go about the world. All this will be passing, as it were, behind the act drop of our first experience, behind this first picture of the urbanised Urseren valley. The literature of the subject will be growing and developing with the easy swiftness of an eagle's swoop as we come down the hillside; unseen in that twilight, unthought of by us until this moment, a thousand men at a thousand glowing desks, a busy specialist press, will be perpetually sifting, criticising, condensing, and clearing the

* In the *New Atlantis*.

ground for further speculation. Those who are concerned with the problems of public locomotion will be following these aeronautic investigations with a keen and enterprising interest, and so will the physiologist and the sociologist. That Utopian research will, I say, go like an eagle's swoop in comparison with the blind-man's fumbling of our terrestrial way. Even before our own brief Utopian journey is out, we may get a glimpse of the swift ripening of all this activity that will be in progress at our coming. Tomorrow, perhaps, or in a day or so, some silent, distant thing will come gliding into view over the mountains, will turn and soar and pass again beyond our astonished sight . . .

6

But my friend and his great trouble turn my mind from these questions of locomotion and the freedoms that cluster about them. In spite of myself I find myself framing his case. He is a lover, the most conventional of Anglican lovers, with a heart that has had its training, I should think, in the clean but limited schoolroom of Mrs Henry Wood . . .

In Utopia I think they will fly with stronger pinions, it will not be in the superficialities of life merely that movement will be wide and free, they will mount higher and swoop more steeply than he in his cage can believe. What will their range be, their prohibitions? what jars to our preconceptions will he and I receive here?

My mind flows with the free, thin flow that it has at the end of an eventful day, and as we walk along in silence towards our inn I rove from issue to issue, I find myself ranging amidst the fundamental things of the individual life and all the perplexity of desires and passions. I turn my questionings to the most difficult of all sets of compromises, those mitigations of spontaneous freedom that constitute the marriage laws, the mystery of balancing justice against the good of the future, amidst these violent and elusive passions. Where falls the balance of freedoms here? I pass for a time from Utopianising altogether, to ask the question that, after all, Schopenhauer failed completely to answer, why sometimes in the case of hurtful, pointless, and destructive things we want so vehemently . . .

I come back from this unavailing glance into the deeps to the general question of freedoms in this new relation. I find myself far adrift from the case of the Frognal botanist, and asking how far a modern Utopia will deal with personal morals.

As Plato demonstrated long ago, the principles of the relation of State control to personal morals may be best discussed in the case of intoxication, the most isolated and least complicated of all this group of problems. But Plato's treatment of this issue as a question of who may or may not have the use of wine, though suitable enough in considering a small State in which everybody was the effectual inspector of everybody, is entirely beside the mark under modern conditions, in which we are to have an extraordinarily higher standard of individual privacy and an amplitude and quantity of migration inconceivable to the Academic imagination. We may accept his principle and put this particular freedom (of the use of wine) among the distinctive privileges of maturity, and still find all that a modern would think of as the Drink Question untouched.

That question in Utopia will differ perhaps in the proportion of its factors, but in no other respect, from what it is upon earth. The same desirable ends will be sought, the maintenance of public order and decency, the reduction of inducements to form this bad and wasteful habit to their lowest possible minimum, and the complete protection of the immature. But the modern Utopians, having systematised their sociology, will have given some attention to the psychology of minor officials, a matter altogether too much neglected by the social reformer on earth. They will not put into the hands of a common policeman powers direct and indirect that would be dangerous to the public in the hands of a judge. And they will have avoided the immeasurable error of making their control of the drink traffic a source of public revenue. Privacies they will not invade, but they will certainly restrict the public consumption of intoxicants to specified licensed places and the sale of them to unmistakable adults, and they will make the temptation of the young a grave offence. In so migratory a population as the modern Utopian, the licensing of inns and bars would be under the same control as the railways and high roads. Inns exist for the stranger and not for the locality, and we shall meet with nothing there to correspond with our terrestrial absurdity of Local Option.

The Utopians will certainly control this trade, and as certainly punish personal excesses. Public drunkenness (as distinguished from the mere elation that follows a generous but controlled use of wine) will be an offence against public decency, and will be dealt with in some very drastic manner. It will, of course, be an aggravation of, and not an excuse for, crime.

But I doubt whether the State will go beyond that. Whether an adult shall use wine or beer or spirits, or not, seems to me entirely a matter for his doctor and his own private conscience. I doubt if we explorers shall meet any drunken men, and I doubt not we shall meet many who have never availed themselves of their adult freedom in this respect. The conditions of physical happiness will be better understood in Utopia, it will be worthwhile to be well there, and the intelligent citizen will watch himself closely. Half and more of the drunkenness of earth is an attempt to lighten dull days and hopelessly sordid and disagreeable lives, and in Utopia they do not suffer these things. Assuredly Utopia will be temperate, not only drinking, but eating with the soundest discretion. Yet I do not think wine and good ale will be altogether wanting there, nor good, mellow whisky, nor, upon occasion, the engaging various liqueur. I do not think so. My botanist, who abstains altogether, is of another opinion. We differ here and leave the question to the earnest reader. I have the utmost respect for all Teetotallers, Prohibitionists, and Haters and Persecutors of Innkeepers, their energy of reform awakens responsive notes in me, and to their species I look for a large part of the urgent repair of our earth; yet for all that –

There is Burgundy, for example, a bottle of soft and kindly Burgundy, taken to make a sunshine on one's lunch when four strenuous hours of toil have left one on the further side of appetite. Or ale, a foaming tankard of ale, ten miles of sturdy tramping in the sleet and slush as a prelude, and then good bread and good butter and a ripe hollow Stilton and celery and ale – ale with a certain quantitative freedom. Or, again, where is the sin in a glass of tawny port three or four times, or it may be five, a year, when the walnuts come round in their season? If you drink no port, then what are walnuts for? Such things I hold for the reward of vast intervals of abstinence; they justify your wide, immaculate margin, which is else a mere unmeaning blankness on the page of palate God has given you! I write of these things as a fleshly man, confessedly and knowingly fleshly, and more than usually aware of my liability to err; I know myself for a gross creature more given to sedentary world-mending than to brisk activities, and not one-tenth as active as the dullest newspaper boy in London. Yet still I have my uses, uses that vanish in monotony, and still I must ask why should we bury the talent of these bright sensations altogether? Under no circumstances can I think of my Utopians maintaining their fine order of life on ginger ale and lemonade and the ale that is Kops'. Those terrible Temperance Drinks, solutions of qualified sugar mixed with vast volumes of gas, as, for example, soda, seltzer, lemonade, and fire-extinguishing hand grenades – *minerals*, they call such stuff in England – fill a man with wind and self-righteousness. Indeed they do! Coffee destroys brain and kidney, a fact now universally recognised and advertised throughout America; and tea, except for a kind of green tea best used with discretion in punch, tans the entrails and turns honest stomachs into leather bags. Rather would I be Metchnikoffed at once and have a clean, good stomach of German silver. No! If we are to have no ale in Utopia, give me the one clean temperance drink that is worthy to set beside wine, and that is simple water. Best it is when not quite pure and with a trace of organic matter, for then it tastes and sparkles . . .

My botanist would still argue.

Thank Heaven this is my book, and that the ultimate decision rests with me. It is open to him to write his own Utopia and arrange that everybody shall do nothing except by the consent of the savants of the Republic, either in his eating, drinking, dressing or lodging, even as Cabet proposed. It is open to him to try a *News from Nowhere* Utopia with the wine left out. I have my short way with him here quite effectually. I turn in the entrance of our inn to the civil but by no means obsequious landlord, and with a careful ambiguity of manner – for the thing may be considered an outrage, and I try to make it possible the idea is a jest – put my test demand . . .

'You see, my dear Teetotaller? – he sets before me tray and glass and . . . ' Here follows the necessary experiment and a deep sigh . . . 'Yes, a bottle of quite *excellent* light beer! So there are also cakes and ale in Utopia! Let us in this saner and more beautiful world drink perdition to all earthly excesses. Let us drink more particularly to the coming of the day when men beyond there will learn to distinguish between qualitative and quantitative questions, to temper good intentions with good intelligence, and righteousness with wisdom. One of the darkest evils of our world is surely the unteachable wildness of the Good.'

7

So presently to bed and to sleep, but not at once to sleep. At first my brain, like a dog in unfamiliar quarters, must turn itself round for a time or so before it lies down. This strange mystery of a world of which I have seen so little as yet – a mountain slope, a twilit road, a traffic of ambiguous vehicles and dim shapes, the window lights of many homes – fills me with curiosities. Figures and incidents come and go, the people we have passed, our landlord, quietly attentive and yet, I feel, with the

---

*   See *The Nature of Man*, by Professor Elie Metchnikoff.]

keenest curiosity peeping from his eyes, the unfamiliar forms of the house parts and furnishings, the unfamiliar courses of the meal. Outside this little bedroom is a world, a whole unimagined world. A thousand million things lie outside in the darkness beyond this lit inn of ours, unthought-of possibilities, overlooked considerations, surprises, riddles, incommensurables, a whole monstrous intricate universe of consequences that I have to do my best to unravel. I attempt impossible recapitulations and mingle the weird quality of dream stuff with my thoughts.

Athwart all this tumult of my memory goes this queer figure of my unanticipated companion, so obsessed by himself and his own egotistical love that this sudden change to another world seems only a change of scene for his gnawing, uninvigorating passion. It occurs to me that she also must have an equivalent in Utopia, and then that idea and all ideas grow thin and vague, and are dissolved at last in the rising tide of sleep . . .

CHAPTER THREE

Utopian Economics

1

These modern Utopians with the universally diffused good manners, the universal education, the fine freedoms we shall ascribe to them, their world unity, world language, worldwide travellings, worldwide freedom of sale and purchase, will remain mere dream stuff, incredible even by twilight, until we have shown that at that level the community will still sustain itself. At any rate, the common liberty of the Utopians will not embrace the common liberty to be unserviceable, the most perfect economy of organisation still leaves the fact untouched that all order and security in a State rests on the certainty of getting work done. How will the work of this planet be done? What will be the economics of a modern Utopia?

Now in the first place, a state so vast and complex as this world Utopia, and with so migratory a people, will need some handy symbol to check the distribution of services and commodities. Almost certainly they will need to have money. They will have money, and it is not inconceivable that, for all his sorrowful thoughts, our botanist, with his trained observation, his habit of looking at little things upon the ground, would be the one to see and pick up the coin that has fallen from some wayfarer's pocket. (This, in our first hour or so before we reach the inn in the Urserenthal.) You figure us upon the high Gotthard road, heads together over the little disc that contrives to tell us so much of this strange world.

It is, I imagine, of gold, and it will be a convenient accident if it is sufficient to make us solvent for a day or so, until we are a little more informed of the economic system into which we have come. It is, moreover, of a fair round size, and the inscription declares it one Lion, equal to 'twaindy' bronze Crosses. Unless the ratio of metals is very different here, this latter must be a token coin, and therefore legal tender for but a small amount. (That would be pain and pleasure to Mr Wordsworth Donisthorpe if he were to chance to join us, for once he planned a Utopian coinage,* and the words Lion and Cross are his.

---

* *A System of Measures*, by Wordsworth Donisthorpe.

But a token coinage and 'legal tender' he cannot abide. They make him argue.) And being in Utopia, that unfamiliar 'twaindy' suggests at once we have come upon that most Utopian of all things, a duodecimal system of counting.

My author's privilege of details serves me here. This Lion is distinctly a beautiful coin, admirably made, with its value in fine, clear letters circling the obverse side, and a head thereon – of Newton, as I live! One detects American influence here. Each year, as we shall find, each denomination of coins celebrates a centenary. The reverse shows the universal goddess of the Utopian coinage – Peace, as a beautiful woman, reading with a child out of a great book, and behind them are stars, and an hour-glass, halfway run. Very human these Utopians, after all, and not by any means above the obvious in their symbolism!

So for the first time we learn definitely of the World State, and we get our first clear hint, too, that there is an end to Kings. But our coin raises other issues also. It would seem that this Utopia has no simple community of goods, that there is, at any rate, a restriction upon what one may take, a need for evidences of equivalent value, a limitation to human credit.

It dates – so much of this present Utopia of ours dates. Those former Utopists were bitterly against gold. You will recall the undignified use Sir Thomas More would have us put it to, and how there was no money at all in the Republic of Plato, and in that later community for which he wrote his 'Laws' an iron coinage of austere appearance and doubtful efficacy . . . It may be these great gentlemen were a little hasty with a complicated difficulty, and not a little unjust to a highly respectable element.

Gold is abused and made into vessels of dishonour, and abolished from ideal society as though it were the cause instead of the instrument of human baseness; but, indeed, there is nothing bad in gold. Making gold into vessels of dishonour and banishing it from the State is punishing the hatchet for the murderer's crime. Money, did you but use it right, is a good thing in life, a necessary thing in civilised human life, as complicated, indeed, for its purposes, but as natural a growth as the bones in a man's wrist, and I do not see how one can imagine anything at all worthy of being called a civilisation without it. It is the water of the body social, it distributes and receives, and renders growth and assimilation and movement and recovery possible. It is the re-conciliation of human interdependence with liberty. What other device will give a man so great a freedom with so strong an inducement to effort? The economic history of the world, where it is not the history of the theory of property, is very largely the record of the abuse, not so much of money as of credit devices to supplement money, to amplify the scope of this most precious invention; and no device of labour credits* or free demand of commodities from a central store† or the like has ever been suggested that does not give ten thousand times more scope for that inherent moral dross in man that must be reckoned with in any sane Utopia we may design and plan . . . Heaven knows where progress may not end, but at any rate this developing State, into which we two men have fallen, this twentieth-century Utopia, has still not passed beyond money and the use of coins.

2

Now if this Utopian world is to be in some degree parallel to contemporary thought, it must have been concerned, it may be still concerned, with many unsettled problems of currency, and with the problems that centre about a standard of value. Gold is perhaps of all material substances the best adapted to the monetary purpose, but even at that best it falls far short of an imaginable ideal. It undergoes spasmodic and irregular cheapening through new discoveries of gold, and at any time it may undergo very extensive and sudden and disastrous depreciation through the discovery of some way of transmuting less valuable elements. The liability to such depreciations introduces an undesirable speculative element into the relations of debtor and creditor. When, on the one hand, there is for a time a check in the increase of the available stores of gold, or an increase in the energy applied to social purposes, or a checking of the public security that would impede the free exchange of credit and necessitate a more frequent production of gold in evidence, then there comes an undue appreciation of money as against the general commodities of life, and an automatic impoverishment of the citizens in general as against the creditor class. The common people are mortgaged into the bondage of debt. And on the other hand an unexpected spate of gold production, the discovery of a single nugget as big as St Paul's, let us say – a quite possible thing – would result in a sort of jail delivery of debtors and a financial earthquake.

It has been suggested by an ingenious thinker that it is possible to use as a standard of monetary value no substance whatever, but instead, force, and that value might be measured in units of energy. An

* Edward Bellamy's *Looking Backward*, Ch. IX.
† More's *Utopia* and Cabet's *Icaria*.

excellent development this, in theory, at any rate, of the general idea of the modern State as kinetic and not static; it throws the old idea of the social order and the new into the sharpest antithesis. The old order is presented as a system of institutions and classes ruled by men of substance; the new, of enterprises and interests led by men of power.

Now I glance at this matter in the most incidental manner, as a man may skim through a specialist's exposition in a popular magazine. You must figure me, therefore, finding from a casual periodical paper in our inn, with a certain surprise at not having anticipated as much, the Utopian self of that same ingenious person quite conspicuously a leader of thought, and engaged in organising the discussion of the currency changes Utopia has under consideration. The article, as it presents itself to me, contains a complete and lucid, though occasionally rather technical, explanation of his newest proposals. They have been published, it seems, for general criticism, and one gathers that in the modern Utopia the administration presents the most elaborately detailed schemes of any proposed alteration in law or custom, some time before any measure is taken to carry it into effect, and the possibilities of every detail are acutely criticised, flaws anticipated, side issues raised, and the whole minutely tested and fined down by a planetful of critics, before the actual process of legislation begins.

The explanation of these proposals involves an anticipatory glance at the local administration of a modern Utopia. To anyone who has watched the development of technical science during the last decade or so, there will be no shock in the idea that a general consolidation of a great number of common public services over areas of considerable size is now not only practicable, but very desirable. In a little while heating and lighting and the supply of power for domestic and industrial purposes and for urban and inter-urban communications will all be managed electrically from common generating stations. And the trend of political and social speculation points decidedly to the conclusion that so soon as it passes out of the experimental stage, the supply of electrical energy, just like drainage and the supply of water, will fall to the local authority. Moreover, the local authority will be the universal landowner. Upon that point so extreme an individualist as Herbert Spencer was in agreement with the Socialist. In Utopia we conclude that, whatever other types of property may exist, all natural sources of force, and indeed all strictly natural products, coal, water power, and the like, are inalienably vested in the local authorities (which, in order to secure the maximum of convenience and administrative efficiency, will probably control areas as large sometimes as half England); they will generate electricity by water power, by combustion, by wind or tide or whatever other natural force is available, and this electricity will be devoted, some of it to the authority's lighting and other public works, some of it, as a subsidy, to the World-State authority which controls the high roads, the great railways, the inns and other apparatus of world communication, and the rest will pass on to private individuals or to distributing companies at a uniform fixed rate for private lighting and heating, for machinery and industrial applications of all sorts. Such an arrangement of affairs will necessarily involve a vast amount of book-keeping between the various authorities, the World-State government and the customers, and this bookkeeping will naturally be done most conveniently in units of physical energy.

It is not incredible that the assessment of the various local administrations for the central world government would be already calculated upon the estimated total of energy, periodically available in each locality, and booked and spoken of in these physical units. Accounts between central and local governments could be kept in these terms. Moreover, one may imagine Utopian local authorities making contracts in which payment would be no longer in coinage upon the gold basis, but in notes good for so many thousands or millions of units of energy at one or other of the generating stations.

Now the problems of economic theory will have undergone an enormous clarification if, instead of measuring in fluctuating money values, the same scale of energy units can be extended to their discussion, if, in fact, the idea of trading could be entirely eliminated. In my Utopia, at any rate, this has been done, the production and distribution of common commodities have been expressed as a problem in the conversion of energy, and the scheme that Utopia was now discussing was the application of this idea of energy as the standard of value to the entire Utopian coinage. Every one of those giant local authorities was to be free to issue energy notes against the security of its surplus of saleable available energy, and to make all its contracts for payment in those notes up to a certain maximum defined by the amount of energy produced and disposed of in that locality in the previous year. This power of issue was to be renewed just as rapidly as the notes came in for redemption. In a world without boundaries, with a population largely migratory and emancipated from locality, the price of the energy notes of these various local bodies would constantly tend to be uniform, because employment would constantly shift into the areas where energy was cheap. Accordingly, the price of so many millions of units of energy at any particular moment in coins of the gold currency would be approximately the same throughout the world. It was proposed to select some particular day when the economic atmosphere was distinctly equable, and to declare a fixed ratio between the gold coinage and the energy notes; each gold Lion and each Lion of credit representing exactly the number of energy units it could buy on that day. The old gold coinage was at once to cease to be legal tender beyond certain defined limits, except to the central government, which would not reissue it as it came in. It was, in fact, to become a temporary token coinage, a token coinage of full value for the day of conversion at any rate, if not afterwards, under the new standard of energy, and to be replaceable by an ordinary token coinage as time went on. The old computation by Lions and the values of the small change of daily life were therefore to suffer no disturbance whatever.

The economists of Utopia, as I apprehended them, had a different method and a very different system of theories from those I have read on earth, and this makes my exposition considerably more difficult. This article upon which I base my account floated before me in an unfamiliar, perplexing, and dreamlike phraseology. Yet I brought away an impression that here was a rightness that earthly economists have failed to grasp. Few earthly economists have been able to disentangle themselves from patriotisms and politics, and their obsession has always been international trade. Here in Utopia the World State cuts that away from beneath their feet; there are no imports but meteorites, and no exports at all. Trading is the earthly economists' initial notion, and they start from perplexing and insoluble riddles about exchange value, insoluble because all trading finally involves individual preferences which are incalculable and unique. Nowhere do they seem to be handling really defined standards, every economic dissertation and discussion reminds one more strongly than the last of the game of croquet Alice played in Wonderland, when the mallets were flamingoes and the balls were hedgehogs and crawled away, and the hoops were soldiers and kept getting up and walking about. But economics in Utopia must be, it seems to me, not a theory of trading based on bad psychology, but physics applied to problems in the theory of sociology. The general problem of Utopian economics is to state the conditions of the most efficient application of the steadily increasing quantities of material energy the progress of science makes available for human service, to the general needs of mankind. Human labour and existing material are dealt with in relation to that. Trading and relative wealth are merely episodical in such a scheme. The trend of the article I read, as I understood it, was that a monetary system based upon a relatively small amount of gold, upon which the business of the whole world had hitherto been done, fluctuated unreasonably and supplied no real criterion of well-being, that the nominal values of things and enterprises had no clear and simple relation to the real physical prosperity of the community, that the nominal wealth of a community in millions of pounds or dollars or Lions, measured nothing but the quantity of hope in the air, and an increase of confidence meant an inflation of credit and a pessimistic phase a collapse of this hallucination of possessions. The new standards, this advocate reasoned, were to alter all that, and it seemed to me they would.

I have tried to indicate the drift of these remarkable proposals, but about them clustered an elaborate mass of keen and temperate discussion. Into the details of that discussion I will not enter now, nor am I sure I am qualified to render the multitudinous aspect of this complicated question at all precisely. I read the whole thing in the course of an hour or two of rest after lunch – it was either the second or third day of my stay in Utopia – and we were sitting in a little inn at the end of the Lake of Uri. We had loitered there, and I had fallen reading because of a shower of rain . . . But certainly as I read it the proposition struck me as a singularly simple and attractive one, and its exposition opened out to me for the first time clearly, in a comprehensive outline, the general conception of the economic nature of the Utopian State.

3

The difference between the social and economic sciences as they exist in our world* and in this Utopia deserves perhaps a word or so more. I write with the utmost diffidence, because upon earth economic science has been raised to a very high level of tortuous abstraction by the industry of its professors, and I can claim neither a patient student's intimacy with their productions nor – what is more serious – anything but the most generalised knowledge of what their Utopian equivalents have achieved. The vital nature of economic issues to a Utopia necessitates, however, some attempt at interpretation between the two.

In Utopia there is no distinct and separate science of economics.

* But see Giddings' *Principles of Sociology*, a modern and richly suggestive American work, imperfectly appreciated by the British student. See also Walter Bagehot's *Economic Studies*.

Many problems that we should regard as economic come within the scope of Utopian psychology. My Utopians make two divisions of the science of psychology, first, the general psychology of individuals, a sort of mental physiology separated by no definite line from physiology proper, and secondly, the psychology of relationship between individuals. This second is an exhaustive study of the reaction of people upon each other and of all possible relationships. It is a science of human aggregations, of all possible family groupings, of neighbours and neighbourhood, of companies, associations, unions, secret and public societies, religious groupings, of common ends and intercourse, and of the methods of intercourse and collective decision that hold human groups together, and finally of government and the State. The elucidation of economic relationships, depending as it does on the nature of the hypothesis of human aggregation actually in operation at any time, is considered to be subordinate and subsequent to this general science of Sociology. Political economy and economics, in our world now, consist of a hopeless muddle of social assumptions and preposterous psychology, and a few geographical and physical generalisations. Its ingredients will be classified out and widely separated in Utopian thought. On the one hand there will be the study of physical economies, ending in the descriptive treatment of society as an organisation for the conversion of all the available energy in nature to the material ends of mankind – a physical sociology which will be already at such a stage of practical development as to be giving the world this token coinage representing energy – and on the other there will be the study of economic problems as problems in the division of labour, having regard to a social organisation whose main ends are reproduction and education in an atmosphere of personal freedom. Each of these enquiries, working unencumbered by the other, will be continually contributing fresh valid conclusions for the use of the practical administrator.

In no region of intellectual activity will our hypothesis of freedom from tradition be of more value in devising a Utopia than here. From its beginning the earthly study of economics has been infertile and unhelpful, because of the mass of unanalysed and scarcely suspected assumptions upon which it rested. The facts were ignored that trade is a by-product and not an essential factor in social life, that property is a plastic and fluctuating convention, that value is capable of impersonal treatment only in the case of the most generalised requirements. Wealth was measured by the standards of exchange. Society was regarded as a practically unlimited number of avaricious adult units incapable of any other subordinate groupings than business partnerships, and the sources of competition were assumed to be inexhaustible. Upon such quicksands rose an edifice that aped the securities of material science, developed a technical jargon and professed the discovery of 'laws'. Our liberation from these false presumptions through the rhetoric of Carlyle and Ruskin and the activities of the Socialists, is more apparent than real. The old edifice oppresses us still, repaired and altered by indifferent builders, underpinned in places, and with a slight change of name. 'Political Economy' has been painted out, and instead we read 'Economics – under entirely new management'. Modern Economics differs mainly from old Political Economy in having produced no Adam Smith. The old 'Political Economy' made certain generalisations, and they were mostly wrong; new Economics evades generalisations, and seems to lack the intellectual power to make them. The science hangs like a gathering fog in a valley, a fog which begins nowhere and goes nowhere, an incidental, unmeaning inconvenience to passers-by. Its most typical exponents display a disposition to disavow generalisations altogether, to claim consideration as 'experts', and to make immediate political application of that conceded claim. Now Newton, Darwin, Dalton, Davy, Joule, and Adam Smith did not affect this 'expert' hankey-pankey, becoming enough in a hairdresser or a fashionable physician, but indecent in a philosopher or a man of science. In this state of impotent expertness, however, or in some equally unsound state, economics must struggle on – a science that is no science, a floundering lore wallowing in a mud of statistics – until either the study of the material organisation of production on the one hand as a development of physics and geography, or the study of social aggregation on the other, renders enduring foundations possible.

4

The older Utopias were all relatively small states; Plato's Republic, for example, was to be smaller than the average English borough, and no distinction was made between the Family, the Local Government, and the State. Plato and Campanella – for all that the latter was a Christian priest – carried communism to its final point and prescribed even a community of husbands and wives, an idea that was brought at last to the test of effectual experiment in the Oneida Community of New York State (1848–79). This latter body did not long survive its founder, at least as a veritable communism, by reason of the insurgent individualism of its vigorous sons. More, too, denied privacy and ruled an absolute community of goods, at any rate, and so, coming to the Victorian Utopias, did Cabet. But Cabet's communism was one of the 'free store' type, and the goods were yours only after you had requisitioned them. That seems the case in the 'Nowhere' of Morris also. Compared with the older writers Bellamy and Morris have a vivid sense of individual separation, and their departure from the old homogeneity is sufficiently marked to justify a doubt whether there will be any more thoroughly communistic Utopias for ever.

A Utopia such as this present one, written in the opening of the twentieth century, and after the most exhaustive discussion – nearly a century long – between Communistic and Socialistic ideas on the one hand, and Individualism on the other, emerges upon a sort of effectual conclusion to those controversies. The two parties have so chipped and amended each other's initial propositions that, indeed, except for the labels still flutteringly adhesive to the implicated men, it is hard to choose between them. Each side established a good many propositions, and we profit by them all. We of the succeeding generation can see quite clearly that for the most part the heat and zeal of these discussions arose in the confusion of a quantitative for a qualitative question. To the onlooker, both Individualism and Socialism are, in the absolute, absurdities; the one would make men the slaves of the violent or rich, the other the slaves of the State official, and the way of sanity runs, perhaps even sinuously, down the intervening valley. Happily the dead past buries its dead, and it is not our function now to adjudicate the preponderance of victory. In the very days when our political and economic order is becoming steadily more Socialistic, our ideals of intercourse turn more and more to a fuller recognition of the claims of individuality. The State is to be progressive, it is no longer to be static, and this alters the general condition of the Utopian problem profoundly; we have to provide not only for food and clothing, for order and health, but for initiative. The factor that leads the World State on from one phase of development to the next is the interplay of individualities; to speak teleologically, the world exists for the sake of and through initiative, and individuality is the method of initiative. Each man and woman, to the extent that his or her individuality is marked, breaks the law of precedent, transgresses the general formula, and makes a new experiment for the direction of the life force. It is impossible, therefore, for the State, which represents all and is preoccupied by the average, to make effectual experiments and intelligent innovations, and so supply the essential substance of life. As against the individual the State represents the species, in the case of the Utopian World State it absolutely represents the species. The individual emerges from the species, makes his experiment, and either fails, dies, and comes to an end, or succeeds and impresses himself in offspring, in consequences and results, intellectual, material and moral, upon the world.

Biologically the species is the accumulation of the experiments of all its successful individuals since the beginning, and the World State of the Modern Utopist will, in its economic aspect, be a compendium of established economic experience, about which individual enterprise will be continually experimenting, either to fail and pass, or to succeed and at last become incorporated with the undying organism of the World State. This organism is the universal rule, the common restriction, the rising level platform on which individualities stand.

The World State in this ideal presents itself as the sole landowner of the earth, with the great local governments I have adumbrated, the local municipalities, holding, as it were, feudally under it as landlords. The State or these subordinates holds all the sources of energy, and either directly or through its tenants, farmers and agents, develops these sources, and renders the energy available for the work of life. It or its tenants will produce food, and so human energy, and the exploitation of coal and electric power, and the powers of wind and wave and water will be within its right. It will pour out this energy by assignment and lease and acquiescence and what not upon its individual citizens. It will maintain order, maintain roads, maintain a cheap and efficient administration of justice, maintain cheap and rapid locomotion and be the common carrier of the planet, convey and distribute labour, control, let, or administer all natural productions, pay for and secure healthy births and a healthy and vigorous new generation, maintain the public health, coin money and sustain standards of measurement, subsidise research, and reward such commercially unprofitable undertakings as benefit the community as a whole; subsidise when needful chairs of criticism and authors and publications, and collect and distribute information. The energy developed and the employment afforded by the State will descend like water that the sun has sucked out of the sea to fall upon a mountain range, and back to the sea again it will come at last, debouching in ground rent and royalty and licence fees, in the fees of travellers and profits upon carrying and coinage and the like, in death duty, transfer tax, legacy and forfeiture, returning to the sea. Between the clouds and the sea it will run, as a river system runs, down through a great region of individual enterprise and interplay, whose freedom it will sustain. In that intermediate region between the kindred heights and deeps those beginnings and promises will arise that are the essential significance, the essential substance, of life. From our human point of view the mountains and sea exist for the habitable lands that lie between. So likewise the State is for Individualities. The State is for Individuals, the law is for freedoms, the world is for experiment, experience, and change: these are the fundamental beliefs upon which a modern Utopia must go.

5

Within this scheme, which makes the State the source of all energy, and the final legatee, what will be the nature of the property a man may own? Under modern conditions – indeed, under any conditions – a man without some negotiable property is a man without freedom, and the extent of his property is very largely the measure of his freedom. Without any property, without even shelter or food, a man has no choice but to set about getting these things; he is in servitude to his needs until he has secured property to satisfy them. But with a certain small property a man is free to do many things, to take a fortnight's holiday when he chooses, for example, and to try this new departure from his work or that; with so much more, he may take a year of freedom and go to the ends of the earth; with so much more, he may obtain elaborate apparatus and try curious novelties, build himself houses and make gardens, establish businesses and make experiments at large. Very speedily, under terrestrial conditions, the property of a man may reach such proportions that his freedom oppresses the freedom of others. Here, again, is a quantitative question, an adjustment of conflicting freedoms, a quantitative question that too many people insist on making a qualitative one.

The object sought in the code of property laws that one would find in operation in Utopia would be the same object that pervades the whole Utopian organisation, namely, a universal maximum of individual freedom. Whatever far-reaching movements the State or great rich men or private corporations may make, the starvation by any complication of employment, the unwilling deportation, the destruction of alternatives to servile submissions, must not ensue. Beyond such qualifications, the object of Modern Utopian statesmanship will be to secure to a man the freedom given by all his legitimate property, that is to say, by all the values his toil or skill or foresight and courage have brought into being. Whatever he has justly made he has a right to keep, that is obvious enough; but he will also have a right to sell and exchange, and so this question of what may be property takes really the form of what a man may buy in Utopia?

A modern Utopian most assuredly must have a practically unqualified property in all those things that become, as it were, by possession, extensions and expressions of his personality; his clothing, his jewels, the tools of his employment, his books, the objects of art he may have bought or made, his personal weapons (if Utopia have need of such things), insignia, and so forth. All such things that he has bought with his money or acquired – provided he is not a professional or habitual dealer in such property – will be inalienably his, his to give or lend or keep, free even from taxation. So intimate is this sort of property that I have no doubt Utopia will give a man posthumous rights over it – will permit him to assign it to a successor with at the utmost the payment of a small redemption. A horse, perhaps, in certain districts, or a bicycle, or any such mechanical conveyance personally used, the Utopians might find it well to rank with these possessions. No doubt, too, a house and privacy owned and occupied by a man, and even a man's own household furniture, might be held to stand as high or almost as high in the property scale, might be taxed as lightly and transferred under only a slightly heavier redemption, provided he had not let these things on hire, or otherwise alienated them from his intimate self. A thorough-going, Democratic Socialist will no doubt be inclined at first to object that if the Utopians make these things a specially free sort of property in this way, men would spend much more upon them than they would otherwise do, but indeed that will be an excellent thing. We are too much affected by the needy atmosphere of our own mismanaged world. In Utopia no one will have to hunger because some love to make and have made and own and cherish beautiful things. To give this much of property to individuals will tend to make clothing, ornamentation, implements, books, and all the arts finer and more beautiful, because by buying such things a man will secure something inalienable – save in the case of bankruptcy – for himself and for those who belong to him. Moreover, a man may in his lifetime set aside sums to ensure special advantages of education and care for the immature children of himself and others, and in this manner also exercise a posthumous right.*

For all other property, the Utopians will have a scantier respect; even money unspent by a man, and debts to him that bear no interest, will at

---

* But a statute of Mortmain will set a distinct time limit to the continuance of such benefactions. A periodic revision of endowments is a necessary feature in any modern Utopia.

his death stand upon a lower level than these things. What he did not choose to gather and assimilate to himself, or assign for the special education of his children, the State will share in the lion's proportion with heir and legatee.

This applies, for example, to the property that a man creates and acquires in business enterprises, which are presumably undertaken for gain, and as a means of living rather than for themselves. All new machinery, all new methods, all uncertain and variable and non-universal undertakings, are no business for the State; they commence always as experiments of unascertained value, and next after the invention of money, there is no invention has so facilitated freedom and progress as the invention of the limited liability company to do this work of trial and adventure. The abuses, the necessary reforms of company law on earth, are no concern of ours here and now, suffice it that in a modern Utopia such laws must be supposed to be as perfect as mortal laws can possibly be made. *Caveat vendor* will be a sound qualification of *caveat emptor* in the beautifully codified Utopian law. Whether the Utopian company will be allowed to prefer this class of share to that or to issue debentures, whether indeed usury, that is to say lending money at fixed rates of interest, will be permitted at all in Utopia, one may venture to doubt. But whatever the nature of the shares a man may hold, they will all be sold at his death, and whatever he has not clearly assigned for special educational purposes will – with possibly some fractional concession to near survivors – lapse to the State. The 'safe investment', that permanent, undying claim upon the community, is just one of those things Utopia will discourage; which indeed the developing security of civilisation quite automatically discourages through the fall in the rate of interest. As we shall see at a later stage, the State will insure the children of every citizen, and those legitimately dependent upon him, against the inconvenience of his death; it will carry out all reasonable additional dispositions he may have made for them in the same event; and it will insure him against old age and infirmity; and the object of Utopian economics will be to give a man every inducement to spend his surplus money in intensifying the quality of his surroundings, either by economic adventures and experiments, which may yield either losses or large profits, or in increasing the beauty, the pleasure, the abundance and promise of life.

Besides strictly personal possessions and shares in business adventures, Utopia will no doubt permit associations of its citizens to have a property in various sorts of contracts and concessions, in leases of agricultural and other land, for example; in houses they may have built, factories and machinery they may have made, and the like. And if a citizen prefer to adventure into business single-handed, he will have all the freedoms of enterprise enjoyed by a company; in business affairs he will be a company of one, and his single share will be dealt with at his death like any other shares . . . So much for the second kind of property. And these two kinds of property will probably exhaust the sorts of property a Utopian may possess.

The trend of modern thought is entirely against private property in land or natural objects or products, and in Utopia these things will be the inalienable property of the World State. Subject to the rights of free locomotion, land will be leased out to companies or individuals, but – in view of the unknown necessities of the future – never for a longer period than, let us say, fifty years.

The property of a parent in his children, and of a husband in his wife, seems to be undergoing a steadily increasing qualification in the world of today, but the discussion of the Utopian state of affairs in regard to such property may be better reserved until marriage becomes our topic. Suffice it here to remark, that the increasing control of a child's welfare and upbringing by the community, and the growing disposition to limit and tax inheritance are complementary aspects of the general tendency to regard the welfare and free interplay of future generations no longer as the concern of parents and altruistic individuals, but as the predominant issue of statesmanship, and the duty and moral meaning of the world community as a whole.

6

From the conception of mechanical force as coming in from Nature to the service of man, a conception the Utopian proposal of a coinage based on energy units would emphasise, arise profound contrasts between the modern and the classical Utopias. Except for a meagre use of water power for milling, and the wind for sailing – so meagre in the latter case that the classical world never contrived to do without the galley slave – and a certain restricted help from oxen in ploughing, and from horses in locomotion, all the energy that sustained the old-fashioned State was derived from the muscular exertion of toiling men. They ran their world by hand. Continual bodily labour was a condition of social existence. It is only with the coming of coal burning, of abundant iron and steel, and of scientific knowledge that this condition has been changed. Today, I suppose, if it were possible to indicate, in units of energy, the grand total of work upon which the social fabric of the United States or England rests, it would be found that a vastly preponderating moiety is derived from non-human sources, from coal and liquid fuel, and explosives and wind and water. There is every indication of a steady increase in this proportion of mechanical energy, in this emancipation of men from the necessity of physical labour. There appears no limit to the invasion of life by the machine.

Now it is only in the last three hundred years that any human being seems to have anticipated this. It stimulates the imagination to remark how entirely it was overlooked as a modifying cause in human development.* Plato clearly had no ideas about machines at all as a force affecting social organisation. There was nothing in his world to suggest them to him. I suppose there arose no invention, no new mechanical appliance or method of the slightest social importance through all his length of years. He never thought of a State that did not rely for its force upon human muscle, just as he never thought of a State that was not primarily organised for warfare hand to hand. Political and moral inventions he saw enough of and to spare, and in that direction he still stimulates the imagination. But in regard to all material possibilities he deadens rather than stimulates.† An infinitude of nonsense about the Greek mind would never have been written if the distinctive intellectual and artistic quality of Plato's time, its extraordinarily clear definition of certain material conditions as absolutely permanent, coupled with its politico-social instability, had been borne in mind. The food of the Greek imagination was the very antithesis of our own nourishment. We are educated by our circumstances to think no revolution in appliances and economic organisation incredible, our minds play freely about possibilities that would have struck the men of the Academy as outrageous extravagance, and it is in regard to politico-social expedients that our imaginations fail. Sparta, for all the evidence of history, is scarcely more credible to us than a motor car throbbing in the agora would have been to Socrates.

By sheer inadvertence, therefore, Plato commenced the tradition of Utopias without machinery, a tradition we find Morris still loyally following, except for certain mechanical barges and suchlike toys, in his

---

* It is interesting to note how little even Bacon seems to see of this in his *New Atlantis*.

† The lost *Utopia* of Hippodamus provided rewards for inventors, but unless Aristotle misunderstood him, and it is certainly the fate of all Utopias to be more or less misread, the inventions contemplated were political devices.

News from Nowhere. There are some foreshadowings of mechanical possibilities in the New Atlantis, but it is only in the nineteenth century that Utopias appeared in which the fact is clearly recognised that the social fabric rests no longer upon human labour. It was, I believe, Cabet* who first in a Utopian work insisted upon the escape of man from irksome labours through the use of machinery. He is the great primitive of modern Utopias, and Bellamy is his American equivalent. Hitherto, either slave labour (Phaleas),† or at least class distinctions involving unavoidable labour in the lower class, have been assumed – as Plato does, and as Bacon in the *New Atlantis* probably intended to do (More gave his Utopians bondsmen *sans phrase* for their most disagreeable toil); or there is – as in Morris and the outright Return-to-Nature Utopians – a bold make-believe that all toil may be made a joy, and with that a levelling down of all society to an equal participation in labour. But indeed this is against all the observed behaviour of mankind. It needed the Olympian unworldliness of an irresponsible rich man of the shareholding type, a Ruskin or a Morris playing at life, to imagine as much. Road-making under Mr Ruskin's auspices was a joy at Oxford no doubt, and a distinction, and it still remains a distinction; it proved the least contagious of practices. And Hawthorne did not find bodily toil anything more than the curse the Bible says it is, at Brook Farm.‡

If toil is a blessing, never was blessing so effectually disguised, and the very people who tell us that, hesitate to suggest more than a beautiful ease in the endless day of Heaven. A certain amount of bodily or mental exercise, a considerable amount of doing things under the direction of one's free imagination is quite another matter. Artistic production, for example, when it is at its best, when a man is freely obeying himself, and not troubling to please others, is really not toil at all. It is quite a different thing digging potatoes, as boys say, 'for a lark', and digging them because otherwise you will starve, digging them day after day as a dull, unavoidable imperative. The essence of toil is that imperative, and the fact that the attention *must* cramp itself to the work in hand – that it excludes freedom, and not that it involves fatigue. So long as anything but a quasi-savage life depended upon toil, so long was it hopeless to expect mankind to do anything but struggle to confer just as much of this blessing as possible upon one another. But now that the new conditions physical science is bringing about, not only

* Cabet, *Voyage en Icarie*, 1848.
† Aristotle's *Politics*, Bk II, Ch. VIII.
‡ *The Blithedale Romance*, and see also his *Note Books*.

dispense with man as a source of energy but supply the hope that all routine work may be made automatic, it is becoming conceivable that presently there may be no need for anyone to toil habitually at all; that a labouring class – that is to say, a class of workers without personal initiative – will become unnecessary to the world of men.

The plain message physical science has for the world at large is this, that were our political and social and moral devices only as well contrived to their ends as a Linotype machine, an antiseptic operating plant, or an electric tramcar, there need now at the present moment be no appreciable toil in the world, and only the smallest fraction of the pain, the fear, and the anxiety that now make human life so doubtful in its value. There is more than enough for everyone alive. Science stands, a competent servant, behind her wrangling underbred masters, holding out resources, devices, and remedies they are too stupid to use.* And on its material side a modern Utopia must needs present these gifts as taken, and show a world that is really abolishing the need of labour, abolishing the last base reason for anyone's servitude or inferiority.

7

The effectual abolition of a labouring and servile class will make itself felt in every detail of the inn that will shelter us, of the bedrooms we shall occupy. You conceive my awakening to all these things on the morning after our arrival. I shall lie for a minute or so with my nose peeping over the coverlet, agreeably and gently coming awake, and with some vague nightmare of sitting at a common table with an un-avoidable dustman in green and gold called Boffin,† fading out of my mind. Then I should start up. You figure my apprehensive, startled inspection of my chamber. 'Where am I?' that classic phrase, recurs. Then I perceive quite clearly that I am in bed in Utopia.

Utopia! The word is enough to bring anyone out of bed to the nearest window, but thence I see no more than the great mountain mass behind the inn, a very terrestrial-looking mountain mass. I return to the contrivances about me, and make my examination as I dress, pausing garment in hand to hover over first this thing of interest and then that.

* See that most suggestive little book, *Twentieth Century Invention*, by Mr George Sutherland.
† See William Morris's *News from Nowhere*.

The room is, of course, very clear and clean and simple; not by any means cheaply equipped, but designed to economise the labour of redding and repair just as much as is possible. It is beautifully proportioned, and rather lower than most rooms I know on earth. There is no fireplace, and I am perplexed by that until I find a thermometer beside six switches on the wall. Above this switchboard is a brief instruction: one switch warms the floor, which is not carpeted, but covered by a substance like soft oilcloth; one warms the mattress (which is of metal with resistance coils threaded to and fro in it); and the others warm the wall in various degrees, each directing current through a separate system of resistances. The casement does not open, but above, flush with the ceiling, a noiseless rapid fan pumps air out of the room. The air enters by a Tobin shaft. There is a recess dressing-room, equipped with a bath and all that is necessary to one's toilette, and the water, one remarks, is warmed, if one desires it warm, by passing it through an electrically heated spiral of tubing. A cake of soap drops out of a store machine on the turn of a handle, and when you have done with it, you drop that and your soiled towels and so forth, which also are given you by machines, into a little box, through the bottom of which they drop at once, and sail down a smooth shaft. A little notice tells you the price of your room, and you gather the price is doubled if you do not leave the toilette as you found it. Beside the bed, and to be lit at night by a handy switch over the pillow, is a little clock, its face flush with the wall. The room has no corners to gather dirt, wall meets floor with a gentle curve, and the apartment could be swept out effectually by a few strokes of a mechanical sweeper. The door frames and window frames are of metal, rounded and impervious to draught. You are politely requested to turn a handle at the foot of your bed before leaving the room, and forthwith the frame turns up into a vertical position, and the bedclothes hang airing. You stand at the doorway and realise that there remains not a minute's work for anyone to do. Memories of the foetid disorder of many an earthly bedroom after a night's use float across your mind.

And you must not imagine this dustless, spotless, sweet apartment as anything but beautiful. Its appearance is a little unfamiliar of course, but all the muddle of dust-collecting hangings and witless ornament that cover the earthly bedroom, the valances, the curtains to check the draught from the ill-fitting wood windows, the worthless irrelevant pictures, usually a little askew, the dusty carpets, and all the paraphernalia about the dirty, black-leaded fireplace are gone. But the faintly tinted walls are framed with just one clear coloured line, as finely placed as the member of a Greek capital; the door handles and the lines of the panels of the door, the two chairs, the framework of the bed, the writing table, have all that final simplicity, that exquisite finish of contour that is begotten of sustained artistic effort. The graciously shaped windows each frame a picture – since they are draughtless the window seats are no mere mockeries as are the window seats of earth – and on the sill, the sole thing to need attention in the room, is one little bowl of blue Alpine flowers.

The same exquisite simplicity meets one downstairs.

Our landlord sits down at table with us for a moment, and seeing we do not understand the electrically heated coffee-pot before us, shows us what to do. Coffee and milk we have, in the Continental fashion, and some excellent rolls and butter.

He is a swarthy little man, our landlord, and overnight we saw him preoccupied with other guests. But we have risen either late or early by Utopian standards, we know not which, and this morning he has us to himself. His bearing is kindly and inoffensive, but he cannot conceal the curiosity that possesses him. His eye meets ours with a mute enquiry, and then as we fall to, we catch him scrutinising our cuffs, our garments, our boots, our faces, our table manners. He asks nothing at first, but says a word or so about our night's comfort and the day's weather, phrases that have an air of being customary. Then comes a silence that is interrogative.

'Excellent coffee,' I say to fill the gap.

'And excellent rolls,' says my botanist.

Our landlord indicates his sense of our approval.

A momentary diversion is caused by the entry of an elfin-tressed little girl, who stares at us half impudently, half shyly, with bright black eyes, hesitates at the botanist's clumsy smile and nod, and then goes and stands by her father and surveys us steadfastly.

'You have come far?' ventures our landlord, patting his daughter's shoulder.

I glance at the botanist. 'Yes,' I say, 'we have.'

I expand. 'We have come so far that this country of yours seems very strange indeed to us.'

'The mountains?'

'Not only the mountains.'

'You came up out of the Ticino valley?'

'No – not that way.'

'By the Oberalp?'

'No.'

'The Furka?'

'No.'

'Not up from the lake?'

'No.'

He looks puzzled.

'We came,' I say, 'from another world.'

He seems trying to understand. Then a thought strikes him, and he sends away his little girl with a needless message to her mother.

'Ah!' he says. 'Another world – eh? Meaning – ?'

'Another world – far in the deeps of space.'

Then at the expression of his face one realises that a modern Utopia will probably keep its more intelligent citizens for better work than inn-tending. He is evidently inaccessible to the idea we think of putting before him. He stares at us a moment, and then remarks, 'There's the book to sign.'

We find ourselves confronted with a book, a little after the fashion of the familiar hotel visitors' book of earth. He places this before us, and beside it puts pen and ink and a slab, upon which ink has been freshly smeared.

'Thumb-marks,' says my scientific friend hastily in English.

'You show me how to do it,' I say as quickly.

He signs first, and I look over his shoulder.

He is displaying more readiness than I should have expected. The book is ruled in broad transverse lines, and has a space for a name, for a number, and a thumb-mark. He puts his thumb upon the slab and makes the thumb-mark first with the utmost deliberation. Meanwhile he studies the other two entries. The 'numbers' of the previous guests above are complex muddles of letters and figures. He writes his name, then with a calm assurance writes down his number, A.M.a.1607.2.$\alpha\beta\oplus$. I am wrung with momentary admiration. I follow his example, and fabricate an equally imposing signature. We think ourselves very clever. The landlord proffers finger bowls for our thumbs, and his eye goes, just a little curiously, to our entries.

I decide it is advisable to pay and go before any conversation about our formulae arises.

As we emerge into the corridor, and the morning sunlight of the Utopian world, I see the landlord bending over the book.

'Come on,' I say. 'The most tiresome thing in the world is explanations, and I perceive that if we do not get along, they will fall upon us now.'

I glance back to discover the landlord and a gracefully robed woman standing outside the pretty simplicity of the Utopian inn, watching us doubtfully as we recede.

'Come on,' I insist.

8

We should go towards the Schoellenen gorge, and as we went, our fresh morning senses would gather together a thousand factors for our impression of this more civilised world. A modern Utopia will have done with yapping about nationality, and so the ugly fortifications, the barracks and military defilements of the earthly vale of Urseren will be wanting. Instead there will be a great multitude of gracious little houses clustering in college-like groups, no doubt about their common kitchens and halls, down and about the valley slopes. And there will be many more trees, and a great variety of trees – all the world will have been ransacked for winter conifers. Despite the height of the valley there will be a double avenue along the road. This high road with its tramway would turn with us to descend the gorge, and we should hesitate upon the adventure of boarding the train. But now we should have the memory of our landlord's curious eye upon us, and we should decide at last to defer the risk of explanations such an enterprise might precipitate.

We should go by the great road for a time, and note something of the difference between Utopian and terrestrial engineering.

The tramway, the train road, the culverts, and bridges, the Urnerloch tunnel, into which the road plunges, will all be beautiful things.

There is nothing in machinery, there is nothing in embankments and railways and iron bridges and engineering devices to oblige them to be ugly. Ugliness is the measure of imperfection; a thing of human making is for the most part ugly in proportion to the poverty of its constructive thought, to the failure of its producer fully to grasp the purpose of its being. Everything to which men continue to give thought and attention, which they make and remake in the same direction, and with a continuing desire to do as well as they can, grows beautiful inevitably. Things made by mankind under modern conditions are ugly, primarily because our social organisation is ugly, because we live in an atmosphere of snatch and uncertainty, and do everything in an underbred strenuous manner. This is the misfortune of machinery, and not its fault. Art, like some beautiful plant, lives on its atmosphere, and when the atmosphere is good, it will grow everywhere, and when it is bad nowhere. If we smashed and buried every machine, every furnace, every factory in the

A MODERN UTOPIA

world, and without any further change set ourselves to home industries, hand labour, spade husbandry, sheepfolding and pig minding, we should still do things in the same haste, and achieve nothing but dirtiness, inconvenience, bad air, and another gaunt and gawky reflection of our intellectual and moral disorder. We should mend nothing.

But in Utopia a man who designs a tram road will be a cultivated man, an artist craftsman; he will strive, as a good writer or a painter strives, to achieve the simplicity of perfection. He will make his girders and rails and parts as gracious as that first engineer, Nature, has made the stems of her plants and the joints and gestures of her animals. To esteem him a sort of anti-artist, to count every man who makes things with his unaided thumbs an artist, and every man who uses machinery as a brute, is merely a passing phase of human stupidity. This tram road beside us will be a triumph of design. The idea will be so unfamiliar to us that for a time it will not occur to us that it is a system of beautiful objects at all. We shall admire its ingenious adaptation to the need of a district that is buried half the year in snow, the hard bed below, curved and guttered to do its own clearing, the great arched sleeper masses, raising the rails a good two yards above the ground, the easy, simple standards and insulators. Then it will creep in upon our minds, 'But, by Jove! *This is designed!*'

Indeed the whole thing will be designed.

Later on, perhaps, we may find students in an art school working in competition to design an electric tram, students who know something of modern metallurgy, and something of electrical engineering, and we shall find people as keenly critical of a signal box or an iron bridge as they are on earth of – ! Heavens! what *are* they critical about on earth?

The quality and condition of a dress tie!

We should make some unpatriotic comparisons with our own planet, no doubt.

CHAPTER FOUR

The Voice of Nature

1

Presently we recognise the fellow of the earthly Devil's Bridge, still intact as a footway, spanning the gorge, and old memories turn us off the road down the steep ruin of an ancient mule track towards it. It is our first reminder that Utopia too must have a history. We cross it and find the Reuss, for all that it has already lit and warmed and ventilated and cleaned several thousands of houses in the dale above, and for all that it drives those easy trams in the gallery overhead, is yet capable of as fine a cascade as ever it flung on earth. So we come to a rocky path, wild as one could wish, and descend, discoursing how good and fair an ordered world may be, but with a certain un-formulated qualification in our minds about those thumb-marks we have left behind.

'Do you recall the Zermatt valley?' says my friend, 'and how on earth it reeks and stinks with smoke?'

'People make that an argument for obstructing change, instead of helping it forward!'

And here perforce an episode intrudes. We are invaded by a talkative person.

He overtakes us and begins talking forthwith in a fluty, but not unamiable, tenor. He is a great talker, this man, and a fairly respectable gesticulator, and to him it is we make our first ineffectual tentatives at explaining who indeed we are; but his flow of talk washes that all away again. He has a face of that rubicund, knobby type I have heard an indignant mineralogist speak of as botryoidal, and about it waves a quantity of disorderly blond hair. He is dressed in leather doublet and knee breeches, and he wears over these a streaming woollen cloak of faded crimson that gives him a fine dramatic outline as he comes down towards us over the rocks. His feet, which are large and handsome, but bright pink with the keen morning air, are bare, except for sandals of leather. (It was the only time that we saw anyone in Utopia with bare feet.) He salutes us with a scroll-like waving of his stick, and falls in with our slower paces.

'Climbers, I presume?' he says, 'and you scorn these trams of theirs? I like you. So do I! Why a man should consent to be dealt with as a bale of goods holding an indistinctive ticket – when God gave him legs and a face – passes my understanding.'

As he speaks, his staff indicates the great mechanical road that runs across the gorge and high overhead through a gallery in the rock, follows it along until it turns the corner, picks it up as a viaduct far below, traces it until it plunges into an arcade through a jutting crag, and there dismisses it with a spiral whirl. '*No!*' he says.

He seems sent by Providence, for just now we had been discussing how we should broach our remarkable situation to these Utopians before our money is spent.

Our eyes meet, and I gather from the botanist that I am to open our case.

I do my best.

'You came from the other side of space!' says the man in the crimson cloak, interrupting me. 'Precisely! I like that – it's exactly my note! So do I! And you find this world strange! Exactly my case! We are brothers! We shall be in sympathy. I am amazed, I have been amazed as long as I can remember, and I shall die, most certainly, in a state of incredulous amazement, at this remarkable world. Eh? . . . You found yourselves suddenly upon a mountain top! Fortunate men!' He chuckled. 'For my part I found myself in the still stranger position of infant to two parents of the most intractable dispositions!'

'The fact remains,' I protest.

'A position, I can assure you, demanding Tact of an altogether super-human quality!'

We desist for a space from the attempt to explain our remarkable selves, and for the rest of the time this picturesque and exceptional Utopian takes the talk entirely under his control . . .

2

An agreeable person, though a little distracting, he was; and he talked, we recall, of many things. He impressed us, we found afterwards, as a poseur beyond question, a conscious Ishmaelite in the world of wit, and in some subtly inexplicable way as a most consummate ass. He talked first of the excellent and commodious trams that came from over the passes, and ran down the long valley towards middle Switzerland, and of all the growth of pleasant homes and chalets amidst the heights that

made the opening gorge so different from its earthly parallel, with a
fine disrespect. 'But they are beautiful,' I protested. 'They are graciously
proportioned, they are placed in well-chosen positions; they give no
offence to the eye.'

'What do we know of the beauty they replace? They are a mere rash.
Why should we men play the part of bacteria upon the face of our Mother?'

'All life is that!'

'No! not natural life, not the plants and the gentle creatures that live
their wild shy lives in forest and jungle. That is a part of her. That is the
natural bloom of her complexion. But these houses and tramways and
things, all made from ore and stuff torn from her veins – ! You can't
better my image of the rash. It's a morbid breaking out! I'd give it all for
one – what is it? – free and natural chamois.'

'You live at times in a house?' I asked.

He ignored my question. For him, untroubled Nature was the best,
he said, and, with a glance at his feet, the most beautiful. He professed
himself a Nazarite, and shook back his Teutonic poet's shock of hair.
So he came to himself, and for the rest of our walk he kept to himself
as the thread of his discourse, and went over himself from top to toe,
and strung thereon all topics under the sun by way of illustrating
his splendours. But especially his foil was the relative folly, the un-
naturalness and want of logic in his fellow men. He held strong views
about the extreme simplicity of everything, only that men, in their
muddle-headedness, had confounded it all. 'Hence, for example, these
trams! They are always running up and down as though they were
looking for the lost simplicity of nature. "We dropped it here!"'
He earned a living, we gathered, 'some considerable way above the
minimum wage', which threw a chance light on the labour problem –
by perforating records for automatic musical machines – no doubt of
the Pianotist and Pianola kind – and he spent all the leisure he could
gain in going to and fro in the earth lecturing on 'The Need of a
Return to Nature', and on 'Simple Foods and Simple Ways'. He did it
for the love of it. It was very clear to us he had an inordinate impulse
to lecture, and esteemed us fair game. He had been lecturing on these
topics in Italy, and he was now going back through the mountains to
lecture in Saxony, lecturing on the way, to perforate a lot more records,
lecturing the while, and so start out lecturing again. He was un-
disguisedly glad to have us to lecture to by the way.

He called our attention to his costume at an early stage. It was the
embodiment of his ideal of Nature-clothing, and it had been made
especially for him at very great cost. 'Simply because naturalness has

fled the earth, and has to be sought now, and washed out from your crushed complexities like gold.'

'I should have thought,' said I, 'that any clothing whatever was something of a slight upon the natural man.'

'Not at all,' said he, 'not at all! You forget his natural vanity!'

He was particularly severe on our artificial hoofs, as he called our boots, and our hats or hair destructors. 'Man is the real King of Beasts and should wear a mane. The lion only wears it by consent and in captivity.' He tossed his head.

Subsequently while we lunched and he waited for the specific natural dishes he ordered – they taxed the culinary resources of the inn to the utmost – he broached a comprehensive generalisation. 'The animal kingdom and the vegetable kingdom are easily distinguished, and for the life of me I see no reason for confusing them. It is, I hold, a sin against Nature. I keep them distinct in my mind and I keep them distinct in my person. No animal substance inside, no vegetable without; – what could be simpler or more logical? Nothing upon me but leather and all-wool garments; within, cereals, fruit, nuts, herbs, and the like. Classification – order – man's function. He is here to observe and accentuate Nature's simplicity. These people' – he swept an arm that tried not too personally to include us – 'are filled and covered with confusion.'

He ate great quantities of grapes and finished with a cigarette. He demanded and drank a great horn of unfermented grape juice, and it seemed to suit him well.

We three sat about the board – it was in an agreeable little arbour on a hill hard by the place where Wassen stands on earth, and it looked down the valley to the Uri Rothstock, and ever and again we sought to turn his undeniable gift of exposition to the elucidation of our own difficulties.

But we seemed to get little, his style was so elusive. Afterwards, indeed, we found much information and many persuasions had soaked into us, but at the time it seemed to us he told us nothing. He indicated things by dots and dashes, instead of by good hard assertive lines. He would not pause to see how little we knew. Sometimes his wit rose so high that he would lose sight of it himself, and then he would pause, purse his lips as if he whistled, and then till the bird came back to the lure, fill his void mouth with grapes. He talked of the relations of the sexes, and love – a passion he held in great contempt as being in its essence complex and disingenuous – and afterwards we found we had learnt much of what the marriage laws of Utopia allow and forbid.

'A simple natural freedom,' he said, waving a grape in an illustrative manner, and so we gathered the modern Utopia did not at any rate go to that. He spoke, too, of the regulation of unions, of people who were not allowed to have children, of complicated rules and interventions. 'Man,' he said, 'had ceased to be a natural product!'

We tried to check him with questions at this most illuminating point, but he drove on like a torrent, and carried his topic out of sight. The world, he held, was over-managed, and that was the root of all evil. He talked of the over-management of the world, and among other things of the laws that would not let a poor simple idiot, a 'natural', go at large. And so we had our first glimpse of what Utopia did with the feeble and insane. 'We make all these distinctions between man and man, we exalt this and favour that, and degrade and seclude that; we make birth artificial, life artificial, death artificial.'

'You say *We*,' said I, with the first glimmering of a new idea, 'but *you* don't participate?'

'Not I! I'm not one of your samurai, your voluntary noblemen who have taken the world in hand. I might be, of course, but I'm not.'

'Samurai!' I repeated, 'voluntary noblemen!' and for the moment could not frame a question.

He whirled on to an attack on science, that stirred the botanist to controversy. He denounced with great bitterness all specialists whatever, and particularly doctors and engineers.

'Voluntary noblemen!' he said, 'voluntary Gods I fancy they think themselves,' and I was left behind for a space in the perplexed examination of this parenthesis, while he and the botanist – who is sedulous to keep his digestion up to date with all the newest devices – argued about the good of medicine men.

'The natural human constitution,' said the blond-haired man, 'is perfectly simple, with one simple condition – you must leave it to Nature. But if you mix up things so distinctly and essentially separated as the animal and vegetable kingdoms for example, and ram *that* in for it to digest, what can you expect?

'Ill health! There isn't such a thing – in the course of Nature. But you shelter from Nature in houses, you protect yourselves by clothes that are useful instead of being ornamental, you wash – with such abstersive chemicals as soap for example – and above all you consult doctors.' He approved himself with a chuckle. 'Have you ever found anyone seriously ill without doctors and medicine about? Never! You say a lot of people would die without shelter and medical attendance! No doubt – but a natural death. A natural death is better than an artificial life, surely? That's – to be frank with you – the very citadel of my position.'

That led him, and rather promptly, before the botanist could rally to reply, to a great tirade against the laws that forbade 'sleeping out'. He denounced them with great vigour; and alleged that for his own part he broke that law whenever he could, found some corner of moss, shaded from an excess of dew, and there sat up to sleep. He slept, he said, always in a sitting position, with his head on his wrists, and his wrists on his knees – the simple natural position for sleep in man . . . He said it would be far better if all the world slept out, and all the houses were pulled down.

You will understand, perhaps, the subdued irritation I felt, as I sat and listened to the botanist entangling himself in the logical net of this wild nonsense. It impressed me as being irrelevant. When one comes to a Utopia one expects a Cicerone, one expects a person as precise and insistent and instructive as an American advertisement – the advertisement of one of those land agents, for example, who print their own engaging photographs to instil confidence and begin, 'You want to buy real estate.' One expects to find all Utopians absolutely convinced of the perfection of their Utopia, and incapable of receiving a hint against its order. And here was this purveyor of absurdities!

And yet now that I come to think it over, is not this too one of the necessary differences between a modern Utopia and those finite compact settlements of the older school of dreamers? It is not to be a unanimous world any more, it is to have all and more of the mental contrariety we find in the world of the real; it is no longer to be perfectly explicable, it is just our own vast mysterious welter, with some of the blackest shadows gone, with a clearer illumination, and a more conscious and intelligent will. Irrelevance is not irrelevant to such a scheme, and our blond-haired friend is exactly just where he ought to be here.

Still –

3

I ceased to listen to the argumentation of my botanist with this apostle of Nature. The botanist, in his scientific way, was, I believe, defending the learned professions. (He thinks and argues like drawing on squared paper.) It struck me as transiently remarkable that a man who could not be induced to forget himself and his personal troubles on coming into a whole new world, who could waste our first evening in Utopia upon a paltry egotistical love story, should presently become quite heated and impersonal in the discussion of scientific professionalism. He was –

absorbed. I can't attempt to explain these vivid spots and blind spots in the imaginations of sane men; there they are!

'You say,' said the botanist, with a prevalent index finger, and the resolute deliberation of a big siege gun being lugged into action over rough ground by a number of inexperienced men, 'you prefer a natural death to an artificial life. But what is your *definition* (stress) of artificial? . . .'

And after lunch too! I ceased to listen, flicked the end of my cigarette ash over the green trellis of the arbour, stretched my legs with a fine restfulness, leant back, and gave my mind to the fields and houses that lay adown the valley.

What I saw interwove with fragmentary things our garrulous friend had said, and with the trend of my own speculations . . .

The high road, with its tramways and its avenues on either side, ran in a bold curve, and with one great loop of descent, down the opposite side of the valley, and below crossed again on a beautiful viaduct, and dipped into an arcade in the side of the Bristenstock. Our inn stood out boldly, high above the level this took. The houses clustered in their collegiate groups over by the high road, and near the subordinate way that ran almost vertically below us and past us and up towards the valley of the Meien Reuss. There were one or two Utopians cutting and packing the flowery mountain grass in the carefully levelled and irrigated meadows by means of swift, light machines that ran on things like feet and seemed to devour the herbage, and there were many children and a woman or so, going to and fro among the houses near at hand. I guessed a central building towards the high road must be the school from which these children were coming. I noted the health and cleanliness of these young heirs of Utopia as they passed below.

The pervading quality of the whole scene was a sane order, the deliberate solution of problems, a progressive intention steadily achieving itself, and the aspect that particularly occupied me was the incongruity of this with our blond-haired friend.

On the one hand here was a state of affairs that implied a power of will, an organising and controlling force, the co-operation of a great number of vigorous people to establish and sustain its progress, and on the other this creature of pose and vanity, with his restless wit, his perpetual giggle at his own cleverness, his manifest incapacity for comprehensive co-operation.

Now, had I come upon a hopeless incompatibility? Was this the *reductio ad absurdum* of my vision, and must it even as I sat there fade, dissolve, and vanish before my eyes?

There was no denying our blond friend. If this Utopia is indeed to parallel our earth, man for man – and I see no other reasonable choice to that – there must be this sort of person and kindred sorts of persons in great abundance. The desire and gift to see life whole is not the lot of the great majority of men, the service of truth is the privilege of the elect, and these clever fools who choke the avenues of the world of thought, who stick at no inconsistency, who oppose, obstruct, confuse, will find only the freer scope amidst Utopian freedoms.

They argued on, these two, as I worried my brains with riddles. It was like a fight between a cock sparrow and a tortoise; they both went on in their own way, regardless of each other's proceedings. The encounter had an air of being extremely lively, and the moments of contact were few. 'But you mistake my point,' the blond man was saying, disordering his hair – which had become unruffled in the preoccupation of dispute – with a hasty movement of his hand, 'you don't appreciate the position I take up.'

'Ugh!' said I privately, and lighted another cigarette and went away into my own thoughts with that.

The position he takes up! That's the way of your intellectual fool, the Universe over. He takes up a position, and he's going to be the most brilliant, delightful, engaging and invincible of gay delicious creatures defending that position you can possibly imagine. And even when the case is not so bad as that, there still remains the quality. We 'take up our positions', silly little contentious creatures that we are, we will not see the right in one another, we will not patiently state and restate, and honestly accommodate and plan, and so we remain at sixes and sevens. We've all a touch of Gladstone in us, and try to the last moment to deny we have made a turn. And so our poor broken-springed world jolts athwart its trackless destiny. Try to win into line with some fellow weakling, and see the little host of suspicions, aggressions, misrepresentations, your approach will stir – like summer flies on a high road – the way he will try to score a point and claim you as a convert to what he has always said, his fear lest the point should be scored to you.

It is not only such gross and palpable cases as our blond and tenoring friend. I could find the thing negligible were it only that. But when one sees the same thread woven into men who are leaders, men who sway vast multitudes, who are indeed great and powerful men; when one sees how unfair they can be, how unteachable, the great blind areas in their eyes also, their want of generosity, then one's doubts gather like mists across this Utopian valley, its vistas pale, its people become unsubstantial phantoms, all its order and its happiness dim and recede . . .

If we are to have any Utopia at all, we must have a clear common purpose, and a great and steadfast movement of will to override all these incurably egotistical dissentients. Something is needed wide and deep enough to float the worst of egotisms away. The world is not to be made right by acclamation and in a day, and then for ever more trusted to run alone. It is manifest this Utopia could not come about by chance and anarchy, but by co-ordinated effort and a community of design, and to tell of just land laws and wise government, a wisely balanced economic system, and wise social arrangements without telling how it was brought about, and how it is sustained against the vanity and self-indulgence, the moody fluctuations and uncertain imaginations, the heat and aptitude for partisanship that lurk, even when they do not flourish, in the texture of every man alive, is to build a palace without either door or staircase.

I had not this in mind when I began.

Somewhere in the Modern Utopia there must be adequate men, men the very antithesis of our friend, capable of self-devotion, of intentional courage, of honest thought, and steady endeavour. There must be a literature to embody their common idea, of which this Modern Utopia is merely the material form; there must be some organisation, however slight, to keep them in touch one with the other.

Who will these men be? Will they be a caste? a race? an organisation in the nature of a church? . . . And there came into my mind the words of our acquaintance, that he was not one of these 'voluntary noblemen'.

At first that phrase struck me as being merely queer, and then I began to realise certain possibilities that were wrapped up in it.

The animus of our chance friend, at any rate, went to suggest that here was his antithesis. Evidently what he is not, will be the class to contain what is needed here. Evidently.

4

I was recalled from my meditations by the hand of the blond-haired man upon my arm.

I looked up to discover the botanist had gone into the inn.

The blond-haired man was for a moment almost stripped of pose.

'I say,' he said. 'Weren't you listening to me?'

'No,' I said bluntly.

His surprise was manifest. But by an effort he recalled what he had meant to say.

'Your friend,' he said, 'has been telling me, in spite of my sustained interruptions, a most incredible story.'

I wondered how the botanist managed to get it in. 'About that woman?' I said.

'About a man and a woman who hate each other and can't get away from each other.'

'I know,' I said.

'It sounds absurd.'

'It is.'

'Why can't they get away? What is there to keep them together? It's ridiculous. I – '

'Quite.'

'He *would* tell it to me.'

'It's his way.'

'He interrupted me. And there's no point in it. Is he – ' he hesitated, 'mad?'

'There's a whole world of people mad with him,' I answered after a pause.

The perplexed expression of the blond-haired man intensified. It is vain to deny that he enlarged the scope of his enquiry, visibly if not verbally. 'Dear me!' he said, and took up something he had nearly forgotten. 'And you found yourselves suddenly on a mountainside? . . . I thought you were joking.'

I turned round upon him with a sudden access of earnestness. At least I meant my manner to be earnest, but to him it may have seemed wild.

'You,' I said, 'are an original sort of man. Do not be alarmed. Perhaps you will understand . . . We were not joking.'

'But, my dear fellow!'

'I mean it! We come from an inferior world! Like this, but out of order.'

'No world could be more out of order – '

'You play at that and have your fun. But there's no limit to the extent to which a world of men may get out of gear. In our world – '

He nodded, but his eye had ceased to be friendly.

'Men die of starvation; people die by the hundred thousand need-lessly and painfully; men and women are lashed together to make hell for each other; children are born – abominably, and reared in cruelty and folly; there is a thing called war, a horror of blood and vileness. The whole thing seems to me at times a cruel and wasteful wilderness of muddle. You in this decent world have no means of understanding – '

'No?' he said, and would have begun, but I went on too quickly.

'No! When I see you dandering through this excellent and hopeful world, objecting, obstructing, and breaking the law, displaying your wit on science and order, on the men who toil so ingloriously to swell and use the knowledge that is salvation, this salvation for which *our* poor world cries to heaven – '

'You don't mean to say,' he said, 'that you really come from some other world where things are different and worse?'

'I do.'

'And you want to talk to me about it instead of listening to me?'

'Yes.'

'Oh, nonsense!' he said abruptly. 'You can't do it – really. I can assure you this present world touches the nadir of imbecility. You and your friend, with his love for the lady who's so mysteriously tied – you're romancing! People could not possibly do such things. It's – if you'll excuse me – ridiculous. *He* began – he would begin. A most tiresome story – simply bore me down. We'd been talking very agreeably before that, or rather *I* had, about the absurdity of marriage laws, the interference with a free and natural life, and so on, and suddenly he burst like a dam. No!' He paused. 'It's really impossible. You behave perfectly well for a time, and then you begin to interrupt . . . And such a childish story, too!'

He spun round upon his chair, got up, glanced at me over his shoulder, and walked out of the arbour. He stepped aside hastily to avoid too close an approach to the returning botanist. 'Impossible,' I heard him say. He was evidently deeply aggrieved by us. I saw him presently a little way off in the garden, talking to the landlord of our inn, and looking towards us as he talked – they both looked towards us – and after that, without the ceremony of a farewell, he disappeared, and we saw him no more. We waited for him a little while, and then I expounded the situation to the botanist . . .

'We are going to have a very considerable amount of trouble explaining ourselves,' I said in conclusion. 'We are here by an act of the imagination, and that is just one of those metaphysical operations that are so difficult to make credible. We are, by the standard of bearing and clothing I remark about us, unattractive in dress and deportment. We have nothing to produce to explain our presence here, no bit of a flying machine or a space-travelling sphere or any of the apparatus customary on these occasions. We have no means beyond a dwindling amount of small change out of a gold coin, upon which I suppose in ethics and the law some native Utopian had a better claim. We may already have got ourselves into trouble with the authorities with that confounded number of yours!'

'You did one too!'

'All the more bother, perhaps, when the thing is brought home to us. There's no need for recriminations. The thing of moment is that we find ourselves in the position – not to put too fine a point upon it – of tramps in this admirable world. The question of all others of importance to us at present is what do they do with their tramps? Because sooner or later, and the balance of probability seems to incline to sooner, whatever they do with their tramps that they will do with us.'

'Unless we can get some work.'

'Exactly – unless we can get some work.'

'Get work!'

The botanist leant forward on his arms and looked out of the arbour with an expression of despondent discovery. 'I say,' he remarked; 'this is a strange world – quite strange and new. I'm only beginning to realise just what it means for us. The mountains there are the same, the old Bristenstock and all the rest of it; but these houses, you know, and that roadway, and the costumes, and that machine that is licking up the grass there – only . . .'

He sought expression. 'Who knows what will come in sight round the bend of the valley there? Who knows what may happen to us anywhere? We don't know who rules over us even . . . we don't know that!'

'No,' I echoed, 'we don't know *that*.'

CHAPTER FIVE

Failure in a Modern Utopia

1

The old Utopias – save for the breeding schemes of Plato and Campanella – ignored that reproductive competition among individualities which is the substance of life, and dealt essentially with its incidentals. The endless variety of men, their endless gradation of quality, over which the hand of selection plays, and to which we owe the unmanageable complication of real life, is tacitly set aside. The real world is a vast disorder of accidents and incalculable forces in which men survive or fail. A modern Utopia, unlike its predecessors, dare not pretend to change the last condition; it may order and humanise the conflict, but men must still survive or fail.

Most Utopias present themselves as going concerns, as happiness in being; they make it an essential condition that a happy land can have no history, and all the citizens one is permitted to see are well looking and upright and mentally and morally in tune. But we are under the dominion of a logic that obliges us to take over the actual population of the world with only such moral and mental and physical improvements as lie within their inherent possibilities, and it is our business to ask what Utopia will do with its congenital invalids, its idiots and madmen, its drunkards and men of vicious mind, its cruel and furtive souls, its stupid people, too stupid to be of use to the community, its lumpish, unteachable and unimaginative people? And what will it do with the man who is 'poor' all round, the rather spiritless, rather incompetent low-grade man who on earth sits in the den of the sweater, tramps the streets under the banner of the unemployed, or trembles – in another man's cast-off clothing, and with an infinity of hat-touching – on the verge of rural employment?

These people will have to be in the descendent phase, the species must be engaged in eliminating them; there is no escape from that, and conversely the people of exceptional quality must be ascendant. The better sort of people, so far as they can be distinguished, must have the fullest freedom of public service, and the fullest opportunity of parentage. And it must be open to every man to approve himself worthy of ascendency.

The way of Nature in this process is to kill the weaker and the sillier, to crush them, to starve them, to overwhelm them, using the stronger and more cunning as her weapon. But man is the unnatural animal, the rebel child of Nature, and more and more does he turn himself against the harsh and fitful hand that reared him. He sees with a growing resentment the multitude of suffering ineffectual lives over which his species tramples in its ascent. In the Modern Utopia he will have set himself to change the ancient law. No longer will it be that failures must suffer and perish lest their breed increase, but the breed of failure must not increase, lest they suffer and perish, and the race with them.

Now we need not argue here to prove that the resources of the world and the energy of mankind, were they organised sanely, are amply sufficient to supply every material need of every living human being. And if it can be so contrived that every human being shall live in a state of reasonable physical and mental comfort, without the reproduction of inferior types, there is no reason whatever why that should not be secured. But there must be a competition in life of some sort to determine who are to be pushed to the edge, and who are to prevail and multiply. Whatever we do, man will remain a competitive creature, and though moral and intellectual training may vary and enlarge his conception of success and fortify him with refinements and consolations, no Utopia will ever save him completely from the emotional drama of struggle, from exultations and humiliations, from pride and prostration and shame. He lives in success and failure just as inevitably as he lives in space and time.

But we may do much to make the margin of failure endurable. On earth, for all the extravagance of charity, the struggle for the mass of men at the bottom resolves itself into a struggle, and often a very foul and ugly struggle, for food, shelter, and clothing. Deaths outright from exposure and starvation are now perhaps uncommon, but for the multitude there are only miserable houses, uncomfortable clothes, and bad and insufficient food; fractional starvation and exposure, that is to say. A Utopia planned upon modern lines will certainly have put an end to that. It will insist upon every citizen being properly housed, well nourished, and in good health, reasonably clean and clothed healthily, and upon that insistence its labour laws will be founded. In a phrasing that will be familiar to everyone interested in social reform, it will maintain a standard of life. Any house, unless it be a public monument, that does not come up to its rising standard of healthiness and convenience, the Utopian State will incontinently pull down, and pile the material and charge the owner for the labour; any house unduly crowded or dirty, it must in some effectual manner, directly or indirectly, confiscate and clear and clean. And any citizen indecently dressed, or ragged and dirty, or publicly unhealthy, or sleeping abroad homeless, or in any way neglected or derelict, must come under its care. It will find him work if he can and will work, it will take him to it, it will register him and lend him the money wherewith to lead a comely life until work can be found or made for him, and it will give him credit and shelter him and strengthen him if he is ill. In default of private enterprises it will provide inns for him and food, and it will – by itself acting as the reserve employer – maintain a minimum wage which will cover the cost of a decent life. The State will stand at the back of the economic struggle as the reserve employer of labour. This most excellent idea does, as a matter of fact, underlie the British institution of the workhouse, but it is jumbled up with the relief of old age and infirmity, it is administered parochially and on the supposition that all population is static and localised whereas every year it becomes more migratory; it is administered without any regard to the rising standards of comfort and self-respect in a progressive civilisation, and it is administered grudgingly. The thing that is done is done as unwilling charity by administrators who are often, in the rural districts at least, competing for low-priced labour, and who regard want of employment as a crime. But if it were possible for any citizen in need of money to resort to a place of public employment as a right, and there work for a week or month without degradation upon certain minimum terms, it seems fairly certain that no one would work, except as the victim of some quite exceptional and temporary accident, for less.

The work publicly provided would have to be toilsome, but not cruel or incapacitating. A choice of occupations would need to be afforded, occupations adapted to different types of training and capacity, with some residual employment of a purely laborious and mechanical sort for those who were incapable of doing the things that required intelligence. Necessarily this employment by the State would be a relief of economic pressure, but it would not be considered a charity done to the individual, but a public service. It need not pay, any more than the police need pay, but it could probably be done at a small margin of loss. There is a number of durable things bound finally to be useful that could be made and stored whenever the tide of more highly paid employment ebbed and labour sank to its minimum: bricks, iron from inferior ores, shaped and preserved timber, pins, nails, plain fabrics of cotton and linen, paper, sheet glass, artificial fuel, and so on; new roads could be made and public buildings reconstructed, inconveniences of all sorts removed, until under the stimulus of accumulating material, accumulating investments or other circumstances, the tide of private enterprise flowed again.

The State would provide these things for its citizen as though it was his right to require them; he would receive as a shareholder in the common enterprise and not with any insult of charity. But on the other hand it will require that the citizen who renders the minimum of service for these concessions shall not become a parent until he is established in work at a rate above the minimum, and free of any debt he may have incurred. The State will never press for its debt, nor put a limit to its accumulation so long as a man or woman remains childless; it will not even grudge them temporary spells of good fortune when they may lift their earnings above the minimum wage. It will pension the age of everyone who cares to take a pension, and it will maintain special guest homes for the very old to which they may come as paying guests, spending their pensions there. By such obvious devices it will achieve the maximum elimination of its feeble and spiritless folk in every generation with the minimum of suffering and public disorder.

2

But the mildly incompetent, the spiritless and dull, the poorer sort who are ill, do not exhaust our Utopian problem. There remain idiots and lunatics, there remain perverse and incompetent persons, there are people of weak character who become drunkards, drug takers, and the like. Then there are persons tainted with certain foul and transmissible diseases. All these people spoil the world for others. They may become parents, and with most of them there is manifestly nothing to be done but to seclude them from the great body of the population. You must resort to a kind of social surgery. You cannot have social freedom in your public ways, your children cannot speak to whom they will, your girls and gentlewomen cannot go abroad while some sorts of people go free. And there are violent people, and those who will not respect the property of others, thieves and cheats; they, too, so soon as their nature is confirmed, must pass out of the free life of our ordered world. So soon as there can be no doubt of the disease or baseness of the individual, so soon as the insanity or other disease is assured, or the crime repeated a third time, or the drunkenness or misdemeanour past its seventh occasion (let us say), so soon must he or she pass out of the common ways of men.

The dreadfulness of all such proposals as this lies in the possibility of their execution falling into the hands of hard, dull, and cruel administrators. But in the case of a Utopia one assumes the best possible government, a government as merciful and deliberate as it is powerful and decisive. You must not too hastily imagine these things being done – as they would be done on earth at present – by a number of zealous half-educated people in a state of panic at a quite imaginary 'Rapid Multiplication of the Unfit'.

No doubt for first offenders, and for all offenders under five-and-twenty, the Modern Utopia will attempt cautionary and remedial treatment. There will be disciplinary schools and colleges for the young, fair and happy places, but with less confidence and more restraint than the schools and colleges of the ordinary world. In remote and solitary regions these enclosures will lie, they will be fenced in and forbidden to the common run of men, and there, remote from all temptation, the defective citizen will be schooled. There will be no masking of the lesson; 'which do you value most, the wide world of humanity, or this evil trend in you?' From that discipline at last the prisoners will return.

But the others; what would a saner world do with them?

Our world is still vindictive, but the all-reaching State of Utopia will have the strength that begets mercy. Quietly the outcast will go from among his fellow men. There will be no drumming of him out of the ranks, no tearing off of epaulettes, no smiting in the face. The thing must be just public enough to obviate secret tyrannies, and that is all.

There would be no killing, no lethal chambers. No doubt Utopia will kill all deformed and monstrous and evilly diseased births, but for the rest, the State will hold itself accountable for their being. There is no justice in Nature perhaps, but the idea of justice must be sacred in any good society. Lives that statesmanship has permitted, errors it has not foreseen and educated against, must not be punished by death. If the State does not keep faith, no one will keep faith. Crime and bad lives are the measure of a State's failure, all crime in the end is the crime of the community. Even for murder Utopia will not, I think, kill.

I doubt even if there will be jails. No men are quite wise enough, good enough and cheap enough to staff jails as a jail ought to be staffed. Perhaps islands will be chosen, islands lying apart from the highways of the sea, and to these the State will send its exiles, most of them thanking Heaven, no doubt, to be quit of a world of prigs. The State will, of course, secure itself against any children from these people, that is the primary object in their seclusion, and perhaps it may even be necessary to make these island prisons a system of island monasteries and island nunneries. Upon that I am not competent to speak, but if I may believe the literature of the subject – unhappily a not very well criticised literature – it is not necessary to enforce this separation.*

About such islands patrol boats will go, there will be no freedoms of boat building, and it may be necessary to have armed guards at the creeks and quays. Beyond that the State will give these segregated failures just as full a liberty as they can have. If it interferes any further it will be simply to police the islands against the organisation of serious cruelty, to maintain the freedom of any of the detained who wish it to transfer themselves to other islands, and so to keep a check upon tyranny. The insane, of course, will demand care and control, but there is no reason why the islands of the hopeless drunkard, for example, should not each have a virtual autonomy, have at the most a Resident and a guard. I believe that a community of drunkards might be capable of organising even its own bad habit to the pitch of tolerable existence. I do not see why such an island should not build and order for itself and manufacture and trade. 'Your ways are not our ways,' the World State will say; 'but here is freedom and a company of kindred souls. Elect your jolly rulers, brew if you will, and distil; here are vine cuttings and barley fields; do as it pleases you to do. We will take care of the knives, but for the rest – deal yourselves with God!'

And you see the big convict steamship standing in to the Island of Incurable Cheats. The crew are respectfully at their quarters, ready to lend a hand overboard, but wide awake, and the captain is hospitably on the bridge to bid his guests goodbye and keep an eye on the movables. The new citizens for this particular Alsatia, each no doubt with his personal belongings securely packed and at hand, crowd the deck and study the nearing coast. Bright, keen faces would be there, and we, were we by any chance to find ourselves beside the captain, might recognise the double of this great earthly magnate or that, Petticoat Lane and Park Lane cheek by jowl. The landing part of the jetty is clear of people, only a government man or so stands there to receive the boat and prevent a rush, but beyond the gates a number of engagingly smart-looking individuals loiter speculatively. One figures a remarkable building labelled Custom House, an interesting fiscal revival this population has made, and beyond, crowding up the hill, the painted walls of a number of comfortable inns clamour loudly. One or two inhabitants in reduced circumstances would act as hotel touts, there are several hotel omnibuses and a Bureau de Change,

* See for example Dr W. A. Chapple's *The Fertility of the Unfit*.

certainly a Bureau de Change. And a small house with a large board, aimed point-blank seaward, declares itself a Gratis Information Office, and next to it rises the graceful dome of a small Casino. Beyond, great hoardings proclaim the advantages of many island specialities, a hustling commerce, and the opening of a Public Lottery. There is a large cheap-looking barrack, the school of Commercial Science for gentlemen of inadequate training . . .

Altogether a very go-ahead-looking little port it would be, and though this disembarkation would have none of the flow of hilarious good fellowship that would throw a halo of genial noise about the Islands of Drink, it is doubtful if the new arrivals would feel anything very tragic in the moment. Here at last was scope for adventure after their hearts.

This sounds more fantastic than it is. But what else is there to do, unless you kill? You must seclude, but why should you torment? All modern prisons are places of torture by restraint, and the habitual criminal plays the part of a damaged mouse at the mercy of the cat of our law. He has his little painful run, and back he comes again to a state more horrible even than destitution. There are no Alsatias left in the world. For my own part I can think of no crime, unless it is reckless begetting or the wilful transmission of contagious disease, for which the bleak terrors, the solitudes and ignominies of the modern prison do not seem outrageously cruel. If you want to go so far as that, then kill. Why, once you are rid of them, should you pester criminals to respect an uncongenial standard of conduct? Into such islands of exile as this a modern Utopia will have to purge itself. There is no alternative that I can contrive.

3

Will a Utopian be free to be idle?

Work has to be done, every day humanity is sustained by its collective effort, and without a constant recurrence of effort in the single man as in the race as a whole, there is neither health nor happiness. The permanent idleness of a human being is not only burdensome to the world, but his own secure misery. But unprofitable occupation is also intended by idleness, and it may be considered whether that freedom also will be open to the Utopian. Conceivably it will, like privacy, locomotion, and almost all the freedoms of life, and on the same terms – if he possess the money to pay for it.

That last condition may produce a shock in minds accustomed to the proposition that money is the root of all evil, and to the idea that Utopia necessarily implies something rather oaken and hand-made and primitive in all these relations. Of course, money is not the root of any evil in the world; the root of all evil in the world, and the root of all good too, is the Will to Live, and money becomes harmful only when by bad laws and bad economic organisation it is more easily attained by bad men than good. It is as reasonable to say food is the root of all disease, because so many people suffer from excessive and unwise eating. The sane economic ideal is to make the possession of money the clear indication of public serviceableness, and the more nearly that ideal is attained, the smaller is the justification of poverty and the less the hardship of being poor. In barbaric and disorderly countries it is almost honourable to be indigent and unquestionably virtuous to give to a beggar, and even in the more or less civilised societies of earth, so many children come into life hopelessly handicapped, that austerity to the poor is regarded as the meanest of mean virtues. But in Utopia everyone will have had an education and a certain minimum of nutrition and training; everyone will be insured against ill-health and accidents; there will be the most efficient organisation for balancing the pressure of employment and the presence of disengaged labour, and so to be moneyless will be clear evidence of unworthiness. In Utopia, no one will dream of giving to a casual beggar, and no one will dream of begging.

There will need to be, in the place of the British casual wards, simple but comfortable inns with a low tariff – controlled to a certain extent no doubt, and even in some cases maintained, by the State. This tariff will have such a definite relation to the minimum permissible wage, that a man who has incurred no liabilities through marriage or the like relationship, will be able to live in comfort and decency upon that minimum wage, pay his small insurance premium against disease, death, disablement, or ripening years, and have a margin for clothing and other personal expenses. But he will get neither shelter nor food, except at the price of his freedom, unless he can produce money.

But suppose a man without money in a district where employment is not to be found for him; suppose the amount of employment to have diminished in the district with such suddenness as to have stranded him there. Or suppose he has quarrelled with the only possible employer, or that he does not like his particular work. Then no doubt the Utopian State, which wants everyone to be just as happy as the future welfare of the race permits, will come to his assistance. One imagines him resorting to a neat and businesslike post office, and stating his case to a civil and intelligent official. In any sane State the economic conditions of every quarter of the earth will be watched as constantly as its meteorological phases, and a daily map of the country within a radius of three or four hundred miles showing all the places where labour is needed will hang upon the post-office wall. To this his attention will be directed. The man out of work will decide to try his luck in this place or that, and the public servant, the official, will make a note of his name, verify his identity – the freedom of Utopia will not be incompatible with the universal registration of thumb-marks – and issue passes for travel and coupons for any necessary inn accommodation on his way to the chosen destination. There he will seek a new employer.

Such a free change of locality once or twice a year from a region of restricted employment to a region of labour shortage will be among the general privileges of the Utopian citizen.

But suppose that in no district in the world is there work within the capacity of this particular man?

Before we suppose that, we must take into consideration the general assumption one is permitted to make in all Utopian speculations. All Utopians will be reasonably well educated upon Utopian lines; there will be no illiterates unless they are unteachable imbeciles, no rule-of-thumb toilers as inadaptable as trained beasts. The Utopian worker will be as versatile as any well-educated man is on earth today, and no Trade Union will impose a limit to his activities. The world will be his Union. If the work he does best and likes best is not to be found, there is still the work he likes second best. Lacking his proper employment, he will turn to some kindred trade.

But even with that adaptability, it may be that sometimes he will not find work. Such a disproportion between the work to be done and the people to do it may arise as to present a surplus of labour everywhere. This disproportion may be due to two causes: to an increase of population without a corresponding increase of enterprises, or to a diminution of employment throughout the world due to the completion of great enterprises, to economies achieved, or to the operation of new and more efficient labour-saving appliances. Through either cause, a World State may find itself doing well except for an excess of citizens of mediocre and lower quality.

But the first cause may be anticipated by wise marriage laws . . . The full discussion of these laws will come later, but here one may insist that Utopia will control the increase of its population. Without the determination and ability to limit that increase as well as to stimulate it whenever it is necessary, no Utopia is possible. That was clearly demonstrated by Malthus for all time.

The second cause is not so easily anticipated, but then, though its immediate result in glutting the labour market is similar, its final consequences are entirely different from those of the first. The whole trend of a scientific mechanical civilisation is continually to replace labour by machinery and to increase it in its effectiveness by organisation, and so quite independently of any increase in population labour must either fall in value until it can compete against and check the cheapening process, or if that is prevented, as it will be in Utopia, by a minimum wage, come out of employment. There is no apparent limit to this process. But a surplus of efficient labour at the minimum wage is exactly the condition that should stimulate new enterprises, and that in a State saturated with science and prolific in invention will stimulate new enterprises. An increasing surplus of available labour without an absolute increase of population, an increasing surplus of labour due to increasing economy and not to proliferation, and which, therefore, does not press on and disarrange the food supply, is surely the ideal condition for a progressive civilisation. I am inclined to think that, since labour will be regarded as a delocalised and fluid force, it will be the World State and not the big municipalities ruling the force areas that will be the reserve employer of labour. Very probably it will be convenient for the State to hand over the surplus labour for municipal purposes, but that is another question. All over the world the labour exchanges will be reporting the fluctuating pressure of economic demand and transferring workers from this region of excess to that of scarcity; and whenever the excess is universal, the World State – failing an adequate development of private enterprise – will either reduce the working day and so absorb the excess, or set on foot some permanent special works of its own, paying the minimum wage and allowing them to progress just as slowly or just as rapidly as the ebb and flow of labour dictated. But with sane marriage and birth laws there is no reason to suppose such calls upon the resources and initiative of the world more than temporary and exceptional occasions.

4

The existence of our blond bare-footed friend was evidence enough that in a modern Utopia a man will be free to be just as idle or uselessly busy as it pleases him, after he has earned the minimum wage. He must do that, of course, to pay for his keep, to pay his assurance tax against ill-health or old age, and any charge or debt paternity may have brought upon him. The World State of the modern Utopist is no state of moral compulsions. If, for example, under the restricted Utopian scheme of inheritance, a man inherited sufficient money to release him from the need to toil, he would be free to go where he pleased and do what he liked. A certain proportion of men at ease is good for the world; work as a moral obligation is the morality of slaves, and so long as no one is overworked there is no need to worry because some few are under-worked. Utopia does not exist as a solace for envy. From leisure, in a good moral and intellectual atmosphere, come experiments, come philosophy and the new departures.

In any modern Utopia there must be many leisurely people. We are all too obsessed in the real world by the strenuous ideal, by the idea that the vehement incessant fool is the only righteous man. Nothing done in a hurry, nothing done under strain, is really well done. A State where all are working hard, where none go to and fro, easily and freely, loses touch with the purpose of freedom.

But inherited independence will be the rarest and least permanent of Utopian facts, for the most part that wider freedom will have to be earned, and the inducements to men and women to raise their personal value far above the minimum wage will be very great indeed. Thereby will come privacies, more space in which to live, liberty to go everywhere and do no end of things, the power and freedom to initiate interesting enterprises and assist and co-operate with interesting people, and indeed all the best things of life. The modern Utopia will give a universal security indeed, and exercise the minimum of compulsions to toil, but it will offer some acutely desirable prizes. The aim of all these devices, the minimum wage, the standard of life, provision for all the feeble and unemployed and so forth, is not to rob life of incentives but to change their nature, to make life not less energetic, but less panic-stricken and violent and base, to shift the incidence of the struggle for existence from our lower to our higher emotions, so to anticipate and neutralise the motives of the cowardly and bestial, that the ambitious and energetic imagination which is man's finest quality may become the incentive and determining factor in survival.

5

After we have paid for our lunch in the little inn that corresponds to Wassen, the botanist and I would no doubt spend the rest of the fore-noon in the discussion of various aspects and possibilities of Utopian labour laws. We should examine our remaining change, copper coins of an appearance ornamental rather than reassuring, and we should decide that after what we had gathered from the man with the blond hair, it would, on the whole, be advisable to come to the point with the labour question forthwith. At last we should draw the deep breath of resolution and arise and ask for the Public Office. We should know by this time that the labour bureau sheltered with the post office and other public services in one building.

The Public Office of Utopia would of course contain a few surprises for two men from terrestrial England. You imagine us entering, the botanist lagging a little behind me, and my first attempts to be offhand and commonplace in a demand for work.

The office is in charge of a quick-eyed little woman of six and thirty perhaps, and she regards us with a certain keenness of scrutiny.

'Where are your papers?' she asks.

I think for a moment of the documents in my pocket, my passport chequered with visas and addressed in my commendation and in the name of her late Majesty by *We, Robert Arthur Talbot Gascoigne Cecil, Marquess of Salisbury, Earl of Salisbury, Viscount Cranborne, Baron Cecil,* and so forth, to all whom it may concern, my *Carte d'Identité* (useful on minor occasions) of the Touring Club de France, my green ticket to the Reading Room of the British Museum, and my *lettre d'indication* from the London and County Bank. A foolish humour prompts me to unfold all these, hand them to her and take the consequences, but I resist.

'Lost,' I say, briefly.

'Both lost?' she asks, looking at my friend.

'Both,' I answer.

'How?'

I astonish myself by the readiness of my answer.

'I fell down a snow slope and they came out of my pocket.'

'And exactly the same thing happened to both of you?'

'No. He'd given me his to put with my own.' She raised her eyebrows. 'His pocket is defective,' I add, a little hastily.

Her manners are too Utopian for her to follow that up. She seems to reflect on procedure.

'What are your numbers?' she asks, abruptly.

A vision of that confounded visitors' book at the inn above comes into my mind. 'Let me *see*,' I say, and pat my forehead and reflect, refraining from the official eye before me. 'Let me *see*.'

'What is yours?' she asks the botanist.

'A. B.,' he says, slowly, 'little *a*, nine four seven, I *think* – '

'Don't you know?'

'Not exactly,' says the botanist, very agreeably. 'No.'

'Do you mean to say neither of you know your own numbers?' says the little postmistress, with a rising note.

'Yes,' I say, with an engaging smile and trying to keep up a good social tone. 'It's queer, isn't it? We've both forgotten.'

'You're joking,' she suggests.

'Well,' I temporise.

'I suppose you've got your thumbs?'

'The fact is – ' I say and hesitate. 'We've got our thumbs, of course.'

'Then I shall have to send a thumb-print down to the office and get your number from that. But are you sure you haven't your papers or numbers? It's very queer.'

We admit rather sheepishly that it's queer, and question one another silently.

She turns thoughtfully for the thumb-marking slab, and as she does so, a man enters the office. At the sight of him she asks with a note of relief, 'What am I to do, sir, here?'

He looks from her to us gravely, and his eye lights to curiosity at our dress. 'What is the matter, madam?' he asks, in a courteous voice.

She explains.

So far the impression we have had of our Utopia is one of a quite unearthly sanity, of good management and comprehensive design in every material thing, and it has seemed to us a little incongruous that all the Utopians we have talked to, our host of last night, the postmistress and our garrulous tramp, have been of the most commonplace type. But suddenly there looks out from this man's pose and regard a different quality, a quality altogether nearer that of the beautiful tramway and of the gracious order of the mountain houses. He is a well-built man of perhaps five and thirty, with the easy movement that comes with perfect physical condition, his face is clean shaven and shows the firm mouth of a disciplined man, and his grey eyes are clear and steady. His legs are clad in some woven stuff deep-red in colour, and over this he wears a white shirt fitting pretty closely, and with a woven purple hem. His general effect reminds me somehow of the Knights Templars. On his head is a cap of thin leather and still thinner steel, and with the vestiges of ear-guards – rather like an attenuated version of the caps that were worn by Cromwell's Ironsides.

He looks at us and we interpolate a word or so as she explains and feel a good deal of embarrassment at the foolish position we have made for ourselves. I determine to cut my way out of this entanglement before it complicates itself further.

'The fact is – ' I say.

'Yes?' he says, with a faint smile.

'We've perhaps been disingenuous. Our position is so entirely exceptional, so difficult to explain – '

'What have you been doing?'

'No,' I say, with decision; 'it can't be explained like that.'

He looks down at his feet. 'Go on,' he says.

I try to give the thing a quiet, matter-of-fact air. 'You see,' I say, in the tone one adopts for really lucid explanations, 'we come from another world. Consequently, whatever thumb-mark registration or numbering you have in this planet doesn't apply to us, and we don't know our numbers because we haven't got any. We are really, you know, explorers, strangers – '

'But what world do you mean?'

'It's a different planet – a long way away. Practically at an infinite distance.'

He looks up in my face with the patient expression of a man who listens to nonsense.

'I know it sounds impossible,' I say, 'but here is the simple fact – we *appear* in your world. We appeared suddenly upon the neck of Lucendro – the Piz Lucendro – yesterday afternoon, and I defy you to discover the faintest trace of us before that time. Down we marched into the St Gotthard road and here we are! That's our fact. And as for papers – ! Where in your world have you seen papers like this?'

I produce my pocketbook, extract my passport, and present it to him.

His expression has changed. He takes the document and examines it, turns it over, looks at me, and smiles that faint smile of his again.

'Have some more,' I say, and proffer the card of the TCF.

I follow up that blow with my green British Museum ticket, as tattered as a flag in a knight's chapel.

'You'll get found out,' he says, with my documents in his hand. 'You've got your thumbs. You'll be measured. They'll refer to the central registers, and there you'll be!'

'That's just it,' I say, 'we shan't be.'

He reflects. 'It's a queer sort of joke for you two men to play,' he decides, handing me back my documents.

'It's no joke at all,' I say, replacing them in my pocketbook.

The postmistress intervenes. 'What would you advise me to do?'

'No money?' he asks.

'No.'

He makes some suggestions. 'Frankly,' he says, 'I think you have escaped from some island. How you got so far as here I can't imagine, or what you think you'll do . . . But anyhow, there's the stuff for your thumbs.'

He points to the thumb-marking apparatus and turns to attend to his own business.

Presently we emerge from the office in a state between discomfiture and amusement, each with a tramway ticket for Lucerne in his hand and with sufficient money to pay our expenses until the morrow. We are to go to Lucerne because there there is a demand for comparatively unskilled labour in carving wood, which seems to us a sort of work within our range and a sort that will not compel our separation.

6

The old Utopias are sessile organisations; the new must square itself to the needs of a migratory population, to an endless coming and going, to a people as fluid and tidal as the sea. It does not enter into the scheme of earthly statesmanship, but indeed all local establishments, all definitions of place, are even now melting under our eyes. Presently all the world will be awash with anonymous stranger men.

Now the simple laws of custom, the homely methods of identification that served in the little communities of the past when everyone knew everyone, fail in the face of this liquefaction. If the modern Utopia is indeed to be a world of responsible citizens, it must have devised some scheme by which every person in the world can be promptly and certainly recognised, and by which anyone missing can be traced and found.

This is by no means an impossible demand. The total population of the world is, on the most generous estimate, not more than 1,500,000,000, and the effectual indexing of this number of people, the record of their movement hither and thither, the entry of various material facts, such as marriage, parentage, criminal convictions and the like, the entry of the new-born and the elimination of the dead, colossal task though it would be, is still not so great as to be immeasurably beyond comparison with the work of the post offices in the world of today, or the cataloguing of such libraries as that of the British Museum, or such collections as that of the insects in Cromwell Road. Such an index could be housed quite comfortably on one side of Northumberland Avenue, for example. It is only a reasonable tribute to the distinctive lucidity of the French mind to suppose the central index housed in a vast series of buildings at or near Paris. The index would be classified primarily by some unchanging physical characteristic, such as we are told the thumb-mark and finger-mark afford, and to these would be added any other physical traits that were of material value. The classification of thumb-marks and of inalterable physical characteristics goes on steadily, and there is every reason for assuming it possible that each human being could be given a distinct formula, a number or 'scientific name', under which he or she could be docketed.* About the buildings in which this great main index would be gathered, would be a system of other indices with cross references to the main one, arranged under names, under professional qualifications, under diseases, crimes and the like.

These index cards might conceivably be transparent and so contrived as to give a photographic copy promptly whenever it was needed, and they could have an attachment into which would slip a ticket bearing the name of the locality in which the individual was last reported. A little army of attendants would be at work upon this index day and night. From substations constantly engaged in checking back thumb-marks and numbers, an incessant stream of information would come, of births, of deaths, of arrivals at inns, of applications to post offices for letters, of tickets taken for long journeys, of criminal convictions, marriages, applications for public doles and the like. A filter of offices would sort the stream, and all day and all night for ever a swarm of clerks would go to and fro correcting this central register, and photographing copies of its entries for transmission to the subordinate local stations, in response to their enquiries. So the inventory of the State would watch its every man and the wide world write its history as the fabric of its destiny flowed on. At last, when the citizen died, would come the last entry of all, his age and the cause of his death and the date and place of his cremation, and his card would be taken out and passed on to the universal pedigree, to a place of greater quiet, to the ever-growing galleries of the records of the dead.

Such a record is inevitable if a modern Utopia is to be achieved.

Yet at this, too, our blond-haired friend would no doubt rebel. One of the many things to which some will make claim as a right, is that of going unrecognised and secret whither one will. But that, so far as one's fellow wayfarers were concerned, would still be possible. Only the State would share the secret of one's little concealment. To the

---

* It is quite possible that the actual thumb-mark may play only a small part in the work of identification, but it is an obvious convenience to our thread of story to assume that it is the one sufficient feature.

eighteenth-century Liberal, to the old-fashioned nineteenth-century Liberal, that is to say to all professed Liberals, brought up to be against the Government on principle, this organised clairvoyance will be the most hateful of dreams. Perhaps, too, the Individualist would see it in that light. But these are only the mental habits acquired in an evil time. The old Liberalism assumed bad government, the more powerful the government the worse it was, just as it assumed the natural righteousness of the free individual. Darkness and secrecy were, indeed, the natural refuges of liberty when every government had in it the near possibility of tyranny, and the Englishman or American looked at the papers of a Russian or a German as one might look at the chains of a slave. You imagine that father of the old Liberalism, Rousseau, slinking off from his offspring at the door of the Foundling Hospital, and you can understand what a crime against natural virtue this quiet eye of the State would have seemed to him. But suppose we do not assume that government is necessarily bad, and the individual necessarily good – and the hypothesis upon which we are working practically abolishes either alternative – then we alter the case altogether. The government of a modern Utopia will be no perfection of intentions ignorantly ruling the world . . . *

Such is the eye of the State that is now slowly beginning to apprehend our existence as two queer and inexplicable particles disturbing the fine order of its field of vision, the eye that will presently be focusing itself upon us with a growing astonishment and interrogation. 'Who in the name of Galton and Bertillon,' one fancies Utopia exclaiming, 'are *you*?'

I perceive I shall cut a queer figure in that focus. I shall affect a certain spurious ease of carriage no doubt. 'The fact is,' I shall begin . . .

* In the typical modern State of our own world, with its population of many millions, and its extreme facility of movement, undistinguished men who adopt an alias can make themselves untraceable with the utmost ease. The temptation of the opportunities thus offered has developed a new type of criminality, the Deeming or Crossman type, base men who subsist and feed their heavy imaginations in the wooing, betrayal, ill-treatment, and sometimes even the murder of undistinguished women. This is a large, a growing, and, what is gravest, a prolific class, fostered by the practical anonymity of the common man. It is only the murderers who attract much public attention, but the supply of low-class prostitutes is also largely due to these free adventures of the base. It is one of the by-products of State Liberalism, and at present it is very probably drawing ahead in the race against the development of police organisation.

And now see how an initial hypothesis may pursue and overtake its maker. Our thumb-marks have been taken, they have travelled by pneumatic tube to the central office of the municipality hard by Lucerne, and have gone on thence to the headquarters of the index at Paris. There, after a rough preliminary classification, I imagine them photographed on glass, and flung by means of a lantern in colossal images upon a screen, all finely squared, and the careful experts marking and measuring their several convolutions. And then off goes a brisk clerk to the long galleries of the index building.

I have told them they will find no sign of us, but you see him going from gallery to gallery, from bay to bay, from drawer to drawer, and from card to card. 'Here he is!' he mutters to himself, and he whips out a card and reads. 'But that is impossible!' he says . . .

You figure us returning after a day or so of such Utopian experiences as I must presently describe, to the central office in Lucerne, even as we have been told to do.

I make my way to the desk of the man who has dealt with us before. 'Well?' I say, cheerfully, 'have you heard?'

His expression dashes me a little. 'We've heard,' he says, and adds, 'it's very peculiar.'

'I told you you wouldn't find out about us,' I say, triumphantly.

'But we have,' he says; 'but that makes your freak none the less remarkable.'

'You've heard! You know who we are! Well – tell us! We had an idea, but we're beginning to doubt.'

'You,' says the official, addressing the botanist, 'are – !'

And he breathes his name. Then he turns to me and gives me mine.

For a moment I am dumbfounded. Then I think of the entries we made at the inn in the Urserenthal, and then in a flash I have the truth. I rap the desk smartly with my fingertips and shake my index-finger in my friend's face.

'By Jove!' I say in English. 'They've got our doubles!'

The botanist snaps his fingers. 'Of course! I didn't think of that.'

'Do you mind,' I say to this official, 'telling us some more about ourselves?'

'I can't think why you keep it up,' he remarks, and then almost wearily tells me the facts about my Utopian self. They are a little difficult to understand. He says I am one of the samurai, which sounds Japanese, 'but you will be degraded,' he says, with a gesture almost of despair. He describes my position in this world in phrases that convey very little.

'The queer thing,' he remarks, 'is that you were in Norway only three days ago.'

'I am there still. At least – I'm sorry to be so much trouble to you, but do you mind following up that last clue and enquiring if the person to whom the thumb-mark really belongs isn't in Norway still?'

The idea needs explanation. He says something incomprehensible about a pilgrimage. 'Sooner or later,' I say, 'you will have to believe there are two of us with the same thumb-mark. I won't trouble you with any apparent nonsense about other planets and so forth again. Here I am. If I was in Norway a few days ago, you ought to be able to trace my journey hither. And my friend?'

'He was in India.' The official is beginning to look perplexed.

'It seems to me,' I say, 'that the difficulties in this case are only just beginning. How did I get from Norway hither? Does my friend look like hopping from India to the St Gotthard at one hop? The situation is a little more difficult than that –'

'But here!' says the official, and waves what are no doubt photographic copies of the index cards.

'But we are not those individuals!'

'You *are* those individuals.'

'You will see,' I say.

He dabs his finger argumentatively upon the thumb-marks. 'I see now,' he says.

'There is a mistake,' I maintain, 'an unprecedented mistake. There's the difficulty. If you enquire you will find it begin to unravel. What reason is there for us to remain casual workmen here, when you allege we are men of position in the world, if there isn't something wrong? We shall stick to this wood-carving work you have found us here, and meanwhile I think you ought to enquire again. That's how the thing shapes to me.'

'Your case will certainly have to be considered further,' he says, with the faintest of threatening notes in his tone. 'But at the same time' – hand out to those copies from the index again – 'there you are, you know!'

When my botanist and I have talked over and exhausted every possibility of our immediate position, we should turn, I think, to more general questions.

I should tell him the thing that was becoming more and more apparent in my own mind. Here, I should say, is a world, obviously on the face of it well organised. Compared with our world, it is like a well-oiled engine beside a scrap-heap. It has even got this confounded visual organ swivelling about in the most alert and lively fashion. But that's by the way . . . You have only to look at all these houses below. (We should be sitting on a seat on the Gütsch and looking down on the Lucerne of Utopia, a Lucerne that would, I insist, quite arbitrarily, still keep the Wasserthurm and the Kapellbrücke.) You have only to mark the beauty, the simple cleanliness and balance of this world, you have only to see the free carriage, the unaffected graciousness of even the common people, to understand how fine and complete the arrangements of this world must be. How are they made so? We of the twentieth century are not going to accept the sweetish, faintly nasty slops of Rousseauism that so gratified our great-great-grandparents in the eighteenth. We know that order and justice do not come by Nature – 'if only the policeman would go away'. These things mean intention, will, carried to a scale that our poor vacillating, hot and cold earth has never known. What I am really seeing more and more clearly is the will beneath this visible Utopia. Convenient houses, admirable engineering that is no offence amidst natural beauties, beautiful bodies, and a universally gracious carriage, these are only the outward and visible signs of an inward and spiritual grace. Such an order means discipline. It means triumph over the petty egotisms and vanities that keep men on our earth apart; it means devotion and a nobler hope; it cannot exist without a gigantic process of enquiry, trial, forethought and patience in an atmosphere of mutual trust and concession. Such a world as this Utopia is not made by the chance occasional co-operations of self-indulgent men, by autocratic rulers or by the bawling wisdom of the democratic leader. And an unrestricted competition for gain, an enlightened selfishness, that too fails us . . .

I have compared the system of indexing humanity we have come upon to an eye, an eye so sensitive and alert that two strangers cannot appear anywhere upon the planet without discovery. Now an eye does not see without a brain, an eye does not turn round and look without a will and purpose. A Utopia that deals only with appliances and arrangements is a dream of superficialities; the essential problem here, the body within these garments, is a moral and an intellectual problem. Behind all this material order, these perfected communications, perfected public services and economic organisations, there must be men and women willing these things. There must be a considerable number and a succession of these men and women of will. No single person, no transitory group of people, could order and sustain this vast complexity. They must have a collective if not a common width of aim, and that involves a spoken or written literature, a living literature to sustain the harmony of their general activity. In some way they must have put the more immediate objects of desire into a secondary place, and that means renunciation. They must be effectual in action and persistent in will, and that means discipline. But in the modern world in which progress advances without limits, it will be evident that whatever common creed or formula they have must be of the simplest sort; that whatever organisation they have must be as mobile and flexible as a thing alive. All this follows inevitably from the general propositions of our Utopian dream. When we made those, we bound ourselves helplessly to come to this . . .

The botanist would nod an abstracted assent.

I should cease to talk. I should direct my mind to the confused mass of memories three days in Utopia will have given us. Besides the personalities with whom we have come into actual contact, our various hosts, our foreman and work-fellows, the blond man, the public officials and so on, there will be a great multitude of other impressions. There will be many bright snapshots of little children, for example, of girls and women and men, seen in shops and offices and streets, on quays, at windows and by the wayside, people riding hither and thither and walking to and fro. A very human crowd it has seemed to me. But among them were there any who might be thought of as having a wider interest than the others, who seemed in any way detached from the rest by a purpose that passed beyond the seen?

Then suddenly I recall that clean-shaven man who talked with us for a little while in the public office at Wassen, the man who reminded me of my boyish conception of a Knight Templar, and with him come momentary impressions of other lithe and serious-looking people dressed after the same manner, words and phrases we have read in such scraps of Utopian reading as have come our way, and expressions that fell from the loose mouth of the man with the blond hair . . .

CHAPTER SIX

Women in a Modern Utopia

1

But though I have come to a point where the problem of a Utopia has resolved itself very simply into the problem of government and direction, I find I have not brought the botanist with me. Frankly he cannot think so steadily onward as I can. I feel to think, he thinks to feel. It is I and my kind that have the wider range, because we can be impersonal as well as personal. We can escape ourselves. In general terms, at least, I understand him, but he does not understand me in any way at all. He thinks me an incomprehensible brute because his obsession is merely one of my incidental interests, and wherever my reasoning ceases to be explicit and full, the slightest ellipsis, the most transitory digression, he evades me and is back at himself again. He may have a personal liking for me, though I doubt it, but also he hates me pretty distinctly, because of this bias he cannot understand. My philosophical insistence that things shall be reasonable and hang together, that what can be explained shall be explained, and that what can be done by calculation and certain methods shall not be left to chance, he loathes. He just wants adventurously to feel. He wants to feel the sunset, and he thinks that on the whole he would feel it better if he had not been taught the sun was about ninety-two million miles away. He wants to feel free and strong, and he would rather feel so than be so. He does not want to accomplish great things, but to have dazzling things occur to him. He does not know that there are feelings also up in the clear air of the philosophic mountains, in the long ascents of effort and design. He does not know that thought itself is only a finer sort of feeling than his – good hock to the mixed gin, porter and treacle of his emotions, a perception of similitudes and oppositions that carries even thrills. And naturally he broods on the source of all his most copious feelings and emotions, women, and particularly upon the woman who has most made him feel. He forces me also to that.

Our position is unfortunate for me. Our return to the Utopian equivalent of Lucerne revives in him all the melancholy distresses that so preoccupied him when first we were transferred to this better planet. One day, while we are still waiting there for the public office to decide about us, he broaches the matter. It is early evening, and we are walking beside the lake after our simple dinner. 'About here,' he says, 'the quays would run and all those big hotels would be along here, looking out on the lake. It's so strange to have seen them so recently, and now not to see them at all . . . Where have they gone?'

'Vanished by hypothesis.'

'What?'

'Oh! They're there still. It's we that have come hither.'

'Of course. I forgot. But still – You know, there was an avenue of little trees along this quay with seats, and she was sitting looking out upon the lake . . . I hadn't seen her for ten years.'

He looks about him still a little perplexed. 'Now we are here,' he says, 'it seems as though that meeting and the talk we had must have been a dream.'

He falls musing.

Presently he says: 'I knew her at once. I saw her in profile. But, you know, I didn't speak to her directly. I walked past her seat and on for a little way, trying to control myself . . . Then I turned back and sat down beside her, very quietly. She looked up at me. Everything came back – everything. For a moment or so I felt I was going to cry . . . '

That seems to give him a sort of satisfaction even in the reminiscence.

'We talked for a time just like casual acquaintances – about the view and the weather, and things like that.'

He muses again.

'In Utopia everything would have been different,' I say.

'I suppose it would.'

He goes on before I can say anything more.

'Then, you know, there was a pause. I had a sort of intuition that the moment was coming. So I think had she. You may scoff, of course, at these intuitions – '

I don't, as a matter of fact. Instead, I swear secretly. Always this sort of man keeps up the pretence of highly distinguished and remarkable mental processes, whereas – have not I, in my own composition, the whole diapason of emotional fool? Is not the suppression of these notes my perpetual effort, my undying despair? And then, am I to be accused of poverty?

But to his story.

'She said, quite abruptly, "I am not happy," and I told her, "I knew that the instant I saw you." Then, you know, she began to talk to me very quietly, very frankly, about everything. It was only afterwards I began to feel just what it meant, her talking to me like that.'

I cannot listen to this!

'Don't you understand,' I cry, 'that we are in Utopia. She may be bound unhappily upon earth and you may be bound, but not here. Here I think it will be different. Here the laws that control all these things will be humane and just. So that all you said and did, over there, does not signify here – does not signify here!'

He looks up for a moment at my face, and then carelessly at my wonderful new world.

'Yes,' he says, without interest, with something of the tone of an abstracted elder speaking to a child, 'I dare say it will be all very fine here.' And he lapses, thwarted from his confidences, into musing.

There is something almost dignified in this withdrawal into himself. For a moment I entertain an illusion that really I am unworthy to hear the impalpable inconclusiveness of what he said to her and of what she said to him.

I am snubbed. I am also amazed to find myself snubbed. I become breathless with indignation. We walk along side by side, but now profoundly estranged.

I regard the façade of the Utopian public offices of Lucerne – I had meant to call his attention to some of the architectural features of these – with a changed eye, with all the spirit gone out of my vision. I wish I had never brought this introspective carcass, this mental ingrate, with me.

I incline to fatalistic submission. I suppose I had no power to leave him behind . . . I wonder and I wonder. The old Utopists never had to encumber themselves with this sort of man.

2

How would things be 'different' in the Modern Utopia? After all it is time we faced the riddle of the problems of marriage and mother-hood . . .

The Modern Utopia is not only to be a sound and happy World State, but it is to be one progressing from good to better. But as Malthus* demonstrated for all time, a State whose population continues to increase in obedience to unchecked instinct, can progress only from bad to worse. From the view of human comfort and happiness, the increase of

* 'Essay on the Principles of Population'.

population that occurs at each advance in human security is the greatest evil of life. The way of Nature is for every species to increase nearly to its possible maximum of numbers, and then to improve through the pressure of that maximum against its limiting conditions by the crushing and killing of all the feebler individuals. The way of Nature has also been the way of humanity so far, and except when a temporary alleviation is obtained through an expansion of the general stock of sustenance by invention or discovery, the amount of starvation and of the physical misery of privation in the world, must vary almost exactly with the excess of the actual birthrate over that required to sustain population at a number compatible with a universal contentment. Neither has Nature evolved, nor has man so far put into operation, any device by which paying this price of progress, this misery of a multitude of starved and unsuccessful lives can be evaded. A mere indiscriminating restriction of the birthrate – an end practically attained in the homely, old-fashioned civilisation of China by female infanticide – involves not only the cessation of distresses but stagnation, and the minor good of a sort of comfort and social stability is won at too great a sacrifice. Progress depends essentially on competitive selection, and that we may not escape.

But it is a conceivable and possible thing that this margin of futile struggling, pain and discomfort and death might be reduced to nearly nothing without checking physical and mental evolution, with indeed an acceleration of physical and mental evolution, by preventing the birth of those who would in the unrestricted interplay of natural forces be born to suffer and fail. The method of Nature 'red in tooth and claw' is to degrade, thwart, torture, and kill the weakest and least adapted members of every species in existence in each generation, and so keep the specific average rising; the ideal of a scientific civilisation is to prevent those weaklings being born. There is no other way of evading Nature's punishment of sorrow. The struggle for life among the beasts and uncivilised men means misery and death for the inferior individuals, misery and death in order that they may not increase and multiply; in the civilised State it is now clearly possible to make the conditions of life tolerable for every living creature, provided the inferiors can be prevented from increasing and multiplying. But this latter condition must be respected. Instead of competing to escape death and wretchedness, we may compete to give birth and we may heap every sort of consolation prize upon the losers in that competition. The modern State tends to qualify inheritance, to insist upon education and nurture for children, to come in more and more in the interests of the future between father and child. It is taking over the responsibility of the general welfare of the children more and more, and as it does so, its right to decide which children it will shelter becomes more and more reasonable.

How far will such conditions be prescribed? How far can they be prescribed in a modern Utopia?

Let us set aside at once all nonsense of the sort one hears in certain quarters about the human stud farm.* State breeding of the population was a reasonable proposal for Plato to make, in view of the biological knowledge of his time and the purely tentative nature of his metaphysics; but from anyone in the days after Darwin, it is preposterous. Yet we have it given to us as the most brilliant of modern discoveries by a certain school of sociological writers, who seem totally unable to grasp the modification of meaning 'species' and 'individual' have undergone in the last fifty years. They do not seem capable of the suspicion that the boundaries of species have vanished, and that individuality now carries with it the quality of the unique! To them individuals are still defective copies of a Platonic ideal of the species, and the purpose of breeding no more than an approximation to that perfection. Individuality is indeed a negligible difference to them, an impertinence, and the whole flow of modern biological ideas has washed over them in vain.

But to the modern thinker individuality is the significant fact of life, and the idea of the State, which is necessarily concerned with the average and general, selecting individualities in order to pair them and improve the race, an absurdity. It is like fixing a crane on the plain in order to raise the hill tops. In the initiative of the individual above the average, lies the reality of the future, which the State, presenting the average, may subserve but cannot control. And the natural centre of the emotional life, the cardinal will, the supreme and significant expression of individuality, should lie in the selection of a partner for procreation.

But compulsory pairing is one thing, and the maintenance of general limiting conditions is another, and one well within the scope of State activity. The State is justified in saying, before you may add children to the community for the community to educate and in part to support, you must be above a certain minimum of personal efficiency, and this you must show by holding a position of solvency and independence in the world; you must be above a certain age, and a certain minimum of physical development, and free of any transmissible disease. You must not be a criminal unless you have expiated your offence. Failing these simple qualifications, if you and some person conspire and add to the population of the State, we will, for the sake of humanity, take over

* See *Mankind in the Making*, Ch. II.

the innocent victim of your passions, but we shall insist that you are under a debt to the State of a peculiarly urgent sort, and one you will certainly pay, even if it is necessary to use restraint to get the payment out of you: it is a debt that has in the last resort your liberty as a security, and, moreover, if this thing happens a second time, or if it is disease or imbecility you have multiplied, we will take an absolutely effectual guarantee that neither you nor your partner offend again in this matter.

'Harsh!' you say, and 'Poor Humanity!'

You have the gentler alternative to study in your terrestrial slums and asylums.

It may be urged that to permit conspicuously inferior people to have one or two children in this way would be to fail to attain the desired end, but, indeed, this is not so. A suitably qualified permission, as every statesman knows, may produce the social effects without producing the irksome pressure of an absolute prohibition. Amidst bright and comfortable circumstances, and with an easy and practicable alternative, people will exercise foresight and self-restraint to escape even the possibilities of hardship and discomfort; and free life in Utopia is to be well worth this trouble even for inferior people. The growing comfort, self-respect, and intelligence of the English is shown, for example, in the fall in the proportion of illegitimate births from 2.2 per 1,000 in 1846–50 to 1.2 per 1,000 in 1890–1900, and this without any positive preventive laws whatever. This most desirable result is pretty certainly not the consequence of any great exaltation of our moral tone, but simply of a rising standard of comfort and a livelier sense of consequences and responsibilities. If so marked a change is possible in response to such progress as England has achieved in the past fifty years, if discreet restraint can be so effectual as this, it seems reasonable to suppose that in the ampler knowledge and the cleaner, franker atmosphere of our Utopian planet the birth of a child to diseased or inferior parents, and contrary to the sanctions of the State, will be the rarest of disasters.

And the death of a child, too, that most tragic event, Utopia will rarely know. Children are not born to die in childhood. But in our world, at present, through the defects of our medical science and nursing methods, through defects in our organisation, through poverty and carelessness, and through the birth of children that never ought to have been born, one out of every five children born dies within five years. It may be the reader has witnessed this most distressful of all human tragedies. It is sheer waste of suffering. There is no reason why ninety-nine out of every hundred children born should not live to a ripe age. Accordingly, in any Modern Utopia, it must be insisted they will.

All former Utopias have, by modern standards, erred on the side of over-regulation in these matters. The amount of State interference with the marriage and birth of the citizens of a modern Utopia will be much less than in any terrestrial State. Here, just as in relation to property and enterprise, the law will regulate only in order to secure the utmost freedom and initiative.

Up to the beginning of this chapter, our Utopian speculations, like many Acts of Parliament, have ignored the difference of sex. 'He' indeed is to be read as 'He and She' in all that goes before. But we may now come to the sexual aspects of the modern ideal of a constitution of society in which, for all purposes of the individual, women are to be as free as men. This will certainly be realised in the Modern Utopia, if it can be realised at all – not only for woman's sake, but for man's.

But women may be free in theory and not in practice, and as long as they suffer from their economic inferiority, from the inability to produce as much value as a man for the same amount of work – and there can be no doubt of this inferiority – so long will their legal and technical equality be a mockery. It is a fact that almost every point in which a woman differs from a man is an economic disadvantage to her, her incapacity for great stresses of exertion, her frequent liability to slight illnesses, her weaker initiative, her inferior invention and resourcefulness, her relative incapacity for organisation and combination, and the possibilities of emotional complications whenever she is in economic dependence on men. So long as women are compared economically with men and boys they will be inferior in precisely the measure in which they differ from men. All that constitutes this difference they are supposed not to trade upon except in one way, and that is by winning or luring a man to marry, selling themselves in an almost irrevocable bargain, and then following and sharing his fortunes for 'better or worse'.

But – do not let the proposition in its first crudity alarm you – suppose the Modern Utopia equalises things between the sexes in the only possible way, by insisting that motherhood is a service to the State and a legitimate claim to a living; and that, since the State is to exercise the right of forbidding or sanctioning motherhood, a woman who is, or is becoming, a mother, is as much entitled to wages above the minimum wage, to support, to freedom, and to respect and dignity as a policeman, a solicitor-general, a king, a bishop in the State Church, a Government professor, or anyone else the State sustains. Suppose the State secures to every woman who is, under legitimate sanctions, becoming or likely to become a mother, that is to say who is duly married, a certain wage from her husband to secure her against the need of toil and anxiety, suppose it pays her a certain gratuity upon the birth of a child, and continues to pay at regular intervals sums sufficient to keep her and her child in independent freedom, so long as the child keeps up to the minimum standard of health and physical and mental development. Suppose it pays more upon the child when it rises markedly above certain minimum qualifications, physical or mental, and, in fact, does its best to make thoroughly efficient motherhood a profession worth following. And suppose in correlation with this it forbids the industrial employment of married women and of mothers who have children needing care, unless they are in a position to employ qualified efficient substitutes to take care of their offspring. What differences from terrestrial conditions will ensue?

This extent of intervention will at least abolish two or three salient hardships and evils of the civilised life. It will abolish the hardship of the majority of widows, who on earth are poor and encumbered exactly in proportion as they have discharged the chief distinctive duty of a woman, and miserable, just in proportion as their standard of life and of education is high. It will abolish the hardship of those who do not now marry on account of poverty, or who do not dare to have children. The fear that often turns a woman from a beautiful to a mercenary marriage will vanish from life. In Utopia a career of wholesome motherhood would be, under such conditions as I have suggested, the normal and remunerative calling for a woman, and a capable woman who has borne, bred, and begun the education of eight or nine well-built, intelligent, and successful sons and daughters would be an extremely prosperous woman, quite irrespective of the economic fortunes of the man she has married. She would need to be an exceptional woman, and she would need to have chosen a man at least a little above the average as her partner in life. But his death, or misbehaviour, or misfortunes would not ruin her.

Now such an arrangement is merely the completed induction from the starting propositions that make some measure of education free and compulsory for every child in the State. If you prevent people making profit out of their children – and every civilised State, even that compendium of old-fashioned Individualism, the United States of America, is now disposed to admit the necessity of that prohibition – and if you provide for the aged instead of leaving them to their children's sense of duty, the practical inducements to parentage, except among very wealthy people, are greatly reduced. The sentimental factor in the case rarely leads to more than a solitary child or at most two to a marriage, and with a high and rising standard of comfort and circumspection it is unlikely that the birthrate will ever rise very greatly again. The Utopians will hold that if you keep the children from profitable employment for the sake of the future, then, if you want any but the exceptionally rich, secure, pious, unselfish, or reckless to bear children freely, you must be prepared to throw the cost of their maintenance upon the general community.

In short, Utopia will hold that sound childbearing and rearing is a service done, not to a particular man, but to the whole community, and all its legal arrangements for motherhood will be based on that conception.

4

And after these preliminaries we must proceed to ask, first, what will be the Utopian marriage law, and then what sort of customs and opinions are likely to be superadded to that law?

The trend of our reasoning has brought us to the conclusion that the Utopian State will feel justified in intervening between men and women on two accounts, first on account of paternity, and secondly on account of the clash of freedoms that may otherwise arise. The Utopian State will effectually interfere with and prescribe conditions for all sorts of contract, and for this sort of contract in particular it will be in agreement with almost every earthly State, in defining in the completest fashion what things a man or woman may be bound to do, and what they cannot be bound to do. From the point of view of a statesman, marriage is the union of a man and woman in a manner so intimate as to involve the probability of offspring, and it is of primary importance to the State, first in order to secure good births, and secondly good home conditions, that these unions should not be free, nor promiscuous, nor practically universal throughout the adult population.

Prolific marriage must be a profitable privilege. It must occur only under certain obvious conditions, the contracting parties must be in health and condition, free from specific transmissible taints, above a certain minimum age, and sufficiently intelligent and energetic to have acquired a minimum education. The man at least must be in receipt of a net income above the minimum wage, after any outstanding charges against him have been paid. All this much it is surely reasonable to insist upon before the State becomes responsible for the prospective children. The age at which men and women may contract to marry is difficult to determine. But if we are, as far as possible, to put women on an equality with men, if we are to insist upon a universally educated population, and if we are seeking to reduce the infantile death-rate to zero, it must be much higher than it is in any terrestrial State. The woman should be at least one-and-twenty; the man twenty-six or twenty-seven.

One imagines the parties to a projected marriage first obtaining licences which will testify that these conditions are satisfied. From the point of view of the theoretical Utopian State, these licences are the feature of primary importance. Then, no doubt, that universal register at Paris would come into play. As a matter of justice, there must be no deception between the two people, and the State will ensure that in certain broad essentials this is so. They would have to communicate their joint intention to a public office after their personal licences were granted, and each would be supplied with a copy of the index card of the projected mate, on which would be recorded his or her age, previous marriages, legally important diseases, offspring, domiciles, public appointments, criminal convictions, registered assignments of property, and so forth. Possibly it might be advisable to have a little ceremony for each party, for each in the absence of the other, in which this record could be read over in the presence of witnesses, together with some prescribed form of address of counsel in the matter. There would then be a reasonable interval for consideration and withdrawal on the part of either spouse. In the event of the two people persisting in their resolution, they would after this minimum interval signify as much to the local official and the necessary entry would be made in the registers. These formalities would be quite independent of any religious ceremonial the contracting parties might choose, for with religious belief and procedure the modern State has no concern.

So much for the preliminary conditions of matrimony. For those men and women who chose to ignore these conditions and to achieve any sort of union they liked the State would have no concern, unless offspring were born illegitimately. In that case, as we have already suggested, it would be only reasonable to make the parents chargeable with every duty, with maintenance, education, and so forth, that in the normal course of things would fall to the State. It would be necessary to impose a life assurance payment upon these parents, and to exact effectual guarantees against every possible evasion of the responsibility they had incurred. But the further control of private morality, beyond the protection of the immature from corruption and evil example, will be no concern of the State's. When a child comes in, the future of the species comes in; and the State comes in as the guardian of interests wider than the individual's; but the adult's private life is the entirely private life into which the State may not intrude.

Now what will be the nature of the Utopian contract of matrimony?

From the first of the two points of view named above, that of parentage, it is obvious that one unavoidable condition will be the chastity of the wife. Her infidelity being demonstrated, must at once terminate the marriage and release both her husband and the State from any liability for the support of her illegitimate offspring. That, at any rate, is beyond controversy; a marriage contract that does not involve that, is a triumph of metaphysics over common sense. It will be obvious that under Utopian conditions it is the State that will suffer injury by a wife's misconduct, and that a husband who condones anything of the sort will participate in her offence. A woman, therefore, who is divorced on this account will be divorced as a public offender, and not in the key of a personal quarrel; not as one who has inflicted a private and personal wrong. This, too, lies within the primary implications of marriage.

Beyond that, what conditions should a marriage contract in Utopia involve?

A reciprocal restraint on the part of the husband is clearly of no importance whatever, so far as the first end of matrimony goes, the protection of the community from inferior births. It is no wrong to the State. But it does carry with it a variable amount of emotional offence to the wife; it may wound her pride and cause her violent perturbations of jealousy; it may lead to her neglect, her solitude and unhappiness, and it may even work to her physical injury. There should be an implication that it is not to occur. She has bound herself to the man for the good of the State, and clearly it is reasonable that she should look to the State for relief if it does occur. The extent of the offence given her is the exact measure of her injury; if she does not mind nobody minds, and if her self-respect does not suffer nothing whatever is lost to the world; and so it should rest with her to establish his misconduct, and, if she thinks fit, to terminate the marriage.

A failure on either side to perform the elementary duties of companionship, desertion, for example, should obviously give the other mate the right to relief, and clearly the development of any disqualifying habit, drunkenness, or drug-taking, or the like, or any serious crime or acts of violence, should give grounds for a final release. Moreover, the modern Utopian State intervenes between the sexes only because of the coming generation, and for it to sustain restrictions upon conduct in a continually fruitless marriage is obviously to lapse into purely moral intervention. It seems reasonable, therefore, to set a term to a marriage that remains childless, to let it expire at the end of three or four or five unfruitful years, but with no restriction upon the right of the husband and wife to marry each other again.

These are the fairly easy primaries of this question. We now come to the more difficult issues of the matter. The first of these is the question of the economic relationships of husband and wife, having regard to the fact that even in Utopia women, at least until they become mothers, are likely to be on the average poorer than men. The second is the question of the duration of a marriage. But the two interlock, and are, perhaps, best treated together in one common section. And they both ramify in the most complicated manner into the consideration of the general morale of the community.

5

This question of marriage is the most complicated and difficult in the whole range of Utopian problems. But it is happily not the most urgent necessity that it should be absolutely solved. The urgent and necessary problem is the ruler. With rulers rightly contrived and a provisional defective marriage law a Utopia may be conceived as existing and studying to perfect itself, but without rulers a Utopia is impossible though the theory of its matrimony be complete. And the difficulty in this question is not simply the difficulty of a complicated chess problem, for example, in which the whole tangle of considerations does at least lie in one plane, but a series of problems upon different levels and containing incommensurable factors.

It is very easy to repeat our initial propositions, to recall that we are on another planet, and that all the customs and traditions of the earth are set aside, but the faintest realisation of that demands a feat of psychological insight. We have all grown up into an invincible mould of suggestion about sexual things; we regard this with approval, that with horror, and this again with contempt, very largely because the thing has always been put to us in this light or that. The more emancipated we think ourselves the more subtle are our bonds. The disentanglement of what is inherent in these feelings from what is acquired is an extraordinarily complex undertaking. Probably all men and women have a more or less powerful disposition to jealousy, but what exactly they will be jealous about and what exactly they will suffer seems part of the superposed factor. Probably all men and women are capable of ideal emotions and wishes beyond merely physical desires, but the shape these take are almost entirely a reaction to external images. And you really cannot strip the external off; you cannot get your stark natural man, jealous, but not jealous about anything in particular, imaginative without any imaginings, proud at large. Emotional dispositions can no more exist without form than a man without air. Only a very observant man who had lived all over the planet Earth, in all sorts of social strata, and with every race and tongue, and who was endowed with great imaginative insight, could hope to understand the possibilities and the limitations of human plasticity in this matter, and say what any men and any women could be induced to do willingly, and just exactly what no man and no woman could stand, provided one had the training of them. Though very young men will tell you readily enough. The proceedings of other races and other ages do not seem to carry conviction; what our ancestors did, or what the Greeks or Egyptians did, though it is the direct physical cause of the modern young man or the modern young lady, is apt to impress these remarkable consequences merely as an arrangement of quaint, comical or repulsive proceedings.

But there emerges to the modern enquirer certain ideals and desiderata that at least go some way towards completing and expanding the crude primaries of a Utopian marriage law set out in section 4.

The sound birth being assured, does there exist any valid reason for the persistence of the Utopian marriage union?

There are two lines of reasoning that go to establish a longer duration for marriage. The first of these rests upon the general necessity for a home and for individual attention in the case of children. Children are the results of a choice between individuals; they grow well, as a rule, only in relation to sympathetic and kindred individualities, and no wholesale character-ignoring method of dealing with them has ever had a shadow of the success of the individualised home. Neither Plato nor Socrates, who repudiated the home, seems ever to have had to do with anything younger than a young man. Procreation is only the beginning of parentage, and even where the mother is not the direct nurse and teacher of her child, even where she delegates these duties, her supervision is, in the common case, essential to its welfare. More-over, though the Utopian State will pay the mother, and the mother only, for the being and welfare of her legitimate children, there will be a clear advantage in fostering the natural disposition of the father to associate his child's welfare with his individual egotism, and to dispense some of his energies and earnings in supplementing the common provision of the State. It is an absurd disregard of a natural economy to leave the innate philoprogenitiveness of either sex uncultivated. Unless the parents continue in close relationship, if each is passing through a series of marriages, the dangers of a conflict of rights, and of the frittering away of emotions, become very grave. The family will lose homogeneity, and its individuals will have for the mother varied and perhaps incompatible emotional associations. The balance of social advantage is certainly on the side of much more permanent unions, on the side of an arrangement that, subject to ample provisions for a formal divorce without disgrace in cases of incompatibility, would bind, or at least enforce ideals that would tend to bind, a man and woman together for the whole term of her maternal activity, until, that is, the last born of her children was no longer in need of her help.

The second system of considerations arises out of the artificiality of woman's position. It is a less conclusive series than the first, and it opens a number of interesting side vistas.

A great deal of nonsense is talked about the natural equality or inferiority of women to men. But it is only the same quality that can be measured by degrees and ranged in ascending and descending series, and the things that are essentially feminine are different qualitatively from and incommensurable with the distinctly masculine things. The relationship is in the region of ideals and conventions, and a State is perfectly free to determine that men and women shall come to intercourse on a footing of conventional equality or with either the man or woman treated as the predominating individual. Aristotle's criticism of Plato in this matter, his insistence upon the natural inferiority of slaves and women, is just the sort of confusion between inherent and imposed qualities that was his most characteristic weakness. The spirit of the European people, of almost all the peoples now in the ascendant, is towards a convention of equality; the spirit of the Mahometan world is towards the intensification of a convention that the man alone is a citizen and that the woman is very largely his property. There can be no doubt that the latter of these two convenient fictions is the more primitive way of regarding this relationship. It is quite unfruitful to argue between these ideals as if there were a demonstrable conclusion, the adoption of either is an arbitrary act, and we shall simply follow our age and time if we display a certain bias for the former.

If one looks closely into the various practical expansions of these ideas, we find their inherent falsity works itself out in a very natural way so soon as reality is touched. Those who insist upon equality work in effect for assimilation, for a similar treatment of the sexes. Plato's women of the governing class, for example, were to strip for gymnastics like men, to bear arms and go to war, and follow most of the masculine occupations of their class. They were to have the same education and to be assimilated to men at every doubtful point. The Aristotelian attitude, on the other hand, insists upon specialisation. The men are to rule and fight and toil; the women are to support motherhood in a state of natural inferiority. The trend of evolutionary forces through long centuries of human development has been on the whole in this second direction, has been towards differentiation.* An adult white woman differs far more from a white man than a negress or pigmy woman from her equivalent male. The education, the mental disposition, of a white or Asiatic woman, reeks of sex; her modesty, her decorum is not to ignore sex but to refine and put a point to it; her costume is clamorous with the distinctive elements of her form. The white woman in the materially prosperous nations is more of a sexual specialist than her sister of the poor and austere peoples, of the prosperous classes more so than the peasant woman. The contemporary woman of fashion who sets the tone of occidental intercourse is a stimulant rather than a companion for a man. Too commonly she is an unwholesome stimulant turning a man from wisdom to appearance, from beauty to beautiful pleasures, from form to colour, from persistent aims to belief and stirring triumphs. Arrayed in what she calls distinctly 'dress', scented, adorned, displayed, she achieves by artifice a sexual differentiation profounder than that of any other vertebrated animal. She outshines the peacock's excess above his mate; one must probe among the domestic secrets of the insects and crustacea to find her living parallel. And it is a question by no means easy and yet of the utmost importance, to determine how far the wide and widening differences between the human sexes is inherent and inevitable, and how far it is an accident of social development that may be converted and reduced under a different social regimen. Are we going to recognise and accentuate this difference and to arrange our Utopian organisation to play upon it, are we to have two primary classes of human being, harmonising indeed and reacting, but following essentially different lives, or are we going to minimise this difference in every possible way?

* See Havelock Ellis's *Man and Woman*.

The former alternative leads either to a romantic organisation of society in which men will live and fight and die for wonderful, beautiful, exaggerated creatures, or it leads to the harem. It would probably lead through one phase to the other. Women would be enigmas and mysteries and maternal dignitaries that one would approach in a state of emotional excitement and seclude piously when serious work was in hand. A girl would blossom from the totally negligible to the mystically desirable at adolescence, and boys would be removed from their mother's educational influence at as early an age as possible. Whenever men and women met together, the men would be in a state of inflamed competition towards one another, and the women likewise, and the intercourse of ideas would be in suspense. Under the latter alternative the sexual relation would be subordinated to friendship and companion-ship; boys and girls would be co-educated – very largely under maternal direction, and women, disarmed of their distinctive barbaric adorn-ments, the feathers, beads, lace, and trimmings that enhance their clamorous claim to a directly personal attention, would mingle, according to their quality, in the counsels and intellectual development of men. Such women would be fit to educate boys even up to adolescence. It is obvious that a marriage law embodying a decision between these two sets of ideas would be very different according to the alternative adopted. In the former case a man would be expected to earn and maintain in an adequate manner the dear delight that had favoured him. He would tell her beautiful lies about her wonderful moral effect upon him, and keep her sedulously from all responsibility and knowledge. And, since there is an undeniably greater imaginative appeal to men in the first bloom of a woman's youth, she would have a distinct claim upon his energies for the rest of her life. In the latter case a man would no more pay for and support his wife than she would do so for him. They would be two friends, differing in kind no doubt but differing reciprocally, who had linked themselves in a matrimonial relationship. Our Utopian marriage so far as we have discussed it, is indeterminate between these alternatives.

We have laid it down as a general principle that the private morals of an adult citizen are no concern for the State. But that involves a decision to disregard certain types of bargain. A sanely contrived State will refuse to sustain bargains wherein there is no plausibly fair exchange, and if private morality is really to be outside the scope of the State then the affections and endearments most certainly must not be regarded as negotiable commodities. The State, therefore, will absolutely ignore the distribution of these favours unless children, or at least the possibility

of children, is involved. It follows that it will refuse to recognise any
debts or transfers of property that are based on such considerations. It
will be only consistent, therefore, to refuse recognition in the marriage
contract to any financial obligation between husband and wife, or any
settlements qualifying that contract, except when they are in the nature
of accessory provision for the prospective children.* So far the Utopian
State will throw its weight upon the side of those who advocate the
independence of women and their conventional equality with men.

But to any further definition of the marriage relation the World State
of Utopia will not commit itself. The wide range of relationships that
are left possible, within and without the marriage code, are entirely a
matter for the individual choice and imagination. Whether a man treat
his wife in private as a goddess to be propitiated, as a 'mystery' to be
adored, as an agreeable auxiliary, as a particularly intimate friend, or as
the wholesome mother of his children, is entirely a matter for their
private intercourse: whether he keep her in Oriental idleness or active
co-operation, or leave her to live her independent life, rests with the
couple alone, and all the possible friendships and intimacies outside
marriage also lie quite beyond the organisation of the modern State.
Religious teaching and literature may affect these; customs may arise;
certain types of relationship may involve social isolation; the justice of
the statesman is blind to such things. It may be urged that according to
Atkinson's illuminating analysis† the control of love-making was the
very origin of the human community. In Utopia, nevertheless, love-
making is no concern of the State's beyond the province that the protection of children covers.‡ Change of function is one of the ruling facts

---

*   Unqualified gifts for love by solvent people will, of course, be quite possible
    and permissible, unsalaried services and the like, provided the standard of
    life is maintained and the joint income of the couple between whom the
    services hold does not sink below twice the minimum wage.
†   See Lang and Atkinson's *Social Origins* and *Primal Law*.
‡   It cannot be made too clear that though the control of morality is outside
    the law the State must maintain a general decorum, a systematic suppression
    of powerful and moving examples, and of incitations and temptations of the
    young and inexperienced, and to that extent it will, of course, in a sense,
    exercise a control over morals. But this will be only part of a wider law to
    safeguard the tender mind. For example, lying advertisements, and the like,
    when they lean towards adolescent interests, will encounter a specially
    disagreeable disposition in the law, over and above the treatment of their
    general dishonesty.

in life, the sac that was in our remotest ancestors a swimming bladder is now a lung; and the State which was once, perhaps, no more than the jealous and tyrannous will of the strongest male in the herd, becomes the instrument of justice and equality. The State intervenes now only where there is want of harmony between individuals – individuals who exist or who may presently come into existence.

6

It must be reiterated that our reasoning still leaves Utopian marriage an institution with wide possibilities of variation. We have tried to give effect to the ideal of a virtual equality, an equality of spirit between men and women, and in doing so we have overridden the accepted opinion of the great majority of mankind. Probably the first writer to do as much was Plato. His argument in support of this innovation upon natural human feeling was thin enough – a mere analogy to illustrate the spirit of his propositions; it was his creative instinct that determined him. In the atmosphere of such speculations as this, Plato looms very large indeed, and in view of what we owe to him, it seems reasonable that we should hesitate before dismissing, as a thing prohibited and evil, a type of marriage that he made almost the central feature in the organisation of the ruling class, at least, of his ideal State. He was persuaded that the narrow monogamic family is apt to become illiberal and anti-social, to withdraw the imagination and energies of the citizen from the services of the community as a whole, and the Roman Catholic Church has so far endorsed and substantiated his opinion as to forbid family relations to its priests and significant servants. He conceived of a poetic devotion to the public idea, a devotion of which the mind of Aristotle, as his criticisms of Plato show, was incapable, as a substitute for the warm and tender but illiberal emotions of the home. But while the Church made the alternative to family ties celibacy* and particip-ation in an organisation, Plato was far more in accordance with modern ideas in perceiving the disadvantage that would result from precluding the nobler types of character from offspring. He sought a way to achieve progeny, therefore, without the narrow concentration of the sympathies about the home, and he found it in a multiple marriage in which every member of the governing class was considered to be married to all the

---

* The warm imagination of Campanella, that quaint Calabrian monastic, fired by Plato, reversed this aspect of the Church.

others. But the detailed operation of this system he put tentatively and very obscurely. His suggestions have the experimental inconsistency of an enquiring man. He left many things altogether open, and it is unfair to him to adopt Aristotle's forensic method and deal with his discussion as though it was a fully-worked-out project. It is clear that Plato intended every member of his governing class to be so 'changed at birth' as to leave paternity untraceable; mothers were not to know their children, nor children their parents, but there is nothing to forbid the supposition that he intended these people to select and adhere to congenial mates within the great family. Aristotle's assertion that the Platonic republic left no scope for the virtue of continence shows that he had jumped to just the same conclusions a contemporary London errand boy, hovering a little shamefacedly over Jowett in a public library, might be expected to reach.

Aristotle obscures Plato's intention, it may be accidentally, by speaking of his marriage institution as a community of wives. When reading Plato he could not or would not escape reading in his own conception of the natural ascendency of men, his idea of property in women and children. But as Plato intended women to be conventionally equal to men, this phrase belies him altogether; community of husbands and wives would be truer to his proposal. Aristotle condemns Plato as roundly as any commercial room would condemn him today, and in much the same spirit; he asserts rather than proves that such a grouping is against the nature of man. He wanted to have women property just as he wanted to have slaves property, he did not care to ask why, and it distressed his conception of convenience extremely to imagine any other arrangement. It is no doubt true that the natural instinct of either sex is exclusive of participators in intimacy during a period of intimacy, but it was probably Aristotle who gave Plato an offensive interpretation in this matter. No one would freely submit to such a condition of affairs as multiple marriage carried out, in the spirit of the Aristotelian interpretation, to an obscene completeness, but that is all the more reason why the modern Utopia should not refuse a grouped marriage to three or more freely consenting persons. There is no sense in prohibiting institutions which no sane people could ever want to abuse. It is claimed – though the full facts are difficult to ascertain – that a group marriage of over two hundred persons was successfully organised by John Humphrey Noyes at Oneida Creek.* It is fairly certain in the

* See John H. Noyes's *History of American Socialisms* and his writings generally. The bare facts of this and the other American experiments are given, together

latter case that there was no 'promiscuity', and that the members mated for variable periods, and often for life, within the group. The documents are reasonably clear upon that point. This Oneida community was, in fact, a league of two hundred persons to regard their children as 'common'. Choice and preference were not abolished in the community, though in some cases they were set aside – just as they are by many parents under our present conditions. There seems to have been a premature attempt at 'stirpiculture', at what Mr Francis Galton now calls 'Eugenics', in the mating of the members, and there was also a limitation of offspring. Beyond these points the inner secrets of the community do not appear to be very profound; its atmosphere was almost commonplace, it was made up of very ordinary people. There is no doubt that it had a career of exceptional success throughout the whole lifetime of its founder, and it broke down with the advent of a new generation, with the onset of theological differences, and the loss of its guiding intelligence. The Anglo-Saxon spirit, it has been said by one of the ablest children of the experiment, is too individualistic for communism. It is possible to regard the temporary success of this complex family as a strange accident, as the wonderful exploit of what was certainly a very exceptional man. Its final disintegration into frankly monogamic couples – it is still a prosperous business association – may be taken as an experimental verification of Aristotle's common-sense psychology, and was probably merely the public acknowledgement of conditions already practically established.

Out of respect for Plato we cannot ignore this possibility of multiple marriage altogether in our Utopian theorising, but even if we leave this possibility open we are still bound to regard it as a thing so likely to be rare as not to come at all under our direct observation during our Utopian journeyings. But in one sense, of course, in the sense that the State guarantees care and support for all properly born children, our entire Utopia is to be regarded as a comprehensive marriage group.*

It must be remembered that a modern Utopia must differ from the Utopias of any preceding age in being worldwide; it is not, therefore, to be the development of any special race or type of culture, as Plato's developed an Athenian-Spartan blend, or More, Tudor England. The

---

with more recent matter, by Morris Hillquit, in *The History of Socialism in the United States*.

* The Thelema of Rabelais, with its principle of *Fay ce que vouldras* within the limits of the order, is probably intended to suggest a Platonic complex marriage after the fashion of our interpretation.

modern Utopia is to be, before all things, synthetic. Politically and socially, as linguistically, we must suppose it a synthesis; politically it will be a synthesis of once widely different forms of government; socially and morally, a synthesis of a great variety of domestic traditions and ethical habits. Into the modern Utopia there must have entered the mental tendencies and origins that give our own world the polygamy of the Zulus and of Utah, the polyandry of Tibet, the latitudes of experiment permitted in the United States, and the divorceless wedlock of Comte. The tendency of all synthetic processes in matters of law and custom is to reduce and simplify the compulsory canon, to admit alternatives and freedoms; what were laws before become traditions of feeling and style, and in no matter will this be more apparent than in questions affecting the relations of the sexes.

CHAPTER SEVEN

A Few Utopian Impressions

1

But now we are in a better position to describe the houses and ways of the Utopian townships about the Lake of Lucerne, and to glance a little more nearly at the people who pass. You figure us as curiously settled down in Utopia, as working for a low wage at wood-carving, until the authorities at the central registry in Paris can solve the perplexing problem we have set them. We stay in an inn looking out upon the lake, and go to and fro for our five hours' work a day, with a curious effect of having been born Utopians. The rest of our time is our own.

Our inn is one of those inns and lodging houses which have a minimum tariff, inns which are partly regulated, and, in the default of private enterprise, maintained and controlled by the World State throughout the entire world. It is one of several such establishments in Lucerne. It possesses many hundreds of practically self-cleaning little bedrooms, equipped very much after the fashion of the rooms we occupied in the similar but much smaller inn at Hospenthal, differing only a little in the decoration. There is the same dressing-room recess with its bath, the same graceful proportion in the succinct simplicity of its furniture. This particular inn is a quadrangle after the fashion of an Oxford college; it is perhaps forty feet high, and with about five storeys of bedrooms above its lower apartments; the windows of the rooms look either outward or inward to the quadrangle, and the doors give upon artificially lit passages with staircases passing up and down. These passages are carpeted with a sort of cork carpet, but are otherwise bare. The lower storey is occupied by the equivalent of a London club, kitchens and other offices, dining-room, writing-room, smoking and assembly rooms, a barber's shop, and a library. A colonnade with seats runs about the quadrangle, and in the middle is a grass-plot. In the centre of this a bronze figure, a sleeping child, reposes above a little basin and fountain, in which water lilies are growing. The place has been designed by an architect happily free from the hampering traditions of Greek temple building, and of Roman and Italian palaces; it is simple, unaffected, gracious. The material is some artificial stone with the dull surface and something of the tint of yellow ivory; the colour is a little irregular, and a partial confession of girders and pillars breaks this front of tender colour with lines and mouldings of greenish grey that blend with the tones of the leaden gutters and rain pipes from the light red roof. At one point only does any explicit effort towards artistic effect appear, and that is in the great arched gateway opposite my window. Two or three abundant yellow roses climb over the face of the building, and when I look out of my window in the early morning – for the usual Utopian working day commences within an hour of sunrise – I see Pilatus above this outlook, rosy in the morning sky.

This quadrangle type of building is the prevalent element in Utopian Lucerne, and one may go from end to end of the town along corridors and covered colonnades without emerging by a gateway into the open roads at all. Small shops are found in these colonnades, but the larger stores are usually housed in buildings specially adapted to their needs. The majority of the residential edifices are far finer and more substantial than our own modest shelter, though we gather from such chance glimpses as we get of their arrangements that the labour-saving ideal runs through every grade of this servantless world; and what we should consider a complete house in earthly England is hardly known here.

The autonomy of the household has been reduced far below terrestrial conditions by hotels and clubs, and all sorts of co-operative expedients. People who do not live in hotels seem usually to live in clubs. The fairly prosperous Utopian belongs, in most cases, to one or two residential clubs of congenial men and women. These clubs usually possess in addition to furnished bedrooms more or less elaborate suites of apartments, and if a man prefers it one of these latter can be taken and furnished according to his personal taste. A pleasant boudoir, a private library and study, a private garden plot, are among the commonest of such luxuries. Devices to secure roof gardens, loggias, verandahs, and suchlike open-air privacies to the more sumptuous of these apartments, give interest and variety to Utopian architecture. There are sometimes little cooking corners in these flats – as one would call them on earth – but the ordinary Utopian would no more think of a special private kitchen for his dinners than he would think of a private flour mill or dairy farm. Business, private work, and professional practice go on sometimes in the house apartments, but often in special offices in the great warren of the business quarter. A common garden, an infant school, play rooms, and a playing garden for children, are universal features of the club quadrangles.

Two or three main roads with their tramways, their cyclists' paths, and swift traffic paths, will converge on the urban centre, where the public offices will stand in a group close to the two or three theatres and the larger shops, and hither, too, in the case of Lucerne, the head of the swift railway to Paris and England and Scotland, and to the Rhineland and Germany will run. And as one walks out from the town centre one will come to that mingling of homesteads and open country which will be the common condition of all the more habitable parts of the globe.

Here and there, no doubt, will stand quite solitary homesteads, homesteads that will nevertheless be lit and warmed by cables from the central force station, that will share the common water supply, will have their perfected telephonic connection with the rest of the world, with doctor, shop, and so forth, and may even have a pneumatic tube for books and small parcels to the nearest post office. But the solitary homestead, as a permanent residence, will be something of a luxury – the resort of rather wealthy garden lovers; and most people with a bias for retirement will probably get as much residential solitude as they care for in the hire of a holiday chalet in a forest, by remote lagoons or high up the mountainside.

The solitary house may indeed prove to be very rare indeed in Utopia. The same forces, the same facilitation of communications that will diffuse the towns will tend to little concentrations of the agricultural population over the countryside. The field workers will probably take their food with them to their work during the day, and for the convenience of an interesting dinner and of civilised intercourse after the working day is over, they will most probably live in a college quadrangle with a common room and club. I doubt if there will be any agricultural labourers drawing wages in Utopia. I am inclined to imagine farming done by tenant associations, by little democratic unlimited liability companies working under elected managers, and paying not a fixed rent but a share of the produce to the State. Such companies could reconstruct annually to weed out indolent members.* A minimum standard of efficiency in farming would be ensured by fixing a minimum beneath which the rent must not fall, and perhaps by inspection. The general laws respecting the standard of life would, of course, apply to such associations. This type of co-operation presents itself to me as socially the best arrangement for productive agriculture and horticulture, but such enterprises as stock breeding, seed farming and the stocking and loan of agricultural implements are probably, and agricultural research and experiment certainly, best

* Schemes for the co-operative association of producers will be found in Dr Hertzka's *Freeland*.

handled directly by large companies or the municipality or the State.

But I should do little to investigate this question; these are presented as quite incidental impressions. You must suppose that for the most part our walks and observations keep us within the more urban quarters of Lucerne. From a number of beautifully printed placards at the street corners, adorned with caricatures of considerable pungency, we discover an odd little election is in progress. This is the selection, upon strictly democratic lines, with a suffrage that includes every permanent resident in the Lucerne ward over the age of fifteen, of the ugliest local building. The old little urban and local governing bodies, we find, have long since been superseded by great provincial municipalities for all the more serious administrative purposes, but they still survive to discharge a number of curious minor functions, and not the least among these is this sort of aesthetic ostracism. Every year every minor local governing body pulls down a building selected by local plebiscite, and the greater Government pays a slight compensation to the owner, and resumes possession of the land it occupies. The idea would strike us at first as simply whimsical, but in practice it appears to work as a cheap and practical device for the aesthetic education of builders, engineers, businessmen, opulent persons, and the general body of the public. But when we come to consider its application to our own world we should perceive it was the most Utopian thing we had so far encountered.

2

The factory that employs us is something very different from the ordinary earthly model. Our business is to finish making little wooden toys – bears, cattle men, and the like – for children. The things are made in the rough by machinery, and then finished by hand, because the work of unskilful but interested men – and it really is an extremely amusing employment – is found to give a personality and interest to these objects no machine can ever attain.

We carvers – who are the riffraff of Utopia – work in a long shed together, nominally by time; we must keep at the job for the length of the spell, but we are expected to finish a certain number of toys for each spell of work. The rules of the game as between employer and employed in this particular industry hang on the wall behind us; they are drawn up by a conference of the Common Council of Wages Workers with the employers, a common council which has resulted in Utopia from a synthesis of the old Trades Unions, and which has become a constitutional power; but any man who has skill or humour is presently making his own bargain with our employer more or less above that datum line.

Our employer is a quiet blue-eyed man with a humorous smile. He dresses wholly in an indigo blue, that later we come to consider a sort of voluntary uniform for Utopian artists. As he walks about the workshop, stopping to laugh at this production or praise that, one is reminded inevitably of an art school. Every now and then he carves a little himself or makes a sketch or departs to the machinery to order some change in the rough shapes it is turning out. Our work is by no means confined to animals. After a time I am told to specialise in a comical little Roman-nosed pony; but several of the better-paid carvers work up caricature images of eminent Utopians. Over these our employer is most disposed to meditate, and from them he darts off most frequently to improve the type.

It is high summer, and our shed lies open at either end. On one hand is a steep mountainside down which there comes, now bridging a chasm, now a mere straight groove across a meadow, now hidden among green branches, the water-slide that brings our trees from the purple forest overhead. Above us, but nearly hidden, hums the machine shed, but we see a corner of the tank into which, with a mighty splash, the pine trees are delivered. Every now and then, bringing with him a gust of resinous smell, a white-clad machinist will come in with a basketful of crude, unwrought little images, and will turn them out upon the table from which we carvers select them.

(Whenever I think of Utopia that faint and fluctuating smell of resin returns to me, and whenever I smell resin, comes the memory of the open end of the shed looking out upon the lake, the blue-green lake, the boats mirrored in the water, and far and high beyond floats the atmospheric fairyland of the mountains of Glarus, twenty miles away.)

The cessation of the second and last spell of work comes about midday, and then we walk home, through this beautiful intricacy of a town to our cheap hotel beside the lake.

We should go our way with a curious contentment, for all that we were earning scarcely more than the minimum wage. We should have, of course, our uneasiness about the final decisions of that universal eye which has turned upon us, we should have those ridiculous sham numbers on our consciences; but that general restlessness, that brooding stress that pursues the weekly worker on earth, that aching anxiety that drives him so often to stupid betting, stupid drinking, and violent and mean offences will have vanished out of mortal experience.

I should find myself contrasting my position with my preconceptions about a Utopian visit. I had always imagined myself as standing outside the general machinery of the State – in the distinguished visitors' gallery, as it were – and getting the new world in a series of comprehensive perspective views. But this Utopia, for all the sweeping floats of generalisation I do my best to maintain, is swallowing me up. I find myself going between my work and the room in which I sleep and the place in which I dine, very much as I went to and fro in that real world into which I fell five-and-forty years ago. I find about me mountains and horizons that limit my view, institutions that vanish also without an explanation, beyond the limit of sight, and a great complexity of things I do not understand and about which, to tell the truth, I do not formulate acute curiosities. People, very unrepresentative people, people just as casual as people in the real world, come into personal relations with us, and little threads of private and immediate interest spin themselves rapidly into a thickening grey veil across the general view. I lose the comprehensive interrogation of my first arrival; I find myself interested in the grain of the wood I work, in birds among the tree branches, in little irrelevant things, and it is only now and then that I get fairly back to the mood that takes all Utopia for its picture.

We spend our first surplus of Utopian money in the reorganisation of our wardrobes upon more Utopian lines; we develop acquaintance with several of our fellow workers, and of those who share our table at the inn. We pass insensibly into acquaintanceships and the beginnings of friendships. The World Utopia, I say, seems for a time to be swallowing me up. At the thought of detail it looms too big for me. The question of government, of its sustaining ideas, of race, and the wider future, hang like the arch of the sky over these daily incidents, very great indeed, but very remote. These people about me are everyday people, people not so very far from the minimum wage, accustomed much as the everyday people of earth are accustomed to take their world as they find it. Such enquiries as I attempt are pretty obviously a bore to them, pass outside their range as completely as Utopian speculation on earth outranges a stevedore or a member of Parliament or a working plumber. Even the little things of daily life interest them in a different way. So I get on with my facts and reasoning rather slowly. I find myself looking among the pleasant multitudes of the streets for types that promise congenial conversation.

My sense of loneliness is increased during this interlude by the better social success of the botanist. I find him presently falling into conversation with two women who are accustomed to sit at a table near our own. They wear the loose, coloured robes of soft material that are the usual wear of common adult Utopian women; they are both dark and sallow, and they affect amber and crimson in their garments. Their faces strike me as a little unintelligent, and there is a faint touch of middle-aged coquetry in their bearing that I do not like. Yet on earth we should consider them women of exceptional refinement. But the botanist evidently sees in this direction scope for the feelings that have wilted a little under my inattention, and he begins that petty intercourse of a word, of a slight civility, of vague enquiries and comparisons that leads at last to associations and confidences. Such superficial confidences, that is to say, as he finds satisfactory.

This throws me back upon my private observations.

The general effect of a Utopian population is vigour. Everyone one meets seems to be not only in good health but in training; one rarely meets fat people, bald people, or bent or grey. People who would be obese or bent and obviously aged on earth are here in good repair, and as a consequence the whole effect of a crowd is livelier and more invigorating than on earth. The dress is varied and graceful; that of the women reminds one most of the Italian fifteenth century; they have an abundance of soft and beautifully coloured stuffs, and the clothes, even of the poorest, fit admirably. Their hair is very simply but very carefully and beautifully dressed, and except in very sunny weather they do not wear hats or bonnets. There is little difference in deportment between one class and another; they all are graceful and bear themselves with quiet dignity, and among a group of them a European woman of fashion in her lace and feathers, her hat and metal ornaments, her mixed accumulations of 'trimmings', would look like a barbarian tricked out with the miscellaneous plunder of a museum. Boys and girls wear much the same sort of costume – brown leather shoes, then a sort of combination of hose and close-fitting trousers that reaches from toe to waist, and over this a beltless jacket fitting very well, or a belted tunic. Many slender women wear the same sort of costume. We should see them in it very often in such a place as Lucerne, as they returned from expeditions in the mountains. The older men would wear long robes very frequently, but the greater proportion of the men would go in variations of much the same costume as the children. There would certainly be hooded cloaks and umbrellas for rainy weather, high boots for mud and snow, and cloaks and coats and furry robes for the winter.

There would be no doubt a freer use of colour than terrestrial Europe sees in these days, but the costume of the women at least would be soberer and more practical, and (in harmony with our discussion in the previous chapter) less differentiated from the men's.

But these, of course, are generalisations. These are the mere translation of the social facts we have hypotheticated into the language of costume. There will be a great variety of costume and no compulsions. The doubles of people who are naturally foppish on earth will be foppish in Utopia, and people who have no natural taste on earth will have inartistic equivalents. Everyone will not be quiet in tone, or harmonious, or beautiful. Occasionally, as I go through the streets to my work, I shall turn round to glance again at some robe shot with gold embroidery, some slashing of the sleeves, some eccentricity of cut, or some discord or untidiness. But these will be but transient flashes in a general flow of harmonious graciousness; dress will have scarcely any of that effect of disorderly conflict, of self-assertion qualified by the fear of ridicule, that it has in the crudely competitive civilisations of earth.

I shall have the seeker's attitude of mind during those few days at Lucerne. I shall become a student of faces. I shall be, as it were, looking for someone. I shall see heavy faces, dull faces, faces with an uncongenial animation, alien faces, and among these some with an immediate quality of appeal. I should see desirable men approaching me, and I should think: 'Now, if I were to speak to *you*?' Many of these latter I should note wore the same clothing as the man who spoke to us at Wassen; I should begin to think of it as a sort of uniform . . .

Then I should see grave-faced girls, girls of that budding age when their bearing becomes delusively wise, and the old deception of my youth will recur to me; 'Could you and I but talk together?' I should think. Women will pass me lightly, women with open and inviting faces, but they will not attract me, and there will come beautiful women, women with that touch of claustral preoccupation which forbids the thought of any near approach. They are private and secret, and I may not enter, I know, into their thoughts . . .

I go as often as I can to the seat by the end of old Kapellbrücke, and watch the people passing over.

I shall find a quality of dissatisfaction throughout all these days. I shall come to see this period more and more distinctly as a pause, as a waiting interlude; and the idea of an encounter with my double, which came at first as if it were a witticism, as something verbal and surprising, begins to take substance. The idea grows in my mind that after all this is the 'someone' I am seeking, this Utopian self of mine. I had at first an idea of a grotesque encounter, as of something happening in a looking-glass, but presently it dawns on me that my Utopian self must be a very different person from me. His training will be different, his mental content different. But between us there will be a strange link of essential identity, a sympathy, an understanding. I find the thing rising suddenly to a preponderance in my mind. I find the interest of details dwindling to the vanishing-point. That I have come to Utopia is the lesser thing now; the greater is that I have come to meet myself.

I spend hours trying to imagine the encounter, inventing little dialogues. I go alone to the Bureau to find if any news has come to hand from the Great Index in Paris, but I am told to wait another twenty-four hours. I cease absolutely to be interested in anything else, except so far as it leads towards intercourse with this being who is to be at once so strangely alien and so totally mine.

4

Wrapped up in these preoccupations as I am, it will certainly be the botanist who will notice the comparative absence of animals about us.

He will put it in the form of a temperate objection to the Utopian planet.

He is a professed lover of dogs and there are none. We have seen no horses and only one or two mules on the day of our arrival, and there seems not a cat in the world. I bring my mind round to his suggestion. 'This follows,' I say.

It is only reluctantly that I allow myself to be drawn from my secret musings into a discussion of Utopian pets.

I try to explain that a phase in the world's development is inevitable when a systematic worldwide attempt will be made to destroy for ever a great number of contagious and infectious diseases, and that this will involve, for a time at any rate, a stringent suppression of the free movement of familiar animals. Utopian houses, streets and drains will be planned and built to make rats, mice, and suchlike house parasites impossible; the race of cats and dogs – providing, as it does, living fastnesses to which such diseases as plague, influenza, catarrhs and the like, can retreat to sally forth again – must pass for a time out of freedom, and the filth made by horses and the other brutes of the highway vanish from the face of the earth. These things make an old story to me, and perhaps explicitness suffers through my brevity.

My botanist fails altogether to grasp what the disappearance of diseases means. His mind has no imaginative organ of that compass. As I talk his mind rests on one fixed image. This presents what the botanist would probably call a 'dear old doggie' – which the botanist would make believe did not possess any sensible odour – and it has faithful brown eyes and understands everything you say. The botanist would make believe it understood him mystically, and I figure his long white hand – which seems to me, in my more jaundiced moments, to exist entirely for picking things and holding a lens – patting its head, while the brute looked things unspeakable . . .

The botanist shakes his head after my explanation and says quietly, 'I do not like your Utopia, if there are to be no dogs.'

Perhaps that makes me a little malicious. Indeed I do not hate dogs, but I care ten thousand times more for a man than for all the brutes on the earth, and I can see, what the botanist I think cannot, that a life spent in the delightful atmosphere of many pet animals may have too dear a price . . .

I find myself back again at the comparison of the botanist and myself. There is a profound difference in our imaginations, and I wonder whether it is the consequence of innate character or of training and whether he is really the human type or I. I am not altogether without imagination, but what imagination I have has the most insistent disposition to square itself with every fact in the universe. It hypothesises very boldly, but on the other hand it will not gravely make believe. Now the botanist's imagination is always busy with the most impossible make-believe. That is the way with all children I know. But it seems to me one ought to pass out of it. It isn't as though the world was an untidy nursery; it is a place of splendours indescribable for all who will lift its veils. It may be he is essentially different from me, but I am much more inclined to think he is simply more childish. Always it is make-believe. He believes that horses are beautiful creatures, for example, dogs are beautiful creatures, that some women are inexpressibly lovely, and he makes believe that this is always so. Never a word of criticism of horse or dog or woman! Never a word of criticism of his impeccable friends! Then there is his botany. He makes believe that all the vegetable kingdom is mystically perfect and exemplary, that all flowers smell deliciously and are exquisitely beautiful, that *Drosera* does not hurt flies very much, and that onions do not smell. Most of the universe does not interest this nature lover at all. But I know, and I am querulously incapable of understanding why everyone else does not know, that a horse is beautiful in one way and quite ugly in another, that everything has this shot-silk quality, and is all the finer for that. When people talk of a horse as an ugly animal I think of its beautiful moments, but when I hear a flow of indiscriminate praise of its beauty I think of such an aspect as one gets for example from a dog-cart, the fiddle-shaped back, and that distressing blade of the neck, the narrow clumsy place between the ears, and the ugly glimpse of cheek. There is, indeed, no beauty whatever save that transitory thing that comes and comes again; all beauty is really the beauty of expression, is really kinetic and momentary. That is true even of those triumphs of static endeavour achieved by Greece. The Greek temple, for example, is a barn with a face that at a certain angle of vision and in a certain light has a great calm beauty.

But where are we drifting? All such things, I hold, are cases of more and less, and of the right moment and the right aspect, even the things I most esteem. There is no perfection, there is no enduring treasure. This pet dog's beautiful affection, I say, or this other sensuous or imaginative delight, is no doubt good, but it can be put aside if it is incompatible with some other and wider good. You cannot focus all good things together.

All right action and all wise action is surely sound judgement and courageous abandonment in the matter of such incompatibilities. If I cannot imagine thoughts and feelings in a dog's brain that cannot possibly be there, at least I can imagine things in the future of men that might be there had we the will to demand them . . .

'I don't like this Utopia,' the botanist repeats. 'You don't understand about dogs. To me they're human beings – and more! There used to be such a jolly old dog at my aunt's at Frognal when I was a boy – '

But I do not heed his anecdote. Something – something of the nature of conscience – has suddenly jerked back the memory of that beer I drank at Hospenthal, and puts an accusing finger on the memory.

I never have had a pet animal, I confess, though I have been fairly popular with kittens. But with regard to a certain petting of myself – ?

Perhaps I was premature about that beer. I have had no pet animals, but I perceive if the Modern Utopia is going to demand the sacrifice of the love of animals, which is, in its way, a very fine thing indeed, so much the more readily may it demand the sacrifice of many other indulgences, some of which are not even fine in the lowest degree.

It is curious this haunting insistence upon sacrifice and discipline!

It is slowly becoming my dominant thought that the sort of people whose will this Utopia embodies must be people a little heedless of small pleasures. You cannot focus all good things at the same time. That is my chief discovery in these meditations at Lucerne. Much of the rest of this Utopia I had in a sort of way anticipated, but not this. I wonder if I shall see my Utopian self for long and be able to talk to him freely . . .

We lie in the petal-strewn grass under some Judas trees beside the lake shore, as I meander among these thoughts, and each of us, disregardful of his companion, follows his own associations.

'Very remarkable,' I say, discovering that the botanist has come to an end with his story of that Frognal dog.

'You'd wonder how he knew,' he says.

'You would.'

I nibble a green blade.

'Do you realise quite,' I ask, 'that within a week we shall face our Utopian selves and measure something of what we might have been?'

The botanist's face clouds. He rolls over, sits up abruptly and puts his lean hands about his knees.

'I don't like to think about it,' he says. 'What is the good of reckoning . . . might have beens?'

5

It is pleasant to think of one's puzzling the organised wisdom of so superior a planet as this Utopia, this moral monster State my Frankenstein of reasoning has made, and to that pitch we have come. When we are next in the presence of our Lucerne official, he has the bearing of a man who faces a mystification beyond his powers, an incredible disarrangement of the order of Nature. Here, for the first time in the records of Utopian science, are two cases – not simply one but two, and these in each other's company! – of duplicated thumbmarks. This, coupled with a cock-and-bull story of an instantaneous transfer from some planet unknown to Utopian astronomy. That he and all his world exists only upon a hypothesis that would explain every one of these difficulties absolutely, is scarcely likely to occur to his obviously unphilosophic mind.

The official eye is more eloquent than the official lips and asks almost urgently, 'What in this immeasurable universe have you managed to do to your thumbs? And why?' But he is only a very inferior sort of official indeed, a mere clerk of the post, and he has all the guarded reserve of your thoroughly unoriginal man. 'You are not the two persons I ascertained you were,' he says, with the note of one resigned to communion with unreason; 'because you' – he indicates me – 'are evidently at your residence in London.' I smile. 'That gentleman' – he points a pen at the botanist in a manner that is intended to dismiss my smile once for all – 'will be in London next week. He will be returning next Friday from a special mission to investigate the fungoid parasites that have been attacking the cinchona trees in Ceylon.'

The botanist blesses his heart.

'Consequently' – the official sighs at the burden of such nonsense, 'you will have to go and consult with – the people you ought to be.'

I betray a faint amusement.

'You will have to end by believing in our planet,' I say.

He waggles a negation with his head. He would intimate his position is too responsible a one for jesting, and both of us in our several ways enjoy the pleasure we poor humans have in meeting with intellectual inferiority. 'The Standing Committee of Identification,' he says, with an eye on a memorandum, 'has remitted your case to the Research Professor of Anthropology in the University of London, and they want you to go there, if you will, and talk to him.'

'What else can we do?' says the botanist.

'There's no positive compulsion,' he remarks, 'but your work here will probably cease. Here – ' he pushed the neat slips of paper towards us – 'are your tickets for London, and a small but sufficient supply of money,' – he indicates two piles of coins and paper on either hand of him – 'for a day or so there.' He proceeds in the same dry manner to inform us we are invited to call at our earliest convenience upon our doubles, and upon the Professor who is to investigate our case.

'And then?'

He pulls down the corners of his mouth in a wry deprecatory smile, eyes us obliquely under a crumpled brow, shrugs his shoulders, and shows us the palms of his hands.

On earth, where there is nationality, this would have been a Frenchman – the inferior sort of Frenchman – the sort whose only happiness is in the routine security of Government employment.

6

London will be the first Utopian city centre we shall see.

We shall find ourselves there with not a little amazement. It will be our first experience of the swift long-distance travel of Utopia, and I have an idea – I know not why – that we should make the journey by night. Perhaps I think so because the ideal of long-distance travel is surely a restful translation less suitable for the active hours.

We shall dine and gossip and drink coffee at the pretty little tables under the lantern-lit trees, we shall visit the theatre, and decide to sup in the train, and so come at last to the station. There we shall find pleasant rooms with seats and books – luggage all neatly elsewhere – and doors that we shall imagine give upon a platform. Our cloaks and hats and suchlike outdoor impedimenta will be taken in the hall and neatly labelled for London, we shall exchange our shoes for slippers there, and we shall sit down like men in a club. An officious little bell will presently call our attention to a label 'London' on the doorway, and an excellent phonograph will enforce that notice with infinite civility. The doors will open, and we shall walk through into an equally comfortable gallery.

'Where is the train for London?' we shall ask a uniformed fellow Utopian.

'This is the train for London,' he will say.

There will be a shutting of doors, and the botanist and I, trying not to feel too childish, will walk exploring through the capacious train.

The resemblance to a club will strike us both. 'A *good* club,' the botanist will correct me.

When one travels beyond a certain speed, there is nothing but fatigue in looking out of a window, and this corridor train, twice the width of its poor terrestrial brother, will have no need of that distraction. The simple device of abandoning any but a few windows, and those set high, gives the wall space of the long corridors to books; the middle part of the train is indeed a comfortable library with abundant armchairs and couches, each with its green-shaded light, and soft carpets upon the soundproof floor. Further on will be a newsroom, with a noiseless but busy tape at one corner, printing off messages from the wires by the wayside, and further still, rooms for gossip and smoking, a billiard room, and the dining car. Behind we shall come to bedrooms, bathrooms, the hairdresser, and so forth.

'When shall we start?' I ask presently, as we return, rather like bashful yokels, to the library, and the old gentleman reading the *Arabian Nights* in the armchair in the corner glances up at me with a sudden curiosity.

The botanist touches my arm and nods towards a pretty little lead-paned window, through which we see a village sleeping under cloudy moonlight go flashing by. Then a sky-lit lake, and then a string of swaying lights, gone with the leap of a camera shutter.

Two hundred miles an hour!

We resort to a dignified Chinese steward and secure our berths. It is perhaps terrestrial of us that we do not think of reading the Utopian literature that lines the middle part of the train. I find a bed of the simple Utopian pattern, and lie for a time thinking – quite tranquilly – of this marvellous adventure.

I wonder why it is that to lie securely in bed, with the light out, seems ever the same place, wherever in space one may chance to be? And asleep, there is no space for us at all. I become drowsy and incoherent and metaphysical . . .

The faint and fluctuating drone of the wheels below the car, re-echoed by the flying track, is more perceptible now, but it is not unpleasantly loud, merely a faint tinting of the quiet . . .

No sea crossing breaks our journey; there is nothing to prevent a Channel tunnel in that other planet; and I wake in London.

The train has been in London some time when I awake, for these marvellous Utopians have discovered that it is not necessary to bundle out passengers from a train in the small hours, simply because they have arrived. A Utopian train is just a peculiar kind of hotel corridor that flies about the earth while one sleeps.

7

How will a great city of Utopia strike us?

To answer that question well one must needs be artist and engineer, and I am neither. Moreover, one must employ words and phrases that do not exist, for this world still does not dream of the things that may be done with thought and steel, when the engineer is sufficiently educated to be an artist, and the artistic intelligence has been quickened to the accomplishment of an engineer. How can one write of these things for a generation which rather admires that inconvenient and gawky muddle of ironwork and Flemish architecture, the London Tower Bridge. When before this, temerarious anticipators have written of the mighty buildings that might someday be, the illustrator has blended with the poor ineffectual splutter of the author's words, his powerful suggestion that it amounted simply to something bulbous, florid and fluent in the vein of the onion, and *L'Art Nouveau*. But here, it may be, the illustrator will not intervene.

Art has scarcely begun in the world.

There have been a few forerunners and that is all. Leonardo, Michel-angelo; how they would have exulted in the liberties of steel! There are no more pathetic documents in the archives of art than Leonardo's memoranda. In these, one sees him again and again reaching out as it were, with empty desirous hands, towards the unborn possibilities of the engineer. And Dürer, too, was a Modern, with the same turn towards creative invention. In our times these men would have wanted to make viaducts, to bridge wild and inaccessible places, to cut and straddle great railways athwart the mountain masses of the world. You can see, time after time, in Dürer's work, as you can see in the imaginary architectural landscape of the Pompeian walls, the dream of structures, lighter and bolder than stone or brick can yield . . . These Utopian town buildings will be the realisation of such dreams.

Here will be one of the great meeting places of mankind. Here – I speak of Utopian London – will be the traditional centre of one of the great races in the commonalty of the World State – and here will be its social and intellectual exchange. There will be a mighty University here, with thousands of professors and tens of thousands of advanced students, and here great journals of thought and speculation, mature and splendid books of philosophy and science, and a glorious fabric of literature will be woven and shaped, and with a teeming leisureliness, put forth. Here will be stupendous libraries, and a mighty organisation of museums. About these centres will cluster a great swarm of people, and close at hand will be another centre, for I who am an Englishman must needs stipulate that Westminster shall still be a seat of world Empire, one of several seats, if you will – where the ruling council of the world assembles. Then the arts will cluster round this city, as gold gathers about wisdom, and here Englishmen will weave into wonderful prose and beautiful rhythms and subtly atmospheric forms, the intricate, austere and courageous imagination of our race.

One will come into this place as one comes into a noble mansion. They will have flung great arches and domes of glass above the wider spaces of the town, the slender beauty of the perfect metalwork far overhead will be softened to a fairylike unsubstantiality by the mild London air. It will be the London air we know, clear of filth and all impurity, the same air that gives our October days their unspeakable clarity and makes every London twilight mysteriously beautiful. We shall go along avenues of architecture that will be emancipated from the last memories of the squat temple boxes of the Greek, the buxom curvatures of Rome; the Goth in us will have taken to steel and countless new materials as kindly as once he took to stone. The gay and swiftly moving platforms of the public ways will go past on either hand, carrying sporadic groups of people, and very speedily we shall find ourselves in a sort of central space, rich with palms and flowering bushes and statuary. We shall look along an avenue of trees, down a wide gorge between the cliffs of crowded hotels, the hotels that are still glowing with internal lights, to where the shining morning river streams dawn-lit out to sea.

Great multitudes of people will pass softly to and fro in this central space, beautiful girls and youths going to the University classes that are held in the stately palaces about us, grave and capable men and women going to their businesses, children meandering along to their schools, holidaymakers, lovers, setting out upon a hundred quests; and here we shall ask for the two we more particularly seek. A graceful little tele-phone kiosk will put us within reach of them, and with a queer sense of unreality I shall find myself talking to my Utopian twin. He has heard of me, he wants to see me and he gives me clear directions how to come to him.

I wonder if my own voice sounds like that.

'Yes,' I say, 'then I will come as soon as we have been to our hotel.'

We indulge in no eloquence upon this remarkable occasion. Yet I feel an unusual emotional stir. I tremble greatly, and the telephonic mouthpiece rattles as I replace it.

And thence the botanist and I walk on to the apartments that have been set aside for us, and into which the poor little rolls of the property that has accumulated about us in Utopia, our earthly raiment, and a change of linen and the like, have already been delivered. As we go I find I have little to say to my companion, until presently I am struck by a transitory wonder that he should have so little to say to me.

'I can still hardly realise,' I say, 'that I am going to see myself – as I might have been.'

'No,' he says, and relapses at once into his own preoccupation.

For a moment my wonder as to what he should be thinking about brings me near to a double self-forgetfulness.

I realise we are at the entrance of our hotel before I can formulate any further remark.

'This is the place,' I say.

CHAPTER EIGHT

My Utopian Self

1

It falls to few of us to interview our better selves. My Utopian self is, of course, my better self – according to my best endeavours – and I must confess myself fully alive to the difficulties of the situation. When I came to this Utopia I had no thought of any such intimate self-examination.

The whole fabric of that other universe sways for a moment as I come into his room, into his clear and ordered workroom. I am trembling. A figure rather taller than myself stands against the light.

He comes towards me, and I, as I advance to meet him, stumble against a chair. Then, still without a word, we are clasping hands.

I stand now so that the light falls upon him, and I can see his face better. He is a little taller than I, younger looking and sounder looking; he has missed an illness or so, and there is no scar over his eye. His training has been subtly finer than mine; he has made himself a better face than mine . . . These things I might have counted upon. I can fancy he winces with a twinge of sympathetic understanding at my manifest inferiority. Indeed, I come, trailing clouds of earthly confusion and weakness; I bear upon me all the defects of my world. He wears, I see, that white tunic with the purple band that I have already begun to consider the proper Utopian clothing for grave men, and his face is clean shaven. We forget to speak at first in the intensity of our mutual inspection. When at last I do gain my voice it is to say something quite different from the fine, significant openings of my pre-meditated dialogues.

'You have a pleasant room,' I remark, and look about a little disconcerted because there is no fireplace for me to put my back against, or hearthrug to stand upon. He pushes me a chair, into which I plump, and we hang over an immensity of conversational possibilities.

'I say,' I plunge, 'what do you think of me? You don't think I'm an impostor?'

'Not now that I have seen you. No.'

'Am I so like you?'

'Like me and your story – exactly.'

'You haven't any doubt left?' I ask.

'Not in the least, since I saw you enter. You come from the world beyond Sirius, twin to this. Eh?'

'And you don't want to know how I got here?'

'I've ceased even to wonder how *I* got here,' he says, with a laugh that echoes mine.

He leans back in his chair, and I in mine, and the absurd parody of our attitude strikes us both.

'Well?' we say, simultaneously, and laugh together.

I will confess this meeting is more difficult even than I anticipated.

2

Our conversation at that first encounter would do very little to develop the Modern Utopia in my mind. Inevitably, it would be personal and emotional. He would tell me how he stood in his world, and I how I stood in mine. I should have to tell him things, I should have to explain things –

No, the conversation would contribute nothing to a modern Utopia. And so I leave it out.

3

But I should go back to my botanist in a state of emotional relaxation. At first I should not heed the fact that he, too, had been in some manner stirred. 'I have seen him,' I should say, needlessly, and seem to be on the verge of telling the untellable. Then I should fade off into: 'It's the strangest thing.'

He would interrupt me with his own preoccupation. 'You know,' he would say, 'I've seen someone.'

I should pause and look at him.

'She is in this world,' he says.

'Who is in this world?'

'Mary!'

I have not heard her name before, but I understand, of course, at once.

'I saw her,' he explains.

'Saw her?'

'I'm certain I saw her. Certain. She was far away across those gardens near here – and before I had recovered from my amazement she had gone! But it was Mary.'

He takes my arm. 'You know I did not understand this,' he says. 'I did not really understand that when you said Utopia, you meant I was to meet her – in happiness.'

'I didn't.'

'It works out at that.'

'You haven't met her yet.'

'I shall. It makes everything different. To tell you the truth I've rather hated this Utopia of yours at times. You mustn't mind my saying it, but there's something of the Gradgrind – '

Probably I should swear at that.

'What?' he says.

'Nothing.'

'But you spoke?'

'I was purring. I'm a Gradgrind – it's quite right – anything you can say about Herbert Spencer, vivisectors, materialistic Science or Atheists, applies without correction to me. Begbie away! But now you think better of a modern Utopia? Was the lady looking well?'

'It was her real self. Yes. Not the broken woman I met – in the real world.'

'And as though she was pining for you.'

He looks puzzled.

'Look there!' I say.

He looks.

We are standing high above the ground in the loggia into which our apartments open, and I point across the soft haze of the public gardens to a tall white mass of University buildings that rises with a free and fearless gesture, to lift saluting pinnacles against the clear evening sky. 'Don't you think that rather more beautiful than – say – our National Gallery?'

He looks at it critically. 'There's a lot of metal in it,' he objects. 'What?'

I purred. 'But, anyhow, whatever you can't see in that, you can, I suppose, see that it is different from anything in your world – it lacks the kindly humanity of a red-brick Queen Anne villa residence, with its gables and bulges, and bow windows, and its stained-glass fanlight, and so forth. It lacks the self-complacent unreasonableness of Board of Works classicism. There's something in its proportions – as though someone with brains had taken a lot of care to get it quite right, someone who not only knew what metal can do, but what a University ought to be, somebody who had found the Gothic spirit enchanted, petrified, in a cathedral, and had set it free.'

'But what has this,' he asks, 'to do with her?'

'Very much,' I say. 'This is not the same world. If she is here, she will be younger in spirit and wiser. She will be in many ways more refined – '

'No one – ' he begins, with a note of indignation.

'No, no! She couldn't be. I was wrong there. But she will be different. Grant that at any rate. When you go forward to speak to her, she may not remember – very many things *you* may remember. Things that happened at Frognal – dear romantic walks through the Sunday summer evenings, practically you two alone, you in your adolescent silk hat and your nice gentlemanly gloves . . . Perhaps that did not happen here! And she may have other memories – of things – that down there haven't happened. You noted her costume. She wasn't by any chance one of the samurai?'

He answers, with a note of satisfaction, 'No! She wore a womanly dress of greyish green.'

'Probably under the Lesser Rule.'

'I don't know what you mean by the Lesser Rule. She wasn't one of the samurai.'

'And, after all, you know – I keep on reminding you, and you keep on losing touch with the fact, that this world contains your double.'

He pales, and his countenance is disturbed. Thank Heaven, I've touched him at last!

'This world contains your double. But, conceivably, everything may be different here. The whole romantic story may have run a different course. It was as it was in our world, by the accidents of custom and proximity. Adolescence is a defenceless plastic period. You are a man to form great affections – noble, great affections. You might have met anyone almost at that season and formed the same attachment.'

For a time he is perplexed and troubled by this suggestion.

'No,' he says, a little doubtfully. 'No. It was herself.' . . . Then, emphatically, '*No!*'

4

For a time we say no more, and I fall musing about my strange encounter with my Utopian double. I think of the confessions I have just made to him, the strange admissions both to him and myself. I have stirred up the stagnations of my own emotional life, the pride that has slumbered, the hopes and disappointments that have not troubled me for years. There are things that happened to me in my adolescence that no discipline of reason will ever bring to a just proportion for me, the first humiliations I was made to suffer, the waste of all the fine irrecoverable loyalties and passions of my youth. The dull base caste of my little personal tragi-comedy – I have ostensibly forgiven, I have for the most part forgotten – and yet when I recall them I hate each actor still. Whenever it comes into my mind – I do my best to prevent it – there it is, and these detestable people blot out the stars for me.

I have told all that story to my double, and he has listened with understanding eyes. But for a little while those squalid memories will not sink back into the deeps.

We lean, side by side, over our balcony, lost in such egotistical absorptions, quite heedless of the great palace of noble dreams to which our first enterprise has brought us.

5

I can understand the botanist this afternoon; for once we are in the same key. My own mental temper has gone for the day, and I know what it means to be untempered. Here is a world and a glorious world, and it is for me to take hold of it, to have to do with it, here and now, and behold! I can only think that I am burnt and scarred, and there rankles that wretched piece of business, the mean unimaginative triumph of my antagonist –

I wonder how many men have any real freedom of mind, are, in truth, unhampered by such associations, to whom all that is great and noble in life does not, at times at least, if not always, seem secondary to obscure rivalries and considerations, to the petty hates that are like germs in the blood, to the lust for self-assertion, to dwarfish pride, to affections they gave in pledge even before they were men.

The botanist beside me dreams, I know, of vindications for that woman.

All this world before us, and its order and liberty, are no more than a painted scene before which he is to meet Her at last, freed from 'that scoundrel'.

He expects 'that scoundrel' really to be present and, as it were, writhing under their feet . . .

I wonder if that man *was* a scoundrel. He has gone wrong on earth, no doubt, has failed and degenerated, but what was it sent him wrong? Was his failure inherent, or did some net of cross purposes tangle about his feet? Suppose he is not a failure in Utopia! . . .

I wonder that this has never entered the botanist's head.

He, with his vaguer mind, can overlook – spite of my ruthless reminders – all that would mar his vague anticipations. That, too, if I suggested it, he would overcome and disregard. He has the most amazing power of resistance to uncongenial ideas; amazing that is, to me. He hates the idea of meeting his double, and consequently so soon as I cease to speak of that, with scarcely an effort of his will, it fades again from his mind.

Down below in the gardens two children pursue one another, and one, near caught, screams aloud and rouses me from my reverie.

I follow their little butterfly antics until they vanish beyond a thicket of flowering rhododendra, and then my eyes go back to the great façade of the University buildings.

But I am in no mood to criticise architecture.

Why should a modern Utopia insist upon slipping out of the hands of its creator and becoming the background of a personal drama – of such a silly little drama?

The botanist will not see Utopia in any other way. He tests it entirely by its reaction upon the individual persons and things he knows; he dislikes it because he suspects it of wanting to lethal-chamber his aunt's 'dear old doggie', and now he is reconciled to it because a certain 'Mary' looks much younger and better here than she did on earth. And here am I, near fallen into the same way of dealing!

We agreed to purge this State and all the people in it of traditions, associations, bias, laws, and artificial entanglements, and begin anew; but we have no power to liberate ourselves. Our past, even its accidents, its accidents above all, and ourselves, are one.

CHAPTER NINE

The Samurai

1

Neither my Utopian double nor I love emotion sufficiently to cultivate it, and my feelings are in a state of seemly subordination when we meet again. He is now in possession of some clear, general ideas about my own world, and I can broach almost at once the thoughts that have been growing and accumulating since my arrival in this planet of my dreams. We find our interest in a humanised statecraft makes us, in spite of our vast difference in training and habits, curiously akin.

I put it to him that I came to Utopia with but very vague ideas of the method of government, biased, perhaps, a little in favour of certain electoral devices, but for the rest indeterminate, and that I have come to perceive more and more clearly that the large intricacy of Utopian organisation demands a more powerful and efficient method of control than electoral methods can give. I have come to distinguish among the varied costumes and the innumerable types of personality Utopia presents, certain men and women of a distinctive costume and bearing, and I know now that these people constitute an order, the samurai, the 'voluntary nobility', which is essential in the scheme of the Utopian State. I know that this order is open to every physically and mentally healthy adult in the Utopian State who will observe its prescribed austere rule of living, that much of the responsible work of the State is reserved for it, and I am inclined now at the first onset of realisation to regard it as far more significant than it really is in the Utopian scheme, as being, indeed, in itself and completely the Utopian scheme. My predominant curiosity concerns the organisation of this order. As it has developed in my mind, it has reminded me more and more closely of that strange class of guardians which constitutes the essential substance of Plato's Republic, and it is with an implicit reference to Plato's profound intuitions that I and my double discuss this question.

To clarify our comparison he tells me something of the history of Utopia, and incidentally it becomes necessary to make a correction in the assumptions upon which I have based my enterprise. We are assuming a world identical in every respect with the real planet Earth, except for the profoundest differences in the mental content of life. This implies a different literature, a different philosophy, and a different history, and so soon as I come to talk to him I find that though it remains unavoidable that we should assume the correspondence of the two populations, man for man – unless we would face unthinkable complications – we must assume also that a great succession of persons of extraordinary character and mental gifts, who on earth died in childhood or at birth, or who never learnt to read, or who lived and died amidst savage or brutalising surroundings that gave their gifts no scope, did in Utopia encounter happier chances, and take up the development and application of social theory – from the time of the first Utopists in a steady onward progress down to the present hour.* The differences of condition, therefore, had widened with each successive year. Jesus Christ had been born into a liberal and progressive Roman Empire that spread from the Arctic Ocean to the Bight of Benin, and was to know no Decline and Fall, and Mahomet, instead of embodying the dense prejudices of Arab ignorance, opened his eyes upon an intellectual horizon already nearly as wide as the world.

And through this empire the flow of thought, the flow of intention, poured always more abundantly. There were wars, but they were conclusive wars that established new and more permanent relations, that swept aside obstructions, and abolished centres of decay; there were prejudices tempered to an ordered criticism, and hatreds that merged at last in tolerant reactions. It was several hundred years ago that the great organisation of the samurai came into its present form. And it was this organisation's widely sustained activities that had shaped and established the World State in Utopia.

This organisation of the samurai was a quite deliberate invention. It arose in the course of social and political troubles and complications, analogous to those of our own time on earth, and was, indeed, the last of a number of political and religious experiments dating back to the first dawn of philosophical statecraft in Greece. That hasty despair of specialisation for government that gave our poor world individualism, democratic liberalism, and anarchism, and that curious disregard of the fund of enthusiasm and self-sacrifice in men, which is the fundamental weakness of worldly economics, do not appear in the history of Utopian

---

* One might assume as an alternative to this that amidst the four-fifths of the Greek literature now lost to the world, there perished, neglected, some book of elementary significance, some earlier *Novum Organum*, that in Utopia survived to achieve the profoundest consequences.

thought. All that history is pervaded with the recognition of the fact that self-seeking is no more the whole of human life than the satisfaction of hunger; that it is an essential of a man's existence no doubt, and that under stress of evil circumstances it may as entirely obsess him as would the food hunt during famine, but that life may pass beyond to an illimitable world of emotions and effort. Every sane person consists of possibilities beyond the unavoidable needs, is capable of disinterested feeling, even if it amounts only to enthusiasm for a sport or an industrial employment well done, for an art, or for a locality or class. In our world now, as in the Utopian past, this impersonal energy of a man goes out into religious emotion and work, into patriotic effort, into artistic enthusiasms, into games and amateur employments, and an enormous proportion of the whole world's fund of effort wastes itself in religious and political misunderstandings and conflicts, and in un-satisfying amusements and unproductive occupations. In a modern Utopia there will, indeed, be no perfection; in Utopia there must also be friction, conflicts and waste, but the waste will be enormously less than in our world. And the co-ordination of activities this relatively smaller waste will measure, will be the achieved end for which the order of the samurai was first devised.

Inevitably such an order must have first arisen among a clash of social forces and political systems as a revolutionary organisation. It must have set before itself the attainment of some such Utopian ideal as this modern Utopia does, in the key of mortal imperfection, realise. At first it may have directed itself to research and discussion, to the elaboration of its ideal, to the discussion of a plan of campaign, but at some stage it must have assumed a more militant organisation, and have prevailed against and assimilated the pre-existing political organisations, and to all intents and purposes have become this present synthesised World State. Traces of that militancy would, therefore, pervade it still, and a campaigning quality – no longer against specific disorders, but against universal human weaknesses, and the inanimate forces that trouble man – still remain as its essential quality.

'Something of this kind,' I should tell my double, 'had arisen in our thought' – I jerk my head back to indicate an infinitely distant planet – 'just before I came upon these explorations. The idea had reached me, for example, of something to be called a New Republic, which was to be in fact an organisation for revolution something after the fashion of your samurai, as I understand them – only most of the organisation and the rule of life still remained to be invented. All sorts of people were thinking of something in that way about the time of my coming. The idea, as it reached me, was pretty crude in several respects. It ignored the high possibility of a synthesis of languages in the future; it came from a literary man, who wrote only English, and, as I read him – he was a little vague in his proposals – it was to be a purely English-speaking movement. And his ideas were coloured too much by the peculiar opportunism of his time; he seemed to have more than half an eye for a prince or a millionaire of genius; he seemed looking here and there for support and the structural elements of a party. Still, the idea of a comprehensive movement of disillusioned and illuminated men behind the shams and patriotisms, the spites and personalities of the ostensible world was there.'

I added some particulars.

'Our movement had something of that spirit in the beginning,' said my Utopian double. 'But while your men seem to be thinking disconnectedly, and upon a very narrow and fragmentary basis of accumulated conclusions, ours had a fairly comprehensive science of human association, and a very careful analysis of the failures of preceding beginnings to draw upon. After all, your world must be as full as ours was of the wreckage and decay of previous attempts; churches, aristocracies, orders, cults . . . '

'Only at present we seem to have lost heart altogether, and now there are no new religions, no new orders, no new cults – no beginnings any more.'

'But that's only a resting phase, perhaps. You were saying – '

'Oh! – let that distressful planet alone for a time! Tell me how you manage in Utopia.'

2

The social theorists of Utopia, my double explained, did not base their schemes upon the classification of men into labour and capital, the landed interest, the liquor trade, and the like. They esteemed these as accidental categories, indefinitely amenable to statesmanship, and they looked for some practical and real classification upon which to base organisation.* But, on the other hand, the assumption that men are unclassifiable, because practically homogeneous, which underlies modern democratic methods and all the fallacies of our equal justice, is

---

* In that they seem to have profited by a more searching criticism of early social and political speculations than our earth has yet undertaken. The social

even more alien to the Utopian mind. Throughout Utopia there is, of course, no other than provisional classifications, since every being is regarded as finally unique, but for political and social purposes things have long rested upon a classification of temperaments, which attends mainly to differences in the range and quality and character of the individual imagination.

This Utopian classification was a rough one, but it served its purpose to determine the broad lines of political organisation; it was so far unscientific that many individuals fall between or within two or even three of its classes. But that was met by giving the correlated organisation a compensatory looseness of play. Four main classes of mind were distinguished, called, respectively, the Poietic, the Kinetic, the Dull, and the Base. The former two are supposed to constitute the living tissue of the State; the latter are the fulcra and resistances, the bone and cover of its body. They are not hereditary classes, nor is there any attempt to develop any class by special breeding, simply because the intricate interplay of heredity is untraceable and incalculable. They are classes to which people drift of their own accord. Education is uniform until differentiation becomes unmistakable, and each man (and woman) must establish his position with regard to the lines of this abstract classification by his own quality, choice, and development . . .

The Poietic or creative class of mental individuality embraces a wide range of types, but they agree in possessing imaginations that range beyond the known and accepted, and that involve the desire to bring the discoveries made in such excursions, into knowledge and recognition. The scope and direction of the imaginative excursion may vary very greatly. It may be the invention of something new or the discovery of something hitherto unperceived. When the invention or discovery is primarily beauty then we have the artistic type of Poietic mind; when it is not so, we have the true scientific man. The range of discovery may be narrowed as it is in the art of Whistler or the science of a cytologist, or it may embrace a wide extent of relevance, until at last both artist or scientific enquirer merge in the universal reference of the true philosopher. To the accumulated activities of the Poietic type, reacted upon by circumstances, are due almost all the forms assumed by human thought and feeling. All religious ideas, all ideas of what is good or

---

speculations of the Greeks, for example, had just the same primary defect as the economic speculations of the eighteenth century – they began with the assumption that the general conditions of the prevalent state of affairs were permanent.

beautiful, entered life through the poietic inspirations of man. Except for processes of decay, the forms of the human future must come also through men of this same type, and it is a primary essential to our modern idea of an abundant secular progress that these activities should be unhampered and stimulated.

The Kinetic class consists of types, various, of course, and merging insensibly along the boundary into the less representative constituents of the Poietic group, but distinguished by a more restricted range of imagination. Their imaginations do not range beyond the known, experienced, and accepted, though within these limits they may imagine as vividly or more vividly than members of the former group. They are often very clever and capable people, but they do not do, and they do not desire to do, new things. The more vigorous individuals of this class are the most teachable people in the world, and they are generally more moral and more trustworthy than the Poietic types. They live – while the Poietics are always something of experimentalists with life. The characteristics of either of these two classes may be associated with a good or bad physique, with excessive or defective energy, with exceptional keenness of the senses in some determinate direction or suchlike 'bent', and the Kinetic type, just as the Poietic type, may display an imagination of restricted or of the most universal range. But a fairly energetic Kinetic is probably the nearest thing to that ideal our earthly anthropologists have in mind when they speak of the 'Normal' human being. The very definition of the Poietic class involves a certain abnormality.

The Utopians distinguished two extremes of this Kinetic class according to the quality of their imaginative preferences, the Dan and Beersheba, as it were, of this division. At one end is the mainly intellectual, unoriginal type, which, with energy of personality, makes an admirable judge or administrator and without it an uninventive, laborious, common mathematician, or common scholar, or common scientific man; while at the other end is the mainly emotional, unoriginal man, the type to which – at a low level of personal energy – my botanist inclines. The second type includes, amidst its energetic forms, great actors, and popular politicians and preachers. Between these extremes is a long and wide region of varieties, into which one would put most of the people who form the reputable workmen, the men of substance, the trustworthy men and women, the pillars of society on earth.

Below these two classes in the Utopian scheme of things, and merging insensibly into them, come the Dull. The Dull are persons of altogether inadequate imagination, the people who never seem to learn thoroughly, or hear distinctly, or think clearly. (I believe if everyone is to be carefully educated they would be considerably in the minority in the world, but it is quite possible that will not be the reader's opinion. It is clearly a matter of an arbitrary line.) They are the stupid people, the incompetent people, the formal, imitative people, the people who, in any properly organised State, should, as a class, gravitate towards and below the minimum wage that qualifies for marriage. The laws of heredity are far too mysterious for such offspring as they do produce to be excluded from a fair chance in the world, but for themselves, they count neither for work nor direction in the State.

Finally, with a bold disregard of the logician's classificatory rules, these Utopian statesmen who devised the World State hewed out in theory a class of the Base. The Base may, indeed, be either poietic, kinetic, or dull, though most commonly they are the last, and their definition concerns not so much the quality of their imagination as a certain bias in it, that to a statesman makes it a matter for special attention. The Base have a narrower and more persistent egoistic reference than the common run of humanity; they may boast, but they have no frankness; they have relatively great powers of concealment, and they are capable of, and sometimes have an aptitude and inclination towards, cruelty. In the queer phrasing of earthly psychology with its clumsy avoidance of analysis, they have no 'moral sense'. They count as an antagonism to the State organisation.

Obviously, this is the rudest of classifications, and no Utopian has ever supposed it to be a classification for individual application, a classification so precise that one can say, this man is 'poietic', and that man is 'base'. In actual experience these qualities mingle and vary in every possible way. It is not a classification for Truth, but a classification to an end. Taking humanity as a multitude of unique individuals in mass, one may, for practical purposes, deal with it far more conveniently by disregarding its uniquenesses and its mixed cases altogether, and supposing it to be an assembly of poietic, kinetic, dull, and base people. In many respects it behaves as if it were that. The State, dealing as it does only with non-individualised affairs, is not only justified in disregarding, but is bound to disregard, a man's special distinction, and to provide for him on the strength of his prevalent aspect as being on the whole poietic, kinetic, or what not. In a world of hasty judgements and carping criticism, it cannot be repeated too often that the fundamental ideas of a modern Utopia imply, everywhere and in everything, margins and elasticities, a certain universal compensatory looseness of play.

Now these Utopian statesmen who founded the World State put the problem of social organisation in the following fashion: To contrive a revolutionary movement that shall absorb all existing governments and fuse them with itself, and that must be rapidly progressive and adaptable, and yet coherent, persistent, powerful, and efficient.

The problem of combining progress with political stability had never been accomplished in Utopia before that time, any more than it has been accomplished on earth. Just as on earth, Utopian history was a succession of powers rising and falling in an alternation of efficient conservative with unstable liberal States. Just as on earth, so in Utopia, the kinetic type of men had displayed a more or less unintentional antagonism to the poietic. The general life-history of a State had been the same on either planet. First, through poietic activities, the idea of a community has developed, and the State has shaped itself; poietic men have arisen first in this department of national life, and then that, and have given place to kinetic men of a high type – for it seems to be in their nature that poietic men should be mutually repulsive, and not succeed and develop one another consecutively – and a period of expansion and vigour has set in. The general poietic activity has declined with the development of an efficient and settled social and political organisation; the statesman has given way to the politician who has incorporated the wisdom of the statesman with his own energy, the original genius in arts, letters, science, and every department of activity to the cultivated and scholarly man. The kinetic man of wide range, who has assimilated his poietic predecessor, succeeds with far more readiness than his poietic contemporary in almost every human activity. The latter is by his very nature undisciplined and experimental, and is positively hampered by precedents and good order. With this sub-stitution of the efficient for the creative type, the State ceases to grow, first in this department of activity, and then in that, and so long as its conditions remain the same it remains orderly and efficient. But it has lost its power of initiative and change; its power of adaptation is gone, and with that secular change of conditions which is the law of life, stresses must arise within and without, and bring at last either through revolution or through defeat the release of fresh poietic power. The process, of course, is not in its entirety simple; it may be masked by the fact that one department of activity may be in its poietic stage, while another is in a phase of realisation. In the United States of America, for example, during the nineteenth century, there was great poietic activity in industrial organisation, and none whatever in political philosophy; but a careful analysis of the history of any period will show the rhythm almost invariably present, and the initial problem before the Utopian philosopher, therefore, was whether this was an inevitable alternation, whether human progress was necessarily a series of developments, collapses, and fresh beginnings, after an interval of disorder, unrest, and often great unhappiness, or whether it was possible to maintain a secure, happy, and progressive State beside an unbroken flow of poietic activity.

Clearly they decided upon the second alternative. If, indeed, I am listening to my Utopian self, then they not only decided the problem could be solved, but they solved it.

He tells me how they solved it.

A modern Utopia differs from all the older Utopias in its recognition of the need of poietic activities – one sees this new consideration creeping into thought for the first time in the phrasing of Comte's insistence that 'spiritual' must precede political reconstruction, and in his admission of the necessity of recurrent books and poems about Utopias – and at first this recognition appears to admit only an added complication to a problem already unmanageably complex. Comte's separation of the activities of a State into the spiritual and material does, to a certain extent, anticipate this opposition of poietic and kinetic, but the intimate texture of his mind was dull and hard, the conception slipped from him again, and his suppression of literary activities, and his imposition of a rule of life upon the poietic types, who are least able to sustain it, mark how deeply he went under. To a large extent he followed the older Utopists in assuming that the philosophical and constructive problem could be done once for all, and he worked the results out simply under an organised kinetic government. But what seems to be merely an addition to the difficulty may in the end turn out to be a simplification, just as the introduction of a fresh term to an intricate irreducible mathematical expression will at times bring it to unity.

Now philosophers after my Utopian pattern, who find the ultimate significance in life in individuality, novelty and the undefined, would not only regard the poietic element as the most important in human society, but would perceive quite clearly the impossibility of its organisation. This, indeed, is simply the application to the moral and intellectual fabric of the principles already applied in discussing the State control of reproduction (in Chapter 6, section 2). But just as in the case of births it was possible for the State to frame limiting conditions within which individuality plays more freely than in the void, so the founders of this modern Utopia believed it possible to define conditions under which every individual born with poietic gifts should be enabled and encouraged to give them a full development, in art, philosophy, invention, or discovery. Certain general conditions presented themselves as obviously reasonable: to give every citizen as good an education as he or she could acquire, for example; to so frame it that the directed educational process would never at any period occupy the whole available time of the learner, but would provide throughout a marginal free leisure with opportunities for developing idiosyncrasies, and to ensure by the expedient of a minimum wage for a specified amount of work, that leisure and opportunity did not cease throughout life.

But, in addition to thus making poietic activities universally possible, the founders of this modern Utopia sought to supply incentives, which was an altogether more difficult research, a problem in its nature irresolvably complex, and admitting of no systematic solution. But my double told me of a great variety of devices by which poietic men and women were given honour and enlarged freedoms, so soon as they produced an earnest of their quality, and he explained to me how great an ambition they might entertain.

There were great systems of laboratories attached to every municipal force station at which research could be conducted under the most favourable conditions, and every mine, and, indeed, almost every great industrial establishment, was saddled under its lease with similar obligations. So much for poietic ability and research in physical science. The World State tried the claims of every living contributor to any materially valuable invention, and paid or charged a royalty on its use that went partly to him personally, and partly to the research institution that had produced him. In the matter of literature and the philosophical and sociological sciences, every higher educational establishment carried its studentships, its fellowships, its occasional lectureships, and to produce a poem, a novel, a speculative work of force or merit, was to become the object of a generous competition between rival Universities. In Utopia, any author has the option either of publishing his works through the public bookseller as a private speculation, or, if he is of sufficient merit, of accepting a University endowment and conceding his copyright to the University press. All sorts of grants in the hands of committees of the most varied constitution, supplemented these academic resources, and ensured that no possible contributor to the wide flow of the Utopian mind slipped into neglect. Apart from those who engaged mainly in teaching and administration, my double told me that the worldwide House of Saloman* thus created sustained over a million men. For all the rarity of large fortunes, therefore, no original man with the desire and capacity for material or mental experiments went long without resources and the stimulus of attention, criticism, and rivalry.

'And finally,' said my double, 'our Rules ensure a considerable understanding of the importance of poietic activities in the majority of the samurai, in whose hands as a class all the real power of the world resides.'

'Ah!' said I, 'and now we come to the thing that interests me most. For it is quite clear, in my mind, that these samurai form the real body of the State. All this time that I have spent going to and fro in this planet, it has been growing upon me that this order of men and women, wearing such a uniform as you wear, and with faces strengthened by discipline and touched with devotion, is the Utopian reality; but that for them, the whole fabric of these fair appearances would crumble and tarnish, shrink and shrivel, until at last, back I should be amidst the grime and disorders of the life of earth. Tell me about these samurai, who remind me of Plato's guardians, who look like Knights Templars, who bear a name that recalls the swordsmen of Japan . . . and whose uniform you yourself are wearing. What are they? Are they an hereditary caste, a specially educated order, an elected class? For, certainly, this world turns upon them as a door upon its hinges.'

4

'I follow the Common Rule, as many men do,' said my double, answering my allusion to his uniform almost apologetically. 'But my own work is, in its nature, poietic; there is much dissatisfaction with our isolation of criminals upon islands, and I am analysing the psychology of prison officials and criminals in general with a view to some better scheme. I am supposed to be ingenious with expedients in this direction. Typically, the samurai are engaged in administrative work. Practically the whole of the responsible rule of the world is in their hands; all our head teachers and disciplinary heads of colleges, our judges, barristers, employers of labour beyond a certain limit, practising medical men,

* The *New Atlantis*.

legislators, must be samurai, and all the executive committees, and so forth, that play so large a part in our affairs are drawn by lot exclusively from them. The order is not hereditary – we know just enough of biology and the uncertainties of inheritance to know how silly that would be – and it does not require an early consecration or novitiate or ceremonies and initiations of that sort. The samurai are, in fact, volunteers. Any intelligent adult in a reasonably healthy and efficient state may, at any age after five-and-twenty, become one of the samurai, and take a hand in the universal control.'

'Provided he follows the Rule.'

'Precisely – provided he follows the Rule.'

'I have heard the phrase, "voluntary nobility".'

'That was the idea of our Founders. They made a noble and privileged order – open to the whole world. No one could complain of an unjust exclusion, for the only thing that could exclude from the order was unwillingness or inability to follow the Rule.'

'But the Rule might easily have been made exclusive of special lineages and races.'

'That wasn't their intention. The Rule was planned to exclude the dull, to be unattractive to the base, and to direct and co-ordinate all sound citizens of good intent.'

'And it has succeeded?'

'As well as anything finite can. Life is still imperfect, still a thick felt of dissatisfactions and perplexing problems, but most certainly the quality of all its problems has been raised, and there has been no war, no grinding poverty, not half the disease, and an enormous increase of the order, beauty, and resources of life since the samurai, who began as a private aggressive cult, won their way to the rule of the world.'

'I would like to have that history,' I said. 'I expect there was fighting?' He nodded. 'But first – tell me about the Rule.'

'The Rule aims to exclude the dull and base altogether, to discipline the impulses and emotions, to develop a moral habit and sustain a man in periods of stress, fatigue, and temptation, to produce the maximum co-operation of all men of good intent, and, in fact, to keep all the samurai in a state of moral and bodily health and efficiency. It does as much of this as well as it can, but, of course, like all general propositions, it does not do it in any case with absolute precision. On the whole, it is so good that most men who, like myself, are doing poietic work, and who would be just as well off without obedience, find a satisfaction in adhesion. At first, in the militant days, it was a trifle hard and un-compromising; it had rather too strong an appeal to the moral prig and harshly righteous man, but it has undergone, and still undergoes, revision and expansion, and every year it becomes a little better adapted to the need of a general rule of life that all men may try to follow. We have now a whole literature, with many very fine things in it, written about the Rule.'

He glanced at a little book on his desk, took it up as if to show it me, then put it down again.

'The Rule consists of three parts; there is the list of things that qualify, the list of things that must not be done, and the list of things that must be done. Qualification exacts a little exertion, as evidence of good faith, and it is designed to weed out the duller dull and many of the base. Our schooling period ends now about fourteen, and a small number of boys and girls – about three per cent – are set aside then as unteachable, as, in fact, nearly idiotic; the rest go on to a college or upper school.'

'All your population?'

'With that exception.'

'Free?'

'Of course. And they pass out of college at eighteen. There are several different college courses, but one or other must be followed and a satisfactory examination passed at the end – perhaps ten per cent fail – and the Rule requires that the candidate for the samurai must have passed.'

'But a very good man is sometimes an idle schoolboy.'

'We admit that. And so anyone who has failed to pass the college leaving examination may at any time in later life sit for it again – and again and again. Certain carefully specified things excuse it altogether.'

'That makes it fair. But aren't there people who cannot pass examinations?'

'People of nervous instability – '

'But they may be people of great though irregular poietic gifts.'

'Exactly. That is quite possible. But we don't want that sort of people among our samurai. Passing an examination is a proof of a certain steadiness of purpose, a certain self-control and submission – '

'Of a certain "ordinariness".'

'Exactly what is wanted.'

'Of course, those others can follow other careers.'

'Yes. That's what we want them to do. And, besides these two educational qualifications, there are two others of a similar kind of more debatable value. One is practically not in operation now. Our Founders put it that a candidate for the samurai must possess what they called a Technic, and, as it operated in the beginning, he had to hold the qualification for a doctor, for a lawyer, for a military officer, or an engineer, or teacher, or have painted acceptable pictures, or written a book, or something of the sort. He had, in fact, as people say, to "be something", or to have "done something". It was a regulation of vague intention even in the beginning, and it became catholic to the pitch of absurdity. To play a violin skilfully has been accepted as sufficient for this qualification. There may have been a reason in the past for this provision; in those days there were many daughters of prosperous parents – and even some sons – who did nothing whatever but idle uninterestingly in the world, and the organisation might have suffered by their invasion, but that reason has gone now, and the requirement remains a merely ceremonial requirement. But, on the other hand, another has developed. Our Founders made a collection of several volumes, which they called, collectively, the Book of the Samurai, a compilation of articles and extracts, poems and prose pieces, which were supposed to embody the idea of the order. It was to play the part for the samurai that the Bible did for the ancient Hebrews. To tell you the truth, the stuff was of very unequal merit; there was a lot of very second-rate rhetoric, and some nearly namby-pamby verse. There was also included some very obscure verse and prose that had the trick of seeming wise. But for all such defects, much of the Book, from the very beginning, was splendid and inspiring matter. From that time to this, the Book of the Samurai has been under revision, much has been added, much rejected, and some deliberately rewritten. Now, there is hardly anything in it that is not beautiful and perfect in form. The whole range of noble emotions finds expression there, and all the guiding ideas of our Modern State. We have recently admitted some terse criticism of its contents by a man named Henley.'

'Old Henley!'

'A man who died a little time ago.'

'I knew that man on earth. And he was in Utopia, too! He was a great red-faced man, with fiery hair, a noisy, intolerant maker of enemies, with a tender heart – and he was one of the samurai?'

'He defied the Rules.'

'He was a great man with wine. He wrote like wine; in our world he wrote wine; red wine with the light shining through.'

'He was on the Committee that revised our Canon. For the revising and bracing of our Canon is work for poietic as well as kinetic men. You knew him in your world?'

'I wish I had. But I have seen him. On earth he wrote a thing . . . it would run –

' "Out of the night that covers me,
  Black as the pit from pole to pole,
  I thank whatever Gods may be,
  For my unconquerable soul . . . " '

'We have that here. All good earthly things are in Utopia also. We put that in the Canon almost as soon as he died,' said my double.

5

'We have now a double Canon, a very fine First Canon, and a Second Canon of work by living men and work of inferior quality, and a satisfactory knowledge of both of these is the fourth intellectual qualification for the samurai.'

'It must keep a sort of uniformity in your tone of thought.'

'The Canon pervades our whole world. As a matter of fact, very much of it is read and learnt in the schools . . . Next to the intellectual qualification comes the physical, the man must be in sound health, free from certain foul, avoidable, and demoralising diseases, and in good training. We reject men who are fat, or thin and flabby, or whose nerves are shaky – we refer them back to training. And finally the man or woman must be fully adult.'

'Twenty-one? But you said twenty-five!'

'The age has varied. At first it was twenty-five or over; then the minimum became twenty-five for men and twenty-one for women. Now there is a feeling that it ought to be raised. We don't want to take advantage of mere boy and girl emotions – men of my way of thinking, at any rate, don't – we want to get our samurai with experiences, with a settled mature conviction. Our hygiene and regimen are rapidly pushing back old age and death, and keeping men hale and hearty to eighty and more. There's no need to hurry the young. Let them have a chance of wine, love, and song; let them feel the bite of full-bodied desire, and know what devils they have to reckon with.'

'But there is a certain fine sort of youth that knows the desirability of the better things at nineteen.'

'They may keep the Rule at any time – without its privileges. But a man who breaks the Rule after his adult adhesion at five-and-twenty is no more in the samurai for ever. Before that age he is free to break it and repent.'

'And now, what is forbidden?'

'We forbid a good deal. Many small pleasures do no great harm, but we think it well to forbid them, none the less, so that we can weed out the self-indulgent. We think that a constant resistance to little seductions is good for a man's quality. At any rate, it shows that a man is prepared to pay something for his honour and privileges. We prescribe a regimen of food, forbid tobacco, wine, or any alcoholic drink, all narcotic drugs – '

'Meat?'

'In all the round world of Utopia there is no meat. There used to be. But now we cannot stand the thought of slaughterhouses. And, in a population that is all educated, and at about the same level of physical refinement, it is practically impossible to find anyone who will hew a dead ox or pig. We never settled the hygienic question of meat-eating at all. This other aspect decided us. I can still remember, as a boy, the rejoicings over the closing of the last slaughterhouse.'

'You eat fish.'

'It isn't a matter of logic. In our barbaric past horrible flayed carcasses of brutes, dripping blood, were hung for sale in the public streets.' He shrugged his shoulders.

'They do that still in London – in *my* world,' I said.

He looked again at my laxer, coarser face, and did not say whatever thought had passed across his mind.

'Originally the samurai were forbidden usury, that is to say the lending of money at fixed rates of interest. They are still under that interdiction, but since our commercial code practically prevents usury altogether, and our law will not recognise contracts for interest upon private accommodation loans to unprosperous borrowers, it is now scarcely necessary. The idea of a man growing richer by mere inaction and at the expense of an impoverishing debtor, is profoundly distasteful to Utopian ideas, and our State insists pretty effectually now upon the participation of the lender in the borrower's risks. This, however, is only one part of a series of limitations of the same character. It is felt that to buy simply in order to sell again brings out many unsocial human qualities; it makes a man seek to enhance profits and falsify values, and so the samurai are forbidden to buy to sell on their own account or for any employer save the State, unless some process of manufacture changes the nature of the commodity (a mere change in bulk or packing does not suffice), and they are forbidden salesmanship and all its arts. Consequently they cannot be hotel-keepers, or hotel proprietors, or hotel shareholders, and a doctor – all practising doctors must be samurai – cannot sell drugs except as a public servant of the municipality or the State.'

'That, of course, runs counter to all our current terrestrial ideas,' I said. 'We are obsessed by the power of money. These rules will work out as a vow of moderate poverty, and if your samurai are an order of poor men – '

'They need not be. Samurai who have invented, organised, and developed new industries have become rich men, and many men who have grown rich by brilliant and original trading have subsequently become samurai.'

'But these are exceptional cases. The bulk of your money-making business must be confined to men who are not samurai. You must have a class of rich, powerful outsiders – '

'*Have* we?'

'I don't see the evidences of them.'

'As a matter of fact, we have such people! There are rich traders, men who have made discoveries in the economy of distribution, or who have called attention by intelligent, truthful advertisement to the possibilities of neglected commodities, for example.'

'But aren't they a power?'

'Why should they be?'

'Wealth *is* power.'

I had to explain that phrase.

He protested. 'Wealth,' he said, 'is no sort of power at all unless you make it one. If it is so in your world it is so by inadvertency. Wealth is a State-made thing, a convention, the most artificial of powers. You can, by subtle statesmanship, contrive what it shall buy and what it shall not. In your world it would seem you have made leisure, movement, any sort of freedom, life itself, *purchasable*. The more fools you! A poor working man with you is a man in discomfort and fear. No wonder your rich have power. But here a reasonable leisure, a decent life, is to be had by every man on easier terms than by selling himself to the rich. And rich as men are here, there is no private fortune in the whole world that is more than a little thing beside the wealth of the State. The samurai control the State and the wealth of the State, and by their vows they may not avail themselves of any of the coarser pleasures wealth can still buy. Where, then, is the power of your wealthy man?'

'But, then – where is the incentive – ?'

'Oh! a man gets things for himself with wealth – no end of things. But little or no power over his fellows – unless they are exceptionally weak or self-indulgent persons.'

I reflected. 'What else may not the samurai do?'

'Acting, singing, or reciting are forbidden them, though they may lecture authoritatively or debate. But professional mimicry is not only held to be undignified in a man or woman, but to weaken and corrupt the soul; the mind becomes foolishly dependent on applause, over-skilful in producing tawdry and momentary illusions of excellence; it is our experience that actors and actresses as a class are loud, ignoble, and insincere. If they have not such flamboyant qualities then they are tepid and ineffectual players. Nor may the samurai do personal services, except in the matter of medicine or surgery; they may not be barbers, for example, nor inn waiters, nor boot cleaners. But, nowadays, we have scarcely any barbers or boot cleaners; men do these things for themselves. Nor may a man under the Rule be any man's servant, pledged to do whatever he is told. He may neither be a servant nor keep one; he must shave and dress and serve himself, carry his own food from the helper's place to the table, redd his sleeping room, and leave it clean . . . '

'That is all easy enough in a world as ordered as yours. I suppose no samurai may bet?'

'Absolutely not. He may insure his life and his old age for the better equipment of his children, or for certain other specified ends, but that is all his dealings with chance. And he is also forbidden to play games in public or to watch them being played. Certain dangerous and hardy sports and exercises are prescribed for him, but not competitive sports between man and man or side and side. That lesson was learnt long ago before the coming of the samurai. Gentlemen of honour, according to the old standards, rode horses, raced chariots, fought, and played competitive games of skill, and the dull, cowardly and base came in thousands to admire, and howl, and bet. The gentlemen of honour degenerated fast enough into a sort of athletic prostitute, with all the defects, all the vanity, trickery, and self-assertion of the common actor, and with even less intelligence. Our Founders made no peace with this organisation of public sports. They did not spend their lives to secure for all men and women on the earth freedom, health, and leisure, in order that they might waste lives in such folly.'

'We have those abuses,' I said, 'but some of our earthly games have a fine side. There is a game called cricket. It is a fine, generous game.'

'Our boys play that, and men too. But it is thought rather puerile to give very much time to it; men should have graver interests. It was undignified and unpleasant for the samurai to play conspicuously ill, and impossible for them to play so constantly as to keep hand and eye in training against the man who was fool enough and cheap enough to become an expert. Cricket, tennis, fives, billiards – . You will find clubs

360 A MODERN UTOPIA

and a class of men to play all these things in Utopia, but not the samurai. And they must play their games as games, not as displays; the price of a privacy for playing cricket, so that they could charge for admission, would be overwhelmingly high . . . Negroes are often very clever at cricket. For a time, most of the samurai had their swordplay, but few do those exercises now; and until about fifty years ago they went out for military training, a fortnight in every year, marching long distances, sleeping in the open, carrying provisions, and sham fighting over un-familiar ground dotted with disappearing targets. There was a curious inability in our world to realise that war was really over for good and all.'

'And now,' I said, 'haven't we got very nearly to the end of your prohibitions? You have forbidden alcohol, drugs, smoking, betting, and usury, games, trade, servants. But isn't there a vow of Chastity?'

'That is the Rule for your earthly orders?'

'Yes – except, if I remember rightly, for Plato's Guardians.'

'There is a Rule of Chastity here – but not of Celibacy. We know quite clearly that civilisation is an artificial arrangement, and that all the physical and emotional instincts of man are too strong, and his natural instinct of restraint too weak, for him to live easily in the civilised State. Civilisation has developed far more rapidly than man has modified. Under the unnatural perfection of security, liberty and abundance our civilisation has attained, the normal untrained human being is disposed to excess in almost every direction; he tends to eat too much and too elaborately, to drink too much, to become lazy faster than his work can be reduced, to waste his interest upon displays, and to make love too much and too elaborately. He gets out of training, and concentrates upon egoistic or erotic broodings. The past history of our race is very largely a history of social collapses due to demoralisation by indulgences following security and abundance. In the time of our Founders the signs of a worldwide epoch of prosperity and relaxation were plentiful. Both sexes drifted towards sexual excesses, the men towards sentimental extravagances, imbecile devotions, and the complication and refinement of physical indulgences; the women towards those expansions and differentiations of feeling that find expression in music and costly and distinguished dress. Both sexes became unstable and promiscuous. The whole world seemed disposed to do exactly the same thing with its sexual interest as it had done with its appetite for food and drink – make the most of it.'

He paused.

'Satiety came to help you,' I said.

'Destruction may come before satiety. Our Founders organised motives from all sorts of sources, but I think the chief force to give men self-control is Pride. Pride may not be the noblest thing in the soul, but it is the best King there, for all that. They looked to it to keep a man clean and sound and sane. In this matter, as in all matters of natural desire, they held no appetite must be glutted, no appetite must have artificial whets, and also and equally that no appetite should be starved. A man must come from the table satisfied, but not replete. And, in the matter of love, a straight and clean desire for a clean and straight fellow-creature was our Founders' ideal. They enjoined marriage between equals as the samurai's duty to the race, and they framed directions of the precisest sort to prevent that uxorious inseparableness, that con-nubiality which will reduce a couple of people to something jointly less than either. That Canon is too long to tell you now. A man under the Rule who loves a woman who does not follow it, must either leave the samurai to marry her, or induce her to accept what is called the Woman's Rule, which, while it excepts her from the severer qualific-ations and disciplines, brings her regimen of life into a working harmony with his.'

'Suppose she breaks the Rule afterwards?'

'He must leave either her or the order.'

'There is matter for a novel or so in that.'

'There has been matter for hundreds.'

'Is the Woman's Rule a sumptuary law as well as a regimen? I mean – may she dress as she pleases?'

'Not a bit of it,' said my double. 'Every woman who could command money used it, we found, to make underbred aggressions on other women. As men emerged to civilisation, women seemed going back to savagery – to paint and feathers. But the samurai, both men and women, and the women under the Lesser Rule also, all have a particular dress. No difference is made between women under either the Great or the Lesser Rule. You have seen the men's dress – always like this I wear. The women may wear the same, either with the hair cut short or plaited behind them, or they may have a high-waisted dress of very fine, soft woollen material, with their hair coiled up behind.'

'I have seen it,' I said. Indeed, nearly all the women had seemed to be wearing variants of that simple formula. 'It seems to me a very beautiful dress. The other – I'm not used to. But I like it on girls and slender women.'

I had a thought, and added, 'Don't they sometimes, well – take a good deal of care, dressing their hair?'

My double laughed in my eyes. 'They do,' he said.

'And the Rule?'

'The Rule is never fussy,' said my double, still smiling.

'We don't want women to cease to be beautiful, and consciously beautiful, if you like,' he added. 'The more real beauty of form and face we have, the finer our world. But costly sexualised trappings – '

'I should have thought,' I said, 'a class of women who traded on their sex would have arisen, women, I mean, who found an interest and an advantage in emphasising their individual womanly beauty. There is no law to prevent it. Surely they would tend to counteract the severity of costume the Rule dictates.'

'There are such women. But for all that the Rule sets the key of everyday dress. If a woman is possessed by the passion for gorgeous raiment she usually satisfies it in her own private circle, or with rare occasional onslaughts upon the public eye. Her everyday mood and the disposition of most people is against being conspicuous abroad. And I should say there are little liberties under the Lesser Rule; a discreet use of fine needlework and embroidery, a wider choice of materials.'

'You have no changing fashions?'

'None. For all that, are not our dresses as beautiful as yours?'

'Our women's dresses are not beautiful at all,' I said, forced for a time towards the mysterious philosophy of dress. 'Beauty? That isn't their concern.'

'Then what are they after?'

'My dear man! What is all my world after?'

6

I should come to our third talk with a great curiosity to hear of the last portion of the Rule, of the things that the samurai are obliged to do.

There would be many precise directions regarding his health, and rules that would aim at once at health and that constant exercise of will that makes life good. Save in specified exceptional circumstances, the samurai must bathe in cold water, and the men must shave every day; they have the precisest directions in such matters; the body must be in health, the skin and muscles and nerves in perfect tone, or the samurai must go to the doctors of the order, and give implicit obedience to the regimen prescribed. They must sleep alone at least four nights in five; and they must eat with and talk to anyone in their fellowship who cares for their conversation for an hour, at least, at the nearest clubhouse of the samurai once on three chosen days in every week. Moreover, they must read aloud from the Book of the Samurai for at least ten minutes every day. Every month they must buy and read faithfully through at least one book that has been published during the past five years, and the only intervention with private choice in that matter is the prescription of a certain minimum of length for the monthly book or books. But the full Rule in these minor compulsory matters is voluminous and detailed, and it abounds with alternatives. Its aim is rather to keep before the samurai by a number of sample duties, as it were, the need of, and some of the chief methods towards health of body and mind, rather than to provide a comprehensive rule; and to ensure the maintenance of a community of feeling and interests among the samurai through habit, intercourse, and a living contemporary literature. These minor obligations do not earmark more than an hour in the day. Yet they serve to break down isolations of sympathy, all sorts of physical and intellectual sluggishness and the development of unsocial preoccupations of many sorts.

Women samurai who are married, my double told me, must bear children – if they are to remain married as well as in the order – before the second period for terminating a childless marriage is exhausted. I failed to ask for the precise figures from my double at the time, but I think it is beyond doubt that it is from samurai mothers of the Greater or Lesser Rule that a very large proportion of the future population of Utopia will be derived. There is one liberty accorded to women samurai which is refused to men, and that is to marry outside the Rule, and women married to men not under the Rule are also free to become samurai. Here, too, it will be manifest there is scope for novels and the drama of life. In practice, it seems that it is only men of great poietic distinction outside the Rule, or great commercial leaders, who have wives under it. The tendency of such unions is either to bring the husband under the Rule, or take the wife out of it. There can be no doubt that these marriage limitations tend to make the samurai something of an hereditary class. Their children, as a rule, become samurai. But it is not an exclusive caste; subject to the most reasonable qualific-ations, anyone who sees fit can enter it at any time, and so, unlike all other privileged castes the world has seen, it increases relatively to the total population, and may indeed at last assimilate almost the whole population of the earth.

So much my double told me readily.

But now he came to the heart of all his explanations, to the will and motives at the centre that made men and women ready to undergo discipline, to renounce the richness and elaboration of the sensuous life, to master emotions and control impulses, to keep in the key of effort while they had abundance about them to rouse and satisfy all desires, and his exposition was more difficult.

He tried to make his religion clear to me.

The leading principle of the Utopian religion is the repudiation of the doctrine of original sin; the Utopians hold that man, on the whole, is good. That is their cardinal belief. Man has pride and conscience, they hold, that you may refine by training as you refine his eye and ear; he has remorse and sorrow in his being, coming on the heels of all inconsequent enjoyments. How can one think of him as bad? He is religious; religion is as natural to him as lust and anger, less intense, indeed, but coming with a wide-sweeping inevitableness as peace comes after all tumults and noises. And in Utopia they understand this, or, at least, the samurai do, clearly. They accept Religion as they accept Thirst, as something inseparably in the mysterious rhythms of life. And just as thirst and pride and all desires may be perverted in an age of abundant opportunities, and men may be degraded and wasted by intemperance in drinking, by display, or by ambition, so too the nobler complex of desires that constitutes religion may be turned to evil by the dull, the base, and the careless. Slovenly indulgence in religious inclinations, a failure to think hard and discriminate as fairly as possible in religious matters, is just as alien to the men under the Rule as it would be to drink deeply because they were thirsty, eat until glutted, evade a bath because the day was chilly, or make love to any bright-eyed girl who chanced to look pretty in the dusk. Utopia, which is to have every type of character that one finds on earth, will have its temples and its priests, just as it will have its actresses and wine, but the samurai will be forbidden the religion of dramatically lit altars, organ music, and incense, as distinctly as they are forbidden the love of painted women, or the consolations of brandy. And to all the things that are less than religion and that seek to comprehend it, to cosmogonies and philosophies, to creeds and formulae, to catechisms and easy explanations, the attitude of the samurai, the note of the Book of Samurai, will be distrust. These things, the samurai will say, are part of the indulgences that should come before a man submits himself to the Rule; they are like the early gratifications of young men, experiences to establish renunciation. The samurai will have emerged above these things.

The theology of the Utopian rulers will be saturated with that same philosophy of uniqueness, that repudiation of anything beyond similarities and practical parallelisms, that saturates all their institutions. They will have analysed exhaustively those fallacies and assumptions that arise between the One and the Many, that have troubled philosophy since philosophy began. Just as they will have escaped that delusive unification of every species under its specific definition that has dominated earthly reasoning, so they will have escaped the delusive simplification of God that vitiates all terrestrial theology. They will hold God to be complex and of an endless variety of aspects, to be expressed by no universal formula nor approved in any uniform manner. Just as the language of Utopia will be a synthesis, even so will its God be. The aspect of God is different in the measure of every man's individuality, and the intimate thing of religion must, therefore, exist in human solitude, between man and God alone. Religion in its quintessence is a relation between God and man; it is perversion to make it a relation between man and man, and a man may no more reach God through a priest than love his wife through a priest. But just as a man in love may refine the interpretation of his feelings and borrow expression from the poems and music of poietic men, so an individual man may at his discretion read books of devotion and hear music that is in harmony with his inchoate feelings. Many of the samurai, therefore, will set themselves private regimens that will help their secret religious life, will pray habitually, and read books of devotion, but with these things the Rule of the order will have nothing to do.

Clearly the God of the samurai is a transcendental and mystical God. So far as the samurai have a purpose in common in maintaining the State, and the order and progress of the world, so far, by their discipline and denial, by their public work and effort, they worship God together. But the fount of motives lies in the individual life, it lies in silent and deliberate reflections, and at this, the most striking of all the rules of the samurai aims. For seven consecutive days in the year, at least, each man or woman under the Rule must go right out of all the life of man into some wild and solitary place, must speak to no man or woman, and have no sort of intercourse with mankind. They must go bookless and weaponless, without pen or paper, or money. Provisions must be taken for the period of the journey, a rug or sleeping sack – for they must sleep under the open sky – but no means of making a fire. They may study maps beforehand to guide them, showing any difficulties and dangers in the journey, but they may not carry such helps. They must not go by beaten ways or wherever there are inhabited houses, but into the bare, quiet places of the globe – the regions set apart for them.

This discipline, my double said, was invented to secure a certain stoutness of heart and body in the members of the order, which otherwise might have lain open to too many timorous, merely abstemious, men and women. Many things had been suggested, swordplay and tests that verged on torture, climbing in giddy places and the like, before this was chosen. Partly, it is to ensure good training and sturdiness of body and mind, but partly, also, it is to draw their minds for a space from the insistent details of life, from the intricate arguments and the fretting effort to work, from personal quarrels and personal affections, and the things of the heated room. Out they must go, clean out of the world.

Certain great areas are set apart for these yearly pilgrimages beyond the securities of the State. There are thousands of square miles of sandy desert in Africa and Asia set apart; much of the Arctic and Antarctic circles; vast areas of mountain land and frozen marsh; secluded reserves of forest, and innumerable unfrequented lines upon the sea. Some are dangerous and laborious routes; some merely desolate; and there are even some sea journeys that one may take in the halcyon days as one drifts through a dream. Upon the seas one must go in a little undecked sailing boat, that may be rowed in a calm; all the other journeys one must do afoot, none aiding. There are, about all these desert regions and along most coasts, little offices at which the samurai says goodbye to the world of men, and at which they arrive after their minimum time of silence is overpast. For the intervening days they must be alone with Nature, necessity, and their own thoughts.

'It is good?' I said.

'It is good,' my double answered. 'We civilised men go back to the stark Mother that so many of us would have forgotten were it not for this Rule. And one thinks . . . Only two weeks ago I did my journey for the year. I went with my gear by sea to Tromsö, and then inland to a starting-place, and took my ice-axe and rucksack, and said goodbye to the world. I crossed over four glaciers; I climbed three high mountain passes, and slept on moss in desolate valleys. I saw no human being for seven days. Then I came down through pine woods to the head of a road that runs to the Baltic shore. Altogether it was thirteen days before I reported myself again, and had speech with fellow creatures.'

'And the women do this?'

'The women who are truly samurai – yes. Equally with the men. Unless the coming of children intervenes.'

I asked him how it had seemed to him, and what he thought about during the journey.

'There is always a sense of effort for me,' he said, 'when I leave the world at the outset of the journey. I turn back again and again, and look at the little office as I go up my mountainside. The first day and night I'm a little disposed to shirk the job – every year it's the same – a little disposed, for example, to sling my pack from my back, and sit down, and go through its contents, and make sure I've got all my equipment.'

'There's no chance of anyone overtaking you?'

'Two men mustn't start from the same office on the same route within six hours of each other. If they come within sight of each other, they must shun an encounter, and make no sign – unless life is in danger. All that is arranged beforehand.'

'It would be, of course. Go on telling me of your journey.'

'I dread the night. I dread discomfort and bad weather. I only begin to brace up after the second day.'

'Don't you worry about losing your way?'

'No. There are cairns and skyline signs. If it wasn't for that, of course we should be worrying with maps the whole time. But I'm only sure of being a man after the second night, and sure of my power to go through.'

'And then?'

'Then one begins to get into it. The first two days one is apt to have the events of one's journey, little incidents of travel, and thoughts of one's work and affairs, rising and fading and coming again; but then the perspectives begin. I don't sleep much at nights on these journeys; I lie awake and stare at the stars. About dawn, perhaps, and in the morning sunshine, I sleep! The nights this last time were very short, never more than twilight, and I saw the glow of the sun always, just over the edge of the world. But I had chosen the days of the new moon, so that I could have a glimpse of the stars . . . Years ago, I went from the Nile across the Libyan Desert east, and then the stars – the stars in the later days of that journey – brought me near weeping . . . You begin to feel alone on the third day, when you find yourself out on some shining snowfield, and nothing of mankind visible in the whole world save one landmark, one remote thin red triangle of iron, perhaps, in the saddle of the ridge against the sky. All this busy world that has done so much and so marvellously, and is still so little – you see it little as it is – and far off. All day long you go and the night comes, and it might be another planet.

Then, in the quiet, waking hours, one thinks of one's self and the great external things, of space and eternity, and what one means by God.'

He mused.

'You think of death?'

'Not of my own. But when I go among snows and desolations – and usually I take my pilgrimage in mountains or the north – I think very much of the Night of this World – the time when our sun will be red and dull, and air and water will lie frozen together in a common snow-field where now the forests of the tropics are steaming . . . I think very much of that, and whether it is indeed God's purpose that our kind should end, and the cities we have built, the books we have written, all that we have given substance and a form, should lie dead beneath the snows.'

'You don't believe that?'

'No. But if it is not so – I went threading my way among gorges and precipices, with my poor brain dreaming of what the alternative should be, with my imagination straining and failing. Yet, in those high airs and in such solitude, a kind of exaltation comes to men . . . I remember that one night I sat up and told the rascal stars very earnestly how they should not escape us in the end.'

He glanced at me for a moment as though he doubted I should understand.

'One becomes a personification up there,' he said. 'One becomes the ambassador of mankind to the outer world.

'There is time to think over a lot of things. One puts one's self and one's ambition in a new pair of scales . . .

'Then there are hours when one is just exploring the wilderness like a child. Sometimes perhaps one gets a glimpse from some precipice edge of the plains far away, and houses and roadways, and remembers there is still a busy world of men. And at last one turns one's feet down some slope, some gorge that leads back. You come down, perhaps, into a pine forest, and hear that queer clatter reindeer make – and then, it may be, see a herdsman very far away, watching you. You wear your pilgrim's badge, and he makes no sign of seeing you . . .

'You know, after these solitudes, I feel just the same queer dis-inclination to go back to the world of men that I feel when I have to leave it. I think of dusty roads and hot valleys, and being looked at by many people. I think of the trouble of working with colleagues and opponents. This last journey I outstayed my time, camping in the pine woods for six days. Then my thoughts came round to my proper work again. I got keen to go on with it, and so I came back into the world.

You come back physically clean – as though you had had your arteries and veins washed out. And your brain has been cleaned, too . . . I shall stick to the mountains now until I am old, and then I shall sail a boat in Polynesia. That is what so many old men do. Only last year one of the great leaders of the samurai – a white-haired man, who followed the Rule in spite of his one hundred and eleven years – was found dead in his boat far away from any land, far to the south, lying like a child asleep . . . '

'That's better than a tumbled bed,' said I, 'and some boy of a doctor jabbing you with injections, and distressful people hovering about you.'

'Yes,' said my double; 'in Utopia we who are samurai die better than that . . . Is that how your great men die?'

It came to me suddenly as very strange that, even as we sat and talked, across deserted seas, on burning sands, through the still aisles of forests, and in all the high and lonely places of the world, beyond the margin where the ways and houses go, solitary men and women sailed alone or marched alone, or clambered – quiet, resolute exiles; they stood alone amidst wildernesses of ice, on the precipitous banks of roaring torrents, in monstrous caverns, or steering a tossing boat in the little circle of the horizon amidst the tumbled, incessant sea, all in their several ways communing with the emptiness, the enigmatic spaces and silences, the winds and torrents and soulless forces that lie about the lit and ordered life of men.

I saw more clearly now something I had seen dimly already, in the bearing and the faces of this Utopian chivalry, a faint persistent tinge of detachment from the immediate heats and hurries, the little graces and delights, the tensions and stimulations of the daily world. It pleased me strangely to think of this steadfast yearly pilgrimage of solitude, and how near men might come then to the high distances of God.

8

After that I remember we fell talking of the discipline of the Rule, of the Courts that try breaches of it, and interpret doubtful cases – for, though a man may resign with due notice and be free after a certain time to rejoin again, one deliberate breach may exclude a man for ever – of the system of law that has grown up about such trials, and of the triennial council that revises and alters the Rule. From that we passed to the discussion of the general constitution of this World State. Practically all political power vests in the samurai. Not only are they the only administrators, lawyers, practising doctors, and public officials of almost all kinds, but they are the only voters. Yet, by a curious exception, the supreme legislative assembly must have one-tenth, and may have one-half of its members outside the order, because, it is alleged, there is a sort of wisdom that comes of sin and laxness, which is necessary to the perfect ruling of life. My double quoted me a verse from the Canon on this matter that my unfortunate verbal memory did not retain, but it was in the nature of a prayer to save the world from 'unfermented men'. It would seem that Aristotle's idea of a rotation of rulers, an idea that crops up again in Harrington's *Oceana*, that first Utopia of 'the sovereign people' (a Utopia that, through Danton's readings in English, played a disastrous part in the French Revolution), gets little respect in Utopia. The tendency is to give a practically permanent tenure to good men. Every ruler and official, it is true, is put on his trial every three years before a jury drawn by lot, according to the range of his activities, either from the samurai of his municipal area or from the general catalogue of the samurai, but the business of this jury is merely to decide whether to continue him in office or order a new election. In the majority of cases the verdict is continuation. Even if it is not so the official may still appear as a candidate before the second and separate jury which fills the vacant post . . .

My double mentioned a few scattered details of the electoral methods, but as at that time I believed we were to have a number of further conversations, I did not exhaust my curiosities upon this subject. Indeed, I was more than a little preoccupied and inattentive. The religion of the samurai was after my heart, and it had taken hold of me very strongly . . . But presently I fell questioning him upon the complications that arise in the Modern Utopia through the differences between the races of men, and found my attention returning. But the matter of that discussion I shall put apart into a separate chapter. In the end we came back to the particulars of this great Rule of Life that any man desiring of joining the samurai must follow.

I remember how, after our third bout of talking, I walked back through the streets of Utopian London to rejoin the botanist at our hotel.

My double lived in an apartment in a great building – I should judge about where, in our London, the Tate Gallery squats, and, as the day was fine, and I had no reason for hurry, I went not by the covered mechanical way, but on foot along the broad, tree-set terraces that follow the river on either side.

It was afternoon, and the mellow Thames Valley sunlight, warm and gentle, lit a clean and gracious world. There were many people abroad, going to and fro, unhurrying, but not aimless, and I watched them so attentively that were you to ask me for the most elementary details of the buildings and terraces that lay back on either bank, or of the pinnacles and towers and parapets that laced the sky, I could not tell you them. But of the people I could tell a great deal.

No Utopians wear black, and for all the frequency of the samurai uniform along the London ways the general effect is of a gaily coloured population. You never see anyone noticeably ragged or dirty; the police, who answer questions and keep order (and are quite distinct from the organisation for the pursuit of criminals) see to that; and shabby people are very infrequent. People who want to save money for other purposes, or who do not want much bother with their clothing, seem to wear costumes of rough woven cloth, dyed an unobtrusive brown or green, over fine woollen underclothing, and so achieve a decent comfort in its simplest form. Others outside the Rule of the samurai range the spectrum for colour, and have every variety of texture; the colours attained by the Utopian dyers seem to me to be fuller and purer than the common range of stuffs on earth; and the subtle folding of the woollen materials witness that Utopian Bradford is no whit behind her earthly sister. White is extraordinarily frequent; white woollen tunics and robes into which are woven bands of brilliant colour, abound. Often these ape the cut and purple edge that distinguishes the samurai. In Utopian London the air is as clear and less dusty than it is among high mountains; the roads are made of unbroken surfaces, and not of friable earth; all heating is done by electricity, and no coal ever enters the town; there are no horses or dogs, and so there is not a suspicion of smoke and scarcely a particle of any sort of dirt to render white impossible.

The radiated influence of the uniform of the samurai has been to keep costume simple, and this, perhaps, emphasises the general effect of vigorous health, of shapely bodies. Everyone is well grown and well nourished; everyone seems in good condition; everyone walks well, and has that clearness of eye that comes with cleanness of blood. In London I am apt to consider myself of a passable size and carriage; here I feel small and mean-looking. The faint suspicions of spinal curvatures, skew feet, unequal legs, and ill-grown bones, that haunt one in a London crowd, the plain intimations – in yellow faces, puffy faces, spotted and irregular complexions, in nervous movements and coughs and colds – of bad habits and an incompetent or disregarded medical profession, do not appear here. I notice few old people, but there seems to be a greater proportion of men and women at or near the prime of life.

I hang upon that. I have seen one or two fat people here – they are all the more noticeable because they are rare. But wrinkled age? Have I yet in Utopia set eyes on a bald head?

The Utopians have brought a sounder physiological science than ours to bear upon regimen. People know better what to do and what to avoid, how to foresee and forestall coming trouble, and how to evade and suppress the subtle poisons that blunt the edge of sensation. They have put off the years of decay. They keep their teeth, they keep their digestions, they ward off gout and rheumatism, neuralgia and influenza and all those cognate decays that bend and wrinkle men and women in the middle years of existence. They have extended the level years far into the seventies, and age, when it comes, comes swiftly and easily. The feverish hurry of our earth, the decay that begins before growth has ceased, is replaced by a ripe prolonged maturity. This modern Utopia is an adult world. The flushed romance, the predominant eroticisms, the adventurous uncertainty of a world in which youth prevails, gives place here to a grave deliberation, to a fuller and more powerful emotion, to a broader handling of life.

Yet youth is here.

Amidst the men whose faces have been made fine by thought and steadfast living, among the serene-eyed women, comes youth, gaily coloured, buoyantly healthy, with challenging eyes, with fresh and eager faces . . .

For everyone in Utopia who is sane enough to benefit, study and training last until twenty; then comes the travel year, and many are still students until twenty-four or twenty-five. Most are still, in a sense, students throughout life, but it is thought that, unless responsible action is begun in some form in the early twenties, will undergoes a partial atrophy. But the full swing of adult life is hardly attained until thirty is reached. Men marry before the middle thirties, and the women rather earlier, few are mothers before five-and-twenty. The majority of those who become samurai do so between twenty-seven and thirty-five. And, between seventeen and thirty, the Utopians have their dealings with love, and the play and excitement of love is a chief interest in life. Much freedom of act is allowed them so that their wills may grow freely. For the most part they end mated, and love gives place to some special and more enduring interest, though, indeed, there is love between older men and fresh girls, and between youths and maturer women. It is in these most graceful and beautiful years of life that such freedoms of dress as the atmosphere of Utopia permits are to be seen, and the crude bright will and imagination of youth peeps out in ornament and colour.

Figures come into my sight and possess me for a moment and pass, and give place to others; there comes a dusky little Jewess, red-lipped and amber-clad, with a deep crimson flower – I know not whether real or sham – in the dull black of her hair. She passes me with an unconscious disdain; and then I am looking at a brightly smiling, blue-eyed girl, tall, ruddy, and freckled warmly, clad like a stage Rosalind, and talking gaily to a fair young man, a novice under the Rule. A red-haired mother under the Lesser Rule goes by, green-gowned, with dark green straps crossing between her breasts, and her two shock-headed children, bare-legged and lightly shod, tug at her hands on either side. Then a grave man in a long, fur-trimmed robe, a merchant, maybe, debates some serious matter with a white-tunicked clerk. And the clerk's face – ? I turn to mark the straight, blue-black hair. The man must be Chinese . . .

Then come two short-bearded men in careless indigo-blue raiment, both of them convulsed with laughter – men outside the Rule, who practise, perhaps, some art – and then one of the samurai, in cheerful altercation with a blue-robed girl of eight. 'But you *could* have come back yesterday, Dadda,' she persists. He is deeply sunburnt, and suddenly there passes before my mind the picture of a snowy mountain waste at nightfall and a solitary small figure under the stars . . .

When I come back to the present thing again, my eye is caught at once by a young negro, carrying books in his hand, a prosperous-looking, self-respecting young negro, in a trimly cut coat of purple-blue and silver.

I am reminded of what my double said to me of race.

CHAPTER TEN

Race in Utopia

1

Above the sphere of the elemental cravings and necessities, the soul of man is in a perpetual vacillation between two conflicting impulses: the desire to assert his individual differences, the desire for distinction, and his terror of isolation. He wants to stand out, but not too far out, and, on the contrary, he wants to merge himself with a group, with some larger body, but not altogether. Through all the things of life runs this tortuous compromise, men follow the fashions but resent ready-made uniforms on every plane of their being. The disposition to form aggregations and to imagine aggregations is part of the incurable nature of man; it is one of the great natural forces the statesman must utilise, and against which he must construct effectual defences. The study of the aggregations and of the ideals of aggregations about which men's sympathies will twine, and upon which they will base a large proportion of their conduct and personal policy, is the legitimate definition of sociology.

Now the sort of aggregation to which men and women will refer themselves is determined partly by the strength and idiosyncrasy of the individual imagination, and partly by the reek of ideas that chances to be in the air at the time. Men and women may vary greatly both in their innate and their acquired disposition towards this sort of larger body or that, to which their social reference can be made. The 'natural' social reference of a man is probably to some rather vaguely conceived tribe, as the 'natural' social reference of a dog is to a pack. But just as the social reference of a dog may be educated until the reference to a pack is completely replaced by a reference to an owner, so on his higher plane of educability the social reference of the civilised man undergoes the most remarkable transformations. But the power and scope of his imagination and the need he has of response sets limits to this process. A highly intellectualised mature mind may refer for its data very consistently to ideas of a higher being so remote and in-definable as God, so comprehensive as humanity, so far-reaching as the purpose in things. I write 'may', but I doubt if this exaltation of reference is ever permanently sustained. Comte, in his 'Positive Polity', exposes his soul with great freedom, and the curious may trace how, while he professes and quite honestly intends to refer himself always to his 'Greater Being' Humanity, he narrows constantly to his projected *Western Republic* of civilised men, and quite frequently to the minute indefinite body of Positivist subscribers. And the history of the Christian Church, with its development of orders and cults, sects and dissents, the history of fashionable society with its cliques and sets and every political history with its cabals and inner cabinets, witness to the struggle that goes on in the minds of men to adjust themselves to a body larger indeed than themselves, but which still does not strain and escape their imaginative grasp.

The statesman, both for himself and others, must recognise this inadequacy of grasp, and the necessity for real and imaginary aggregations to sustain men in their practical service of the order of the world. He must be a sociologist; he must study the whole science of aggregations in relation to that World State to which his reason and his maturest thought direct him. He must lend himself to the development of aggregatory ideas that favour the civilising process, and he must do his best to promote the disintegration of aggregations and the effacement of aggregatory ideas, that keep men narrow and unreasonably prejudiced one against another.

He will, of course, know that few men are even rudely consistent in such matters, that the same man in different moods and on different occasions is capable of referring himself in perfect good faith, not only to different, but to contradictory larger beings, and that the more important thing about an aggregatory idea from the State-maker's point of view is not so much what it explicitly involves as what it implicitly repudiates. The natural man does not feel he is aggregating at all, unless he aggregates *against* something. He refers himself to the tribe; he is loyal to the tribe, and quite inseparably he fears or dislikes those others outside the tribe. The tribe is always at least defensively hostile and usually actively hostile to humanity beyond the aggregation. The Anti-idea, it would seem, is inseparable from the aggregatory idea; it is a necessity of the human mind. When we think of the class A as desirable, we think of Not-A as undesirable. The two things are as inevitably connected as the tendons of our hands, so that when we flatten down our little fingers on our palms, the fourth digit, whether we want it or not, comes down halfway. All real working gods, one may remark, all gods that are worshipped emotionally, are tribal gods, and every attempt to universalise the idea of God trails dualism and the devil after it as a moral necessity.

When we enquire, as well as the unformed condition of terrestrial sociology permits, into the aggregatory ideas that seem to satisfy men, we find a remarkable complex, a disorderly complex, in the minds of nearly all our civilised contemporaries. For example, all sorts of aggregatory ideas come and go across the chameleon surfaces of my botanist's mind. He has a strong feeling for systematic botanists as against plant physiologists, whom he regards as lewd and evil scoundrels in this relation, but he has a strong feeling for all botanists, and, indeed, all biologists, as against physicists, and those who profess the exact sciences, all of whom he regards as dull, mechanical, ugly-minded scoundrels in this relation; but he has a strong feeling for all who profess what is called Science as against psychologists, sociologists, philosophers, and literary men, whom he regards as wild, foolish, immoral scoundrels in this relation; but he has a strong feeling for all educated men as against the working man, whom he regards as a cheating, lying, loafing, drunken, thievish, dirty scoundrel in this relation; but so soon as the working man is comprehended together with those others, as Englishmen – which includes, in this case, I may remark, the Scottish and Welsh – he holds them superior to all other sorts of European, whom he regards, etc . . .

Now one perceives in all these aggregatory ideas and rearrangements of the sympathies one of the chief vices of human thought, due to its obsession by classificatory suggestions.* The necessity for marking out classes has brought with it a bias for false and excessive contrast, and we never invent a term but we are at once cramming it with implications beyond its legitimate content. There is no feat of irrelevance that people will not perform quite easily in this way; there is no class, however accidental, to which they will not at once ascribe deeply distinctive qualities. The seventh sons of seventh sons have remarkable powers of insight; people with a certain sort of ear commit crimes of violence; people with red hair have souls of fire; all democratic socialists are trustworthy persons; all people born in Ireland have vivid imaginations and all Englishmen are clods; all Hindus are cowardly liars; all curly-haired people are good-natured; all hunchbacks are energetic and wicked, and all Frenchmen eat frogs. Such stupid generalisations have been believed with the utmost readiness, and acted upon by great numbers of sane, respectable people. And when the class is one's own class, when it expresses one of the aggregations to which one refers one's own activities, then the disposition to divide all qualities between

* See Chapter One, section 5, and the Appendix.

this class and its converse, and to cram one's own class with every desirable distinction, becomes overwhelming.

It is part of the training of the philosopher to regard all such general-isations with suspicion; it is part of the training of the Utopist and statesman – and all good statesmen are Utopists – to mingle something very like animosity with that suspicion. For crude classifications and false generalisations are the curse of all organised human life.

2

Disregarding classes, cliques, sets, castes, and the like minor aggreg-ations, concerned for the most part with details and minor aspects of life, one finds among the civilised peoples of the world certain broad types of aggregatory ideas. There are, firstly, the national ideas, ideas which, in their perfection, require a uniformity of physical and mental type, a common idiom, a common religion, a distinctive style of costume, decoration, and thought, and a compact organisation acting with com-plete external unity. Like the Gothic cathedral, the national idea is never found complete with all its parts; but one has in Russia, with her insistence on political and religious orthodoxy, something approaching it pretty closely, and again in the inland and typical provinces of China, where even a strange pattern of hat arouses hostility. We had it in vigorous struggle to exist in England under the earlier Georges in the minds of those who supported the Established Church. The idea of the fundamental nature of nationality is so ingrained in thought, with all the usual exaggeration of implication, that no one laughs at talk about Swedish painting or American literature. And I will confess and point out that my own detachment from these delusions is so imperfect and discontinuous that in another passage I have committed myself to a short assertion of the exceptionally noble quality of the English imagination.* I am constantly gratified by flattering untruths about English superiority which I should reject indignantly were the applic-ation bluntly personal, and I am ever ready to believe the scenery of England, the poetry of England, even the decoration and music of England, in some mystic and impregnable way, the best. This habit of intensifying all class definitions, and particularly those in which one has a personal interest, is in the very constitution of man's mind. It is

* Chapter Seven, section 6.

part of the defect of that instrument. We may watch against it and prevent it doing any great injustices, or leading us into follies, but to eradicate it is an altogether different matter. There it is, to be reckoned with, like the coccyx, the pineal eye, and the vermiform appendix. And a too consistent attack on it may lead simply to its inversion, to a vindictively pro-foreigner attitude that is equally unwise.

The second sort of aggregatory ideas, running very often across the boundaries of national ideas and in conflict with them, are religious ideas. In Western Europe true national ideas only emerged to their present hectic vigour after the shock of the Reformation had liberated men from the great tradition of a Latin-speaking Christendom, a tradition the Roman Catholic Church has sustained as its modification of the old Latin-speaking Imperialism in the rule of the *pontifex maximus*. There was, and there remains to this day, a profound disregard of local dialect and race in the Roman Catholic tradition, which has made that Church a persistently disintegrating influence in national life. Equally spacious and equally regardless of tongues and peoples is the great Arabic-speaking religion of Mahomet. Both Christendom and Islam are indeed on their secular sides imperfect realisations of a Utopian World State. But the secular side was the weaker side of these cults; they produced no sufficiently great statesmen to realise their spiritual forces, and it is not in Rome under pontifical rule, nor in Munster under the Anabaptists, but rather in Thomas à Kempis and Saint Augustin's *City of God* that we must seek for the Utopias of Christianity.

In the last hundred years a novel development of material forces, and especially of means of communication, has done very much to break up the isolations in which nationality perfected its prejudices and so to render possible the extension and consolidation of such a worldwide culture as mediaeval Christendom and Islam foreshadowed. The first onset of these expansive developments has been marked in the world of mind by an expansion of political ideals – Comte's *Western Republic* (1848) was the first Utopia that involved the synthesis of numerous States – by the development of 'Imperialisms' in the place of national policies, and by the search for a basis for wider political unions in racial traditions and linguistic affinities. Anglo-Saxonism, Pan-Germanism, and the like are such synthetic ideas. Until the eighties, the general tendency of progressive thought was at one with the older Christian tradition which ignored 'race', and the aim of the expansive liberalism movement, so far as it had a clear aim, was to Europeanise the world, to extend the franchise to negroes, put Polynesians into trousers, and train the teeming myriads of India to appreciate the exquisite lilt of

'The Lady of the Lake'. There is always some absurdity mixed with human greatness, and we must not let the fact that the middle Victorians counted Scott, the suffrage and pantaloons among the supreme blessings of life, conceal from us the very real nobility of their dream of England's mission to the world . . .

We of this generation have seen a flood of reaction against such universalism. The great intellectual developments that centre upon the work of Darwin have exacerbated the realisation that life is a conflict between superior and inferior types, it has underlined the idea that specific survival rates are of primary significance in the world's development, and a swarm of inferior intelligences has applied to human problems elaborated and exaggerated versions of these generalisations. These social and political followers of Darwin have fallen into an obvious confusion between race and nationality, and into the natural trap of patriotic conceit. The dissent of the Indian and Colonial governing class to the first crude applications of liberal propositions in India has found a voice of unparalleled penetration in Mr Kipling, whose want of intellectual deliberation is only equalled by his poietic power. The search for a basis for a new political synthesis in adaptable sympathies based on linguistic affinities, was greatly influenced by Max Müller's unaccountable assumption that language indicated kindred, and led straight to wildly speculative ethnology, to the discovery that there was a Keltic race, a Teutonic race, an Indo-European race, and so forth. A book that has had enormous influence in this matter, because of its use in teaching, is J. R. Green's *Short History of the English People*, with its grotesque insistence upon Anglo-Saxonism. And just now, the world is in a sort of delirium about race and the racial struggle. The Briton forgetting his Defoe,* the Jew forgetting the very word proselyte, the German forgetting his anthropometric variations, and the Italian forgetting everything, are obsessed by the singular purity of their blood, and the danger of contamination the mere continuance of other races involves. True to the law that all human aggregation involves the development of a spirit of opposition to whatever is external to the aggregation, extraordinary intensifications of racial definition are going on; the vileness, the inhumanity, the incompatibility of alien races is being steadily exaggerated. The natural tendency of every human being towards a stupid conceit in himself and his kind, a stupid depreciation of all unlikeness, is traded

---

* *The True-born Englishman.*

upon by this bastard science. With the weakening of national references, and with the pause before reconstruction in religious belief, these new arbitrary and unsubstantial race prejudices become daily more formidable. They are shaping policies and modifying laws, and they will certainly be responsible for a large proportion of the wars, hardships, and cruelties the immediate future holds in store for our earth.

No generalisations about race are too extravagant for the inflamed credulity of the present time. No attempt is ever made to distinguish differences in inherent quality – the true racial differences – from artificial differences due to culture. No lesson seems ever to be drawn from history of the fluctuating incidence of the civilising process first upon this race and then upon that. The politically ascendant peoples of the present phase are understood to be the superior races, including such types as the Sussex farm labourer, the Bowery tough, the London hooligan, and the Paris apache; the races not at present prospering politically, such as the Egyptians, the Greeks, the Spanish, the Moors, the Chinese, the Hindus, the Peruvians, and all uncivilised people are represented as the inferior races, unfit to associate with the former on terms of equality, unfit to intermarry with them on any terms, unfit for any decisive voice in human affairs. In the popular imagination of Western Europe, the Chinese are becoming bright gamboge in colour, and unspeakably abominable in every respect; the people who are black – the people who have fuzzy hair and flattish noses, and no calves to speak of – are no longer held to be within the pale of humanity. These superstitions work out along the obvious lines of the popular logic. The depopulation of the Congo Free State by the Belgians, the horrible massacres of Chinese by European soldiery during the Pekin expedition, are condoned as a painful but necessary part of the civilising process of the world. The worldwide repudiation of slavery in the nineteenth century was done against a vast sullen force of ignorant pride, which, reinvigorated by the new delusions, swings back again to power.

'Science' is supposed to lend its sanction to race mania, but it is only 'science' as it is understood by very illiterate people that does anything of the sort – 'scientists'' science, in fact. What science has to tell about 'The Races of Man' will be found compactly set forth by Doctor J. Deniker, in the book published under that title.* From that book one may learn the beginnings of race charity. Save for a few isolated pools of

* See also an excellent paper in the *American Journal of Sociology* for March, 1904, 'The Psychology of Race Prejudice', by W. I. Thomas.

savage humanity, there is probably no pure race in the whole world. The great continental populations are all complex mixtures of numerous and fluctuating types. Even the Jews present every kind of skull that is supposed to be racially distinctive, a vast range of complexion – from blackness in Goa, to extreme fairness in Holland – and a vast mental and physical diversity. Were the Jews to discontinue all intermarriage with 'other races' henceforth for ever, it would depend upon quite unknown laws of fecundity, prepotency, and variability, what their final type would be, or, indeed, whether any particular type would ever prevail over diversity. And, without going beyond the natives of the British Isles, one can discover an enormous range of types, tall and short, straight-haired and curly, fair and dark, supremely intelligent and unteachably stupid, straightforward, disingenuous, and what not. The natural tendency is to forget all this range directly 'race' comes under discussion, to take either an average or some quite arbitrary ideal as the type, and think only of that. The more difficult thing to do, but the thing that must be done if we are to get just results in this discussion, is to do one's best to bear the range in mind.

Let us admit that the average Chinaman is probably different in complexion, and, indeed, in all his physical and psychical proportions, from the average Englishman. Does that render their association upon terms of equality in a World State impossible? What the average China-man or Englishman may be, is of no importance whatever to our plan of a World State. It is not averages that exist, but individuals. The average Chinaman will never meet the average Englishman anywhere; only individual Chinamen will meet individual Englishmen. Now among Chinamen will be found a range of variety as extensive as among Englishmen, and there is no single trait presented by all Chinamen and no Englishman, or vice versa. Even the oblique eye is not universal in China, and there are probably many Chinamen who might have been 'changed at birth', taken away and educated into quite passable English-men. Even after we have separated out and allowed for the differences in carriage, physique, moral prepossessions, and so forth, due to their entirely divergent cultures, there remains, no doubt, a very great difference between the average Chinaman and the average Englishman; but would that amount to a wider difference than is to be found between extreme types of Englishmen?

For my own part I do not think that it would. But it is evident that any precise answer can be made only when anthropology has adopted much more exact and exhaustive methods of enquiry, and a far more precise analysis than its present resources permit.

Be it remembered how doubtful and tainted is the bulk of our evidence in these matters. These are extraordinarily subtle enquiries, from which few men succeed in disentangling the threads of their personal associations – the curiously interwoven strands of self-love and self-interest that affect their enquiries. One might almost say that instinct fights against such investigations, as it does undoubtedly against many necessary medical researches. But while a long special training, a high tradition and the possibility of reward and distinction, enable the medical student to face many tasks that are at once undignified and physically repulsive, the people from whom we get our anthropological information are rarely men of more than average intelligence, and of no mental training at all. And the problems are far more elusive. It surely needs at least the gifts and training of a first-class novelist, combined with a sedulous patience that probably cannot be hoped for in combination with these, to gauge the all-round differences between man and man. Even where there are no barriers of language and colour, understanding may be nearly impossible. How few educated people seem to understand the servant class in England, or the working men! Except for Mr Bart Kennedy's *A Man Adrift*, I know of scarcely any book that shows a really sympathetic and living understanding of the navvy, the longshore sailor man, the rough chap of our own race. Caricatures, luridly tragic or gaily comic, in which the misconceptions of the author blend with the preconceptions of the reader and achieve success, are, of course, common enough. And then consider the sort of people who pronounce judgements on the moral and intellectual capacity of the negro, the Malay, or the Chinaman. You have missionaries, native schoolmasters, employers of coolies, traders, simple downright men, who scarcely suspect the existence of any sources of error in their verdicts, who are incapable of understanding the difference between what is innate and what is acquired, much less of distinguishing them in their interplay. Now and then one seems to have a glimpse of something really living – in Mary Kingsley's buoyant work, for instance – and even that may be no more than my illusion.

For my own part I am disposed to discount all adverse judgements and all statements of insurmountable differences between race and race. I talk upon racial qualities to all men who have had opportunities of close observation, and I find that their insistence upon these differences is usually in inverse proportion to their intelligence. It may be the chance of my encounters, but that is my clear impression. Common sailors will generalise in the profoundest way about Irishmen, and Scotchmen, and Yankees, and Nova Scotians, and 'Dutchies', until one might think one talked of different species of animal, but the educated explorer flings clear of all these delusions. To him men present themselves individualised, and if they classify it is by some skin-deep accident of tint, some trick of the tongue, or habit of gesture, or suchlike superficiality. And after all there exists today available one kind at least of unbiased anthropological evidence. There are photographs. Let the reader turn over the pages of some such copiously illustrated work as *The Living Races of Mankind*,* and look into the eyes of one alien face after another. Are they not very like the people one knows? For the most part, one finds it hard to believe that, with a common language and common social traditions, one would not get on very well with these people. Here or there is a brutish or evil face, but you can find as brutish and evil in the Strand on any afternoon. There are differences no doubt, but fundamental incompatibilities – *no!* And very many of them send out a ray of special resemblance and remind one more strongly of this friend or that, than they do of their own kind. One notes with surprise that one's good friend and neighbour X and an anonymous naked Gold Coast negro belong to one type, as distinguished from one's dear friend Y and a beaming individual from Somaliland, who as certainly belong to another.

In one matter the careless and prejudiced nature of accepted racial generalisations is particularly marked. A great and increasing number of people are persuaded that 'half-breeds' are peculiarly evil creatures – as hunchbacks and bastards were supposed to be in the middle ages. The full legend of the wickedness of the half-breed is best to be learnt from a drunken mean white from Virginia or the Cape. The half-breed, one hears, combines all the vices of either parent, he is wretchedly poor in health and spirit, but vindictive, powerful, and dangerous to an extreme degree, his morals – the mean white has high and exacting standards – are indescribable even in whispers in a saloon, and so on, and so on. There is really not an atom of evidence an unprejudiced mind would accept to sustain any belief of the sort. There is nothing to show that the children of racial admixture are, as a class, inherently either better or worse in any respect than either parent. There is an equally baseless theory that they are better, a theory displayed to a fine degree of foolishness in the article on Shakespeare in the *Encyclopaedia Britannica*. Both theories belong to the vast edifice of sham science that smothers the realities of modern knowledge. It may be that most

* *The Living Races of Mankind*, by H. N. Hutchinson, J. W. Gregory, and R. Lydekker, Hutchinson.

'half-breeds' are failures in life, but that proves nothing. They are, in an enormous number of cases, illegitimate and outcast from the normal education of either race; they are brought up in homes that are the battlegrounds of conflicting cultures; they labour under a heavy premium of disadvantage. There is, of course, a passing suggestion of Darwin's to account for atavism that might go to support the theory of the vileness of half-breeds, if it had ever been proved. But, then, it never has been proved. There is no proof in the matter at all.

3

Suppose, now, there is such a thing as an all-round inferior race. Is that any reason why we should propose to preserve it for ever in a condition of tutelage? Whether there is a race so inferior I do not know, but certainly there is no race so superior as to be trusted with human charges. The true answer to Aristotle's plea for slavery, that there are 'natural slaves', lies in the fact that there are no 'natural' masters. Power is no more to be committed to men without discipline and restriction than alcohol. The true objection to slavery is not that it is unjust to the inferior but that it corrupts the superior. There is only one sane and logical thing to be done with a really inferior race, and that is to exterminate it.

Now there are various ways of exterminating a race, and most of them are cruel. You may end it with fire and sword after the old Hebrew fashion; you may enslave it and work it to death, as the Spaniards did the Caribs; you may set it boundaries and then poison it slowly with deleterious commodities, as the Americans do with most of their Indians; you may incite it to wear clothing to which it is not accustomed and to live under new and strange conditions that will expose it to infectious diseases to which you yourselves are immune, as the missionaries do the Polynesians; you may resort to honest simple murder, as we English did with the Tasmanians; or you can maintain such conditions as conduce to 'race suicide', as the British administration does in Fiji. Suppose, then, for a moment, that there is an all-round inferior race; a Modern Utopia is under the hard logic of life, and it would have to exterminate such a race as quickly as it could. On the whole, the Fijian device seems the least cruel. But Utopia would do that without any clumsiness of race distinction, in exactly the same manner, and by the same machinery, as it exterminates all its own defective and inferior strains; that is to say, as we have already discussed in Chapter Five, section 1, by its marriage laws, and by the laws of the minimum wage. That extinction need never be discriminatory. If any of the race did, after all, prove to be fit to survive, they would survive – they would be picked out with a sure and automatic justice from the over-ready condemnation of all their kind.

Is there, however, an all-round inferior race in the world? Even the Australian black-fellow is, perhaps, not quite so entirely eligible for extinction as a good, wholesome, horse-racing, sheep-farming Australian white may think. These queer little races, the black-fellows, the Pygmies, the Bushmen, may have their little gifts, a greater keenness, a greater fineness of this sense or that, a quaintness of the imagination or what not, that may serve as their little unique addition to the totality of our Utopian civilisation. We are supposing that every individual alive on earth is alive in Utopia, and so all the surviving 'black-fellows' are there. Every one of them in Utopia has had what none has had on earth, a fair education and fair treatment, justice, and opportunity. Suppose that the common idea is right about the general inferiority of these people, then it would follow that in Utopia most of them are childless, and working at or about the minimum wage, and some will have passed out of all possibility of offspring under the hand of the offended law; but still – cannot we imagine some few of these little people – whom you must suppose neither naked nor clothed in the European style, but robed in the Utopian fashion – may have found some delicate art to practise, some peculiar sort of carving, for example, that justifies God in creating them? Utopia has sound sanitary laws, sound social laws, sound economic laws; what harm are these people going to do?

Some may be even prosperous and admired, may have married women of their own or some other race, and so may be transmitting that distinctive thin thread of excellence, to take its due place in the great synthesis of the future.

And, indeed, coming along that terrace in Utopia, I see a little figure, a little bright-eyed, bearded man, inky black, frizzy haired, and clad in a white tunic and black hose, and with a mantle of lemon yellow wrapped about his shoulders. He walks, as most Utopians walk, as though he had reason to be proud of something, as though he had no reason to be afraid of anything in the world. He carries a portfolio in his hand. It is that, I suppose, as much as his hair, that recalls the Quartier Latin to my mind.

I had already discussed the question of race with the botanist at Lucerne.

'But you would not like,' he cried in horror, 'your daughter to marry a Chinaman or a negro?'

'Of course,' said I, 'when you say Chinaman, you think of a creature with a pigtail, long nails, and insanitary habits, and when you say negro you think of a filthy-headed, black creature in an old hat. You do this because your imagination is too feeble to disentangle the inherent qualities of a thing from its habitual associations.'

'Insult isn't argument,' said the botanist.

'Neither is unsound implication. You make a question of race into a question of unequal cultures. You would not like your daughter to marry the sort of negro who steals hens, but then you would also not like your daughter to marry a pure English hunchback with a squint, or a drunken cab tout of Norman blood. As a matter of fact, very few well-bred English girls do commit that sort of indiscretion. But you don't think it necessary to generalise against men of your own race because there are drunken cab touts, and why should you generalise against negroes? Because the proportion of undesirables is higher among negroes, that does not justify a sweeping condemnation. You may have to condemn most, but why *all*? There may be – neither of us knows enough to deny – negroes who are handsome, capable, courageous.'

'Ugh!' said the botanist.

'How detestable you must find Othello!'

It is my Utopia, and for a moment I could almost find it in my heart to spite the botanist by creating a modern Desdemona and her lover sooty black to the lips, there before our eyes. But I am not so sure of my case as that, and for the moment there shall come nothing more than a swart-faced, dusky Burmese woman in the dress of the Greater Rule, with her tall Englishman (as he might be on earth) at her side. That, however, is a digression from my conversation with the botanist.

'And the Chinaman?' said the botanist.

'I think we shall have all the buff and yellow peoples intermingling pretty freely.'

'Chinamen and white women, for example.'

'Yes,' I said, 'you've got to swallow that, anyhow; you *shall* swallow that.'

He finds the idea too revolting for comment.

I try and make the thing seem easier for him. 'Do try,' I said, 'to grasp a Modern Utopian's conditions. The Chinaman will speak the same language as his wife – whatever her race may be – he will wear costume of the common civilised fashion, he will have much the same education as his European rival, read the same literature, bow to the same traditions. And you must remember a wife in Utopia is singularly not subject to her husband . . . '

The botanist proclaims his invincible conclusion: 'Everyone would cut her!'

'This is Utopia,' I said, and then sought once more to tranquillise his mind. 'No doubt among the vulgar, coarse-minded people outside the Rule there may be something of the sort. Every earthly moral block-head, a little educated, perhaps, is to be found in Utopia. You will, no doubt, find the "cut" and the "boycott", and all those nice little devices by which dull people get a keen edge on life, in their place here, and their place here is somewhere – '

I turned a thumb earthward. 'There!'

The botanist did not answer for a little while. Then he said, with some temper and great emphasis: 'Well, I'm jolly glad anyhow that I'm not to be a permanent resident in this Utopia, *if our daughters are to be married to Hottentots* by regulation. I'm jolly glad.'

He turned his back on me.

Now did I say anything of the sort? . . .

I had to bring him, I suppose; there's no getting away from him in this life. But, as I have already observed, the happy ancients went to their Utopias without this sort of company.

5

What gives the botanist so great an advantage in all his Anti-Utopian utterances is his unconsciousness of his own limitations. He thinks in little pieces that lie about loose, and nothing has any necessary link with anything else in his mind. So that I cannot retort upon him by asking him, if he objects to this synthesis of all nations, tongues and peoples in a World State, what alternative ideal he proposes.

People of this sort do not even feel the need of alternatives. Beyond the scope of a few personal projects, meeting Her again, and things like that, they do not feel that there is a future. They are unencumbered by any baggage of convictions whatever, in relation to that. That, at least, is the only way in which I can explain our friend's high intellectual mobility. Attempts to correlate statesmanship, which they regard with interest as a dramatic interplay of personalities, with any secular movement of humanity, they class with the differential calculus and Darwinism, as things far too difficult to be anything but finally and subtly wrong.

So the argument must pass into a direct address to the reader.

If you are not prepared to regard a worldwide synthesis of all cultures and polities and races into one World State as the desirable end upon which all civilising efforts converge, what do you regard as the desirable end? Synthesis, one may remark in passing, does not necessarily mean fusion, nor does it mean uniformity.

The alternatives fall roughly under three headings. The first is to assume there is a best race, to define as well as one can that best race, and to regard all other races as material for extermination. This has a fine, modern, biological air ('Survival of the Fittest'). If you are one of those queer German professors who write insanity about Welt-Politik, you assume the best race is the 'Teutonic'; Cecil Rhodes affected that triumph of creative imagination, the 'Anglo-Saxon race'; my friend, Moses Cohen, thinks there is much to be said for the Jew. On its premises, this is a perfectly sound and reasonable policy, and it opens out a brilliant prospect for the scientific inventor for what one might call Welt-Apparat in the future, for national harrowing and reaping machines, and race-destroying fumigations. The great plain of China ('Yellow Peril') lends itself particularly to some striking wholesale undertaking; it might, for example, be flooded for a few days, and then disinfected with volcanic chlorine. Whether, when all the inferior races have been stamped out, the superior race would not proceed at once, or after a brief millennial period of social harmony, to divide itself into sub-classes, and begin the business over again at a higher level, is an interesting residual question into which we need not now penetrate.

That complete development of a scientific Welt-Politik is not, however, very widely advocated at present, no doubt from a want of confidence in the public imagination. We have, however, a very audible and influential school, the Modern Imperialist school, which distinguishes its own race – there is a German, a British, and an Anglo-Saxon section in the school, and a wider teaching which embraces the whole 'white race' in one remarkable tolerance – as the superior race, as one, indeed, superior enough to own slaves, collectively, if not individually; and the exponents of this doctrine look with a resolute, truculent, but slightly indistinct eye to a future in which all the rest of the world will be in subjection to these elect. The ideals of this type are set forth pretty clearly in Mr Kidd's *Control of the Tropics*. The

whole world is to be administered by the 'white' Powers – Mr Kidd
did not anticipate Japan – who will see to it that their subjects do not
'prevent the utilisation of the immense natural resources which they
have in charge'. Those other races are to be regarded as children,
recalcitrant children at times, and without any of the tender emotions
of paternity. It is a little doubtful whether the races lacking 'in the
elementary qualities of social efficiency' are expected to acquire them
under the chastening hands of those races which, through 'strength
and energy of character, humanity, probity, and integrity, and a single-
minded devotion to conceptions of duty', are developing 'the resources
of the richest regions of the earth' over their heads, or whether this is
the ultimate ideal.

Next comes the rather incoherent alternative that one associates in
England with official Liberalism.

Liberalism in England is not quite the same thing as Liberalism in
the rest of the world; it is woven of two strands. There is Whiggism, the
powerful tradition of seventeenth-century Protestant and republican
England, with its great debt to republican Rome, its strong constructive
and disciplinary bias, its broad and originally very living and intelligent
outlook; and interwoven with this there is the sentimental and logical
Liberalism that sprang from the stresses of the eighteenth century, that
finds its early scarce differentiated expression in Harrington's Oceana,
and after fresh draughts of the tradition of Brutus and Cato and
some elegant trifling with noble savages, budded in 'La Cité Morellyste',
flowered in the emotional democratic naturalism of Rousseau, and bore
abundant fruit in the French Revolution. These are two very distinct
strands. Directly they were freed in America from the grip of conflict
with British Toryism, they came apart as the Republican and
Democratic parties respectively. Their continued union in Great Britain
is a political accident. Because of this mixture, the whole career of
English-speaking Liberalism, though it has gone to one unbroken strain
of eloquence, has never produced a clear statement of policy in relation
to other peoples politically less fortunate. It has developed no definite
ideas at all about the future of mankind. The Whig disposition, which
once had some play in India, was certainly to attempt to anglicise the
'native', to assimilate his culture, and then to assimilate his political
status with that of his temporary ruler. But interwoven with this
anglicising tendency, which was also, by the by, a Christianising
tendency, was a strong disposition, derived from the Rousseau strand,
to leave other peoples alone, to facilitate even the separation and
autonomy of detached portions of our own peoples, to disintegrate

finally into perfect, because lawless, individuals. The official exposition of British 'Liberalism' today still wriggles unstably because of these conflicting constituents, but on the whole the Whig strand now seems the weaker. The contemporary Liberal politician offers cogent criticism upon the brutality and conceit of modern imperialisms, but that seems to be the limit of his service. Taking what they do not say and do not propose as an indication of Liberal intentions, it would seem that the ideal of the British Liberals and of the American Democrats is to favour the existence of just as many petty, loosely allied, or quite independent nationalities as possible, just as many languages as possible, to deprecate armies and all controls, and to trust to the innate goodness of disorder and the powers of an ardent sentimentality to keep the world clean and sweet. The Liberals will not face the plain consequence that such a state of affairs is hopelessly unstable, that it involves the maximum risk of war with the minimum of permanent benefit and public order. They will not reflect that the stars in their courses rule inexorably against it. It is a vague, impossible ideal, with a rude sort of unworldly moral beauty, like the gospel of the Doukhobors. Besides that charm it has this most seductive quality to an official British Liberal, that it does not exact intellectual activity nor indeed activity of any sort whatever. It is, by virtue of that alone, a far less mischievous doctrine than the crude and violent Imperialism of the popular Press.

Neither of these two schools of policy, neither the international laissez-faire of the Liberals, nor 'hustle to the top' Imperialism, promise any reality of permanent progress for the world of men. They are the resort, the moral reference, of those who will not think frankly and exhaustively over the whole field of this question. Do that, insist upon solutions of more than accidental applicability, and you emerge with one or other of two contrasted solutions, as the consciousness of kind or the consciousness of individuality prevails in your mind. In the former case you will adopt aggressive Imperialism, but you will carry it out to its 'thorough' degree of extermination. You will seek to develop the culture and power of your kind of men and women to the utmost in order to shoulder all other kinds from the earth. If on the other hand you appreciate the unique, you will aim at such a synthesis as this Utopia displays, a synthesis far more credible and possible than any other Welt-Politik. In spite of all the pageant of modern war, synthesis is in the trend of the world. To aid and develop it, could be made the open and secure policy of any great modern empire now. Modern war, modern international hostility is, I believe, possible only through the stupid illiteracy of the mass of men and the conceit and intellectual indolence of rulers and those who feed the public mind. Were the will of the mass of men lit and conscious, I am firmly convinced it would now burn steadily for synthesis and peace.

It would be so easy to bring about a world peace within a few decades, was there but the will for it among men! The great empires that exist need but a little speech and frankness one with another. Within, the riddles of social order are already half solved in books and thought, there are the common people and the subject peoples to be educated and drilled, to be led to a common speech and a common literature, to be assimilated and made citizens; without, there is the possibility of treaties. Why, for example, should Britain and France, or either and the United States, or Sweden and Norway, or Holland, or Denmark, or Italy, fight any more for ever? And if there is no reason, how foolish and dangerous it is still to sustain linguistic differences and custom houses, and all sorts of foolish and irritating distinctions between their various citizens! Why should not all these peoples agree to teach some common language, French, for example, in their common schools, or to teach each other's languages reciprocally? Why should they not aim at a common literature, and bring their various common laws, their marriage laws, and so on, into uniformity? Why should they not work for a uniform minimum of labour conditions through all their communities? Why, then, should they not – except in the interests of a few rascal plutocrats – trade freely and exchange their citizenship freely throughout their common boundaries? No doubt there are difficulties to be found, but they are quite finite difficulties. What is there to prevent a parallel movement of all the civilised Powers in the world towards a common ideal and assimilation?

Stupidity – nothing but stupidity, a stupid brute jealousy, aimless and unjustifiable.

The coarser conceptions of aggregation are at hand, the hostile, jealous patriotisms, the blare of trumpets and the pride of fools; they serve the daily need though they lead towards disaster. The real and the immediate has us in its grip, the accidental personal thing. The little effort of thought, the brief sustained effort of will, is too much for the contemporary mind. Such treaties, such sympathetic international movements, are but dream stuff yet on earth, though Utopia has realised them long since and already passed them by.

CHAPTER ELEVEN

The Bubble Bursts

1

As I walk back along the river terrace to the hotel where the botanist awaits me, and observe the Utopians I encounter, I have no thought that my tenure of Utopia becomes every moment more precarious. There float in my mind vague anticipations of more talks with my double and still more, of a steady elaboration of detail, of interesting journeys of exploration. I forget that a Utopia is a thing of the imagination that becomes more fragile with every added circumstance, that, like a soap-bubble, it is most brilliantly and variously coloured at the very instant of its dissolution. This Utopia is nearly done. All the broad lines of its social organisation are completed now, the discussion of all its general difficulties and problems. Utopian individuals pass me by, fine buildings tower on either hand; it does not occur to me that I may look too closely. To find the people assuming the concrete and individual, is not, as I fondly imagine, the last triumph of realisation, but the swimming moment of opacity before the film gives way. To come to individual emotional cases, is to return to the earth.

I find the botanist sitting at a table in the hotel courtyard.

'Well?' I say, standing before him.

'I've been in the gardens on the river terrace,' he answers, 'hoping I might see her again.'

'Nothing better to do?'

'Nothing in the world.'

'You'll have your double back from India tomorrow. Then you'll have conversation.'

'I don't want it,' he replies, compactly.

I shrug my shoulders, and he adds, 'At least with him.'

I let myself down into a seat beside him.

For a time I sit restfully enjoying his companionable silence, and thinking fragmentarily of those samurai and their Rules. I entertain something of the satisfaction of a man who has finished building a bridge; I feel that I have joined together things that I had never joined before. My Utopia seems real to me, very real, I can believe in it, until the metal chair-back gives to my shoulder blades, and Utopian sparrows twitter and hop before my feet. I have a pleasant moment of unhesitating self-satisfaction; I feel a shameless exultation to be there. For a moment I forget the consideration the botanist demands; the mere pleasure of completeness, of holding and controlling all the threads possesses me.

'You *will* persist in believing,' I say, with an aggressive expository note, 'that if you meet this lady she will be a person with the memories and sentiments of her double on earth. You think she will understand and pity, and perhaps love you. Nothing of the sort is the case.' I repeat with confident rudeness, 'Nothing of the sort is the case. Things are different altogether here; you can hardly tell even now how different are – '

I discover he is not listening to me.

'What is the matter?' I ask abruptly.

He makes no answer, but his expression startles me.

'What is the matter?' and then I follow his eyes.

A woman and a man are coming through the great archway – and instantly I guess what has happened. She it is arrests my attention first – long ago I knew she was a sweetly beautiful woman. She is fair, with frank blue eyes, that look with a sort of tender receptivity into her companion's face. For a moment or so they remain, greyish figures in the cool shadow, against the sunlit greenery of the gardens beyond.

'It is Mary,' the botanist whispers with white lips, but he stares at the form of the man. His face whitens, it becomes so transfigured with emotion that for a moment it does not look weak. Then I see that his thin hand is clenched.

I realise how little I understand his emotions.

A sudden fear of what he will do takes hold of me. He sits white and tense as the two come into the clearer light of the courtyard. The man, I see, is one of the samurai, a dark, strong-faced man, a man I have never seen before, and she is wearing the robe that shows her a follower of the Lesser Rule.

Some glimmering of the botanist's feelings strikes through to my slow sympathies. Of course – a strange man! I put out a restraining hand towards his arm. 'I told you,' I say, 'that very probably, most probably, she would have met some other. I tried to prepare you.'

'Nonsense,' he whispers, without looking at me. 'It isn't that. It's – that scoundrel – '

He has an impulse to rise. 'That scoundrel,' he repeats.

'He isn't a scoundrel,' I say. 'How do you know? Keep still! Why are you standing up?'

He and I stand up quickly, I as soon as he. But now the full meaning of the group has reached me. I grip his arm. 'Be sensible,' I say, speaking very quickly, and with my back to the approaching couple. 'He's not a scoundrel here. This world is different from that. It's caught his pride somehow and made a man of him. Whatever troubled them there –'

He turns a face of white wrath on me, of accusation, and for the moment of unexpected force. 'This is *your* doing,' he says. 'You have done this to mock me. He – of all men!' For a moment speech fails him, then; 'You – you have done this to mock me.'

I try to explain very quickly. My tone is almost propitiatory.

'I never thought of it until now. But he's – How did I know he was the sort of man a disciplined world has a use for?'

He makes no answer, but he looks at me with eyes that are positively baleful, and in the instant I read his mute but mulish resolve that Utopia must end.

'Don't let that old quarrel poison all this,' I say almost entreatingly. 'It happened all differently here – everything is different here. Your double will be back tomorrow. Wait for him. Perhaps then you will understand –'

He shakes his head, and then bursts out with, 'What do I want with a double? Double! What do I care if things have been different here? This –'

He thrusts me weakly back with his long, white hand. 'My God!' he says almost forcibly, 'what nonsense all this is! All these dreams! All Utopias! There she is – ! Oh, but I have dreamt of her! And now –'

A sob catches him. I am really frightened by this time. I still try to keep between him and these Utopians, and to hide his gestures from them.

'It's different here,' I persist. 'It's different here. The emotion you feel has no place in it. It's a scar from the earth – the sore scar of your past –'

'And what are we all but scars? What is life but a scarring? It's *you* – you who don't understand! Of course we are covered with scars, we live to be scarred, we are scars! We are the scars of the past! These *dreams*, these childish dreams – !'

He does not need to finish his sentence, he waves an unteachable destructive arm.

My Utopia rocks about me.

For a moment the vision of that great courtyard hangs real. There the Utopians live real about me, going to and fro, and the great archway blazes with sunlight from the green gardens by the riverside. The man who is one of the samurai, and his lady, whom the botanist loved on earth, pass out of sight behind the marble flower-set Triton that spouts coolness in the middle of the place. For a moment I see two working men in green tunics sitting on a marble seat in the shadow of the colonnade, and a sweet little silver-haired old lady, clad all in violet, and carrying a book, comes towards us, and lifts a curious eye at the botanist's gestures. And then –

'Scars of the past! Scars of the past! These fanciful, useless dreams!'

2

There is no jerk, no sound, no hint of material shock. We are in London, and clothed in the fashion of the town. The sullen roar of London fills our ears . . .

I see that I am standing beside an iron seat of poor design in that grey and gawky waste of asphalt – Trafalgar Square, and the botanist, with perplexity in his face, stares from me to a poor, shrivelled, dirt-lined old woman – my God! what a neglected thing she is! – who proffers a box of matches . . .

He buys almost mechanically, and turns back to me.

'I was saying,' he says, 'the past rules us absolutely. These dreams – '

His sentence does not complete itself. He looks nervous and irritated.

'You have a trick at times,' he says instead, 'of making your suggestions so vivid – '

He takes a plunge. 'If you don't mind,' he says in a sort of quavering ultimatum, 'we won't discuss that aspect of the question – the lady, I mean – further.'

He pauses, and there still hangs a faint perplexity between us.

'But – ' I begin.

For a moment we stand there, and my dream of Utopia runs off me like water from an oiled slab. Of course – we lunched at our club. We came back from Switzerland by no dream train but by the ordinary Bâle express. We have been talking of that Lucerne woman he harps upon, and I have made some novel comment on his story. I have touched certain possibilities.

'You can't conceivably understand,' he says.

'The fact remains,' he goes on, taking up the thread of his argument again with an air of having defined our field, 'we are the scars of the past. That's a thing one can discuss – without personalities.'

'No,' I say rather stupidly, 'no.'

'You are always talking as though you could kick the past to pieces; as though one could get right out from oneself and begin afresh. It is your weakness – if you don't mind my being frank – it makes you seem harsh and dogmatic. Life has gone easily for you; you have never been badly tried. You have been lucky – you do not understand the other way about. You are – hard.'

I answer nothing.

He pants for breath. I perceive that in our discussion of his case I must have gone too far, and that he has rebelled. Clearly I must have said something wounding about that ineffectual love story of his.

'You don't allow for my position,' he says, and it occurs to me to say, 'I'm obliged to look at the thing from my own point of view . . . '

One or other of us makes a move. What a lot of filthy, torn paper is scattered about the world! We walk slowly side by side towards the dirt-littered basin of the fountain, and stand regarding two grimy tramps who sit and argue on a further seat. One holds a horrible old boot in his hand, and gesticulates with it, while his other hand caresses his rag-wrapped foot. 'Wot does Cham'lain *si*?' his words drift to us. 'W'y, 'e says, wot's the good of 'nvesting your kepital where these 'ere Americans may dump it flat any time they like? . . . '

(Were there not two men in green sitting on a marble seat?)

3

We walk on, our talk suspended, past a ruthlessly clumsy hoarding, towards where men and women and children are struggling about a string of omnibuses. A newsvendor at the corner spreads a newspaper placard upon the wood pavement, pins the corners down with stones, and we glimpse something about:

MASSACRE IN ODESSA.

DISCOVERY OF HUMAN REMAINS AT CHERTSEY.

SHOCKING LYNCHING OUTRAGE IN NEW YORK STATE.

GERMAN INTRIGUES GET A SET-BACK.

THE BIRTHDAY HONOURS. – FULL LIST.

Dear old familiar world!

An angry parent in conversation with a sympathetic friend jostles against us. 'I'll knock his blooming young 'ed orf if 'e cheeks me again. It's these 'ere brasted Board Schools – '

An omnibus passes, bearing on a board beneath an incorrectly drawn Union Jack an exhortation to the true patriot to 'Buy Bumper's British-Boiled Jam' ...

I am stunned beyond the possibility of discussion for a space. In this very place it must have been that the high terrace ran with the gardens below it, along which I came from my double to our hotel. I am going back, but now through reality, along the path I passed so happily in my dream. And the people I saw then are the people I am looking at now – with a difference.

The botanist walks beside me, white and nervously jerky in his movements, his ultimatum delivered.

We start to cross the road. An open carriage drives by, and we see a jaded, red-haired woman, smeared with paint, dressed in furs, and petulantly discontented. Her face is familiar to me, her face, with a difference.

Why do I think of her as dressed in green?

Of course! – she it was I saw leading her children by the hand!

Comes a crash to our left, and a running of people to see a cab-horse down on the slippery, slanting pavement outside St Martin's Church.

We go on up the street.

A heavy-eyed young Jewess, a draggled prostitute – no crimson flower for her hair, poor girl! – regards us with a momentary speculation, and we get a whiff of foul language from two newsboys on the kerb.

'We can't go on talking,' the botanist begins, and ducks aside just in time to save his eye from the ferule of a stupidly held umbrella. He is going to treat our little tiff about that lady as closed. He has the air of picking up our conversation again at some earlier point.

He steps into the gutter, walks round outside a negro hawker, just escapes the wheel of a hansom, and comes to my side again.

'We can't go on talking of your Utopia,' he says, 'in a noise and crowd like this.'

We are separated by a portly man going in the opposite direction, and join again. 'We can't go on talking of Utopia,' he repeats, 'in London ... Up in the mountains – and holiday-time – it was all right. We let ourselves go!'

'I've been living in Utopia,' I answer, tacitly adopting his tacit proposal to drop the lady out of the question.

'At times,' he says, with a queer laugh, 'you've almost made me live there too.'

He reflects. 'It doesn't do, you know. *No!* And I don't know whether, after all, I want – '

We are separated again by half a dozen lifted flagstones, a burning brazier, and two engineers concerned with some underground business or other – in the busiest hour of the day's traffic.

'Why shouldn't it do?' I ask.

'It spoils the world of everyday to let your mind run on impossible perfections.'

'I wish,' I shout against the traffic, 'I could *smash* the world of everyday.'

My note becomes quarrelsome. 'You may accept *this* as the world of reality, *you* may consent to be one scar in an ill-dressed compound wound, but so – not I! This is a dream too – this world. *Your* dream, and you bring me back to it – out of Utopia – '

The crossing of Bow Street gives me pause again.

The face of a girl who is passing westward, a student girl, rather carelessly dressed, her books in a carrying-strap, comes across my field of vision. The westward sun of London glows upon her face. She has eyes that dream, surely no sensuous nor personal dream.

After all, after all, dispersed, hidden, disorganised, undiscovered, unsuspected even by themselves, the samurai of Utopia are in this world, the motives that are developed and organised there stir dumbly here and stifle in ten thousand futile hearts . . .

I overtake the botanist, who got ahead at the crossing by the advantage of a dustcart.

'You think this is real because you can't wake out of it,' I say. 'It's all a dream, and there are people – I'm just one of the first of a multitude – between sleeping and waking – who will presently be rubbing it out of their eyes.'

A pinched and dirty little girl, with sores upon her face, stretches out a bunch of wilting violets, in a pitifully thin little fist, and interrupts my speech. 'Bunch o' vi'lets – on'y a penny.'

'No!' I say curtly, hardening my heart.

A ragged and filthy nursing mother, with her last addition to our Imperial People on her arm, comes out of a drink shop, and stands a little unsteadily, and wipes mouth and nose comprehensively with the back of a red chapped hand . . .

'Isn't *that* reality?' says the botanist, almost triumphantly, and leaves me aghast at his triumph.

'*That!*' I say belatedly. 'It's a thing in a nightmare!'

He shakes his head and smiles – exasperatingly.

I perceive quite abruptly that the botanist and I have reached the limits of our intercourse.

'The world dreams things like that,' I say, 'because it suffers from an indigestion of such people as you.'

His low-toned self-complacency, like the faded banner of an obstinate fort, still flies unconquered. And you know, he's not even a happy man with it all!

For ten seconds or more I am furiously seeking in my mind for a word, for a term of abuse, for one compendious verbal missile that shall smash this man for ever. It has to express total inadequacy of imagination and will, spiritual anaemia, dull respectability, gross sentimentality, a cultivated pettiness of heart . . .

That word will not come. But no other word will do. Indeed the word does not exist. There is nothing with sufficient vituperative concentration for this moral and intellectual stupidity of educated people . . .

'Er – ' he begins.

No! I can't endure him.

With a passionate rapidity of movement, I leave his side, dart between a carriage and a van, duck under the head of a cab-horse, and board a bus going westward somewhere – but anyhow, going in exactly the reverse direction to the botanist. I clamber up the steps and thread my swaying way to the seat immediately behind the driver.

'There!' I say, as I whack myself down on the seat and pant.

When I look round the botanist is out of sight.

5

But I am back in the world for all that, and my Utopia is done.

It is good discipline for the Utopist to visit this world occasionally.

But from the front seat on the top of an omnibus on a sunny September afternoon, the Strand, and Charing Cross corner, and Whitehall, and the great multitude of people, the great uproar of vehicles, streaming in all directions, is apt to look a world altogether too formidable. It has a glare, it has a tumult and vigour that shouts one down. It shouts one down, if shouting is to carry it. What good was it to trot along the pavement through this noise and tumult of life, pleading Utopia to that botanist? What good would it be to recommend Utopia in this driver's preoccupied ear?

There are moments in the life of every philosopher and dreamer when he feels himself the flimsiest of absurdities, when the Thing in Being has its way with him, its triumphant way, when it asks in a roar, unanswerably, with a fine solid use of the current vernacular, 'What Good is all this – Rot about Utopias?'

One inspects the Thing in Being with something of the diffident speculation of primitive man, peering from behind a tree at an angry elephant.

(There is an omen in that image. On how many occasions must that ancestor of ours have had just the Utopist's feeling of ambitious unreality, have decided that on the whole it was wiser to go very quietly home again, and leave the big beast alone? But, in the end, men rode upon the elephant's head, and guided him this way or that . . . The Thing in Being that roars so tremendously about Charing Cross corner seems a bigger antagonist than an elephant, but then we have better weapons than chipped flint blades . . .)

After all, in a very little time everything that impresses me so mightily this September afternoon will have changed or passed away for ever, everything. These omnibuses, these great, stalwart, crowded, many-coloured things that jostle one another, and make so handsome a clatter-clamour, will all have gone; they and their horses and drivers and organisation; you will come here and you will not find them. Something else will be here, some different sort of vehicle, that is now perhaps the mere germ of an idea in some engineer student's brain. And this road and pavement will have changed, and these impressive great buildings; other buildings will be here, buildings that are as yet more impalpable than this page you read, more formless and flimsy by far than anything that is reasoned here. Little plans sketched on paper, strokes of a pen or of a brush, will be the first materialisations of what will at last obliterate every detail and atom of these re-echoing actualities that overwhelm us now. And the clothing and gestures of these innumerable people, the character of their faces and bearing, these too will be recast in the spirit of what are now obscure and impalpable beginnings.

The new things will be indeed of the substance of the thing that is, but differing just in the measure of the will and imagination that goes to make them. They will be strong and fair as the will is sturdy and organised and the imagination comprehensive and bold; they will be ugly and smeared with wretchedness as the will is fluctuating and the imagination timid and mean.

Indeed Will is stronger than Fact, it can mould and overcome Fact. But this world has still to discover its will, it is a world that slumbers inertly, and all this roar and pulsation of life is no more than its heavy breathing . . . My mind runs on to the thought of an awakening.

As my omnibus goes lumbering up Cockspur Street through the clatter-rattle of the cabs and carriages, there comes another fancy in my mind . . . Could one but realise an apocalyptic image and suppose an angel, such as was given to each of the seven churches of Asia, given for a space to the service of the Greater Rule! I see him as a towering figure of flame and colour, standing between earth and sky, with a trumpet in his hands, over there above the Haymarket, against the October glow; and when he sounds, all the samurai, all who are samurai in Utopia, will know themselves and one another . . .

(Whup! says a motor brougham, and a policeman stays the traffic with his hand.)

All of us who partake of the samurai would know ourselves and one another!

For a moment I have a vision of this resurrection of the living, of a vague, magnificent answer, of countless myriads at attention, of all that is fine in humanity at attention, round the compass of the earth.

Then that philosophy of individual uniqueness resumes its sway over my thoughts, and my dream of a world's awakening fades.

I had forgotten . . .

Things do not happen like that. God is not simple, God is not theatrical, the summons comes to each man in its due time for him, with an infinite subtlety of variety . . .

If that is so, what of my Utopia?

This infinite world must needs be flattened to get it on one retina. The picture of a solid thing, although it is flattened and simplified, is not necessarily a lie. Surely, surely, in the end, by degrees, and steps, something of this sort, some such understanding, as this Utopia must come. First here, then there, single men and then groups of men will fall into line – not indeed with my poor faulty hesitating suggestions – but with a great and comprehensive plan wrought out by many minds and in many tongues. It is just because my plan is faulty, because it mis-states so much, and omits so much, that they do not now fall in. It will not be like *my* dream, the world that is coming. My dream is just my own poor dream, the thing sufficient for me. We fail in comprehension, we fail so variously and abundantly. We see as much as it is serviceable for us to see, and we see no further. But the fresh undaunted generations come to take on our work beyond our utmost effort, beyond the range of our ideas. They will learn with certainty things that to us are guesses and riddles . . .

There will be many Utopias. Each generation will have its new version of Utopia, a little more certain and complete and real, with its problems lying closer and closer to the problems of the Thing in Being. Until at last from dreams Utopias will have come to be working drawings, and the whole world will be shaping the final World State, the fair and great and fruitful World State, that will only not be a Utopia because it will be this world. So surely it must be –

The policeman drops his hand. 'Come up,' says the bus driver, and the horses strain; 'Clitter, clatter, cluck, clak,' the line of hurrying hansoms overtakes the omnibus going west. A dexterous lad on a bicycle with a bale of newspapers on his back dodges nimbly across the head of the column and vanishes up a side street.

The omnibus sways forward. Rapt and prophetic, his plump hands clasped round the handle of his umbrella, his billycock hat a trifle askew, this irascible little man of the Voice, this impatient dreamer, this scolding Optimist, who has argued so rudely and dogmatically about economics and philosophy and decoration, and indeed about everything under the sun, who has been so hard on the botanist and fashionable women, and so reluctant in the matter of beer, is carried onward, dreaming dreams, dreams that with all the inevitable ironies of difference, may be realities when you and I are dreams.

He passes, and for a little space we are left with his egoisms and idiosyncrasies more or less in suspense.

But why was he intruded? you ask. Why could not a modern Utopia be discussed without this impersonation – impersonally? It has confused the book, you say, made the argument hard to follow, and thrown a quality of insincerity over the whole. Are we but mocking at Utopias, you demand, using all these noble and generalised hopes as the backcloth against which two bickering personalities jar and squabble? Do I mean we are never to view the promised land again except through a foreground of fellow-travellers? There is a common notion that the reading of a Utopia should end with a swelling heart and clear resolves, with lists of names, formation of committees, and even the commencement of subscriptions. But this Utopia began upon a philosophy of fragmentation, and ends, confusedly, amidst a gross tumult of immediate realities, in dust and doubt, with, at the best, one individual's aspiration.

Utopias were once in good faith, projects for a fresh creation of the world and of a most unworldly completeness; this so-called Modern Utopia is a mere story of personal adventures among Utopian philosophies.

Indeed, that came about without the writer's intention. So it was the summoned vision came. For I see about me a great multitude of little souls and groups of souls as darkened, as derivative as my own; with the passage of years I understand more and more clearly the quality of the motives that urge me and urge them to do whatever we do . . . Yet that is not all I see, and I am not altogether bounded by my littleness. Ever and again, contrasting with this immediate vision, come glimpses of a comprehensive scheme, in which these personalities float, the scheme of a synthetic wider being, the great State, mankind, in which we all move and go, like blood corpuscles, like nerve cells, it may be at times like brain cells, in the body of a man. But the two visions are not seen consistently together, at least by me, and I do not surely know that they exist consistently together. The motives needed for those wider issues come not into the interplay of my vanities and wishes. That greater scheme lies about the men and women I know, as I have tried to make the vistas and spaces, the mountains, cities, laws, and order of Utopia lie about my talking couple, too great for their sustained comprehension. When one focuses upon these two that wide landscape becomes indistinct and distant, and when one regards that then the real persons one knows grow vague and unreal. Nevertheless, I cannot separate these two aspects of human life, each commenting on the other. In that incongruity between great and individual inheres the incompatibility I could not resolve, and which, therefore, I have had to present in this conflicting form. At times that great scheme does seem to me to enter certain men's lives as a passion, as a real and living motive; there are those who know it almost as if it was a thing of desire; even for me, upon occasion, the little lures of the immediate life are seen small and vain, and the soul goes out to that mighty Being, to apprehend it and serve it and possess. But this is an illumination that passes as it comes, a rare transitory lucidity, leaving the soul's desire suddenly turned to presumption and hypocrisy upon the lips. One grasps at the Universe and attains – Bathos. The hungers, the jealousies, the prejudices and habits have us again, and we are forced back to think that it is so, and not otherwise, that we are meant to serve the mysteries; that in these blinkers it is we are driven to an end we cannot understand. And then, for measured moments in the night watches or as one walks alone or while one sits in thought and speech with a friend, the wider aspirations glow again with a sincere emotion, with the colours of attainable desire . . .

That is my all about Utopia, and about the desire and need for Utopia, and how that planet lies to this planet that bears the daily lives of men.

Scepticism of the Instrument

A portion of a paper read to the Oxford Philosophical Society, November 8, 1903, and reprinted, with some revision, from the version given in *Mind*, vol. xiii (N.S.), No. 51.

(See also Chapter One, section 6, and Chapter Ten, sections 1 and 2.)

It seems to me that I may most propitiously attempt to interest you this evening by describing very briefly the particular metaphysical and philosophical system in which I do my thinking, and more particularly by setting out for your consideration one or two points in which I seem to myself to differ most widely from current accepted philosophy.

You must be prepared for things that will strike you as crude, for a certain difference of accent and dialect that you may not like, and you must be prepared too to hear what may strike you as the clumsy statement of my ignorant rediscovery of things already beautifully thought out and said. But in the end you may incline to forgive me some of this first offence . . . It is quite unavoidable that, in setting out these intellectual foundations of mine, I should lapse for a moment or so towards autobiography.

A convergence of circumstances led to my having my knowledge of concrete things quite extensively developed before I came to philosophical examination at all. I have heard someone say that a savage or an animal is mentally a purely objective being, and in that respect I was like a savage or an animal until I was well over twenty. I was extremely unaware of the subjective or introverted element in my being. I was a Positivist without knowing it. My early education was a feeble one; it was one in which my private observation, enquiry and experiment were far more important factors than any instruction, or rather perhaps the instruction I received was less even than what I learnt for myself, and it terminated at thirteen. I had come into pretty intimate contact with the harder realities of life, with hunger in various forms, and many base and disagreeable necessities, before I was fifteen. About that age, following the indication of certain theological and speculative curiosities, I began to learn something of what I will call deliberately and justly, Elementary

Science – stuff I got out of *Cassell's Popular Educator* and cheap text-books – and then, through accidents and ambitions that do not matter in the least to us now, I came to three years of illuminating and good scientific work. The central fact of those three years was Huxley's course in Comparative Anatomy at the school in Exhibition Road. About that as a nucleus I arranged a spacious digest of facts. At the end of that time I had acquired what I still think to be a fairly clear, and complete and ordered view of the ostensibly real universe. Let me try to give you the chief things I had. I had man definitely placed in the great scheme of space and time. I knew him incurably for what he was, finite and not final, a being of compromises and adaptations. I had traced his lungs, for example, from a swimming bladder, step by step, with scalpel and probe, through a dozen types or more, I had seen the ancestral caecum shrink to that disease nest, the appendix of today, I had watched the gill slit patched slowly to the purposes of the ear and the reptile jaw suspension utilised to eke out the needs of a sense organ taken from its native and natural water. I had worked out the development of those extraordinarily unsatisfactory and untrustworthy instruments, man's teeth, from the skin scutes of the shark to their present function as a basis for gold stoppings, and followed the slow unfolding of the complex and painful process of gestation through which man comes into the world. I had followed all these things and many kindred things by dissection and in embryology – I had checked the whole theory of development again in a year's course of palaeontology, and I had taken the dimensions of the whole process, by the scale of the stars, in a course of astronomical physics. And all that amount of objective elucidation came before I had reached the beginnings of any philosophical or meta-physical enquiry, any enquiry as to why I believed, how I believed, what I believed, or what the fundamental stuff of things was.

Now following hard upon this interlude with knowledge, came a time when I had to give myself to teaching, and it became advisable to acquire one of those Teaching Diplomas that are so widely and so foolishly despised, and that enterprise set me to a superficial, but suggestive study of educational method, of educational theory, of logic, of psychology, and so at last, when the little affair with the diploma was settled, to philosophy. Now to come to logic over the bracing uplands of comparative anatomy is to come to logic with a lot of very natural preconceptions blown clean out of one's mind. It is, I submit, a way of taking logic in the flank. When you have realised to the marrow, that all the physical organs of man and all his physical structure are what they are through a series of adaptations and approximations, and that they are kept up to a level of practical efficiency only by the elimination of death, and that this is true also of his brain and of his instincts and of many of his mental predispositions, you are not going to take his thinking apparatus unquestioningly as being in any way mysteriously different and better. And I had read only a little logic before I became aware of implications that I could not agree with, and assumptions that seemed to me to be altogether at variance with the general scheme of objective fact established in my mind.

I came to an examination of logical processes and of language with the expectation that they would share the profoundly provisional character, the character of irregular limitation and adaptation that pervades the whole physical and animal being of man. And I found the thing I had expected. And as a consequence I found a sort of intellectual hardihood about the assumptions of logic, that at first confused me and then roused all the latent scepticism in my mind.

My first quarrel with the accepted logic I developed long ago in a little paper that was printed in the *Fortnightly Review* in July 1891. It was called the 'Rediscovery of the Unique', and re-reading it I perceive not only how bad and even annoying it was in manner – a thing I have long known – but also how remarkably bad it was in expression. I have good reason for doubting whether my powers of expression in these uses have very perceptibly improved, but at any rate I am doing my best now with that previous failure before me.

That unfortunate paper, among other oversights I can no longer regard as trivial, disregarded quite completely the fact that a whole literature upon the antagonism of the one and the many, of the specific ideal and the individual reality, was already in existence. It defined no relations to other thought or thinkers. I understand now, what I did not understand then, why it was totally ignored. But the idea underlying that paper I cling to today. I consider it an idea that will ultimately be regarded as one of primary importance to human thought, and I will try and present the substance of that early paper again now very briefly, as the best opening of my general case. My opening scepticism is essentially a doubt of *the objective reality of classification*. I have no hesitation in saying that is the first and primary proposition of my philosophy.

I have it in my mind that classification is a necessary condition of the working of the mental implement, but that it is a departure from the objective truth of things, that classification is very serviceable for the practical purposes of life but a very doubtful preliminary to those fine penetrations the philosophical purpose, in its more arrogant moods, demands. All the peculiarities of my way of thinking derive from that.

A mind nourished upon anatomical study is of course permeated with the suggestion of the vagueness and instability of biological species. A biological species is quite obviously a great number of unique individuals which is separable from other biological species only by the fact that an enormous number of other linking individuals are inaccessible in time – are in other words dead and gone – and each new individual in that species does, in the distinction of its own individuality, break away in however infinitesimal degree from the previous average properties of the species. There is no property of any species, even the properties that constitute the specific definition, that is not a matter of more or less. If, for example, a species be distinguished by a single large red spot on the back, you will find if you go over a great number of specimens that red spot shrinking here to nothing, expanding there to a more general redness, weakening to pink, deepening to russet and brown, shading into crimson, and so on, and so on. And this is true not only of biological species. It is true of the mineral specimens constituting a mineral species, and I remember as a constant refrain in the lectures of Professor Judd upon rock classification, the words 'they pass into one another by insensible gradations'. That is true, I hold, of all things.

You will think perhaps of atoms of the elements as instances of identically similar things, but these are things not of experience but of theory, and there is not a phenomenon in chemistry that is not equally well explained on the supposition that it is merely the immense quantities of atoms necessarily taken in any experiment that mask by the operation of the law of averages the fact that each atom also has its unique quality, its special individual difference. This idea of uniqueness in all individuals is not only true of the classifications of material science; it is true, and still more evidently true, of the species of common thought, it is true of common terms. Take the word 'chair'. When one says chair, one thinks vaguely of an average chair. But collect individual instances, think of armchairs and reading chairs, and dining-room chairs and kitchen chairs, chairs that pass into benches, chairs that cross the boundary and become settees, dentists' chairs, thrones, opera stalls, seats of all sorts, those miraculous fungoid growths that cumber the floor of the Arts and Crafts Exhibition, and you will perceive what a lax bundle in fact is this simple straightforward term. In co-operation with an intelligent joiner I would undertake to defeat any definition of chair or chairishness that you gave me. Chairs just as much as individual organisms, just as much as mineral and rock specimens, are unique things – if you know them well enough you will find an individual difference even in a set of machine-made chairs – and it is only because we do not possess minds of unlimited capacity, because our brain has only a limited number of pigeon-holes for our correspondence with an unlimited universe of objective uniques, that we have to delude ourselves into the belief that there is a chairishness in this species common to and distinctive of all chairs.

Let me repeat; this is of the very smallest importance in all the practical affairs of life, or indeed in relation to anything but philosophy and wide generalisations. But in philosophy it matters profoundly. If I order two new-laid eggs for breakfast, up come two unhatched but still unique avian individuals, and the chances are they serve my rude physiological purpose. I can afford to ignore the hens' eggs of the past that were not quite so nearly this sort of thing, and the hens' eggs of the future that will accumulate modification age by age; I can venture to ignore the rare chance of an abnormality in chemical composition and of any startling aberration in my physiological reaction; I can, with a confidence that is practically perfect, say with unqualified simplicity 'two eggs', but not if my concern is not my morning's breakfast but the utmost possible truth.

Now let me go on to point out whither this idea of uniqueness tends. I submit to you that syllogism is based on classification, that all hard logical reasoning tends to imply and is apt to imply a confidence in the objective reality of classification. Consequently in denying that I deny the absolute validity of logic. Classification and number, which in truth ignore the fine differences of objective realities, have in the past of human thought been imposed upon things. Let me for clearness' sake take a liberty here – commit, as you may perhaps think, an unpardonable insolence. Hindu thought and Greek thought alike impress me as being overmuch obsessed by an objective treatment of certain necessary preliminary conditions of human thought – number and definition and class and abstract form. But these things, number, definition, class and abstract form, I hold, are merely unavoidable conditions of mental activity – regrettable conditions rather than essential facts. *The forceps of our minds are clumsy forceps, and crush the truth a little in taking hold of it.*

It was about this difficulty that the mind of Plato played a little inconclusively all his life. For the most part he tended to regard the *idea* as the something behind reality, whereas it seems to me that the idea is the more proximate and less perfect thing, the thing by which the mind, by ignoring individual differences, attempts to comprehend an otherwise unmanageable number of unique realities.

Let me give you a rough figure of what I am trying to convey in this first attack upon the philosophical validity of general terms. You have seen the results of those various methods of black and white reproduction that involve the use of a rectangular net. You know the sort of process picture I mean – it used to be employed very frequently in reproducing photographs. At a little distance you really seem to have a faithful reproduction of the original picture, but when you peer closely you find not the unique form and masses of the original, but a multitude of little rectangles, uniform in shape and size. The more earnestly you go into the thing, the closer you look, the more the picture is lost in reticulations. I submit the world of reasoned enquiry has a very similar relation to the world I call objectively real. For the rough purposes of every day the network picture will do, but the finer your purpose the less it will serve, and for an ideally fine purpose, for absolute and general knowledge that will be as true for a man at a distance with a telescope as for a man with a microscope it will not serve at all.

It is true you can make your net of logical interpretation finer and finer, you can fine your classification more and more – up to a certain limit. But essentially you are working in limits, and as you come closer, as you look at finer and subtler things, as you leave the practical purpose for which the method exists, the element of error increases. Every species is vague, every term goes cloudy at its edges, and so in my way of thinking, relentless logic is only another phrase for a stupidity – for a sort of intellectual pig-headedness. If you push a philosophical or metaphysical enquiry through a series of valid syllogisms – never committing any generally recognised fallacy – you nevertheless leave a certain rubbing and marginal loss of objective truth and you get deflections that are difficult to trace, at each phase in the process. Every species waggles about in its definition, every tool is a little loose in its handle, every scale has its individual error. So long as you are reasoning for practical purposes about the finite things of experience, you can every now and then check your process, and correct your adjustments. But not when you make what are called philosophical and theological enquiries, when you turn your implement towards the final absolute truth of things. Doing that is like firing at an inaccessible, unmarkable and indestructible target at an unknown distance, with a defective rifle and variable cartridges. Even if by chance you hit, you cannot know that you hit, and so it will matter nothing at all.

This assertion of the necessary untrustworthiness of all reasoning processes arising out of the fallacy of classification in what is quite conceivably a universe of uniques, forms only one introductory aspect of my general scepticism of the Instrument of Thought.

I have now to tell you of another aspect of this scepticism of the instrument which concerns negative terms.

Classes in logic are not only represented by circles with a hard firm outline, whereas they have no such definite limits, but also there is a constant disposition to think of negative terms as if they represented positive classes. With words just as with numbers and abstract forms there are definite phases of human development. There is, you know, with regard to number, the phase when man can barely count at all, or counts in perfect good faith and sanity upon his fingers. Then there is the phase when he is struggling with the development of number, when he begins to elaborate all sorts of ideas about numbers, until at last he develops complex superstitions about perfect numbers and imperfect numbers, about threes and sevens and the like. The same is the case with abstracted forms, and even today we are scarcely more than heads out of the vast subtle muddle of thinking about spheres and ideally perfect forms and so on, that was the price of this little necessary step to clear thinking. You know better than I do how large a part numerical and geometrical magic, numerical and geometrical philosophy has played in the history of the mind. And the whole apparatus of language and mental communication is beset with like dangers. The language of the savage is, I suppose, purely positive; the thing has a name, the name has a thing. This indeed is the tradition of language, and even today, we, when we hear a name, are predisposed – and sometimes it is a very vicious disposition – to imagine forthwith something answering to the name. *We are disposed, as an incurable mental vice, to accumulate intension in terms.* If I say to you Wodget or Crump, you find yourself passing over the fact that these are nothings, these are, so to speak, mere blankety blanks, and trying to think what sort of thing a Wodget or a Crump may be. And where this disposition has come in, in its most alluring guise, is in the case of negative terms. Our instrument of knowledge persists in handling even such openly negative terms as the Absolute, the Infinite, as though they were real existences, and when the negative element is ever so little disguised, as it is in such a word as Omniscience, then the illusion of positive reality may be complete.

Please remember that I am trying to tell you my philosophy, and not arguing about yours. Let me try and express how in my mind this matter of negative terms has shaped itself. I think of something which I may perhaps best describe as being off the stage or out of court, or as the Void without Implications, or as Nothingness or as Outer Darkness.

This is a sort of hypothetical Beyond to the visible world of human thought, and thither I think all negative terms reach at last, and merge and become nothing. Whatever positive class you make, whatever boundary you draw, straight away from that boundary begins the corresponding negative class and passes into the illimitable horizon of nothingness. You talk of pink things, you ignore, if you are a trained logician, the more elusive shades of pink, and draw your line. Beyond is the not pink, known and knowable, and still in the not pink region one comes to the Outer Darkness. Not blue, not happy, not iron, all the *not* classes meet in that Outer Darkness. That same Outer Darkness and nothingness is infinite space, and infinite time, and any being of infinite qualities, and all that region I rule out of court in my philosophy altogether. I will neither affirm nor deny if I can help it about any *not* things. I will not deal with not things at all, except by accident and inadvertence. If I use the word 'infinite' I use it as one often uses 'countless', 'the countless hosts of the enemy' – or 'immeasurable' – 'immeasurable cliffs' – that is to say as the limit of measurement rather than as the limit of imaginary measurability, as a convenient equivalent to as many times this cloth yard as you can, and as many again and so on and so on. Now a great number of apparently positive terms are, or have become, practically negative terms and are under the same ban with me. A considerable number of terms that have played a great part in the world of thought, seem to me to be invalidated by this same defect, to have no content or an undefined content or an unjustifiable content. For example, that word Omniscient, as implying infinite knowledge, impresses me as being a word with a delusive air of being solid and full, when it is really hollow with no content whatever. I am persuaded that knowing is the relation of a conscious being to something not itself, that the thing known is defined as a system of parts and aspects and relationships, that knowledge is comprehension, and so that only finite things can know or be known. When you talk of a being of infinite extension and infinite duration, omniscient and omnipotent and Perfect, you seem to me to be talking in negatives of nothing whatever. When you speak of the Absolute you speak to me of nothing. If however you talk of a great yet finite and thinkable being, a being not myself, extending beyond my imagination in time and space, knowing all that I can think of as known and capable of doing all that I can think of as done, you come into the sphere of my mental operations, and into the scheme of my philosophy . . .

These then are my first two charges against our Instrument of Knowledge, firstly, that it can work only by disregarding individuality and treating uniques as identically similar objects in this respect or that, so as to group them under one term, and that once it has done so it tends automatically to intensify the significance of that term, and secondly, that it can only deal freely with negative terms by treating them as though they were positive. But I have a further objection to the Instrument of Human Thought, that is not correlated to these former objections and that is also rather more difficult to convey.

Essentially this idea is to present a sort of stratification in human ideas. I have it very much in mind that various terms in our reasoning lie, as it were, at different levels and in different planes, and that we accomplish a large amount of error and confusion by reasoning terms together that do not lie or nearly lie in the same plane.

Let me endeavour to make myself a little less obscure by a most flagrant instance from physical things. Suppose someone began to talk seriously of a man seeing an atom through a microscope, or better perhaps of cutting one in half with a knife. There are a number of non-analytical people who would be quite prepared to believe that an atom could be visible to the eye or cut in this manner. But anyone at all conversant with physical conceptions would almost as soon think of killing the square root of 2 with a rook rifle as of cutting an atom in half with a knife. Our conception of an atom is reached through a process of hypothesis and analysis, and in the world of atoms there are no knives and no men to cut. If you have thought with a strong consistent mental movement, then when you have thought of your atom under the knife blade, your knife blade has itself become a cloud of swinging grouped atoms, and your microscope lens a little universe of oscillatory and vibratory molecules. If you think of the universe, thinking at the level of atoms, there is neither knife to cut, scale to weigh nor eye to see. The universe *at that plane to which the mind of the molecular physicist descends* has none of the shapes or forms of our common life whatever. This hand with which I write is in the universe of molecular physics a cloud of warring atoms and molecules, combining and recombining, colliding, rotating, flying hither and thither in the universal atmosphere of ether.

You see, I hope, what I mean, when I say that the universe of molecular physics is at a different level from the universe of common experience; – what we call stable and solid is in that world a freely moving system of interlacing centres of force, what we call colour and sound is there no more than this length of vibration or that. We have reached to a conception of that universe of molecular physics by a great enterprise of organised analysis, and our universe of daily experiences stands in relation to that elemental world as if it were a synthesis of those elemental things.

I would suggest to you that this is only a very extreme instance of the general state of affairs, that there may be finer and subtler differences of level between one term and another, and that terms may very well be thought of as lying obliquely and as being twisted through different levels.

It will perhaps give a clearer idea of what I am seeking to convey if I suggest a concrete image for the whole world of a man's thought and knowledge. Imagine a large clear jelly, in which at all angles and in all states of simplicity or contortion his ideas are imbedded. They are all valid and possible ideas as they lie, none in reality incompatible with any. If you imagine the direction of up or down in this clear jelly being as it were the direction in which one moves by analysis or by synthesis, if you go down for example from matter to atoms and centres of force and up to men and states and countries – if you will imagine the ideas lying in that manner – you will get the beginning of my intention. But our Instrument, our process of thinking, like a drawing before the discovery of perspective, appears to have difficulties with the third dimension, appears capable only of dealing with or reasoning about ideas by projecting them upon the same plane. It will be obvious that a great multitude of things may very well exist together in a solid jelly, which would be overlapping and incompatible and mutually destructive, when projected together upon one plane. Through the bias in our Instrument to do this, through reasoning between terms not in the same plane, an enormous amount of confusion, perplexity and mental deadlocking occurs.

The old theological deadlock between predestination and free will serves admirably as an example of the sort of deadlock I mean. Take life at the level of common sensation and common experience and there is no more indisputable fact than man's freedom of will, unless it is his complete moral responsibility. But make only the least penetrating of analyses and you perceive a world of inevitable consequences, a rigid succession of cause and effect. Insist upon a flat agreement between the two, and there you are! The Instrument fails.

It is upon these three objections, and upon an extreme suspicion of abstract terms which arises materially out of my first and second objections, that I chiefly rest my case for a profound scepticism of the remoter possibilities of the Instrument of Thought. It is a thing no more perfect than the human eye or the human ear, though like those other instruments it may have undefined possibilities of evolution towards increased range, and increased power.

So much for my main contention. But before I conclude I may – since I am here – say a little more in the autobiographical vein, and with a view to your discussion to show how I reconcile this fundamental scepticism with the very positive beliefs about worldwide issues I possess, and the very definite distinction I make between right and wrong.

I reconcile these things by simply pointing out to you that if there is any validity in my image of that three-dimensional jelly in which our ideas are suspended, such a reconciliation as you demand in logic, such a projection of the things as being in accordance upon one plane, is totally unnecessary and impossible. They can never come together upon one plane.

This insistence upon the element of uniqueness in being, this subordination of the class to the individual difference, not only destroys the universal claim of philosophy, but the universal claim of ethical imperatives, the universal claim of any religious teaching. If you press me back upon my fundamental position I must confess I put faith and standards and rules of conduct upon exactly the same level as I put my belief of what is right in art, and what I consider right practice in art. I have arrived at a certain sort of self-knowledge and there are, I find, very distinct imperatives for me, but I am quite prepared to admit there is no proving them imperative on anyone else. One's political proceedings, one's moral acts are, I hold, just as much self-expression as one's poetry or painting or music. But since life has for its primordial elements assimilation and aggression, I try not only to obey my imperatives, but to put them persuasively and convincingly into other minds, to bring about *my* good and to resist and overcome *my* evil as though they were the universal Good and the universal Evil in which unthinking men believe. And it is obviously in no way contradictory to this philosophy, for me, if I find others responding sympathetically to any notes of mine or if I find myself responding sympathetically to notes sounding about me, to give that common resemblance between myself and others a name, to refer these others and myself in common to this thing as if it were externalised and spanned us all.

Scepticism of the Instrument is for example not incompatible with religious association and with organisation upon the basis of a common faith. It is possible to regard God as a Being synthetic in relation to men and societies, just as the idea of a universe of atoms and molecules and inorganic relationships is analytical in relation to human life.

The repudiation of demonstration in any but immediate and verifiable cases that this Scepticism of the Instrument amounts to, the abandonment of any universal validity for moral and religious propositions, brings ethical, social and religious teaching into the province of poetry, and does something to correct the estrangement between knowledge and beauty that is a feature of so much mental existence at this time. All these things are self-expression. Such an opinion sets a new and greater value on that penetrating and illuminating quality of mind we call insight, insight which when it faces towards the contradictions that arise out of the imperfections of the mental instrument is called humour. In these innate, unteachable qualities I hold – in humour and the sense of beauty – lies such hope of intellectual salvation from the original sin of our intellectual instrument as we may entertain in this uncertain and fluctuating world of unique appearances . . .

So frankly I spread my little equipment of fundamental assumptions before you, heartily glad of the opportunity you have given me of taking them out, of looking at them with the particularity the presence of hearers ensures, and of hearing the impression they make upon you. Of course, such a sketch must have an inevitable crudity of effect. The time I had for it – I mean the time I was able to give in preparation – was altogether too limited for any exhaustive finish of presentation; but I think on the whole I have got the main lines of this sketch map of my mental basis true. Whether I have made myself comprehensible is a different question altogether. It is for you rather than me to say how this sketch map of mine lies with regard to your own more systematic cartography.